D0298396

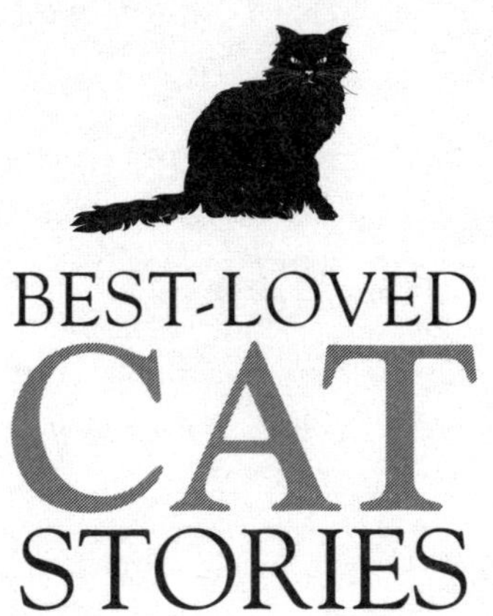

BEST-LOVED CAT STORIES

The colour pictures in this volume are by Ditz who was born in Vienna but has lived in England for over twenty-five years. She has shown her pictures at many major exhibitions and is a regular contributor to the Royal Academy Summer Exhibition. Her pictures hang in private and public collections in many countries.

The pictures in this collection are some of her favourite cats.

BEST-LOVED CAT STORIES

Edited by

LESLEY O'MARA

Illustrations by

WILLIAM GELDART

MICHAEL O'MARA BOOKS LIMITED

First published in Great Britain in 1997 by
Michael O'Mara Books Limited
9 Lion Yard, Tremadoc Road
London SW4 7NQ

A CIP catalogue record for this book
is available from the British Library

ISBN 1-85479-251-2

1 3 5 7 9 10 8 6 4 2

Designed and typeset by Martin Bristow

Printed and bound in England
by Clays Ltd, St Ives plc

CONTENTS

THE CAT'S PARADISE

Emile Zola

I WAS THEN TWO YEARS OLD, and was at the same time the fattest and most naive cat in existence. At that tender age I still had all the presumptuousness of an animal who is disdainful of the sweetness of home.

How fortunate I was, indeed, that providence had placed me with your aunt! That good woman adored me. I had at the bottom of a wardrobe a veritable sleeping salon, with feather cushions and triple covers. My food was equally excellent; never just bread, or soup, but always meat, carefully chosen meat.

Well, in the midst of all this opulence, I had only one desire, one dream, and that was to slip out of the upper window and escape on to the roofs. Caresses annoyed me, the softness of my bed nauseated me, and I was so fat that it was disgusting even to myself. In short, I was bored the whole day long just with being happy.

I must tell you that by stretching my neck a bit, I had seen the roof directly in front of my window. That day four cats were playing with each other up there; their fur bristling, their tails high, they were romping around with every indication of joy on the blue roof slates baked by the sun. I had never before watched such an extraordinary spectacle. And from then on I had a definitely fixed belief: out there on that roof was true happiness, out there beyond the window which was always closed so carefully. In proof of that contention I remembered that the doors of the chest in which the meat was kept were also closed, just as carefully!

I resolved to flee. After all there had to be other things in life besides a comfortable bed. Out there was the unknown, the ideal. And then one day they forgot to close the kitchen window. I jumped out on to the small roof above it.

How beautiful the roofs were! The wide eaves bordering them exuded delicious smells. Carefully I followed those eaves, where my feet sank into fine mud that smelled tepid and infinitely sweet. It felt as if I were walking on velvet. And the sun shone with a good warmth that caressed my plumpness.

I will not hide from you the fact that I was trembling all over. There was something overwhelming in my joy. I remember particularly the tremendous emotional upheaval which actually made me lose my footing on the slates, when three cats rolled down from the ridge of the roof and approached with excited miaows. But when I showed signs of fear, they told me I was a silly fat goose and insisted that their miaowing was only laughter.

I decided to join them in their caterwauling. It was fun, even though the three stalwarts weren't as fat as I was and made fun of me when I rolled like a ball over the roof heated by the sun.

An old tomcat belonging to the gang honoured me particularly with his friendship. He offered to take care of my education, an offer which I accepted with gratitude.

Oh, how far away seemed all the soft things of your aunt! I drank from the gutters, and never did sugared milk taste half as fine! Everything was good and beautiful.

A female cat passed by, a ravishing she, and the very sight of her filled me with strange emotions. Only in my dreams had I up to then seen such an exquisite creature with such a magnificently arched back. We dashed forward to meet the newcomer, my three companions and myself. I was actually ahead of the others in paying the enchanting female my compliments; but then one of my comrades gave me a nasty bite in the neck, and I let out a shriek of pain.

'Pshaw!' said the old tomcat, dragging me away. 'You will meet plenty of others.'

After a walk that lasted an hour I had a ravenous appetite.

'What does one eat on these roofs?' I asked my friend the tom.

'Whatever one finds,' he replied laconically.

This answer embarrassed me somewhat for, hunt as I might, I couldn't find a thing. Finally I looked through a dormer window and saw a young workman preparing his breakfast. On the table, just above the windowsill, lay a chop of a particularly succulent red.

'There is my chance,' I thought, rather naively.

So I jumped on to the table and snatched the chop. But the workingman saw me and gave me a terrific wallop across my back with a broom. I dropped the meat, cursed rather vulgarly and escaped.

'What part of the world do you come from?' asked the tomcat. 'Don't you know that meat on tables is meant only to be admired from afar? What we've got to do is look in the gutters.'

I have never been able to understand why kitchen meat shouldn't belong to cats. My stomach began to complain quite bitterly. The tom tried to console me by saying it would only be necessary to wait for the night. Then, he said, we would climb down from the roofs into the streets and forage in the garbage heaps.

Wait for the night! Confirmed philosopher that he was, he said it calmly while the very thought of such a protracted fast made me positively faint.

Night came ever so slowly, a misty night that made me shiver. To make things worse, rain began to fall, a thin, penetrating rain whipped up by brisk howling gusts of wind.

How desolate the streets looked to me! There was nothing left of the good warmth, of the big sun, of those roofs where one could play so pleasantly. My paws slipped on the slimy pavement, and I began to think with some longing of my triple covers and my feather pillow.

We had hardly reached the street when my friend, the tom, began to tremble. He made himself small, quite small, and glided surreptitiously along the walls of the houses, warning me under his breath to be quick about it. When we reached the shelter of a house door, he hid behind it and purred with satisfaction. And when I asked him the reason for his strange conduct, he said:

'Did you see that man with the hook and the basket?'

'Yes.'

'Well, if he had seen us, we would have been caught, fried on the spit and eaten!'

'Fried on the spit and eaten!' I exclaimed. 'Why, then the street is really not for the likes of us. One does not eat, but is eaten instead!'

In the meantime, however, they had begun to put the garbage out on the sidewalks. I inspected it with growing despair. All I found there were two or three dry bones that had obviously been thrown in among the ashes. And then and there I realized how succulent a dish of fresh meat really is!

My friend, the tom, went over the heaps of garbage with consummate artistry. He made me rummage around until morning, inspecting every cobblestone, without the least trace of hurry. But after ten hours of almost incessant rain my whole body was trembling. Damn the street, I thought, damn liberty! And how I longed for my prison!

When day came, the tomcat noticed that I was weakening.

'You've had enough, eh?' he asked in a strange voice.

'Oh, yes,' I replied.

'Do you want to go home?'

'I certainly do. But how can I find my house?'

'Come along. Yesterday morning when I saw you come out I knew immediately that a cat as fat as you isn't made for the joys of liberty. I know where you live. I'll take you back to your door.'

He said this all simply enough, the good, dignified tom. And when we finally got there, he added, without the slightest show of emotion:

'Goodbye, then.'

'No, no!' I protested. 'I shall not leave you like this. You come with me! We shall share bed and board. My mistress is a good woman . . .

He didn't even let me finish.

'Shut up!' he said brusquely. 'You are a fool. I'd die in that stuffy softness. Your abundant life is for weaklings. Free cats will never buy your comforts and your featherbeds at the price of being imprisoned. Goodbye!'

With these words he climbed back on to the roof. I saw his proud thin shadow shudder deliciously as it began to feel the warmth of the morning sun.

When I came home your aunt acted the martinet and administered a corrective which I received with profound joy. I revelled in being punished and voluptuously warm. And while she cuffed me, I thought with delight of the meat she would give me directly afterwards.

You see – an afterthought, while stretched out before the embers – true happiness, paradise, my master, is where one is locked up and beaten, wherever there is meat.

I speak for cats.

AMOURS

Colette

THE ROBIN HAD WON. Now he celebrated his victory in little dry chirps, safe in the depths of a chestnut tree. He was proud that he had not fled from the cat. He had hovered above her buzzing like an angry bee. His taunts, to anyone who understood his chirping, were fiercesome.

'I, Robin red-breast, will peck out your eyes if you take one more step towards the nest which holds my precious eggs.'

I was watching, ready to intervene, but the cat understands that the robin is not to be touched. She understands so many things. Still, she thinks that in allowing the bird to insult her with impunity, she risks being made to look a fool. So, she thrashes her tail like a lion and arches her back. In the end she leaves the frantic bird and we continue on our walk through the dusk.

It is a slow, pleasurable amble in which we both make discoveries. Well, she is making discoveries to be honest. She stops and stares fixedly at something in the distance which I cannot see. She crouches and leaps at a noise I do not hear. I have to guess what she is finding so fascinating.

Being with a cat is always stimulating but did I set out fifty years ago to seek the company of cats? It never seemed that I had to look for them. They were always there at my feet. They came in so many guises: lost and starving, hunting and being hunted, the library cat embalmed in ink, dairy cats and butcher's cats well-fed but with paws cold from the tiled floor. There are flabby bourgeois cats,

self-satisfied cats and despot cats who tyrannize over Paul Morand, Claude Farrere and me. They all come to me with pleasure but without surprise.

One day I noticed a poor thin cat being pushed to and fro by the crowd which pours each evening out of the Autreuil metro. In fact it was she who recognized me. 'There you are at last,' she said. 'You are very late. Where is your home? Do not worry, I will follow you.'

When we got home my house seemed to frighten her, perhaps because I lived there with someone else. She soon settled in, however. She lived with me for four years before dying in an accident.

But I must not forget my dogs, just as loving, just as vulnerable. How could I live without you? I am indispensable to you. You make me realise how truly valuable I am to you. Is there anyone else of whom I can say the same? You comfort me with your devotion though maybe you are almost too loving, your eyes too beseeching. I do not know much about a dog's sex life; because, out of my favourite ten breeds, I prefer those unable to breed. For instance, sometimes the bitch of the Brabant terrier, the French type of bulldog – pug-nosed with a huge head – instinctively refuses to mate. It knows that giving birth is dangerous because of its size and shape.

Two bitches I had, used to bite dogs who tried to mate outside 'safe periods'. One poodle was happy to feed a rubber puppy instead of the real thing. Though I have owned many dogs, cats have always been more important to me. From them I have learnt to be reserved, self-disciplined and intolerant of noise.

The cat which has meant most to me and was different from all others was the one I mentioned at the beginning. And yet, because she was so special I cannot say too much about her. Only when she was sexually active did she cease to be mine and rejoined the cat world. I can only guess what she saw in the tomcat who raped and abused her. Sex not love brought forth her terrible wails and bird-like cries, insulting and threatening her mate.

In the country she is flirtatious and promiscuous, delighting in her freedom to be truly catlike and not the human's 'best friend'. To me she is warm, faithful and sensitive – the opposite of all she is to her cat lovers.

In town, in the narrow walled garden of my Paris house, she played happily, sometimes full of energy, sometimes content to dream. She restrained her natural instincts, haughtily rejecting would-be mates. There is the old striped conqueror, thin as a rake, bald in places but highly experienced. He is decisive, respected by his rivals, confident of success.

Then there is a young cat, stupid and self-satisfied, enjoying his own beauty – the beauty of the tiger. Finally, there is the farm cat who appears on the top of the wall as though awakened from a dream by an urgent mating call.

She gives all three a hard time, using her paws without mercy to slap their faces when they push too hard. Then she rolls around in front of them but follows that exhibition with freezing contempt. She climbs onto a crumbling pillar from which she can pour scorn on her assailants. When she decides to rejoin her three slaves she does so with hauteur. She allows one of her admirers to kiss her nose but when this goes on too long she puts a stop to it with an imperious cry impossible to describe.

The three tomcats jump back in surprise. My cat, seeming to forget her lovers, goes back to grooming herself. Depressed by their long courtship, the male cats begin to fight amongst themselves to pass the time. My cat leaves them to it, renouncing her flirtatious games, pleased to rejoin the humans.

While I work, my cat lies beside me under the warmth of the reading lamp, silent, watchful, content – my she-cat, my friend.

A SHIP OF SOLACE

Eleanor Mordaunt

The cat stands alone, distinct – out-individualizing every individual. 'Let us agree with the world in general that a cat has nine lives,' pursued Charlotte; 'and that this cat has nine different individualities to its nine different lives – that makes fourteen people on board this ship that really count, the cat being half.'

When Charlotte talks in that way she reminds me of Plato – of course, she is not so deep, but she is just as mystifying and convincing. 'For instance, when a man, by feeling, hearing, or perceiving a thing by any of the senses, knows what it is that thus strikes the senses, and at the same time imagines to himself another thing (independent of that knowledge, by virtue of a quite different knowledge), do we not justly say that the man remembers the thing that comes into his mind?' Charlotte has heard that cats have nine lives; she feels that there can be no individuality without life; she perceives that the ship's cat has individuality to a striking degree, and (independent of that knowledge, by virtue of a quite different knowledge – namely, a woman's genius for jumping at conclusions) argues that the cat is fully the equal of the nine other individuals on board this ship. The line of argument is distinctly Charlotte, notwithstanding that the sentences between the inverted commas are to be found in the 'Phaedo'.

And yet, after all, even without the wisdom of the ages to support her line of argument, she is right. There are many men – of sorts – on board, but there is only one cat, and *such* a cat! She is always spoken of as 'he', in spite of the fact that on the return voyage last trip she brought in the world a family of kittens, during a most unholy gale off Cape Horn; though the Captain tells me that she treated them with the barest toleration, 'being such an arrant scoundrel, such a hard case, that he is a deal more like a boy than a girl'.

But the ship's cat is not only more like a 'he' than a 'she', it has also more of the characteristics of a dog than any cat I ever met before, the chief of them being its unswerving and undivided devotion to the Captain; and that in spite of being teased and tormented, and, worst of all, laughed at, in a way that would alienate most cats' affections for ever.

We – that is, the cat and the Captain – keep cocks and hens on board, which during the fine weather parade the decks in the most exasperatingly consequential manner. Still, they are popularly supposed to be held within certain bounds, these bounds being the delight of the cat. Let the Lord of the Harem lead his train of wives up on to the poop-deck and he pays dearly for his temerity. 'Boy' does not at once take matters into his own hands, but if the Captain is below will deliberately walk down the companion and into his cabin, stare him in the face for a moment, and then make his exit, walking backwards, and with weird emphatic mews entreating him to come and witness the scandal that is disgracing 'their' ship. Even then he awaits orders, at the side of his master, up on the poop-deck, the whole of his muscular little body, with its precise tiger-like markings, tense and rigid, the pupils of his clear green eyes contracted to mere pin-points by the intensity of his feelings as he watches, not the intruders, but the eye of his god. Then suddenly, without a word, some electric current seems to pass between them, his back arches, he crouches a little, ready for a spring, so ready that he is off, like a bolt from a tightly strung catapult, almost before the words 'At 'em, Boy!' are out of the Captain's mouth.

For a moment the cock may face him – feathers ruffled, beak agape, wings spread – but it is only for the moment, during which his hysterical female belongings are scattering, Boy's one care being that they shall not go over the rail. Then comes their lord's turn, and he is harried on all sides, the furred fury that attacks him

A *Ship of Solace*

appearing a mere blurred mist of many cats, so swiftly does he circle and leap and dart, scratch and spit. The cock's wings are spread as a protection, no longer in defiance, his erstwhile brilliant and erect comb becomes pale and flaccid, his curving tail feathers, that but a moment before would not have disgraced a Field-Marshal's hat, trail on the deck. With ducking head he runs to and fro, then suddenly throws all pretence of dignity to the winds, flings out his long ungainly legs and hurtles over the break of the poop after his departing fair, who are fleeing to their own quarters in the midships, with their tails blown over their heads like inverted crinolines.

To see Boy play ball with a piece of cork is a truly wonderful study in curves and intensest vitality. He crouches just about three yards from his master, the pupils of his eyes expanded till they look like black wells, with the merest rim of green, his tail beating the deck with a regular circular movement.

'Ready, Boy!' cries the Captain, and he stiffens himself with a joyous quiver which runs through the whole of the lithe little body, in which every atom of life is gathered for the spring; it is for the time a matter of life and death, and his whole being is aflame with ardour; there is he himself, and the cork, and, incidentally, the man who throws – nothing else, and no one else in the whole of the wide world.

'Now!' The cork is flung and Boy springs, stretched to his full length, then gathered to a ball in mid air, with front paws upraised like a cricketer's hands, full a yard from the deck, catches the cork between his white-stockinged feet, and rolls on the deck, kicking at it in a perfect transport of delight with his hind-feet.

But if he misses? Ah, that is another matter. Supposing we are too well-mannered to laugh, he simply appears oblivious of the bauble having been thrown at all, but walks the deck a little, goes up to it in a leisurely fashion, sniffs as if to say, 'What in the world can this be?' looks at his master – 'a game, eh?' and finally picking it up, deposits it at his feet, asking, as an obviously new idea, that it shall be thrown. But if anyone, other than his master, has laughed, the game is over for the day, and off goes his Highness in a fit of sulks,

which is, in its intensity, another sign of how great a mistake his real sex has been, for women seldom sulk: they usually have too much to say on any matter which annoys them.

At such times as this he delights in getting into the most dangerous positions, on the taffrail, or up on the boats, with the air of one who says to himself: 'I'll give them a good fright for once, and they'll be sorry for this levity, then they'll wish they hadn't.'

'Come down out of that!' shouts the Captain. But Boy merely cocks an eye at him and does not budge an inch, till his master stoops for a coil of rope, when he is off like a flash to a safer position, for he knows quite well that he is not allowed in certain places, even though the ship is, so to speak, his own.

When a sheep has been killed the fresh meat is hung just below the boats on the main-deck, and draws Boy like a magnet, though nothing on earth would tempt him to help himself. But if we are all on the poop-deck, including him, of course, for he hates solitude, and the Captain so much as takes his knife out of his pocket, he mews wildly and trembles all over with excitement. There is an example of self-control! He wants it terribly; so terribly that he is almost mad with excitement at the prospect of even the merest morsel. He could help himself easily any hour of the day or night; yet he never does so. Now, tell me, is morality a matter of the soul, which is allowed to the inveterate drunkard, the irreclaimable thief, and is yet denied to Boy? In the saloon it is the same: the Captain has only to pick up his cap and the cat is rubbing himself against his legs mewing, 'Meat, meat, meat – meat – *please*, dear.'

Yet it is not merely cupboard love, for however warm the saloon fire, however wet the deck, however rainy and stormy the weather, if the Captain is up on deck, there the cat must be also. Sometimes his courage will half fail him, and he will wait to see if his idol has not merely gone up to take a look at the weather and then return again; but he cannot rest, and after a moment or so of anxious watching he throws comfort to the winds and is off, not to return to the warmth and light till his master returns too. A few nights ago he was caught by a heavy sea and washed backwards and forwards over the deck, hopelessly, helplessly, till he was secured by the mate and brought to the saloon, a dejected wisp of misery, to be washed in fresh water and dried by the fire. But even then he could not rest; his eyes, as he lay on my lap, were for ever on the door, and he was off again before he was one-half dry.

It is not even as though he has an easy time with his idol, for he is always getting his tail and ears pulled, and his little toes pinched, though he but seldom retaliates with claw or tooth, while if he does he is so bitterly ashamed of himself that it is really heart-breaking to see his utter dejection.

When first we came on board, Boy regarded us with the utmost suspicion; perhaps we reminded him of his own sex, or perhaps it was sheer dislike of petticoats fluttering aboard his ship. But since that first night, when Charlotte was so ill, all this has changed. While the Captain made poultices, Boy was constantly in and out, clambering on to the bunk, and clamouring strenuously for notice and explanations, for puss is feminine enough in this – he will know the why and wherefore of everything. And now, having found that we are tolerated, to say the least of it, by his master, he tolerates us too, and will make himself quite at home on my knee, occasionally even placing two soft little front-paws on my chest, and inviting me amicably to rub noses. But this is only when he cannot sit on his master's knee, which he infinitely prefers, uncomfortable as it always looks, and must be, with no nice warm spread of dress for him to repose on.

INCIDENT ON EAST NINTH

Jill Drower

I LEANED MY HEAD against the cool metal of the reinforced door. Something was digging into my temple – the spy-hole. I pictured Arnold peeping through from the other side, squinting at me with a cold, cold eye, resentful, gloating, wishing me dead. He loathed me. I realized it the first moment we were introduced. Arnold got me into this. It was all his fault.

It was hot – somewhere in the eighties. This was a smart apartment block in the East Village, but the corridor still looked like it belonged to cell block B at a state pen. It was stifling but I was shaking more than a leaf on a Dutch elm. Was it embarrassment or shock? Every few minutes the elevator would chime and ping out another group of homecomers. They would glance over in my direction and then look away indifferently. What was the matter? Didn't I look weird enough for them? Dishevelled, furtive, I pressed up close to the apartment door in a feeble attempt to conceal myself behind the architrave.

The T-shirt I was wearing was a little tatty, but it was as bright-white as new. It came down just below my navel and it had giant sans serif letters across the chest which spelt out the word 'RELAX'. This was my first night in New York and I was locked out of my friend's apartment. I was telling myself to calm down. Difficult. Apart from the T-shirt, all I was wearing was a pair of gold-hoop earrings.

Arnold's relationship with Laura was entirely platonic. Having shared the apartment for some years they were now as close as brother and sister. Laura was relieved to find a flatmate who accepted her as she was, someone who didn't squabble about petty things like who did the washing-up. Besides, living in New York was a lonely business and Arnold was entertaining company. The problem was, he was jealous of her friends. Maybe he thought that, if she found someone and fell in love, she might want to get married and 'the other man' would boot him out. Whatever it was, Arnold made it his business to frighten away any friends whom she invited in. She had taken to visiting singles bars, and this brought a fairly high number of invitations from her to 'come back to my place for coffee'. Arnold developed what he called his 'spooking-out technique' which, after a couple of evenings, he had down to a fine art. Laura, unsuspecting, would disappear into the kitchen to fix the percolator. Arnold, very friendly, would join the visitor on the sofa and, at a given moment, he would put on this stare and become strangely menacing. When Laura returned with the tray, he was back to being the nice guy and would make a big ceremony of leaving the room tactfully to let them sit alone together on the sofa. After one visit, these poor hopefuls never returned.

I was in New York principally to meet a number of old friends who were now living there but, as this was my first visit to the city, I wanted to see as much of Manhattan as possible in the ten days I had.

'You're welcome to stay at my place, if you like, so long as you don't mind sleeping on the sofa.' I took Laura up on her offer. She lived on East Ninth, somewhere near the bottom of Fifth Avenue and near enough to Washington Square Park for us to go jogging there every morning.

The journey from La Guardia to Laura's apartment had me in a trance. It was all exactly like those cop shows and Scorcese films I'd seen, only much more so. It was all so different from the ribbons of mock Tudor en route from Heathrow or Gatwick. I took it all in: the weatherboard houses, the freeways, the automobiles, the 'last exit to . . .' signs and the bluntness of the yellow cab driver who

took me from the bus terminal to Laura's place. Like the uninitiated in any major city, I saw the place as a series of clichés. All that was missing was the steam coming out of subway gratings, but I suppose I had the wrong time of year for that. This was summer in the city and fire-hydrant-unlocking time. Firecrackers snapped all around, a constant reminder that July the 4th was only a day away.

Laura was a model host. She took me for brunch and a short walk through the Village. Being an architect, she was able to talk interestingly about the brownstone buildings around. She did warn me briefly about Arnold, saying he was a bit fractious, but no more was said about him that afternoon. Anyway, I reckoned I could manage to soften him up easily enough and that, in no time, we'd be getting along fine.

That first evening a whole group of us ate out in Little Italy to celebrate the reunion of an old gang of friends. I had Conchiglie alla Siciliana which seemed to me the most wonderful dish I had ever tried. We toasted the chef and then drank to absent friends. The man who served us was attentive and gave me a special smile which made him look like a member of the Corleone family. 'I haven't said goodbye to the waiter,' I exclaimed as we were leaving the building. 'He'll live,' said the manageress in the kind of Brooklyn accent I'd kill for if I were an actress. We all laughed and linked arms walking briskly back past the down and outs on the Bowery.

'Do come with us,' said Emil. 'You're only here for a few days.' He wanted me to join them for a late-night showing of *Kiss Me Kate* in 3D. 'No, I'm really too tired, I haven't slept for nineteen hours,' I made my excuses, trying to draw some sympathy. 'I'll see you all tomorrow when the jet lag's worn off.' They accompanied me as far as the junction of Astor Place and Broadway. Laura explained once more how the spare key worked. 'If you get stuck, ask the super.' I looked blank. 'The janitor,' she translated. 'What's a janitor?' I joked in my most pompous English accent.

I let myself in without difficulty and walked over to the window. It was wide open. Just level with the bottom of the frame was a large expanse of flat roofing. At the far end was the ironwork of a fire escape. 'Fire escapes,' I thought. 'Now I know I'm in New York.

Cookie, elevator, faucet, super, janitor, I wonder if they have their own word for fire escape too.'

On the sofa was a neat pile of sheets. I managed to assemble it all into some sort of order and struggle into my T-shirt ready for bed. As I lay there half-asleep, I wondered mildly why Laura was so lax about security, but I was too sleepy to get up and close the window. I sank under the cover and within a few seconds I had drifted into sleep.

I woke with a start and lay there for several minutes listening to the whoop-whoop-whoop of police patrol cars and watching the thin curtains billow in the grimy night air.

At some point, I realized I was not alone. The intruder was there somewhere in the room. I stumbled through the darkness towards the door, upsetting a table as I went. I felt something sharp slash my flesh as I groped madly around the wall for a light switch and found it. Then we were looking straight at each other in the lighted room. My attacker, with his vicious penetrating eyes, was standing a few feet away, holding my gaze with his, pinning me to the spot with nothing more than his burning, piercing, hating eyes.

I knew that, if I moved, my assailant would try another slash. We stayed frozen like that for a few moments – musical statues without the music – blood dripping down from the deep gashes in my legs. I had to protect my body from the next attack. Beside me on the floor was a pile of old copies of *Rolling Stone* magazine. Moving quickly, I tried to whip the newsprint in front of me as a shield, but he was far quicker on the draw and cut through the backs of my hands in a trice. He was now taking systematic swipes at any exposed part of me that he could reach. I was no match.

I grappled with the front-door latch and shot through to the hallway. This time Arnold was not quite quick enough. I pulled the door until I heard a gentle click as the latch locked home.

I don't know how long I stood there in that Greenwich Village hallway, half-naked, in a state of trembling indecision.

At last, I crept down to the basement by the back stairs and followed the sound of an early hours news channel reporting preparations for the Independence Day celebration fireworks on

Incident on East Ninth

the West Side. The janitor looked me slowly up and down, but more down than up.

'Do you happen to have a first-aid box?' I asked meekly. 'And something for me to wear?' He shuffled about and produced a large paint-spattered sheet which I wrapped around me like a toga. After further searching he came up with an old rag, stiff with dried metal polish. After dabbing at the gashes with it for a few moments, I managed to work out that it had once been some kind of undergarment.

'I've been attacked by a cat,' I explained. 'Lady,' he replied, 'you got problems.' He wasn't planning to solve them for me, just commenting. He went back to listening to the broadcast. 'I've also been locked out of apartment number 208. I don't suppose you've got a spare key, have you?'

He dug a credit card out of his wallet and I followed him back up to the flat. He started to work away with the plastic. He seemed amazingly skilled at breaking in and I began to wonder what he did for a living before he was a janitor. Still, this was not the moment to doubt the man whose help I badly needed. My assistant was the silent type, so I did all the talking. 'As soon as the door opens, I'll throw this in.' I waved the polishing-rag undies. 'Don't leave until I've got past him into the bedroom.' I rolled them up tight into a ball and got ready to throw.

The door swung wide open. Arnold was across the other side, eyeing me, quivering in readiness. Ignoring the janitor, he waited for me to make my move. I bowled the brasso ball, medium speed, with a bit of spin. While he was savaging it, I slipped past into Laura's bedroom and shut the door, calling out my thanks to the indifferent janitor. Wasting no time, I took a ladderback chair and tucked it smartly under the door handle.

I switched on the TV. It was tuned to a Spanish language programme. 'Adónde vas? A que no te atreves a besarme?' I flicked the button to the next channel number. Behind me the bedroom-door handle was rattling and jerking. I checked the chair back was still tightly wedged in position, and then settled down to the programme. It was a threesome gameshow. The secretary was called

Barbara. She knew far more about husband Bob than wife Connie did. Still, Connie was being very sporting about it; even when it emerged that it was Barbara, not Bob, who had chosen her tenth anniversary present, she laughed ecstatically and applauded her humiliation along with the studio audience.

All this time, Arnold was still pounding on the handle, trying to hurry up the metal fatigue. I turned the volume up to maximum and set my face to the screen. Then suddenly nothing. Silence outside.

I heard the front latch turn and heard Laura's voice. 'Hi, Arnold, how yer been?' She walked in to greet me wearing cardboard glasses, one red side, one green. She stopped in her tracks. 'Looks like you've been having some 3D effects in here.' She looked round at all the furniture in disarray.

Over the next few days Laura did what she could to try to make Arnold see me in a more positive light. These efforts included getting me to give him a bowl of Nine Lives Formula, a plan which went disastrously wrong. Simple tasks like walking to the bathroom or making a cup of coffee were now a nerve-wracking ordeal. 'Try and relax,' Laura would encourage me as I started my journey across the room. 'Are you sure this is a good idea? Couldn't we lock Arnold away just till I go out?' I pleaded. Then I'd hear him scurrying along after me and feel his claws as they found their way through the denim to my tender flesh.

Laura eventually brought in a cat psychiatrist because she was seriously worried about his worsening behaviour. A neighbour had already threatened litigation after Arnold took a swipe one afternoon. 'I'd better do something or, sooner or later, someone is going to take me to court. Suing someone you know is our most popular national pastime. People take classes in it at night school.'

A series of appointments were set up with a very nice Argentinean therapist called Graciela. 'She says I am Arnold's emotional blanket,' Laura confided after one of these consultations. 'And she thinks he's suffering from an abandonment complex.' I felt this was all a very pricey way to find out the obvious, but I kept these thoughts to myself.

The therapist explained what single-cat syndrome was, and suggested that Laura buy Arnold his own little kitten to play with. He was also put on a course of Valium. With half a tablet he was still attacking me. On one whole pill he couldn't quite coordinate enough, so he would just stare at me. In fact, Arnold did a lot of staring over the next few days. At primary school, I can remember a huge portrait of the Queen which hung in the dining-room. I noticed that it didn't matter which table I sat at, her eyes would always be looking directly at me. Having Arnold around was a bit like that, only it wasn't a case of wherever I looked from but whenever I looked. From time to time, it might be two minutes or twenty, I would glance up from my guide book or Manhattan street plan, and there he'd be, eyeballing me. I never saw him blink.

Laura followed all the advice she was given except the bit about buying Arnold his own little kitten. Somehow, she never got around to visiting that pet store on Hudson Street. It would, on reflection, have been a bad idea. Picture Arnold patting and putting the fluffy little thing around the room like an outsize mouse.

This story does have a happy ending (for Arnold at any rate) because, after a few days, I gave up and moved to a hotel. He celebrated his victory by becoming docile and lovable once more. He continued to preside over Laura's spinsterhood, but now with increased confidence.

As for Laura, she carried on her social life outside the flat and rarely invited people back. The offers of a bed to visiting tourist friends ceased after my trip which, for someone living in such a sought-after spot on the globe, must have come as something of a relief. It certainly gave her more time to concentrate on her work and later that year she was promoted, so I suppose there was a happy ending for her too.

'I've landed this incredible job,' she phoned me about a year later. 'It's a complete renovation of an art gallery in SoHo.'

'How's Arnold these days?' I asked.

'Oh, he couldn't be better. He's right by my side, can't you hear him purring?'

HOW A CAT PLAYED ROBINSON CRUSOE

Charles G. D. Roberts

THE ISLAND WAS A MERE SANDBANK off the low, flat coast. Not a tree broke its bleak levels – not even a shrub. But the long, gritty stalks of the marsh grass clothed it everywhere above tide-mark; and a tiny rivulet of sweet water, flowing from a spring at its centre, drew a ribbon of inland herbage and tenderer green across the harsh and sombre yellow grey of the grass. Few would have chosen the island as a place to live, yet at its seaward end, where the changing tides were never still, stood a spacious, one-storied, wide-verandaed cottage, with a low shed behind it. The virtue of this lone plot of sand was coolness. When the neighbour mainland would be sweltering day and night alike under a breathless heat, out here on the island there was always a cool wind blowing. Therefore a wise city dweller had appropriated the sea waif and built his summer home thereon, where the tonic airs might bring back the rose to the pale cheeks of his children.

The family came to the island toward the end of June. In the first week of September they went away, leaving every door and window of house and shed securely shuttered, bolted or barred against the winter's storms. A roomy boat, rowed by two fishermen, carried them across the half mile of racing tides that separated them from the mainland. The elders of the household were not sorry to get back to the world of men, after two months of mere wind, and sun, and waves, and waving grass tops. But the children went with tear-stained faces. They were leaving behind them their favourite pet, the accustomed comrade of their migrations, a handsome, moon-faced cat, striped like a tiger. The animal had mysteriously disappeared two days before, vanishing from the face of the island without leaving a trace behind. The only reasonable explanation seemed to be that she had been snapped up by a passing eagle. The cat, meanwhile, was a fast prisoner at the other end of the island, hidden beneath a broken barrel and some hundredweight of drifted sand.

The old barrel, with the staves battered out of one side, had stood, half buried, on the crest of a sand ridge raised by a long prevailing wind. Under its lee the cat had found a sheltered hollow, full of sun, where she had been wont to lie curled up for hours at a time, basking and sleeping. Meanwhile the sand had been steadily piling itself higher and higher behind the unstable barrier. At last it had piled too high; and suddenly, before a stronger gust, the barrel had come toppling over beneath a mass of sand, burying the sleeping cat out of sight and light. But at the same time the sound half of the barrel had formed a safe roof to her prison, and she was neither crushed nor smothered. When the children in their anxious search all over the island chanced upon the mound of fine, white sand they gave it but one careless look. They could not hear the faint cries that came, at intervals, from the close darkness within. So they went away sorrowfully, little dreaming that their friend was imprisoned almost beneath their feet.

For three days the prisoner kept up her appeals for help. On the third day the wind changed and presently blew up a gale. In a few hours it had uncovered the barrel. At one corner a tiny spot of light appeared.

Eagerly the cat stuck her paw through the hole. When she withdrew it again the hole was much enlarged. She took the hint and fell to scratching. At first her efforts were rather aimless; but presently, whether by good luck or quick sagacity, she learned to make her scratching more effective. The opening rapidly enlarged, and at last she was able to squeeze her way out.

The wind was tearing madly across the island, filled with flying sand. The seas hurled themselves trampling up the beach, with the

uproar of a bombardment. The grasses lay bowed flat in long quivering ranks. Over the turmoil the sun stared down from a deep, unclouded blue. The cat, when first she met the full force of the gale, was fairly blown off her feet. As soon as she could recover herself she crouched low and darted into the grasses for shelter. But there was little shelter there, the long stalks being held down almost level. Through their lashed lines, however, she sped straight before the gale, making for the cottage at the other end of the island, where she would find, as she fondly imagined, not only food and shelter but also loving comfort to make her forget her terrors.

Still and desolate in the bright sunshine and the tearing wind, the house frightened her. She could not understand the tight-closed shutters, the blind, unresponding doors that would no longer open to her anxious appeal. The wind swept her savagely across the naked veranda. Climbing with difficulty to the dining-room windowsill, where so often she had been let in, she clung there a few moments and yowled heartbrokenly. Then, in a sudden panic, she jumped down and ran to the shed. That, too, was closed. Never before had she seen the shed doors closed, and she could not understand it. Cautiously she crept around the foundations – but those had been built honestly: there was no such thing as getting in that way. On every side it was nothing but a blank, forbidding face that the old familiar house confronted her with.

The cat had always been so coddled and pampered by the children that she had had no need to forage for herself; but, fortunately for her, she had learned to hunt the marsh mice and grass sparrows for amusement. So now, being ravenous from her long fast under the sand, she slunk mournfully away from the deserted house and crept along under the lee of a sand ridge to a little grassy hollow which she knew. Here the gale caught only the tops of the grasses; and here, in the warmth and comparative calm, the furry little marsh folk, mice and shrews, were going about their business undisturbed.

The cat, quick and stealthy, soon caught one and eased her hunger. She caught several. And then, making her way back to the house, she spent hours in heartsick prowling around it and around, sniffing and peering, yowling piteously on the threshold and windowsill; and every now and then being blown ignominiously across the smooth, naked expanse of the veranda floor. At last, hopelessly discouraged, she curled herself up beneath the children's window and went to sleep.

In spite of her loneliness and grief the life of the island prisoner during the next two or three weeks was by no means one of hardship. Besides her abundant food of birds and mice she quickly learned to catch tiny fish in the mouth of the rivulet, where salt water and fresh water met. It was an exciting game, and she became expert at dashing the grey tom-cod and blue-and-silver sand-lance far up the slope with a sweep of her armed paw. But when the equinoctial storms roared down upon the island, with furious rain, and low, black clouds torn to shreds, then life became more difficult for her. Game all took to cover, where it was hard to find. It was difficult to get around in the drenched and lashing grass; and, moreover, she loathed wet. Most of the time she went hungry, sitting sullen and desolate under the lee of the house, glaring out defiantly at the rush and battling tumult of the waves.

The storm lasted nearly ten days before it blew itself clean out. On the eighth day the abandoned wreck of a small Nova Scotia schooner drove ashore, battered out of all likeness to a ship. But hulk as it was it had passengers of a sort. A horde of rats got through the surf and scurried into the hiding of the grass roots. They promptly made themselves at home, burrowing under the grass and beneath old, half-buried timbers, and carrying panic into the ranks of the mice and shrews.

When the storm was over the cat had a decided surprise in her first long hunting expedition. Something had rustled the grass heavily and she trailed it, expecting a particularly large, fat marsh mouse. When she pounced and alighted upon an immense old ship's rat, many-voyaged and many-battled, she got badly bitten. Such an experience had never before fallen to her lot. At first she felt so injured that she was on the point of backing out and running away. Then her latent pugnacity awoke, and the fire of far-off ancestors. She flung herself into the fight with a rage that took no accounting of the wounds she got; and the struggle was soon over.

Stakes

'The cat stands alone, distinct – out-individualizing every individual.'
A Ship of Solace

The Window Cat

'Sunbathing on my windowsill meant nothing to her.
She was there because she liked the shelter it afforded her.'
CATS OF MY CHILDHOOD

Thomas

'He conveyed the impression of being a cat of deep reserves.'
THE STORY OF WEBSTER

The Carpet-Cat

'The animal which the Egyptians worshipped as divine, which the Romans venerated as a symbol of liberty . . .'

THE ACHIEVEMENT OF THE CAT

Her wounds, faithfully licked, quickly healed themselves in that clean and tonic air; and after that, having learned how to handle such big game, she no more got bitten.

During the first full moon after her abandonment – the first week in October – the island was visited by still weather with sharp night frosts. The cat discovered then that it was most exciting to hunt by night and do her sleeping in the daytime. She found that now, under the strange whiteness of the moon, all her game was astir – except the birds, which had fled to the mainland during the storm, gathering for the southward flight. The blanched grasses, she found, were now everywhere a-rustle; and everywhere dim little shapes went darting with thin squeaks across ghostly-white sands. Also she made the acquaintance of a new bird, which she regarded at first uneasily and then with vengeful wrath. This was the brown marsh owl, which came over from the mainland to do some autumn mouse hunting. There were two pairs of these big, downy-winged, round-eyed hunters, and they did not know there was a cat on the island.

The cat, spying one of them as it swooped soundlessly hither and thither over the silvered grass tops, crouched with flattened ears. With its wide spread of wing it looked bigger than herself; and the great round face, with hooked beak and wild, staring eyes, appeared extremely formidable. However, she was no coward; and presently, though not without reasonable caution, she went about her hunting. Suddenly the owl caught a partial glimpse of her in the grass – probably of her ears or head. He swooped; and at the same instant she sprang upward to meet the assault, spitting and growling harshly and striking with unsheathed claws. With a frantic flapping of his great wings the owl checked himself and drew back into the air, just escaping the clutch of those indignant claws. After that the marsh owls were careful to give her a wide berth. They realized that the black-striped animal with the quick spring and the clutching claws was not to be interfered with. They perceived that she was some relation to that ferocious prowler, the lynx.

In spite of all this hunting, however, the furry life of the marsh grass was so teeming, so inexhaustible, that the depredations of cat, rats and owls were powerless to make more than a passing impression upon it. So the hunting and the merrymaking went on side by side under the indifferent moon.

As the winter deepened – with bursts of sharp cold and changing winds that forced the cat to be continually changing her refuge – she grew more and more unhappy. She felt her homelessness keenly. Nowhere on the whole island could she find a nook where she might feel secure from both wind and rain. As for the old barrel, the first cause of her misfortunes, there was no help in that. The winds had long ago turned it completely over, open to the sky, then drifted it full of sand and reburied it. And in any case the cat would have been afraid to go near it again. So it came about that she alone of all the island dwellers had no shelter to turn to when the real winter arrived, with snows that smothered the grass tops out of sight, and frosts that lined the shore with grinding ice cakes. The

rats had their holes under the buried fragments of wreckage; the mice and shrews had their deep, warm tunnels; the owls had nests in hollow trees far away in the forests of the mainland. But the cat, shivering and frightened, could do nothing but crouch against the blind walls of the unrelenting house and let the snow whirl itself and pile itself about her.

And now, in her misery, she found her food cut off. The mice ran secure in their hidden runways, where the grass roots on each side of them gave them easy and abundant provender. The rats, too, were out of sight – digging burrows themselves in the soft snow in the hope of intercepting some of the tunnels of the mice, and now and then snapping up an unwary passer-by. The ice fringe, crumbling and heaving under the ruthless tide, put an end to her fishing. She would have tried to capture one of the formidable owls in her hunger, but the owls no longer came to the island. They would return, no doubt, later in the season when the snow had hardened and the mice had begun to come out and play on the surface. But for the present they were following an easier chase in the deeps of the upland forest.

When the snow stopped falling and the sun came out again there fell such keen cold as the cat had never felt before. The day, as it chanced, was Christmas; and if the cat had had any idea as to the calendar she would certainly have marked the day in her memory as it was an eventful one for her. Starving as she was she could not sleep, but kept ceaselessly on the prowl. This was fortunate, for had she gone to sleep without any more shelter than the wall of the house she would never have wakened again. In her restlessness she wandered to the farther side of the island where, in a somewhat sheltered and sunny recess of the shore facing the mainland, she found a patch of bare sand, free of ice cakes and just uncovered by the tide. Opening upon this recess were the tiny entrances to several of the mouse tunnels.

Close beside one of these holes in the snow the cat crouched, quiveringly intent. For ten minutes or more she waited, never so much as twitching a whisker. At last a mouse thrust out its little pointed head. Not daring to give it time to change its mind or take alarm, she pounced. The mouse, glimpsing the doom ere it fell, doubled back upon itself in the narrow runway. Hardly realizing what she did in her desperation the cat plunged head and shoulders into the snow, reaching blindly after the vanished prize. By great good luck she caught it.

It was her first meal in four bitter days. The children had always tried to share with her their Christmas cheer and enthusiasm, and had usually succeeded in interesting her by an agreeable lavishness in the matter of cream; but never before had she found a Christmas feast so good.

Now she had learned a lesson. Being naturally clever and her wits sharpened by her fierce necessities, she had grasped the idea that it was possible to follow her prey a little way into the snow. She had not realized that the snow was so penetrable. She had quite wiped out the door of this particular runway; so she went and crouched beside a similar one, but here she had to wait a long time before an adventurous mouse came to peer out. But this time she showed that she had grasped her lesson. It was straight at the side of the entrance that she pounced, where instinct told her that the body of the mouse would be. One outstretched paw thus cut off the quarry's retreat. Her tactics were completely successful; and as her head went plunging into the fluffy whiteness she felt the prize between her paws.

Her hunger now fairly appeased, she found herself immensely excited over this new fashion of hunting. Often before had she waited at mouse holes, but never had she found it possible to break down the walls and invade the holes themselves. It was a thrilling idea. As she crept toward another hole a mouse scurried swiftly up the sand and darted into it. The cat, too late to catch him before he disappeared, tried to follow him. Scratching clumsily but hopefully she succeeded in forcing the full length of her body into the snow. She found no sign of the fugitive, which was by this time racing in safety down some dim transverse tunnel. Her eyes, mouth, whiskers and fur full of the powdery white particles, she backed out, much disappointed. But in that moment she had realized that it was much warmer in there beneath the snow than out in the stinging air. It

was a second and vitally important lesson; and though she was probably unconscious of having learned it she instinctively put the new lore into practice a little while later.

Having succeeded in catching yet another mouse for which her appetite made no immediate demand, she carried it back to the house and laid it down in tribute on the veranda steps while she meowed and stared hopefully at the desolate, snow-draped door. Getting no response she carried the mouse down with her to the hollow behind the drift which had been caused by the bulging front of the bay-window on the end of the house. Here she curled herself up forlornly, thinking to have a wink of sleep.

But the still cold was too searching. She looked at the sloping wall of snow beside her and cautiously thrust her paw into it. It was very soft and light. It seemed to offer practically no resistance. She pawed away in an awkward fashion till she had scooped out a sort of tiny cave. Gently she pushed herself into it, pressing back the snow on every side till she had room to turn around.

Then turn around she did several times, as dogs do in getting their beds arranged to their liking. In this process she not only packed down the snow beneath her, but she also rounded out for herself a snug chamber with a comparatively narrow doorway. From this snowy retreat she gazed forth with a solemn air of possession; then she went to sleep with a sense of comfort, of 'homeyness', such as she had never before felt since the disappearance of her friends.

Having thus conquered misfortune and won herself the freedom of the winter wild, her life though strenuous was no longer one of any terrible hardship. With patience at the mouse holes she could catch enough to eat; and in her snowy den she slept warm and secure. In a little while, when a crust had formed over the surface, the mice took to coming out at night and holding revels on the snow. Then the owls, too, came back; and the cat, having tried to catch one, got sharply bitten and clawed before she realized the propriety of letting it go. After this experience she decided that owls, on the whole, were meant to be let alone. But for all that she found it fine hunting, out there on the bleak, unfenced, white reaches of the snow.

Thus, mistress of the situation, she found the winter slipping by without further serious trials. Only once, toward the end of January, did Fate send her another bad quarter of an hour. On the heels of a peculiarly bitter cold snap a huge white owl from the Arctic Barrens came one night to the island. The cat, taking observations from the corner of the veranda, caught sight of him. One look was enough to assure her that this was a very different kind of visitor from the brown marsh owls. She slipped inconspicuously down into her burrow; and until the great white owl went away, some twenty-four hours later, she kept herself discreetly out of sight.

When spring came back to the island, with the nightly shrill chorus of fluting frogs in the shallow, sedgy pools and the young grass alive with nesting birds, the prisoner's life became almost luxurious in its easy abundance. But now she was once more homeless, since her snug den had vanished with the snow. This did not much matter to her, however, for the weather grew warmer and more tranquil day by day; and moreover, she herself, in being forced back upon her instincts, had learned to be as contented as a tramp. Nevertheless, with all her capacity for learning and adapting herself she had not forgotten anything. So when, one day in June, a crowded boat came over from the mainland, and children's voices, clamouring across the grass tops, broke the desolate silence of the island, the cat heard and sprang up out of her sleep on the veranda steps.

For one second she stood, listening intently. Then, almost as a dog would have done, and as few of her supercilious tribe ever condescend to do, she went racing across to the landing place – to be snatched up into the arms of four happy children at once, and to have her fine fur ruffled to a state which it would cost her an hour's assiduous toilet to put in order.

OLLY AND GINNY

James Herriot

IT IRKED ME, as a cat lover, that my own cats couldn't stand the sight of me. Ginny and Olly were part of the family now. We were devoted to them and whenever we had a day out the first thing Helen did on our return was to open the back door and feed them. The cats knew this very well and were either sitting on the flat top of the wall, waiting for her, or ready to trot down from the log shed which was their home.

We had been to Brawton on our half-day and they were there as usual as Helen put out a dish of food and a bowl of milk for them on the wall.

'Olly, Ginny,' she murmured as she stroked the furry coats. The days had long gone when they refused to let her touch them. Now they rubbed against her hand in delight, arching and purring and, when they were eating, she ran her hand repeatedly along their backs. They were such gentle little animals, their wildness expressed only in fear, and now, with her, that fear had gone. My children and some from the village had won their confidence, too, and were allowed to give them a careful caress, but they drew the line at Herriot.

Like now, for instance, when I quietly followed Helen out and moved towards the wall, immediately they left the food and retreated to a safe distance where they stood, still arching their backs but, as ever, out of reach. They regarded me without hostility but as I held out a hand they moved further away.

'Look at the little beggars!' I said. 'They still won't have anything to do with me.'

It was frustrating since, throughout my years in veterinary practice, cats had always intrigued me and I had found that this helped me in my dealings with them. I felt I could handle them more easily than most people because I liked them and they sensed it. I rather prided myself on my cat technique, a sort of feline bedside manner, and was in no doubt that I had an empathy with the entire species and that they all liked me. In fact, if the truth were told, I fancied myself as a cats' pin-up. Not so, ironically, with these two – the ones to whom I had become so deeply attached.

It was a bit hard, I thought, because I had doctored them and probably saved their lives when they had cat flu. Did they

remember that, I wondered, but if they did it still didn't give me the right apparently to lay a finger on them. And, indeed, what they certainly did seem to remember was that it was I who had netted them and then shoved them into a cage before I neutered them. I had the feeling that whenever they saw me, it was that net and cage which was uppermost in their minds.

I could only hope that time would bring an understanding between us but, as it turned out, fate was to conspire against me for a long time still. Above all, there was the business of Olly's coat. Unlike his sister, he was a longhaired cat and as such was subject to constant tangling and knotting of his fur. If he had been an ordinary domesticated feline, I would have combed him out as soon as trouble arose but since I couldn't even get near him I was helpless. We had had him about two years when Helen called me to the kitchen.

'Just look at him!' she said. 'He's a dreadful sight!'

I peered through the window. Olly was indeed a bit of a scarecrow with his matted fur and dangling knots in cruel contrast with his sleek and beautiful little sister.

'I know, I know. But what can I do?' I was about to turn away when I noticed something. 'Wait a minute, there's a couple of horrible big lumps hanging below his neck. Take these scissors and have a go at them – a couple of quick snips and they'll be off.'

Helen gave me an anguished look. 'Oh, we've tried this before. I'm not a vet and anyway, he won't let me do that. He'll let me pet him, but this is something else.'

'I know that, but have a go. There's nothing to it, really.' I pushed a pair of curved scissors into her hand and began to call instructions through the window. 'Right now, get your fingers behind that big dangling mass. Fine, fine! Now up with your scissors and –'

But at the first gleam of steel, Olly was off and away up the hill. Helen turned to me in despair. 'It's no good, Jim, it's hopeless – he won't let me cut even one lump off and he's covered with them.'

I looked at the dishevelled little creature standing at a safe distance from us. 'Yes, you're right. I'll have to think of something.'

Thinking of something entailed doping Olly so that I could get at him, and my faithful Nembutal capsules sprang immediately to mind. This oral anaesthetic had been a valued ally on countless occasions where I had to deal with unapproachable animals, but this was different. With the other cases, my patients had been behind closed doors but Olly was outside with all the wide countryside to roam in. I couldn't have him going to sleep somewhere out there where a fox or other predator might get him. I would have to watch him all the time.

It was a time for decisions, and I drew myself up. 'I'll have a go at him this Sunday,' I told Helen. 'It's usually a bit quieter and I'll ask Siegfried to stand in for me in an emergency.'

When the day arrived, Helen went out and placed two meals of chopped fish on the wall, one of them spiked with the contents of my Nembutal capsule. I crouched behind the window; watching intently as she directed Olly to the correct portion, and holding my breath as he sniffed at it suspiciously. His hunger soon overcame his caution and he licked the bowl clean with evident relish.

Now we started the tricky part. If he decided to explore the fields as he often did I would have to be right behind him. I stole out of the house as he sauntered back up the slope to the open log shed and to my vast relief he settled down in his own particular indentation in the straw and began to wash himself.

As I peered through the bushes I was gratified to see that very soon he was having difficulty with his face, licking his hind paw then toppling over as he brought it up to his cheek.

I chuckled to myself. This was great. Another few minutes and I'd have him.

And so it turned out. Olly seemed to conclude that he was tired of falling over and it wouldn't be a bad idea to have a nap. After gazing drunkenly around him, he curled up in the straw.

I waited a short time, then, with all the stealth of an Indian brave on the trail, I crept from my hiding place and tiptoed to the shed. Olly wasn't flat out – I hadn't dared give him the full anaesthetic dose in case I had been unable to track him – but he was deeply sedated. I could pretty well do what I wanted with him.

As I knelt down and began to snip away with my scissors, he opened his eyes and made a feeble attempt to struggle, but it was no good and I worked my way quickly through the ravelled fur. I wasn't able to make a particularly tidy job because he was wriggling slightly all the time, but I clipped off all the huge unsightly knots which used to get caught in the bushes, and must have been horribly uncomfortable, and soon had a growing heap of black hair by my side.

I noticed that Olly wasn't only not moving, he was watching me. Dazed as he was, he knew me all right and his eyes told me all. 'It's you again!' he was saying. 'I might have known!'

When I had finished, I lifted him into a cat cage and placed it on the straw. 'Sorry, old lad,' I said, 'but I can't let you go free till you've wakened up completely.'

Olly gave me a sleepy stare, but his sense of outrage was evident. 'So you've dumped me in here again. You don't change much, do you?'

By teatime he was fully recovered and I was able to release him. He looked so much better without the ugly tangles but he didn't seem impressed, and as I opened the cage he gave me a single disgusted look and sped away.

Helen was enchanted with my handiwork and she pointed eagerly at the two cats on the wall next morning. 'Doesn't he look smart! Oh, I'm so glad you managed to do him, it was really worrying me. And he must feel so much better.'

I felt a certain smug satisfaction as I looked through the window. Olly indeed was almost unrecognizable as the scruffy animal of yesterday and there was no doubt I had dramatically altered his life and relieved him of a constant discomfort, but my burgeoning bubble of self-esteem was pricked the instant I put my head round the back door. He had just started to enjoy his breakfast but at the sight of me he streaked away faster than ever before and disappeared far over the hill-top. Sadly, I turned back into the kitchen. Olly's opinion of me had dropped several more notches. Wearily I poured a cup of tea. It was a hard life.

MY BOSS THE CAT

Paul Gallico

IF YOU ARE THINKING of acquiring a cat at your house and would care for a quick sketch of what your life will be like under *Felis domesticus*, you have come to the right party. I have figured out that, to date, I have worked for – and I mean *worked* for – thirty-nine of these four-legged characters, including one memorable period when I was doing the bidding of some twenty-three assorted resident felines all at the same time.

Cats are, of course, no good. They're chisellers and panhandlers, sharpers and shameless flatterers. They're as full of schemes and plans, plots and counterplots, wiles and guiles as any confidence man. They can read your character better than a $50-an-hour psychiatrist. They know to a milligram how much of the old oil to pour on to break you down. They are definitely smarter than I am, which is one reason why I love 'em.

Cat-haters will try to floor you with the old argument, 'If cats are so smart, why can't they do tricks, the way dogs do?' It isn't that cats can't do tricks; it's that they *won't*. They're far too hep to stand up and beg for food when they know in advance you'll give it to them anyway. And as for rolling over, or playing dead, or 'speaking', what's in it for pussy that isn't already hers?

Cats, incidentally, are a great warm-up for a successful marriage – they teach you your place in the household. The first thing Kitty does is to organize your home on a comfortable basis – *her* basis. She'll eat when she wants to; she'll go out at her pleasure. She'll come in when she gets good and ready, if at all.

She wants attention when she wants it and darned well means to be let alone when she has other things on her mind. She is jealous; she won't have you showering attentions or caresses on any other minxes, whether two or four-footed.

She gets upset when you come home late and when you go away on a business trip. But when *she* decides to stay out a couple of nights, it is none of your darned business where she's been or what she's been up to. Either you trust her or you don't.

She hates dirt, bad smells, poor food, loud noises and people you bring home unexpectedly to dinner.

Kitty also has her share of small-child obstinacy. She enjoys seeing you flustered, fussed, red in the face and losing your temper. Sometimes, as she hangs about watching, you get the feeling that it is all she can do to keep from busting out laughing. And she's got the darndest knack for putting the entire responsibility for everything on *you*.

For instance, Kitty pretends that she can neither talk nor understand you, and that she is therefore nothing but a poor helpless dumb animal. What a laugh! Any self-respecting racket-working cat can make you understand at all times exactly what she wants. She has one voice for 'Let's eat,' another for wanting out, still a third for 'You don't happen to have seen my toy mouse around here, the one with the tail chewed off?' and a host of other easily identifiable speeches. She can also understand you perfectly, if she thinks there's profit in it.

I once had a cat I suspected of being able to read. This was a gent named Morris, a big tabby with topaz eyes who lived with me when I was batching it in a New York apartment. One day I had just finished writing to a lady who at that time was the object of my devotion. Naturally I brought considerable of the writer's art into telling her this. I was called to the telephone for a few minutes. When I returned, Morris was sitting on my desk reading the letter. At least, he was staring down at it, looking a little ill. He gave me that long, baffled look of which cats are capable, and immediately meowed to be let out. He didn't come back for three days. Thereafter I kept my private correspondence locked up.

The incident reminds me of another highly discriminating cat I had down on the farm by the name of Tante Hedwig. One Sunday a guest asked me whether I could make a cocktail called a Mexican. I said I thought I could, and proceeded to blend a horror of gin, pineapple juice, vermouth, bitters, and other ill-assorted ingredients. Pouring out a trial glass, I spilled it on the grass. Tante Hedwig came over, sniffed and, with a look of shameful embarrassment, solicitously covered it over. Everybody agreed later that she had something there.

Let me warn you not to put too much stock in the theory that animals do not think and that they act only by instinct. Did you ever try to keep a cat out that wanted to come in, or vice versa? I once locked a cat in the cellar. He climbed a straight, smooth cement wall, hung on with his paws (I saw the claw marks to prove

it); unfastened the window-hook with his nose and climbed out.

Cats have fabulous memories, I maintain, and also the ability to measure and evaluate what they remember. Take, for instance, our two Ukrainian greys, Chin and Chilla. My wife brought them up on a medicine dropper. We gave them love and care and a good home on a farm in New Jersey.

Eventually we had to travel abroad, so Chin and Chilla went to live with friends in Glenview, III., a pretty snazzy place. Back in the United States, we went out to spend Thanksgiving in Glenview. We looked forward, among other things, to seeing our two cats. When we arrived at the house, Chin and Chilla were squatting at the top of a broad flight of stairs. As we called up a tender greeting to them, we saw an expression of horror come over their faces. 'Great heavens! It's those *paupers*! Run!' With that, they vanished and could not be found for five hours. They were frightened to death we had come to take them back to the squalor of a country estate in New Jersey, and deprive them of a room of their own in Illinois, with glassed-in sun porch, screens for their toilets and similar super-luxuries.

After a time they made a grudging appearance and consented to play the old games and talk over old times, guardedly. But when the hour arrived for our departure, they vanished once more. Our hostess wrote us that apparently they got hold of a timetable somewhere and waited until our train was past Elkhart before coming out.

It was this same Chilla who, one day on the farm after our big ginger cat, Wuzzy, had been missing for forty-eight hours, led us to where he was, a half mile away, out of sight and out of hearing, caught in a trap. Every so often Chilla would look back to see if we were coming. Old Wuz was half-dead when we got there, but when he saw Chilla he started to purr.

Two-Timing, or Leading the Double Life, is something you may be called upon to face with your cat. It means simply that Kitty manages to divide her time between two homes sufficiently far apart that each home-owner thinks she is his.

I discovered this when trying to check up on the unaccountable absences of Lulu II, a seal-point Siamese. I finally located her at the other end of the bay, mooching on an amiable spinster. When I said, 'Oh, I hope that my Lulu hasn't been imposing on you,' she replied indignantly, '*Your* Lulu! You mean *our* dear little Pitipoo! We've been wondering where she went when she disappeared occasionally. We do hope she hasn't been annoying *you*.'

The shocking part of this story, of course, is that, for the sake of a hand-out, Lulu, with a pedigree as long as your arm, was willing to submit to being called Pitipoo.

Of all things a smart cat does to whip you into line, the gift of the captured mouse is the cleverest and most touching. There was Limpy, the wild barn cat down on the farm who lived off what she caught in the fields. We were already supporting four cats, but in the winter, when we went to town, we brought her along.

We had not been inside the apartment ten minutes before Limpy caught a mouse, or probably *the* mouse, and at once brought it over and laid it at our feet. Now, as indicated before, Limpy had hunted to survive. To Limpy a dead mouse was Big and Little Casino, a touch-down home run and Grand Slam. Yet this one she gave to us.

How can you mark it up except as rent, or thanks, or 'Here, looka; this is the most important thing I do. You take it because I like you'? You can teach a dog to retrieve and bring you game, but only a cat will voluntarily hand over its kill to you as an unsolicited gift.

How come Kitty acts not like the beast of prey she is but like a better-class human being? I don't know the answer. The point is, she does it – and makes you her slave ever after. Once you have been presented with a mouse by your cat, you will never be the same again. She can use you for a door-mat. And she will, too.

THE KITTEN'S TAILOR

Peggy Bacon

ONCE THERE WAS a young tailor's apprentice with blue eyes and brown hair, who in due time became a tailor, and delightedly acquired a small shop of his own, with a green door and a shiny window and a real sign outside in red and gold. Inside this establishment were a small room with a counter, and a still smaller room with a shelf. And here, when the day arrived, came the tailor with a kitten and a thimble; and having arranged upon the shelf the mug and plate that were his, and the bowl that was the kitten's, he composed himself to wait for a customer.

It was not long before one came – a very grand gentleman – and the tailor's heart gave an important throb as he hurried in to take his first order. There was a fine suit to make, of white satin and silver lace, and the gentleman was eager to have it the day after next. So when he was gone, down sat the tailor to his work, and down sat the kitten beside him.

While his master was busy snipping, the kitten played with the thimble; what mattered it, since the tailor was not using it then? And when he finally needed it, the thimble was soon found. But when the young man began to sew, he could not help wishing that the kitten would not squeeze quite so close to his right elbow, though the little creature obviously sat there because of a very flattering interest in the work.

In fact, from time to time it would reach out a tentative paw towards the long thread with which the tailor was stitching. But the latter always managed to elude it until – quite suddenly – the kitten made a little lunge, caught the thread, and gave it such a pull that the seam puckered and the tailor must rip out and start afresh. Upon a repetition of this offence, he removed the animal to the back room. But there the kitten felt so lonely and wailed so piteously that the tailor let him in again, rebuking it, however, with: 'Crumpet, be good!' Whereat the kitten sat down at a little distance from the tailor and looked wistfully at the thread.

Noticing the disconsolate air of the kitten, the tailor tossed it an empty spool; and while Crumpet played, the young man worked on busily, letting his thoughts wander to the baker's daughter, who, for some inexplicable reason, refused to marry him. He had gone to see her only the day before, hoping that since he was become a real tailor with a new shop – and such a nice one – she would at last accept his proposals. But, though she admitted her love for him, she still refused, and he came away disappointed and puzzled.

The young man was soon roused from these thoughts by sounds from the table; and looking up, discovered to his excessive annoyance that Crumpet, having unwound a skein of silk, was at the moment engaged in tangling the silver lace. Dodging the now almost angry tailor with mischievous agility, the kitten sprang to the bale of white satin, swiftly sharpened its claws therein, and then rolled over on its back with disarming coyness, batting a derisive paw at his friend. But, steeling his heart, the latter opened the shop door, and depositing Crumpet with all possible gentleness in the street without, he returned hastily to his work. As the day was chilly, Crumpet clambered on to the window-ledge, mewing sadly and pressing an impotent little nose against the pane; so that the tailor, conscience-stricken, opened the door and recalled the kitten, who charged in wildly, and then, recollecting itself, halted just in time to wash its face. After which, with an air of virtuous reform, it curled up in a corner and went to sleep.

The tailor surveyed his work. The suit was indeed barely started, owing to constant interruptions; and when he considered the bale of satin, pricked and pulled by the naughty claws, the silk hopelessly snarled, the silver lace torn and bitten, he was forced to admit that much damage had been done that morning. And as it was now noon, he left his work, laid out the mug, the plate and the bowl, and summoned Crumpet. Together they ate their meal of bread and milk, then speedily set to work again, the tailor endeavouring to make up for the loss of the morning, the kitten slyly rooting in the button-box, which, of course, soon upset, and cost the poor man some thirty minutes of angry grubbing.

During the remainder of the day the kitten was expelled from the room four times and four times recalled in recognition of its hearty protests. Its offences were varied, for it distributed its attentions impartially among the spools, the scissors and the beeswax, which last it evidently fancied edible, chewing it up very small and spitting it out disappointedly with much coughing and choking, thereby causing the tailor no little anxiety for its windpipe. The tray of pins that the tailor always kept within convenient reach was soon overturned, and the contents scattered far and wide. Indeed, if there had been six little kittens, the pins could not have been scattered further, for the tailor found them in the far recesses of the room.

It is hard to punish a fat little kitten – 'And that kitten an orphan!' so thought the tailor with a sympathetic pang. And the end of the day found a very discouraged young man and a not very chastened puss. As the occurrences of the first day were repeated the next, it is easy to see that the suit was not nearly ready when the fine gentleman called for it. Excuses were in vain; abuse was heaped on the head of the poor tailor, and the gentleman stormed himself off.

That evening the tailor faced the facts with a serious mind, and after a small struggle with himself, decided to give up the thought of being a tailor; and as a grocery is a pleasant place for a kitten, being always warm and full of amusement, he determined to turn grocer. Acting on this resolution, he sought out his uncle who owned a large grocery store in the next street. 'Splendid!' cried the old man, upon hearing the tailor's plan. 'I have long been wanting a partner in my business, and who could be a fitter one than my own nephew?'

And so the young tailor became a young grocer, and he and the kitten went to live in the grocery store. As they were both very fond of cheese, they easily reconciled themselves to the change, and very comfortable they were to be sure. Crumpet could sleep on the flour bags, on the counter, in the sunny window, or in his own soft basket behind the stove, and he soon cultivated a taste for dried fish. There were plenty of potatoes and walnuts for him to play with and as he grew older he learned to appreciate the rats and mice.

As for the tailor, or rather the grocer, he presently plucked up courage to ask again for the plump hand of the baker's daughter, and this time to his great joy it was not denied him. 'Now that you are a grocer, my love,' cried she, 'I have no objections at all; but I would never marry a tailor. To sit like a Turk is undignified and barbarous, and I have heard it makes them bowlegged.' And so they were married.

THE CHESHIRE CAT

Lewis Carroll

THE ONLY THINGS in the kitchen that did not sneeze were the cook, and a large cat which was sitting on the hearth and grinning from ear to ear.

'Please, would you tell me,' said Alice a little timidly, for she was not quite sure whether it was good manners for her to speak first, 'why your cat grins like that?'

'It's a Cheshire cat,' said the Duchess, 'and that's why. Pig!'

She said the last word with such sudden violence that Alice quite jumped; but she saw in another moment that it was addressed to the baby, and not to her, so she took courage and went on again:

'I didn't know that Cheshire cats always grinned; in fact, I didn't know that cats *could* grin.'

'They all can,' said the Duchess, 'and most of 'em do.'

'I don't know of any that do,' Alice said very politely, feeling quite pleased to have got into a conversation.

'You don't know much,' said the Duchess, 'and that's a fact.'

Alice did not at all like the tone of this remark, and thought it would be as well to introduce some other subject of conversation. While she was trying to fix on one, the cook took the cauldron of soup off the fire, and at once set to work throwing everything within her reach at the Duchess and the baby – the fire-irons came first; then followed a shower of saucepans, plates and dishes. The Duchess took no notice of them even when they hit her; and the baby was howling so much already that it was quite impossible to say whether the blows hurt it or not.

'Oh, *please* mind what you're doing!' cried Alice, jumping up and down in an agony of terror. 'Oh, there goes his *precious* nose,' as an unusually large saucepan flew close by it, and very nearly carried it off.

'If everybody minded their own business,' the Duchess said in a hoarse growl, 'the world would go round a deal faster than it does.'

'Which would *not* be an advantage,' said Alice, who felt very glad to get an opportunity of showing off a little of her knowledge. 'Just think what work it would make with the day and night! You see the earth takes twenty-four hours to turn round on its axis –'

'Talking of axes,' said the Duchess, 'chop off her head!'

Alice glanced rather anxiously at the cook, to see if she meant to take the hint; but the cook was busily engaged in stirring the soup, and did not seem to be listening, so she ventured to go on again: 'Twenty-four hours, I *think*; or is it twelve? I –'

'Oh, don't bother *me*,' said the Duchess. 'I never could abide figures!' And with that she began nursing her child again, singing a sort of lullaby to it as she did so, and giving it a violent shake at the end of every line:

Speak roughly to your little boy,
And beat him when he sneezes:
He only does it to annoy,
Because he knows it teases.

Chorus (which the cook and the baby joined):

Wow! wow! wow!

While the Duchess sang the second verse of the song, she kept tossing the baby violently up and down, and the poor little thing howled so, that Alice could hardly hear the words:

I speak severely to my boy,
I beat him when he sneezes;
For he can thoroughly enjoy
The pepper when he pleases!

Chorus:

Wow! wow! wow!

'Here! You may nurse it a bit, if you like!' the Duchess said to Alice, flinging the baby at her as she spoke. 'I must go and get ready to play croquet with the Queen,' and she hurried out of the room. The cook threw a frying-pan after her as she went out, but it just missed her.

Alice caught the baby with some difficulty, as it was a queer-shaped little creature and held out its arms and legs in all directions, 'just like a star-fish', thought Alice. The poor little thing was snorting like a steam-engine when she caught it, and kept doubling itself up and straightening itself out again, so that altogether, for the first minute or two, it was as much as she could do to hold it.

As soon as she made out the proper way of nursing it (which was to twist it up into a sort of knot, and then keep tight hold of its right ear and left foot, so as to prevent its undoing itself), she carried it out into the open air. 'If I don't take this child away with me,' thought Alice, 'they're sure to kill it in a day or two; wouldn't it be murder to leave it behind?' She said the last words out loud, and the little thing grunted in reply (it had left off sneezing by this time). 'Don't grunt,' said Alice, 'that's not at all a proper way of expressing yourself.'

The baby grunted again, and Alice looked very anxiously into its face to see what was the matter with it. There could be no doubt that it had a *very* turn-up nose, much more like a snout than a real nose; also its eyes were getting extremely small for a baby. Altogether, Alice did not like the look of the thing at all. 'But perhaps it was only sobbing,' she thought, and looked into its eyes again to see if there were any tears.

No, there were no tears. 'If you're going to turn into a pig, my dear,' said Alice, seriously, 'I'll have nothing more to do with you. Mind now!' The poor little thing sobbed again (or grunted, it was impossible to say which), and they went on for some while in silence.

Alice was just beginning to think to herself, 'Now, what am I to do with this creature when I get it home?' when it grunted again, so violently, that she looked down into its face in some alarm. This time there could be *no* mistake about it: it was neither more nor less than a pig, and she felt that it would be quite absurd for her to carry it any further.

So she set the little creature down, and felt quite relieved to see it trot away quietly into the wood. 'If it had grown up,' she said to herself, 'it would have made a dreadfully ugly child; but it makes rather a handsome pig, I think.' And she began thinking over other children she knew, who might do very well as pigs, and was just saying to herself, 'If one only knew the right way to change them –' when she was a little startled by seeing the Cheshire Cat sitting on a bough of a tree a few yards off.

The Cat only grinned when it saw Alice. It looked good-natured, she thought; still, it had *very* long claws and a great many teeth, so she felt that it ought to be treated with respect.

'Cheshire Puss,' she began, rather timidly, as she did not at all know whether it would like the name; however, it only grinned a little wider. 'Come, it's pleased so far,' thought Alice, and she went on: 'Would you tell me, please, which way I ought to go from here?'

'That depends a good deal on where you want to get to,' said the Cat.

'I don't much care where –' said Alice.

'Then it doesn't matter which way you go,' said the Cat.

'– so long as I get *somewhere*,' Alice added as an explanation.

'Oh, you're sure to do that,' said the Cat, 'if you only walk long enough.'

Alice felt that this could not be denied so, she tried another question: 'What sort of people live about here?'

'In *that* direction,' the Cat said, waving its right paw round, 'lives a Hatter; and in *that* direction,' waving the other paw, 'lives a March Hare. Visit either you like; they're both mad.'

'But I don't want to go among mad people,' Alice remarked.

'Oh, but you can't help that,' said the Cat: 'We're all mad here. I'm mad. You're mad.'

'How do you know I'm mad?' said Alice.

'You must be,' said the Cat, 'or you wouldn't have come here.'

Alice didn't think that proved it at all; however, she went on. 'And how do you know that you're mad?'

'To begin with,' said the Cat, 'a dog's not mad. You grant that?'

'I suppose so,' said Alice.

'Well, then,' the Cat went on, 'you see a dog growls when it's angry, and wags its tail when it's pleased. Now I growl when I'm pleased, and wag my tail when I'm angry. Therefore, I'm mad.'

'I call it purring, not growling,' said Alice.

'Call it what you like,' said the Cat. 'Do you play croquet with the Queen today?'

'I should like it very much,' said Alice, 'but I haven't been invited yet.'

'You'll see me there,' said the Cat, and vanished.

Alice was not much surprised at this, she was getting so used to queer things happening. While she was looking at the place where it had been, it suddenly appeared again.

'By the by, what became of the baby?' said the Cat. 'I'd nearly forgotten to ask.'

'It turned into a pig,' Alice quietly said, just as if it had come back in a natural way.

'I thought it would,' said the Cat, and vanished again.

Alice waited a little, half expecting to see it again, but it did not appear, and after a minute or two she walked on in the direction in which the March Hare was said to live. 'I've seen hatters before,' she said to herself; 'the March Hare will be much the most interesting, and perhaps, as this is May, it won't be raving mad – at least not so mad as it was in March.' As she said this, she looked up, and there was the Cat again, sitting on a branch of a tree.

'Did you say pig, or fig?' said the Cat.

'I said pig,' replied Alice, 'and I wish you wouldn't keep appearing and vanishing so suddenly. You make one quite giddy.'

'All right,' said the Cat; and this time it vanished quite slowly, beginning with the end of the tail and ending with the grin, which remained some time after the rest of it had gone.

'Well! I've often seen a cat without a grin,' thought Alice, 'but a grin without a cat! It's the most curious thing I ever saw in all my life!'

* * *

Alice began to feel very uneasy; to be sure she had not, as yet, had any dispute with the Queen, but she knew that it might happen any minute, 'and then,' thought she, 'what would become of me? They're dreadfully fond of beheading people here; the great wonder is that there's anyone left alive!'

She was looking about for some way of escape, and wondering whether she could get away without being seen, when she noticed a curious appearance in the air. It puzzled her very much at first, but, after watching it a minute or two, she made it out to be a grin, and she said to herself, 'It's the Cheshire Cat; now I shall have somebody to talk to.'

'How are you getting on?' said the Cat, as soon as there was mouth enough for it to speak with.

Alice waited till the eyes appeared, and then nodded, 'It's no use speaking to it,' she thought, 'till its ears have come, or at least one of them.' In another minute the whole head appeared, and then Alice put down her flamingo and began an account of the game, feeling very glad she had someone to listen to her. The Cat seemed to think that there was enough of it now in sight, and no more of it appeared.

'I don't think they play at all fairly,' Alice began, in rather a complaining tone, 'and they all quarrel so dreadfully one can't hear oneself speak – and they don't seem to have any rules in particular; at least, if there are, nobody attends to them – and you've no idea how confusing it is all the things being alive; for instance, there's the arch I've got to go through next walking about at the other end of the ground – and I should have croqueted the Queen's hedgehog just now, only it ran away when it saw mine coming!'

'How do you like the Queen?' said the Cat in a low voice.

'Not at all,' said Alice; 'she's so extremely –' Just then she noticed that the Queen was close behind her listening, so she went

on, ' – likely to win, that it's hardly worth while finishing the game.'

The Queen smiled and passed on.

'Who *are* you talking to?' said the King, coming up to Alice, and looking at the Cat's head with great curiosity.

'It's a friend of mine – a Cheshire Cat,' said Alice, 'allow me to introduce it.'

'I don't like the look of it at all,' said the King; 'however, it may kiss my hand if it likes.'

'I'd rather not,' the Cat remarked.

'Don't be impertinent,' said the King, 'and don't look at me like that!' He got behind Alice as he spoke.

'A cat may look at a king,' said Alice. 'I've read that in some book, but I don't remember where.'

'Well, it must be removed,' said the King very decidedly, and he called to the Queen who was passing at the moment. 'My dear! I wish you would have this cat removed!'

The Queen had only one way of settling all difficulties, great or small. 'Off with his head!' she said, without even looking around.

'I'll fetch the executioner myself,' said the King eagerly, and he hurried off.

Alice thought she might as well go back and see how the game was going on as she heard the Queen's voice in the distance, screaming with passion. She had already heard her sentence three of the players to be executed for having missed their turns, and she did not like the look of things at all, as the game was in such confusion that she never knew whether it was her turn or not. So she went in search of her hedgehog.

The hedgehog was engaged in a fight with another hedgehog, which seemed to Alice an excellent opportunity for croqueting one of them with the other; the only difficulty was that her flamingo was gone across to the other side of the garden where Alice could see it trying in a helpless sort of way to fly up into one of the trees.

By the time she had caught the flamingo and brought it back, the fight was over and both the hedgehogs were out of sight. 'But it doesn't matter much,' thought Alice, 'as all the arches are gone from this side of the ground.' So she tucked it under her arm, that it

might not escape again, and went back for a little more conversation with her friend.

When she got back to the Cheshire Cat she was surprised to find quite a large crowd collected around it; there was a dispute going on between the executioner, the King, and the Queen, who were all talking at once, while all the rest were quite silent and looked very uncomfortable.

The moment Alice appeared, she was appealed to by all three to settle the question, and they repeated their arguments to her, though as they all spoke at once, she found it very hard to make out exactly what they said.

The executioner's argument was, that you couldn't cut off a head unless there was a body to cut it off from; that he had never had to do such a thing before, and he wasn't going to begin at *his* time of life.

The King's argument was, that anything that had a head could be beheaded, and that you weren't to talk nonsense.

The Queen's argument was, that if something wasn't done about it in less than no time, she'd have everybody executed, all round. (It was this last remark that had made the whole party look so grave and anxious.)

Alice could think of nothing else to say but, 'It belongs to the Duchess; you'd better ask *her* about it.'

'She's in prison,' the Queen said to the executioner, 'fetch her here.' And the executioner went off like an arrow.

The Cat's head began fading away the moment he was gone and, by the time he had come back with the Duchess, it had entirely disappeared.

MING'S BIGGEST PREY

Patricia Highsmith

MING WAS RESTING COMFORTABLY on the foot of his mistress's bunk, when the man picked him up by the back of the neck, stuck him out on the deck and closed the cabin door. Ming's blue eyes widened in shock and brief anger, then nearly closed again because of the brilliant sunlight. It was not the first time Ming had been thrust out of the cabin rudely, and Ming realized that the man did it when his mistress, Elaine, was not looking.

The sailboat now offered no shelter from the sun, but Ming was not yet too warm. He leapt easily to the cabin roof and stepped on to the coil of rope just behind the mast. Ming liked the rope coil as a couch, because he could see everything from the height, the cup shape of the rope protected him from strong breezes, and also minimized the swaying and sudden changes of angle of the *White Lark*, since it was more or less the centre point. But just now the sail had been taken down, because Elaine and the man had eaten lunch, and often they had a siesta afterward, during which time, Ming knew, that man didn't like him in the cabin. Lunchtime was all right. In fact, Ming had just lunched on delicious grilled fish and a bit of lobster. Now, lying in a relaxed curve on the coil of rope, Ming opened his mouth in a great yawn, then with his slant eyes almost closed against the strong sunlight, gazed at the beige hills and the white and pink houses and hotels that circled the bay of Acapulco. Between the *White Lark* and the shore where people

plashed inaudibly, the sun twinkled on the water's surface like thousands of tiny electric lights going on and off. A water-skier went by, skimming up white spray behind him. Such activity! Ming half dozed, feeling the heat of the sun sink into his fur. Ming was from New York, and he considered Acapulco a great improvement over his environment in the first weeks of his life. He remembered a sunless box with straw on the bottom, three or four other kittens in with him, and a window behind which giant forms paused for a few moments, tried to catch his attention by tapping, then passed on. He did not remember his mother at all. One day a young woman who smelled of something pleasant came into the place and took him away – away from the ugly, frightening smell of dogs, of medicine and parrot dung. Then they went on what Ming now knew was an aeroplane. He was quite used to aeroplanes now and rather liked them. On aeroplanes he sat on Elaine's lap, or slept on her lap, and there were always titbits to eat if he was hungry.

Elaine spent much of the day in a shop in Acapulco, where dresses and slacks and bathing suits hung on all the walls. This place smelled clean and fresh, there were flowers in pots and in boxes out front, and the floor was of cool blue and white tiles. Ming had perfect freedom to wander out into the patio behind the shop, or to sleep in his basket in a corner. There was more sunlight in front of the shop, but mischievous boys often tried to grab him if he sat in front, and Ming could never relax there.

Ming liked best lying in the sun with his mistress on one of the long canvas chairs on their terrace at home. What Ming did not like were the people she sometimes invited to their house, people who spent the night, people by the score who stayed up very late eating and drinking, playing the gramophone or the piano – people who separated him from Elaine. People who stepped on his toes, people who sometimes picked him up from behind before he could do anything about it, so that he had to squirm and fight to get free, people who stroked him roughly, people who closed a door somewhere, locking him in. *People*! Ming detested people. In all the world, he liked only Elaine. Elaine loved him and understood him.

Especially this man called Teddie Ming detested now. Teddie was around all the time lately. Ming did not like the way Teddie looked at him, when Elaine was not watching. And sometimes Teddie, when Elaine was not near, muttered something which Ming knew was a threat. Or a command to leave the room. Ming took it calmly. Dignity was to be preserved. Besides, wasn't his mistress on his side? The man was the intruder. When Elaine was watching, the man sometimes pretended a fondness for him, but Ming always moved gracefully but unmistakably in another direction.

Ming's nap was interrupted by the sound of the cabin door opening. He heard Elaine and the man laughing and talking. The big red-orange sun was near the horizon.

'Ming!' Elaine came over to him. 'Aren't you getting *cooked*, darling? I thought you were *in*!'

'So did I!' said Teddie.

Ming purred as he always did when he awakened. She picked him up gently, cradled him in her arms, and took him below into the suddenly cool shade of the cabin. She was talking to the man, and not in a gentle tone. She set Ming down in front of his dish of water, and though he was not thirsty, he drank a little to please her. Ming did feel addled by the heat, and he staggered a little.

Elaine took a wet towel and wiped Ming's face, his ears and his four paws. Then she laid him gently on the bunk that smelled of Elaine's perfume but also of the man whom Ming detested.

Now his mistress and the man were quarrelling, Ming could tell from the tone. Elaine was staying with Ming, sitting on the edge of the bunk. Ming at last heard the splash that meant Teddie had dived into the water. Ming hoped he stayed there, hoped he drowned, hoped he never came back. Elaine wet a bathtowel in the aluminium sink, wrung it out, spread it on the bunk, and lifted Ming on to it. She brought water, and now Ming was thirsty, and drank. She left him to sleep again while she washed and put away the dishes. These were comfortable sounds that Ming liked to hear.

But soon there was another *plash* and *plop*, Teddie's wet feet on the deck, and Ming was awake again.

The tone of quarrelling recommenced. Elaine went up the few

steps on to the deck. Ming, tense but with his chin still resting on the moist bathtowel, kept his eyes on the cabin door. It was Teddie's feet that he heard descending. Ming lifted his head slightly, aware that there was no exit behind him, that he was trapped in the cabin. The man paused with a towel in his hands, staring at Ming.

Ming relaxed completely, as he might do preparatory to a yawn, and this caused his eyes to cross. Ming then let his tongue slide a little way out of his mouth. The man started to say something, looked as if he wanted to hurl the wadded towel at Ming, but he wavered, whatever he had been going to say never got out of his mouth, and he threw the towel in the sink, then bent to wash his face. It was not the first time Ming had let his tongue slide out at Teddie. Lots of people laughed when Ming did this, if they were people at a party, for instance, and Ming rather enjoyed that. But Ming sensed that Teddie took it as a hostile gesture of some kind, which was why Ming did it deliberately to Teddie, whereas among other people, it was often an accident when Ming's tongue slid out.

The quarrelling continued. Elaine made coffee. Ming began to feel better, and went on deck again, because the sun had now set. Elaine had started the motor, and they were gliding slowly towards the shore. Ming caught the song of birds, the odd screams, like shrill phrases, of certain birds that cried only at sunset. Ming looked forward to the adobe house on the cliff that was his and his mistress's home. He knew that the reason she did not leave him at home (where he would have been more comfortable) when she went on the boat, was because she was afraid that people might trap him, even kill him. Ming understood. People had tried to grab him from almost under Elaine's eyes. Once he had been suddenly hauled away in a cloth bag and, though fighting as hard as he could, he was not sure he would have been able to get out if Elaine had not hit the boy herself and grabbed the bag from him.

Ming had intended to jump up on the cabin roof again but, after glancing at it, he decided to save his strength, so he crouched on the warm, gently sloping deck with his feet tucked in, and gazed at the approaching shore. Now he could hear guitar music from the beach. The voices of his mistress and the man had come to a halt.

For a few moments, the loudest sound was the *chug-chug-chug* of the boat's motor. Then Ming heard the man's bare feet climbing the cabin steps. Ming did not turn his head to look at him, but his ears twitched back a little, involuntarily. Ming looked at the water just the distance of a short leap in front of him and below him. Strangely, there was no sound from the man behind him. The hair on Ming's neck prickled, and Ming glanced over his right shoulder.

At that instant, the man bent forward and rushed at Ming with his arms outspread.

Ming was on his feet at once, darting straight towards the man, which was the only direction of safety on the rail-less deck, and the man swung his left arm and cuffed Ming in the chest. Ming went flying backward, claws scraping the deck, but his hind legs went over the edge. Ming clung with his front feet to the sleek wood which gave him little hold, while his hind legs worked to heave him up, worked at the side of the boat which sloped to Ming's disadvantage.

The man advanced to shove a foot against Ming's paws, but Elaine came up the cabin steps just then.

'What's happening? *Ming*!'

Ming's strong hind legs were getting him on to the deck little by little. The man had knelt as if to lend a hand. Elaine had fallen on to her knees also, and had Ming by the back of the neck now.

Ming relaxed, hunched on the deck. His tail was wet.

'He fell overboard!' Teddie said. 'It's true, he's groggy. Just lurched over and fell when the boat gave a dip.'

'It's the sun. Poor *Ming*!' Elaine held the cat against her breast, and carried him into the cabin. 'Teddie – could you steer?'

The man came down into the cabin. Elaine had Ming on the bunk and was talking softly to him. Ming's heart was still beating fast. He was alert against the man at the wheel, even though Elaine was with him. Ming was aware that they had entered the little cove where they always went before getting off the boat.

Here were the friends and allies of Teddie, whom Ming detested by association, although these were merely Mexican boys. Two or three boys in shorts called 'Señor Teddie!' and offered a hand to

Elaine to climb on to the dock, took the rope attached to the front of the boat, offered to carry '*Ming*! – *Ming*!' Ming leapt on to the dock himself and crouched, waiting for Elaine, ready to dart away from any other hand that might reach for him. And there were several brown hands making a rush for him, so that Ming had to keep jumping aside. There were laughs, yelps, stomps of bare feet on wooden boards. But there was also the reassuring voice of Elaine warning them off. Ming knew she was busy carrying off the plastic satchels, locking the cabin door. Teddie with the aid of one of the Mexican boys was stretching the canvas over the cabin now. And Elaine's sandalled feet were beside Ming. Ming followed her as she walked away. A boy took the things Elaine was carrying, then she picked Ming up.

They got into the big car without a roof that belonged to Teddie, and drove up the winding road towards Elaine's and Ming's house. One of the boys was driving. Now the tone in which Elaine and Teddie were speaking was calmer, softer. The man laughed. Ming sat tensely on his mistress's lap. He could feel her concern for him in the way she stroked him and touched the back of his neck. The man reached out to put his fingers on Ming's back, and Ming gave a low growl that rose and fell and rumbled deep in his throat.

'Well, well,' said the man, pretending to be amused, and took his hand away.

Elaine's voice had stopped in the middle of something she was saying. Ming was tired, and wanted nothing more than to take a nap on the big bed at home. The bed was covered with a red and white striped blanket of thin wool.

Hardly had Ming thought of this, when he found himself in the cool, fragrant atmosphere of his own home, being lowered gently on to the bed with the soft woollen cover. His mistress kissed his cheek, and said something with the word hungry in it. Ming understood, at any rate. He was to tell her when he was hungry.

Ming dozed, and awakened at the sound of voices on the terrace a couple of yards away, past the open glass doors. Now it was dark. Ming could see one end of the table, and could tell from the quality of the light that there were candles on the table. Concha, the servant who slept in the house, was clearing the table. Ming heard her voice, then the voices of Elaine and the man. Ming smelled cigar smoke. Ming jumped to the floor and sat for a moment looking out of the door towards the terrace. He yawned, then arched his back and stretched, and limbered up his muscles by digging his claws into the thick straw carpet. Then he slipped out to the right of the terrace and glided silently down the long stairway of broad stones to the garden below. The garden was like a jungle or a forest. Avocado trees and mango trees grew as high as the terrace itself, there were bougainvillaea against the wall, orchids in the trees, and magnolias and several camellias which Elaine had planted. Ming could hear birds twittering and stirring in their nests. Sometimes he climbed trees to get at their nests, but tonight he was not in the mood, though he was no longer tired. The voices of his mistress and the man disturbed him. His mistress was not a friend of the man's tonight, that was plain.

Concha was probably still in the kitchen, and Ming decided to go in and ask her for something to eat. Concha liked him. One maid who had not liked him had been dismissed by Elaine. Ming thought he fancied barbecued pork. That was what his mistress and the

man had eaten tonight. The breeze blew fresh from the ocean, ruffling Ming's fur slightly. Ming felt completely recovered from the awful experience of nearly falling into the sea.

Now the terrace was empty of people. Ming went left, back into the bedroom, and was at once aware of the man's presence, though there was no light on and Ming could not see him. The man was standing by the dressing table, opening a box. Again involuntarily Ming gave a low growl which rose and fell, and Ming remained frozen in the position he had been in when he first became aware of the man, his right front paw extended for the next step. Now his ears were back, he was prepared to spring in any direction, although the man had not seen him.

'*Ssss-st!* Damn you!' the man said in a whisper. He stamped his foot, not very hard, to make the cat go away.

Ming did not move at all. Ming heard the soft rattle of the white necklace which belonged to his mistress. The man put it into his pocket, then moved to Ming's right, out of the door that went into the big living-room. Ming now heard the clink of a bottle against glass, heard liquid being poured. Ming went through the same door and turned left towards the kitchen.

Here he miaowed, and was greeted by Elaine and Concha. Concha had her radio turned on to music.

'Fish? – Pork. He likes pork,' Elaine said, speaking the odd form of words which she used with Concha.

Ming, without much difficulty, conveyed his preference for pork, and got it. He fell to with a good appetite. Concha was exclaiming 'Ah-eee-ee!' as his mistress spoke with her, spoke at length. Then Concha bent to stroke him, and Ming put up with it, still looking down at his plate, until she left off and he could finish his meal. Then Elaine left the kitchen. Concha gave him some of the tinned milk, which he loved, in his now empty saucer, and Ming lapped this up. Then he rubbed himself against her bare leg by way of thanks and went out of the kitchen, made his way cautiously into the living-room en route to the bedroom. But now Elaine and the man were out on the terrace. Ming had just entered the bedroom, when he heard Elaine call:

'Ming? Where are you?'

Ming went to the terrace door and stopped, and sat on the threshold.

Elaine was sitting sideways at the end of the table, and the candle-light was bright on her long fair hair, on the white of her trousers. She slapped her thigh, and Ming jumped on to her lap.

The man said something in a low tone, something not nice.

Elaine replied something in the same tone. But she laughed a little.

Then the telephone rang.

Elaine put Ming down, and went into the living-room towards the telephone.

The man finished what was in his glass, muttered something at Ming, then set the glass on the table. He got up and tried to circle Ming, or to get him towards the edge of the terrace, Ming realized, and Ming also realized that the man was drunk – therefore moving slowly and a little clumsily. The terrace had a parapet about as high as the man's hips, but it was broken by grilles in three places, grilles with bars wide enough for Ming to pass through, though Ming never did, merely looked through the grilles sometimes. It was plain to Ming that the man wanted to drive him through one of the grilles, or grab him and toss him over the terrace parapet. There was nothing easier for Ming than to elude him. Then the man picked up a chair and swung it suddenly, catching Ming on the hip. That had been quick, and it hurt. Ming took the nearest exit, which was down the outside steps that led to the garden.

The man started down the steps after him. Without reflecting, Ming dashed back up the few steps he had come, keeping close to the wall which was in shadow. The man hadn't seen him, Ming knew. Ming leapt to the terrace parapet, sat down and licked a paw once to recover and collect himself. His heart beat fast as if he were in the middle of a fight. And hatred ran in his veins. Hatred burned his eyes as he crouched and listened to the man uncertainly climbing the steps below him. The man came into view.

Ming tensed himself for a jump, then jumped as hard as he could, landing with all four feet on the man's right arm near the shoulder. Ming clung to the cloth of the man's white jacket, but they were

both falling. The man groaned. Ming hung on. Branches crackled. Ming could not tell up from down. Ming jumped off the man, became aware of direction and of the earth too late, and landed on his side. Almost at the same time, he heard the thud of the man hitting the ground, then of his body rolling a little way, then there was silence. Ming had to breathe fast with his mouth open until his chest stopped hurting. From the direction of the man, he could smell drink, cigar, and the sharp odour that meant fear. But the man was not moving.

Ming could now see quite well. There was even a bit of moonlight. Ming headed for the steps again, had to go a long way through the bush, over stones and sand, to where the steps began. Then he glided up and arrived once more upon the terrace.

Elaine was just coming on to the terrace.

'Teddie?' she called. Then she went back into the bedroom where she turned on a lamp. She went into the kitchen. Ming followed her. Concha had left the light on, but Concha was now in her own room, where the radio played.

Elaine opened the front door.

The man's car was still in the driveway, Ming saw. Now Ming's hip had begun to hurt, or now he had begun to notice it. It caused him to limp a little. Elaine noticed this, touched his back, and asked him what was the matter. Ming only purred.

'Teddie? – Where are you?' Elaine called.

She took a torch and shone it down into the garden, down among the great trunks of the avocado trees, among the orchids and the lavender and pink blossoms of the bougainvillaeas. Ming, safe beside her on the terrace parapet, followed the beam of the torch with his eyes and purred with content. The man was not below here, but below and to the right. Elaine went to the terrace steps and carefully, because there was no rail here, only broad steps, pointed the beam of the light downward. Ming did not bother looking. He sat on the terrace where the steps began.

'Teddie!' she said. '*Teddie!*' Then she ran down the steps.

Ming still did not follow her. He heard her draw in her breath. Then she cried:

'*Concha!*'

Elaine ran back up the steps.

Concha had come out of her room. Elaine spoke to Concha. Then Concha became excited. Elaine went to the telephone, and spoke for a short while, then she and Concha went down the steps together. Ming settled himself with his paws tucked under him on the terrace, which was still faintly warm from the day's sun. A car arrived. Elaine came up the steps, and went and opened the front door. Ming kept out of the way on the terrace, in a shadowy corner, as three or four strange men came out on the terrace and tramped down the steps. There was a great deal of talk below, noises of feet, breaking of bushes, and then the smell of all of them mounted the steps, the smell of tobacco, sweat, and the familiar smell of blood. The man's blood. Ming was pleased, as he was pleased when he killed a bird and created this smell of blood under his own teeth. This was big prey. Ming, unnoticed by any of the others, stood up to his full height as the group passed with the corpse, and inhaled the aroma of his victory with a lifted nose.

Then suddenly the house was empty. Everyone had gone, even Concha. Ming drank a little water from his bowl in the kitchen, then went to his mistress's bed, curled against the slope of the pillows, and fell fast asleep. He was awakened by the *rr-rr-r* of an unfamiliar car. Then the front door opened, and he recognized the step of Elaine and then Concha. Ming stayed where he was. Elaine and Concha talked softly for a few minutes. Then Elaine came into the bedroom. The lamp was still on. Ming watched her slowly open the box on her dressing table, and into it she let fall the white necklace that made a little clatter. Then she closed the box. She began to unbutton her shirt, but before she had finished, she flung herself on the bed and stroked Ming's head, lifted his left paw and pressed it gently so that the claws came forth.

'Oh, Ming – Ming,' she said.

Ming recognized the tones of love.

DICK BAKER'S CAT

Mark Twain

ONE OF MY COMRADES THERE – another of those victims of eighteen years of unrequited toil and blighted hopes – was one of the gentlest spirits that ever bore its patient cross in a weary exile; grave and simple Dick Baker, pocket-miner of Dead-Horse Gulch. He was forty-six, grey as a rat, earnest, thoughtful, slenderly educated, slouchily dressed and clay-soiled, but his heart was finer metal than any gold his shovel ever brought to light – than any, indeed, that ever was mined or minted.

Whenever he was out of luck and a little down-hearted, he would fall to mourning over the loss of a wonderful cat he used to own (for where women and children are not, men of kindly impulses take up with pets, for they must love something). And he always spoke of the strange sagacity of that cat with the air of a man who believed in his secret heart that there was something human about it – maybe even supernatural.

I heard him talking about this animal once. He said:

'Gentlemen, I used to have a cat here, by the name of Tom Quartz, which you'd 'a' took an interest in, I reckon – most anybody would. I had him here eight year – and he was the remarkablest cat I ever see. He was a large grey one of the Tom specie, an' he had more hard, natchral sense than any man in this camp – 'n' a *power* of dignity he wouldn't let the Gov'ner of Californy be familiar with him. He never ketched a rat in his life – 'peered to be above it. He never cared for nothing but mining. He knowed more about mining, that cat did, than any man I ever, ever see. You couldn't tell *him* noth'n' 'bout placer-diggin's – 'n' as for pocket-mining, why he was just born for it. He would dig out after me an' Jim when we went over the hills prospect'n', and he would trot along behind us for as much as five mile, if we went so fur. An' he had the best judgment about mining-ground – why, you never see anything like it. When we went to work, he'd scatter a glance round, 'n' if he didn't think much of the indications, he would give a look as much as to say, "Well, I'll have to get you to excuse *me*" – 'n' without another word he'd hyste his nose in the air 'n' shove for home. But if the ground suited him, he would lay low 'n' keep dark till the first pan was washed, 'n' then he would sidle up 'n' take a look, an' if there was about six or seven grains of gold *he* was satisfied – he didn't want no better prospect 'n' that – 'n' then he would lay down on our coats and snore like a steamboat till we'd struck the pocket, an' then get up 'n' superintend. He was nearly lightin' on superintending.

'Well, by an' by, up comes this yer quartz excitement. Everybody was into it – everybody was pick'n' 'n' blast'n' instead of shovellin' dirt on the hillside – everbody was putt'n' down a shaft instead of scrapin' the surface. Noth'n' would do Jim, but *we* must tackle the ledges, too, 'n' so we did. We commenced putt'n' down a shaft, 'n' Tom Quartz he begin to wonder what in the dickens it was all about. *He* hadn't ever seen any mining like that before, 'n' he was all upset, as you may say – he couldn't come to a right understanding of it no way – it was too many for *him*. He was down on it too, you bet you – he was down on it powerful – 'n' always appeared to consider it the cussedest foolishness out. But that cat, you know, was *always* agin' new-fangled arrangements – somehow he never could abide 'em. *You* know how it is with old habits. But by an' by Tom Quartz begin to git sort of reconciled a little though he never *could* altogether understand that eternal sinkin' of a shaft an' never pannin' out anything. At last he got to comin' down in the shaft, hisself, to try to cipher it out. An' when he'd git the blues, 'n' feel kind o' scruffy, 'n' aggravated 'n' disgusted – knowin' as he did, that

the bills was runnin' up all the time an' we warn's makin' a cent – he would curl up on a gunny-sack in the corner an' go to sleep. Well, one day when the shaft was down about eight foot, the rock got so hard that we had to put in a blast – the first blast'n' we'd ever done since Tom Quartz was born. An' then we lit the fuse 'n' crumb out 'n' got off 'bout fifty yards – 'n' forgot 'n' left Tom Quartz sound asleep on the gunny-sack. In 'bout a minute we seen a puff of smoke bust up out of the hole, 'n' then everything let go with an awful crash, 'n' about four million ton of rocks 'n' dirt 'n' smoke 'n' splinters shot up 'bout a mile an' a half into the air, an' by George, right in the dead centre of it was old Tom Quartz a-goin' end over end, an' a-snortin' an' a-sneez'n, an' a-clawin' an' a-reach'n' for things like all possessed. But it warn't no use, you know, it warn't no use. An' that was the last we see of *him* for about two minutes 'n' a half, an' then all of a sudden it begin to rain rocks and rubbage an' directly he come down leer-whoop about ten foot off f'm where we stood. Well, I reckon he was p'raps the orneriest-lookin' beast you ever see. One ear was sot back on his neck, 'n' his tail was stove up, 'n' his eye-winkers were singed off, 'n' he was all blacked up with powder an' smoke, an' all sloppy with mud 'n' slush f'm one end to the other. Well, sir, it warn't no use to try to apologize – we couldn't say a word. He took a sort of disgusted look at hisself, 'n' then he looked at us – an' it was just exactly the same as if he had said – "Gents, maybe *you* think it's smart to take advantage of a cat that ain't had no experience of quartz-minin', but I think *different*" – an' then he turned on his heel 'n' marched off home without ever saying another word.

'That was jest his style. An' maybe you won't believe it, but after that you never see a cat so prejudiced agin' quartz-mining as what he was. An' by an' by when he *did* get to goin' down in the shaft agin', you'd 'a' been astonished at his sagacity. The minute we'd fetch off a blast 'n' the fuse'd begin to sizzle, he'd give a look as much as to say, "Well, I'll have to git you to excuse *me*," an' it was surpris'n' the way he'd shin out of that hole 'n' go f'r a tree. Sagacity? It ain't no name for it. 'Twas inspiration!'

I said, 'Well, Mr Baker, his prejudice against quartz-mining was remarkable, considering how he came by it. Couldn't you ever cure him of it?'

'*Cure him*! No! When Tom Quartz was sot once, he was *always* sot – and you might 'a' browed him up as much as three million times 'n' you'd never 'a' broken him of his cussed prejudice agin' quartz-mining.'

CALVIN, THE CAT

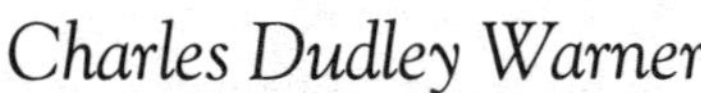

Charles Dudley Warner

CALVIN IS DEAD. His life, long to him, but short for the rest of us, was not marked by startling adventures, but his character was so uncommon and his qualities were so worthy of imitation that I have been asked by those who personally knew him to set down my recollections of his career.

His origin and ancestry were shrouded in mystery; even his age was a matter of pure conjecture. Although he was of the Maltese race, I have reason to suppose that he was American by birth as he certainly was in sympathy. Calvin was given to me eight years ago by Mrs Stowe, but she knew nothing of his age or origin. He walked into her house one day out of the great unknown and became at once at home, as if he had been always a friend of the family. He appeared to have artistic and literary tastes, and it was as if he had enquired at the door if that was the residence of the author of *Uncle Tom's Cabin* and, upon being assured that it was, had decided to dwell there. This is, of course, fanciful, for his antecedents were wholly unknown, but in his time he could hardly have been in any household where he would not have heard *Uncle Tom's Cabin* talked about.

When he came to Mrs Stowe, he was as large as he ever was, and apparently as old as he ever became. Yet there was in him no appearance of age; he was in the happy maturity of all his powers and you would rather have said, in that maturity, he had found the secret of perpetual youth. And it was as difficult to believe that he would ever be aged as it was to imagine that he had ever been in immature youth. There was in him a mysterious perpetuity.

After some years, when Mrs Stowe made her winter home in Florida, Calvin came to live with us. From the first moment, he fell into the ways of the house and assumed a recognized position in the family – I say recognized, because after he became known he was always enquired for by visitors, and in the letters from other members of the family he always received a message. Although the least obtrusive of beings, his individuality always made itself felt.

His personal appearance had much to do with this, for he was of royal mould and had an air of high breeding. He was large, but he had nothing of the fat grossness of the celebrated Angora family; though powerful, he was exquisitely proportioned and as graceful in every movement as a young leopard. When he stood up to open a door – he opened all the doors with old-fashioned latches – he was portentously tall, and when he stretched on the rug before the fire he seemed too long for this world – as indeed he was. His coat was the finest and softest I have ever seen, a shade of quiet Maltese; and from his throat downwards, underneath, to the white tips of his feet, he wore the whitest and most delicate ermine; and no person was ever more fastidiously neat. In his finely formed head you saw something of his aristocratic character; the ears were small and cleanly cut, there was a tinge of pink in the nostrils, his face was handsome and the expression of his countenance exceedingly intelligent – I should call it even a sweet expression if the term were not inconsistent with his look of alertness and sagacity.

It is difficult to convey a just idea of his gaiety in connection with his dignity and gravity, which his name expressed. As we know nothing of his family, of course it will be understood that Calvin was his Christian name. He had times of relaxation into utter playfulness, delighting in a ball of yarn, catching sportively at stray ribbons when his mistress was at her toilet, and pursuing his own tail, with hilarity, for lack of anything better. He could amuse himself by the hour, and he did not care for children; perhaps something in his past was present to his memory. He had absolutely no bad habits, and his disposition was perfect. I never saw him exactly angry, though I have seen his tail grow to an enormous size when a

strange cat appeared upon his lawn. He disliked cats, evidently regarding them as feline and treacherous, and he had no association with them. Occasionally there would be heard a night concert in the shrubbery. Calvin would ask to have the door opened, and then you would hear a rush and a 'pestzt', and the concert would explode, and Calvin would quietly come in and resume his seat on the hearth. There was no trace of anger in his manner, but he wouldn't have any of that about the house.

He had the rare virtue of magnanimity. Although he had fixed notions about his own rights, and extraordinary persistency in getting them, he never showed temper at a repulse; he simply and firmly persisted till he had what he wanted. His diet was one point; his idea was that of the scholars about dictionaries – to 'get the best'. He knew as well as anyone what was in the house, and would refuse beef if turkey was to be had; and if there were oysters, he would wait over the turkey to see if the oysters would not be forthcoming. And yet he was not a gross gourmand; he would eat bread if he saw me eating it, and thought he was not being imposed on. His habits of feeding, also, were refined; he never used a knife, and he would put up his hand and draw the fork down to his mouth as gracefully as a grown person. Unless necessity compelled, he would not eat in the kitchen, but insisted upon his meals in the dining-room, and would wait patiently, unless a stranger were present; and then he was sure to importune the visitor, hoping that the latter was ignorant of the rule of the house, and would give him something. They used to say that he preferred as his tablecloth on the floor a certain well-known Church journal; but this was said by an Episcopalian.

So far as I know, he had no religious prejudices, except that he did not like the association with Romanists. He tolerated the servants, because they belonged to the house, and would sometimes linger by the kitchen stove; but the moment visitors came in he arose, opened the door and marched into the drawing-room. Yet he enjoyed the company of his equals, and never withdrew, no matter how many callers – whom he recognized as of his society – might come into the drawing-room. Calvin was fond of company, but he wanted to choose it; and I have no doubt that his was an aristocratic fastidiousness rather than one of faith. It is so with most people.

The intelligence of Calvin was something phenomenal, in his rank of life. He established a method of communicating his wants, and even some of his sentiments; and he could help himself in many things. There was a furnace register in a retired room, where he used to go when he wished to be alone, that he always opened when he desired more heat; but never shut it, any more than he shut the door after himself. He could do almost everything but speak; and you would declare sometimes that you could see a pathetic longing to do that in his intelligent face. I have no desire

to overdraw his qualities but, if there was one thing in him more noticeable than another, it was his fondness for nature. He could content himself for hours at a low window, looking into the ravine and at the great trees, noting the smallest stir there; he delighted, above all things, to accompany me walking about the garden, hearing the birds, getting the smell of the fresh earth, and rejoicing in the sunshine. He followed me and gambolled like a dog, rolling over on the turf and exhibiting his delight in a hundred ways. If I worked, he sat and watched me, or looked off over the bank and kept his ear open to the twitter in the cherry trees. When it stormed, he was sure to sit at the windows, keenly watching the rain or the snow, glancing up and down at its falling; and a winter tempest always delighted him.

I think he was genuinely fond of birds but, so far as I know, he usually confined himself to one a day; he never killed, as some sportsmen do, for the sake of killing, but only as civilized people do – from necessity. He was intimate with the flying-squirrels who dwelt in the chestnut tree – too intimate, for almost every day in the summer he would bring in one, until he nearly discouraged them. He was, indeed, a superb hunter, and would have been a devastating one if his bump of destructiveness had not been offset by a bump of moderation. There was very little of the brutality of the lower animals about him; I don't think he enjoyed rats for themselves, but he knew his business and, for the first few months of his residence with us, waged an awful campaign against the horde and, after that, his simple presence was sufficient to deter them from coming on the premises. Mice amused him, but he usually considered them too small game to be taken seriously; I have seen him play for an hour with a mouse and then let him go with a royal condescension. In this whole matter of 'getting a living', Calvin was a great contrast to the rapacity of the age in which he lived.

I hesitate to speak of his capacity for friendship and the affectionateness of his nature, for I know from his own reserve that he would not care to have it much talked about. We understood each other perfectly, but we never made any fuss about it; when I spoke his name and snapped my fingers, he came to me; when I returned home at night, he was pretty sure to be waiting for me near the gate, and would rise and saunter along the walk, as if his being there were purely accidental – so shy was he commonly of showing feeling; and when I opened the door he never rushed in, like a cat, but loitered and lounged, as if he had had no intention of going in, but would condescend to. And yet, the fact was, he knew dinner was ready, and he was bound to be there. He kept the run of dinner-time. It happened sometimes, during our absence in the summer, that dinner would be early, and Calvin, walking about the grounds, missed it and came in late. But he never made a mistake the second day. There was one thing he never did – he never rushed through an open doorway. He never forgot his dignity. If he had asked to have the door opened, and was eager to go out, he always went deliberately; I can see him now, standing on the sill, looking about at the sky as if he was thinking whether it were worth while to take an umbrella, until he was near having his tail shut in.

His friendship was rather constant than demonstrative. When we returned from an absence of nearly two years Calvin welcomed us with evident pleasure, but showed his satisfaction rather by tranquil happiness than by fuming about. He had the faculty of making us glad to get home. It was his constancy that was so attractive. He liked companionship, but he wouldn't be petted, or fussed over, or sit in anyone's lap a moment; he always extricated himself from such familiarity with dignity and with no show of temper. If there was any petting to be done, however, he chose to do it. Often he would sit looking at me and then, moved by a delicate affection, come and pull at my coat and sleeve until he could touch my face with his nose, and then go away contented. He had a habit of coming to my study in the morning sitting quietly by my side or on the table for hours, watching the pen run over the paper, occasionally swinging his tail round for a blotter and then going to sleep among the papers by the inkstand. Or, more rarely, he would watch the writing from a perch on my shoulder. Writing always interested him and, until he understood it, he wanted to hold the pen.

He always held himself in a kind of reserve with his friend, as if he had said, 'Let us respect our personality and not make a "mess"

of friendship.' He saw, with Emerson, the risk of degrading it to trivial conveniency. 'Why insist on rash personal relations with your friends. Leave this touching and clanging.' Yet I would not give an unfair notion of his aloofness, his fine sense of the sacredness of the me and the not-me. And, at the risk of not being believed, I will relate an incident which was often repeated. Calvin had the practice of passing a portion of the night in the contemplation of its beauties and would come into our chamber over the roof of the conservatory through the open window, summer and winter, and go to sleep at the foot of my bed. He would do this always exactly in this way; he never was content to stay in the chamber if we compelled him to go upstairs and through the door. He had the obstinacy of General Grant. But this is by the way. In the morning, he performed his toilet and went down to breakfast with the rest of the family. Now, when the mistress was absent from home, and at no other time, Calvin would come in the morning, when the bell rang, to the head of the bed, put up his feet and look into my face, follow me about when I rose, 'assist' at the dressing, and in many purring ways show his fondness, as if he had plainly said, 'I know that she has gone away, but I am here.' Such was Calvin in rare moments.

He had his limitations. Whatever passion he had for nature, he had no conception of art. There was sent to him once a fine and very expressive cat's head in bronze, by Frémiet. I placed it on the floor. He regarded it intently, approached it cautiously and crouchingly, touched it with his nose, perceived the fraud, turned away abruptly and never would notice it afterwards.

On the whole, his life was not only a successful one, but a happy one. He never had but one fear, so far as I know; he had a mortal and a reasonable terror of plumbers. He would never stay in the house when they were here. No coaxing could quiet him. Of course, he didn't share our fear about their charges, but he must have had some dreadful experience with them in that portion of his life which is unknown to us. A plumber was to him the devil, and I have no doubt that, in his scheme, plumbers were foreordained to do him mischief.

In speaking of his worth, it has never occurred to me to estimate Calvin by the worldly standard. I know that it is customary now, when anyone dies, to ask how much he was worth, and that no obituary in the newspapers is considered complete without such an estimate. The plumbers in our house were one day overheard to say that, 'They say that she says that he says that he wouldn't take $100 for him.' It is unnecessary to say that I never made such a remark, and that, so far as Calvin was concerned, there was no purchase in money.

As I look back upon it, Calvin's life seems to me a fortunate one, for it was natural and unforced. He ate when he was hungry, slept when he was sleepy, and enjoyed existence to the very tips of his toes and the end of his expressive and slow-moving tail. He delighted to roam about the garden, and stroll among the trees, and to lie on the green grass and luxuriate in all the sweet influences of summer. You could never accuse him of idleness, and yet he knew the secret of repose. The poet who wrote so prettily of him that his little life was rounded with a sleep, understated his felicity; it was rounded with a good many. His conscience never seemed to interfere with his slumbers. In fact, he had good habits and a contented mind. I can see him now walk in at the study door, sit down by my chair, bring his tail artistically about his feet, and look up at me with unspeakable happiness in his handsome face.

I often thought that he felt the dumb limitation which denied him the power of language. But since he was denied speech, he scorned the inarticulate mouthings of the lower animals. The vulgar mewing and yowling of the cat species was beneath him; he sometimes uttered a sort of articulate and well-bred ejaculation, when he wished to call attention to something that he considered remarkable, or to some want of his, but he never went whining about. He would sit for hours at a closed window, when he desired to enter, without a murmur, and when it was opened he never admitted that he had been impatient by 'bolting' in. Though speech he had not, and the unpleasant kind of utterance given to his race he would not use, he had a mighty power of purr to express his measureless content with congenial society. There was in him a

musical organ with stops of varied power and expression, upon which I have no doubt he could have performed Scarlatti's celebrated cat's fugue.

Whether Calvin died of old age, or was carried off by one of the diseases incident to youth, it is impossible to say; for his departure was as quiet as his advent was mysterious. I only know that he appeared to us in the world in his perfect stature and beauty, and that after a time, like Lohengrin, he withdrew. In his illness there was nothing more to be regretted than in all his blameless life. I suppose there never was an illness that had more dignity and sweetness and resignation in it. It came on gradually, in a kind of listlessness and want of appetite. An alarming symptom was his preference for the warmth of a furnace register to the lively sparkle of the open wood fire. Whatever pain he suffered, he bore it in silence, and seemed only anxious not to obtrude his malady. We tempted him with the delicacies of the season, but it soon became impossible for him to eat, and for two weeks he ate or drank scarcely anything. Sometimes he made an effort to take something, but it was evident that he made the effort to please us. The neighbours – and I am convinced that the advice of neighbours is never good for anything – suggested catnip. He wouldn't even smell it. We had the attendance of an amateur practitioner of medicine, whose real office was the cure of souls, but nothing touched his case. He took what was offered, but it was with the air of one to whom the time for pellets was passed. He sat or lay day after day almost motionless, never once making a display of those vulgar convulsions or contortions of pain which are so disagreeable to society. His favourite place was on the brightest spot of a Smyrna rug by the conservatory, where the sunlight fell and he could hear the fountain play. If we went to him and exhibited our interest in his condition, he always purred in recognition of our sympathy. And when I spoke his name, he looked up with an expression that said, 'I understand it, old fellow, but it's no use.' He was to all who came to visit him a model of calmness and patience in affliction.

I was absent from home at the last, but heard by daily postal card of his failing condition; and never again saw him alive. One sunny morning he rose from his rug, went into the conservatory (he was very thin then), walked around it deliberately, looking at all the plants he knew, and then went to the bay-window in the dining-room and stood a long time looking out upon the little field, now brown and sere, and towards the garden where perhaps the happiest hours of his life had been spent. It was a last look. He

turned and walked away, laid himself down upon the bright spot in the rug, and quietly died.

It is not too much to say that a little shock went through the neighbourhood when it was known that Calvin was dead, so marked was his individuality; and his friends, one after another, came in to see him. There was no sentimental nonsense about his obsequies; it was felt that any parade would have been distasteful to him. John, who acted as undertaker, prepared a candle-box for him, and I believe assumed a professional decorum; but there may have been the usual levity underneath, for I heard that he remarked in the kitchen that it was the 'driest wake he ever attended'. Everybody, however, felt a fondness for Calvin and regarded him with a certain respect. Between him and Bertha there existed a great friendship, and she apprehended his nature; she used to say that sometimes she was afraid of him, he looked at her so intelligently; she was never certain that he was what he appeared to be.

When I returned, they had laid Calvin on a table in an upper chamber by an open window. It was February. He reposed in a candle-box, lined about the edge with evergreen, and at his head stood a little wine glass with flowers. He lay with his head tucked down in his arms – a favourite position of his before the fire – as if asleep in the comfort of his soft and exquisite fur. It was the involuntary exclamation of those who saw him, 'How natural he looks!' As for myself, I said nothing. John buried him under the twin hawthorn trees – one white and the other pink – in a spot where Calvin was fond of lying and listening to the hum of summer insects and the twitter of birds.

Perhaps I have failed to make appear the individuality of character that was so evident to those who knew him. At any rate, I have set down nothing concerning him but the literal truth. He was always a mystery. I did not know whence he came; I do not know whither he has gone. I would not weave one spray of falsehood in the wreath I lay upon his grave.

LUCKY CAT

Charlotte Wallace

GERALD FAWNSLEY WAS UNHAPPY and a little drunk as he came back to the flat about two in the morning. He threw down his coat which was sleek and black just like Basil's. 'Well old fellow,' he said, gathering him up into his arms and nuzzling his cheek against the cat's fur, 'I made a fool of myself tonight. You remember that girl who said you gave her asthma and that, if she married me, you would be the first thing to go? She's just said she never wants to see me again as long as she lives. She told me I had to choose: her or "that bloody cat". I don't know why but, at that moment, I knew there was really no competition. I chose you. She burst into tears and said she hated me and that was that.'

Basil couldn't understand it. He knew he was supposed to be lucky, being so black, but anytime Gerald got keen on a girl, he seemed quite unwittingly to break up the relationship. For instance, there was the French girl Marie-Claire who was such a good cook Gerald began to get fat and Basil, on the leftovers, grew so rotund he could barely jump up on to the sofa. One evening – it must have been the young lovers' third month together – as Marie-Claire was cooking, she confessed to Basil, she was going to make Gerald ask her to marry him.

When Gerald got back from work, he was greeted by Marie-Claire's loving kiss and would have been happy to have tumbled into bed with her. His heart rather sank when he saw the candlelit table, the single rose in its elegant little vase, the gleaming silver. Obviously, he was in for a special meal and, though he loved good

food, he had eaten an awful lot recently and it had so happened he had had to take some clients out to lunch. The curry he had eaten with so much gusto three hours before was still very much 'in situ' but he had a suspicion that that might not be the case for long.

Still, he dutifully sat down to salmon mousse. Basil could never resist salmon mousse, particularly one as good as Marie-Claire's. He made to leap on to Gerald's lap but, being much less agile than he remembered, he missed Gerald and had to make a grab at the tablecloth. The tablecloth, the salmon mousse, the white wine, the rose, the silver followed Basil on to the floor. It did not need Marie-Claire's shrieks to warn Basil he was going to be unpopular. He got to his feet and made for the door but he was still embraced by the tablecloth. However much he thrashed about he could not get free. When at last he managed to poke his head out, he saw that Gerald was laughing fit to burst but Marie-Claire was crying with rage. She grabbed the saucepan off the stove and threw it at Basil missing him by miles. She had forgotten there was still sauce in the pan and this now spotted Gerald's Charvet tie and splashed down his trousers. Gerald's laughter now turned to rage and so sudden was his change of mood, it precipitated digestive revolt; he shot the whole of his curry down his already pink-sauced suit.

'She had no sense of humour,' Gerald confided to Basil later. Anyway, I could never have married her. I would have had a heart attack by the time I was forty.'

Still, Basil had felt a bit guilty. Half a dozen other promising romances followed, none of which survived Basil's efforts to be helpful, courteous and kind. He really did want his master to marry and be happy.

The idea eventually came to him to go out and find someone to suit his master. It was self-evident that Gerald was not himself capable of finding a mate, so the responsibility lay with his friends to do it for him. He took his quest seriously, often spending nights away from home much to Gerald's concern. 'Where *have* you been, Basil?' he cried in alarm after the cat had returned from one such trip, scarred and weary, his usually sleek fur bedraggled and dull. Of course, Basil could not explain but he looked so sorrowfully at his master, Gerald, misunderstanding, said: 'Don't worry old fellow, I'll never leave you. We'll be two crusty bachelors together and women can go hang. But I think I will put a collar and address on you, just in case you get lost again.'

Although he spoke with spirit, Basil thought he could detect a tremor in his voice. He noticed his master was looking almost as bedraggled as himself. His suit was crumpled. He hadn't brushed his hair and his eyes were rather glassy. He was clutching a glass of whisky which he refilled far too frequently. Basil had tasted whisky once, thinking it was water, and he knew it was poison. 'I can't bear it if you aren't here when I come in, Basil. If you go and if I lose my job, which seems quite on the cards, I think I'll commit suicide.'

Basil was seriously worried. On none of his trips had he seen anyone he remotely liked the look of. After all, human-beings weren't prepossessing at the best of times.

Dolefully, Basil slunk out of the flat and straight into the path of a hurrying girl. She tripped over him and fell heavily. The noise brought Gerald out on to the landing. 'Basil!' he yelled. 'What have you done?' Rushing to the young lady's side he gently cradled her in his arms. She had been momentarily stunned but now her eyes opened. As Gerald met her gaze he fell utterly, hopelessly, in love.

As she tried to get up, she let out a cry of pain. 'Oh, my ankle!' she gasped, catching hold of Gerald for support. 'I think it must be broken.'

'Here let me help you into my flat and then I'll call the doctor,' urged Gerald solicitously.

'Oh but I'm late already. I really must be going.'

'I'm afraid, thanks to Basil here, you can't go anywhere,' said Gerald firmly, drinking in the loveliness of the young goddess who had fallen into his arms as though she were a gift from heaven. 'I'm Gerald Fawnsley. Who were you going to see, Miss . . . Miss . . . Let me ring and explain.'

'Ouch!' the girl ejaculated, proving Gerald's point. 'I was meeting my father. He hates me to be late. He's such a busy man, when he makes the time to see me, I feel I have to . . .'

'Please, don't distress yourself,' said Gerald wretchedly, as the girl began to cry again. 'Do you know what his telephone number is?'

'Oh yes. I have it here in my diary. But . . . where is my handbag?' she wailed.

Then followed a mad hunt by Gerald for the bag which was eventually found two flights of stairs down. It had burst open and much of what it contained, which seemed an unbelievable amount to Gerald, had spilled down a further flight. At last, however everything had been gathered up and the diary located.

'730 234,' she read out to Gerald.

'Who shall I ask for?' he queried as he dialled.

'My father, of course!' she answered crossly.

'Forgive me,' said Gerald humbly, 'but I don't know his name.'

'Oh sorry, yes . . . but I quite forgot we were strangers.' She flashed him such a brilliant smile his heart turned a couple of somersaults. 'I'm Caroline Spry and my father is Sir Godfrey Spry,' she said.

He could not prevent his surprise showing on his face. The goddess's father was one of the best-known industrialists in England. Gerald was a little down-hearted. She must be an heiress and her father would want something better than a not very successful stockbroker as a son-in-law. Oh God! he checked himself. There he was again, rushing ahead of himself. He was already imagining asking Sir Godfrey for his daughter's hand and he had only known her five minutes.

'Oh yes,' said the girl dryly, 'everyone knows my father, except me I sometimes think. I really should not say this to a complete stranger but my father is someone I hardly know at all. That is why I am so anxious about not missing my appointment with him.'

By this time Gerald had got through on the telephone to a fierce sounding lady who said she was Miss Walmsley, Sir Godfrey's personal assistant. When Gerald had finished telling her about Caroline's mishap there was a silence.

'Hello? Are you still there?' asked Gerald. 'Oh yes,' said the woman, 'I'm here but I'm afraid Sir Godfrey isn't. He is in Geneva. He had to go quite suddenly and I'm afraid he quite forgot he had asked Miss Caroline to lunch. She is in the room with you now, is she?'

'Yes indeed,' said Gerald uncomfortably.

'Perhaps,' said Miss Walmsley, 'it would be better if you did not say her father had forgotten she was coming today.'

'Can I speak to Daddy?' demanded Caroline from the chair.

'I don't think . . . I mean . . .' stammered Gerald. The girl, suddenly resolute, hopped across the room and seized the telephone out of his hands. 'Miss Walmsley? It's Caroline Spry here. May I

speak to my father?' Gerald could not hear what Miss Walmsley answered but the girl suddenly seemed to crumple. Gently, Gerald took the telephone out of her hand and helped her back to the chair. 'He had forgotten all about me,' she said in little more than a whisper. Suddenly, theatrically, she bent her face to her hands and sobbed wildly.

'Please Miss . . . please Caroline . . .' said Gerald going down on his knees. 'Please don't cry. Why don't I ring your mother?'

Caroline gulped down her sobs and tried to pull herself together. 'I am sorry Mr Fawnsley,' and even at that moment Gerald could not help a leap of pleasure to find she had remembered his name, 'You must think me such a fool. I don't know why I'm crying. It must be delayed shock or something. I'm afraid I haven't got a mother. She died when I was five, but I'm quite all right, honestly.'

'No please, Miss Spry . . . Caroline, Basil and I will look after you. You have had a horrid shock and it was all my fault or rather Basil's.' He scowled at the cat but Basil could see he wasn't really cross. 'Let us escort you to your flat and settle you in. You have taken the flat above this one, haven't you?'

'Yes, number 5. I have only been here a week and you are the first resident I have met. I hope all the others aren't as dangerous as you,' she smiled. 'Ought I to take out medical insurance, do you think?'

Basil and Gerald helped her back to her own flat and Caroline, catching sight of herself in the mirror exclaimed: 'Oh dear! I look like something the cat brought home.' Then, seeing Basil, added quickly, 'I'm sorry Basil, I was only joking. I love cats and I think we are going to be great friends.'

Basil purred appreciatively. He liked this girl. She sat in a big armchair with her leg on a stool and Basil sat in her lap and she stroked him. Gerald stood at the door and was jealous.

Several weeks passed. Things seemed to be getting better at work and Gerald had even been commended for sorting out a particularly complicated problem connected with a client's off-shore fund. In fact he was so busy he was often not home until after nine in the evenings. Basil spent most of his time with Caroline. She was mobile now but did not go out much during the day. It was Gerald's habit to knock on Caroline's door, maybe have a drink and then take Basil down to have their supper together unless Caroline had a date. At weekends Caroline went away to stay with friends of whom, rather to Gerald's chagrin, she seemed to have a large circle.

Coming back from work one Monday about a couple of months after the accident, Gerald went as usual to pick up Basil. He was rather put out to find Caroline with a glass of wine in one hand, her other arm round a good looking young man whose face was disfigured, in Gerald's eyes, by a grin of self-congratulation. 'I have just come to pick up Basil,' said Gerald uncertainly.

'Oh, Gerald,' Caroline trilled as Basil leapt into his arms, 'come and be introduced to my fiancé.'

Gerald could remember nothing of what followed except that the man he now hated most in all the world was called Monty Braggot. Caroline's fiancé! The word with its frenchified coyness made him want to vomit. Oh God! Why had he not spoken of his love before? Now it was too late. No gentleman could speak of love to a girl who had introduced him, without a trace of embarrassment, to her fiancé. But it had always been impossible. Of course he had loved the girl from the first moment he had seen her lying on the floor half-stunned but somehow, despite the propitious circumstances of their first meeting, the relationship had never developed. As far as Gerald knew, she looked on him as just a kindly neighbour with a cat to trip over.

As the days passed, Basil became increasingly concerned at his master's downward spiral through self-pity to depression. The wedding, to which Gerald had been invited, was scheduled for early March and, as the day approached, Gerald went into something worse than mere depression. Caroline was hardly in the flat, she was so busy with preparations for her great day. So, evening after evening, Gerald sat in his chair staring glumly into space, hugging Basil. He did not eat or wash or even sleep.

One such evening, two or three days before the wedding, when Gerald had at last fallen into an uneasy doze, Basil slipped out of the flat with no object in view except to get some air and maybe

forage for some food. In his grief, Gerald had forgotten to feed him. Two blocks away there was a particularly toothsome dustbin which he had often visited before. He was just preparing to leap on to it and push off the lid to see what good things it held – he thought he could smell sardines – when he noticed, going into the house next door, the man who had, to his disgust, won the affections of his beloved Caroline. He knew that the girl was adored by his master and that this man was the cause of his master's sadness.

On a whim, he turned from the dustbin and walked over to the door through which he had seen his master's enemy, and therefore his own, disappear. The door was firmly closed but at a glance he saw that for a cat of his agility there would be no difficulty in gaining entrance by a half-open window on the first floor. After thinking about it for a few minutes, he leapt softly on to a convenient drainpipe and from thence through the window. The room into which he had jumped was a bedroom and in the bed were two humans. They were so tangled up in the sheets that he could only see a bare arm and a shapely leg and then a mop of golden curls. After a moment, the girl stopped wrestling with the bedclothes and, glancing towards the window, saw Basil. 'Why, Monty!' she cried. 'There's a lucky black cat. It must have got in by the window.' The other person in the bed reluctantly raised his head from the girl's breast. His eyes met Basil's and his face went bright red. 'Monty darling,' said the girl, 'why are you blushing? Do you recognize the cat?'

'Of course not!' said Monty sulkily, 'and I'm not blushing.'

'Yes you are,' insisted the girl. 'You do know this cat. I'm sure of it. Why does he bother you?'

'I tell you,' said the wretched Monty getting up from the bed, 'I've never seen the bloody cat in my life and now I am going to throw it out.'

'Oh no you're not,' said the girl jumping up. She looked quite ravishingly beautiful in her nakedness and for a moment Basil could see what Monty could see. He allowed the girl to pick him up in her arms and read the label on his collar. 'He lives just round the corner. When you've gone I will take him back to his home.'

'Oh, for God's sake, Sukie,' cried Monty impatiently, 'leave the cat alone. It doesn't need you to take it home. Come back to bed, there's a good girl! I've only got five minutes then I have to be going.'

'Well,' said the girl hotly, 'you can bloody well spend the five minutes playing with yourself. I refuse to be a quickie for you, my lad.'

'Come on Sukie, I didn't mean it that way,' he coaxed. 'I just meant we haven't got much time and . . . Oh, to hell with it then.'

Seeing there was no chance of persuading the girl back to bed, he got up and began dressing himself. Putting on his tie, he said carelessly, 'Give the cat to me. I'll take him home.'

'No,' said the girl still naked, hugging the cat to her breasts, 'I don't trust you, Monty. I will do it. You get on back to the office. Isn't your "meeting" supposed to be over by now? We don't want didydums to get into trouble do we?'

A little later, the girl, now dressed in expensive jeans and a man's shirt which seemed to emphasize just those attributes it might have been supposed to have concealed, rang the bell of Gerald's flat. Gerald was out at work but Caroline happened to be coming down the stairs. 'Were you looking for Mr Fawnsley?' she asked. 'Ah, is that Basil?'

'You know the cat?' said Sukie. 'Yes I found him in my flat and I thought I would bring him home.'

'How very kind of you,' said Caroline. 'He belongs to my neighbour, Gerald Fawnsley. He – Basil I mean, not Gerald – is always gallivanting. I know Gerald will be so pleased to have him back. Why don't you bring him up to my flat? Perhaps you have time for a coffee?'

The two girls cooing over Basil went into Caroline's flat and Caroline went into the kitchen to put on the kettle. While she was out of the room Sukie glanced at the framed photographs on the mantelpiece. She immediately noticed the photograph of Monty who had been caught by the photographer in the act of kissing Caroline. It was Caroline's particular favourite. As she came back into the room Sukie said: 'What a small world! I see you know Monty. When was that photo taken?'

Ben Youssef's Staircase

'Of all the things a smart cat does to whip you into line, the gift of the captured mouse is the cleverest and most touching.'

My Boss the Cat

Noah's Cats, 1995

'Cats, as a class, have never completely got over the snootiness caused by the fact that in Ancient Egypt they were worshipped as gods.'

THE STORY OF WEBSTER

The Essaouira-Bird

'I think he was genuinely fond of birds but, so far as I know, he usually confined himself to one a day.'

CALVIN, THE CAT

The Frog

'He was domesticated, too, and never objected to having his whiskers pulled.'
CATS OF MY CHILDHOOD

'Oh, a month ago. Why, do you know my fiancé?'

'Your fiancé,' exclaimed Sukie. 'You must be mistaken! Monty and I have been together for a year now and we are planning to get married next August.'

Caroline dropped the coffee.

Basil left them to sort it out and they did not notice him leaving. 'Another human relationship I have put an end to,' he growled to himself. 'I don't think I can be a lucky cat.'

'He was only after my money,' said Caroline, snuggling into Gerald's shoulder. I see that now.'

It was six months later and they were honeymooning at Lake Garda. It had all been so simple in the end. Gerald had come back to find Caroline in tears sitting hunched up on the stairs outside his flat. He had lifted her into his arms and comforted her. She had told him what Basil had done and Gerald had said that he had never liked the look of the man – he could not bring himself to give him a name. Gerald, breathing in her scent as though it were nectar, and knowing that it was wrong to take advantage of her distress, told her he loved her and said she should marry him instead. She must, he opined, know he loved her, always had and always would. He said much else but nothing that Basil could listen to without embarrassment.

She replied she had always loved him but had never suspected . . . And then he stopped her speaking with kisses.

And so there they were: married and in bliss. 'Your father was awfully good about it in the end,' Gerald murmured, generous in victory. 'He might have cut up a bit rough.'

'Oh,' said Caroline in a small voice, 'I don't think he minded as long as I was off his hands.'

Gerald hardly heard her. 'I wonder how Basil's getting on without us,' he said, letting his hand travel down her flat stomach. 'I expect he's destroying somebody's love affair.'

She turned and nestled deeper against his chest. 'He brought us together,' she went on comfortably. 'For us he is a lucky cat and always will be.'

THE SLUM CAT

Ernest Thompson Seton

LIFE I

THE LITTLE SLUM KITTEN was not six weeks old yet, but she was alone in the old junk-yard. Her mother had gone to seek food among the garbage-boxes the night before, and had never returned, so when the second evening came she was very hungry. A deep-laid instinct drove her forth from the old cracker-box to seek something to eat. Feeling her way silently among the rubbish she smelt everything that seemed eatable, but without finding food. At length she reached the wooden steps leading down into Jap Malee's bird store underground at the far end of the yard. The door was open a little, and she walked in. A Negro sitting idly on a box in a corner watched her curiously. She wandered past some rabbits; they paid no heed. She came to a wide-barred cage in which was a fox. He crouched low; his eyes glowed. The kitten wandered, sniffing, up to the bars, put her head in, sniffed again, then made straight toward the feed-pan, to be seized in a flash by the crouching fox. She gave a frightened 'mew', and the Negro also sprang forward, spitting with such copious vigour in the Fox's face that he dropped the kitten and returned to the corner, there to sit blinking his eyes in sullen fear.

The Negro pulled the kitten out. She tottered in a circle a few times, then revived, and a few minutes later, when Jap Malee came back, she was purring in the Negro's lap, apparently none the worse.

Jap was not an Oriental; he was a full-blooded Cockney; but his eyes were such little accidental slits aslant in his round, flat face that his first name was forgotten in the highly descriptive title of 'Jap'. He was not especially unkind to the birds and beasts which furnished his living, but he did not want the slum kitten.

The Negro gave her all the food she could eat and then carried her to a distant block and dropped her in an iron-yard. Here she lived and somehow found food enough to grow till, weeks later, an extended exploration brought her back to her old quarters in the junk-yard and, glad to be at home, she at once settled down.

Kitty was now fully grown. She was a striking-looking cat of the tiger type. Her marks were black on a pale grey, and the four beauty spots of white, on nose, ears and tail-tip, lent a certain distinction. She was expert now at getting a living, yet she had some days of starvation and had so far failed in her ambition to catch a sparrow. She was quite alone, but a new force was coming into her life.

She was lying in the sun one September day when a large black cat came walking along the top of a wall in her direction. By his torn ear she recognized him at once as an old enemy. She slunk into her box and hid. He picked his way gingerly, bounded lightly to a shed that was at the end of the yard, and was crossing the roof when a yellow cat rose up. The black tom glared and growled; so did the yellow tom. Their tails lashed from side to side. Strong throats growled and yowled. They approached with ears laid back, with muscles a-tense.

'Yow – yow – ow,' said the black one.

'Wow – w – w –' was the slightly deeper answer.

'Ya – wow – wow – wow –' said the black one, edging up an inch nearer.

'Yow – w – w –' was the yellow answer, as the blond cat rose to full height and stepped with vast dignity a whole inch forward. 'Yow – w,' and he went another inch, while his tail went swish, thump, from one side to the other.

'Ya – wow – yow – w,' screamed the black in a rising tone, and he backed the eighth of an inch as he marked the broad, unshrinking beast before him.

Windows opened all around, human voices were heard, but the cat scene went on.

'Yow – yow – ow,' rumbled the yellow peril, his voice deepening as the other's rose. 'Yow,' and he advanced another step.

Now their noses were but three inches apart; they stood sidewise, both ready to clinch, but each waiting for the other. They glared at each other for three minutes in silence, and like statues, except that each tail-tip was twisting.

The yellow began again. 'Yow – ow – ow,' in deep tone.

'Ya-a-a-a-a,' screamed the black with intent to strike terror by his yell, but he retreated one-sixteenth of an inch. The yellow walked up a whole long inch; their whiskers were mixing now; another advance, and their noses almost touched.

'Yo – w – w,' said yellow like a deep moan.

'Ya–a–a–a–a,' screamed black, but he retreated a thirty-second of an inch, and the yellow warrior closed and clinched like a demon.

Oh, how they rolled and bit and tore – especially the yellow one!

How they pitched and gripped and hugged – but especially the yellow one!

Over and over, sometimes one on top, sometimes the other, but usually the yellow one, and over they rolled till off the roof, amid cheers from all the windows. They lost not a second in that fall into the junk-yard; they tore and clawed all the way down, but especially the yellow one; and when they struck the ground, still fighting, the one on top was chiefly the yellow one; and before they separated both had had as much as they wanted, especially the black one! He scaled the wall and, bleeding and growling, disappeared, while the news was passed from window to window that Cayley's 'Nig' had been licked by 'Orange Billy'.

Either the yellow cat was a very clever seeker, or else slum Kitty did not hide very hard, for he discovered her among the boxes and she made no attempt to get away, probably because she had witnessed the fight. There is nothing like success in warfare to win the female heart, and thereafter the yellow tom and Kitty became very good friends, not sharing each other's lives or food – cats do not do

that much – but recognizing each other as entitled to special friendly privileges.

When October's shortening days were on an event took place in the old cracker-box. If 'Orange Billy' had come he would have seen five little kittens curled up in the embrace of their mother, the little slum Kitty. It was a wonderful thing for her. She felt all the elation an animal mother can feel – all the delight – as she tenderly loved them and licked them.

She had added a joy to her joyless life, but she had also added a heavy burden. All her strength was taken now to find food. And one day, led by a tempting smell, she wandered into the bird cellar and into an open cage. Everything was still, there was meat ahead, and she reached forward to seize it; the cage door fell with a snap and she was a prisoner. That night the Negro put an end to the kittens and was about to do the same with the mother when her unusual markings attracted the attention of the bird man, who decided to keep her.

LIFE II

Jap Malee was as disreputable a little Cockney bantam as ever sold cheap canary birds in a cellar. He was extremely poor, and the Negro lived with him because the 'Henglishman' was willing to share bed and board. Jap was perfectly honest, according to his lights, but he had no lights and there is little doubt that his chief revenue was derived from storing and restoring stolen dogs and cats. The fox and the half a dozen canaries were mere blinds. The 'Lost and Found' columns of the papers were the only ones of interest to Jap, but he noticed and saved a clipping about breeding for fur. This was stuck on the wall of his den and, under its influence, he set about making an experiment with the slum cat. First he soaked her dirty fur with stuff to kill the two or three kinds of creepers she wore and, when it had done its work, he washed her thoroughly. Kitty was savagely indignant, but a warm and happy glow spread over her as she dried off in a cage near the stove, and her fur began to fluff out with wonderful softness and whiteness. Jap and his assistant were much pleased. But this was preparatory. 'Nothing is so good for growing fur as plenty of oily food and continued exposure to cold weather,' said the clipping. Winter was at hand, and Jap Malee put Kitty's cage out in the yard, protected only from the rain and the direct wind, and fed her with all the oil cake and fish heads she could eat. In a week the change began to show. She was rapidly getting fat. She had nothing to do but get fat and dress her fur. Her cage was kept clean, and Nature responded to the chill weather and oily food by making Kitty's coat thicker and glossier every day so that, by Christmas, she was an unusually beautiful cat in the fullest and finest of fur with markings that were at least a rarity.

Why not send the slum cat to the show now coming on?

"T'won't do, ye kneow, Sammy, to henter 'er as a Tramp Cat, ye kneow,' Jap observed to his help; 'but it kin be arranged to suit the Knickerbockers. Nothink like a good noime, ye kneow. Ye see now, it had orter be "Royal" somethink or other – nothink goes with the Knickerbockers like "Royal" anythink. Now, "Royal Dick" or "Royal Sam": 'ow's that? But 'owld on: them's tom names. Oi say, Sammy, wot's the noime of that island where you were born?'

'Analostan Island, sah, was my native vicinity, sah.'

'Oi say, now, that's good, ye kneow. "Royal Analostan," by Jove! The onliest pedigreed Royal Analostan in the howle sheow, ye kneow. Ain't that capital?' and they mingled their cackles.

'But we'll 'ave to 'ave a pedigree, ye kneow;' so a very long fake pedigree on the recognized lines was prepared.

One afternoon Sam, in a borrowed silk hat, delivered the cat and the pedigree at the show door. He had been a barber, and he could put on more pomp in five minutes than Jap Malee could have displayed in a lifetime, and this, doubtless, was one reason for the respectful reception awarded the Royal Analostan at the cat show.

Jap had all the Cockney's reverence for the upper class. He was proud to be an exhibitor but when, on the opening day, he went to the door he was overpowered to see the array of carriages and silk

hats. The gateman looked at him sharply but passed him on his ticket, doubtless taking him for a stable boy to some exhibitor. The hall had velvet carpets before the long rows of cages. Jap was sneaking down the side row, glancing at the cats of all kinds, noting the blue ribbons and the reds, glancing about but not daring to ask for his own exhibit, inwardly trembling to think what the gorgeous gathering of fashion would say if they discovered the trick he was playing on them. But he saw no sign of slum Kitty.

In the middle of the centre aisle were the high-class cats. A great throng was there. The passage was roped and two policemen were there to keep the crowd moving. Jap wriggled in among them; he was too short to see over, but he gathered from the remarks that the gem of the show was there.

'Oh, isn't she a beauty!' said one tall woman.

'Ah! what distinction!' was the reply.

'One cannot mistake the air that comes only from ages of the most refined surroundings.'

'How I should like to own that superb creature!'

Jap pushed near enough to get a glimpse of the cage and read a placard which announced that 'The Blue Ribbon and Gold Medal of the Knickerbocker High Society Cat and Pet Show had been awarded to the thoroughbred pedigreed Royal Analostan, imported and exhibited by J. Malee, Esquire, the well-known fancier. Not for sale.' Jap caught his breath; he stared – yes, surely, there, high in a gilded cage on velvet cushions, with two policemen for guards, her fur bright black and pale grey, her bluish eyes slightly closed, was his slum Kitty, looking the picture of a cat that was bored to death.

Jap Malee lingered around that cage for hours, drinking a draught of glory such as he had never before known. But he saw that it would be wise for him to remain unknown; his 'butler' must do all the business.

It was slum Kitty who made that show a success. Each day her value went up in the owner's eye. He did not know what prices had been given for cats and thought that he was touching a record pitch when his 'butler' gave the director authority to sell the cat for $100.

This is how it came about that the slum cat found herself transferred to a Fifth Avenue mansion. She showed a most unaccountable wildness, as well as other peculiarities. Her retreat from the lap dog to the centre of the dinner-table was understood to express a deep-rooted, though mistaken, idea of avoiding a defiling touch. The patrician way in which she would get the cover off a milk-can was especially applauded, while her frequent wallowings in the garbage-pail were understood to be the manifestation of a little pardonable high-born eccentricity. She was fed and pampered, shown and praised, but she was not happy. She clawed at that blue ribbon around her neck till she got it off; she jumped against the plate glass because that seemed the road to outside; and she would sit and gaze out on the roofs and back yards at the other side of the window and wish she could be among them for a change.

She was strictly watched – was never allowed outside – so that all the happy garbage-pail moments occurred while these receptacles of joy were indoors. But one night in March, as they were being set out a-row for the early scavenger, the Royal Analostan saw her chance, slipped out of the door, and was lost to view.

Of course there was a grand stir, but pussy neither knew nor cared anything about that. Her one thought was to go home. A raw east wind had been rising and now it came to her with a particularly friendly message. Man would have called it an unpleasant smell of the docks, but to pussy it was a welcome message from her own country. She trotted on down the long street due east, threading the rails of front gardens, stopping like a statue for an instant, or crossing the street in search of the darkest side. She came at length to the docks and to the water, but the place was strange. She could go north or south; something turned her southward and, dodging among docks and dogs, carts and cats, crooked arms of the bay and straight board fences, she got in an hour or two into familiar scenes and smells and, before the sun came up, she crawled back, weary and footsore, through the same old hole in the same old fence, and over a wall into her junk-yard back of the bird cellar, yes, back into the very cracker-box where she was born.

After a long rest she came quietly down from the cracker-box towards the steps leading to the cellar, and engaged in her old-time pursuit of seeking for eatables. The door opened and there stood the Negro. He shouted to the bird-man inside:

'Say, Boss, come hyar! Ef dere ain't dat afar Royal Ankalostan comed back!'

Jap came in time to see the Cat jumping the wall. The Royal Analostan had been a windfall for him; had been the means of adding many comforts to the cellar and several prisoners to the cages. It was now of the utmost importance to recapture Her Majesty. Stale fish heads and other infallible lures were put out till pussy was induced to chew at a large fish head in a box trap. The Negro, in watching, pulled the string that dropped the lid, and a minute later the Analostan was again in a cage in the cellar. Meanwhile, Jap had been watching the 'Lost and Found' column. There it was: 'Twenty-five dollars reward,' etc. That night Mr Malee's 'butler' called at the Fifth Avenue mansion with the missing cat. 'Mr Malee's compliments, sah.' Of course, Mr Malee would not be rewarded, but the 'butler' was evidently open to any offer.

Kitty was guarded carefully after that but, so far from being disgusted with the old life of starving and glad of her care, she became wilder and more dissatisfied.

The spring was on in full power now and the Fifth Avenue family were thinking of their country residence. They packed up, closed house and moved off to the summer home some fifty miles away, and Pussy, in a basket, went with them.

The basket was put on the back seat of a carriage. New sounds and passing smells were entered and left. Then a roaring of many feet, more swinging of the basket, then some clicks, some bangs, a long, shrill whistle, and door-bells of a very big front door, a rumbling, a whizzling, an unpleasant smell; then there was a succession of jolts, roars, jars, stops, clicks, clacks, smells, jumps, shakes, more smells, more shakes, big shakes, little shakes, gases, smoke, screeches, door-bells, tremblings; roars, thunders, and some new smells, raps, taps, heavings, rumbling and more smells. When at last it all stopped the sun came twinkling through the basket lid.

The Royal Cat was lifted into another carriage and they turned aside from their past course. Very soon the carriage swerved, the noises of its wheels were grittings and rattlings, a new and horrible sound was added – the barking of dogs, big and little, and dreadfully close. The basket was lifted, and slum Kitty had reached her country home.

Everyone was officiously kind. All wanted to please the Royal Cat, but, somehow, none of them did, except possibly the big, fat cook that Kitty discovered on wandering into the kitchen. That greasy woman smelt more like a slum than anything she had met for months and the Royal Analostan was proportionately attracted. The cook, when she learned that fears were entertained about the cat's staying, said: 'Shure, she'd 'tind to shot; wanst a cat licks her futs shure she's at home.' So she deftly caught the unapproachable Royalty in her apron and committed the horrible sacrilege of greasing the soles of her feet with pot grease. Of course, Kitty resented it; she resented everything in the place; but, on being set down, she began to dress her paws and found evident satisfaction in that grease. She licked all four feet for an hour, and the cook triumphantly announced that now 'shure she's be apt to sthay'; and stay she did, but she showed a most surprising and disgusting preference for the kitchen and the cook and the garbage-pail.

The family, though distressed by these high-born eccentricities, were glad to see the Royal Analostan more contented and approachable. They guarded her from every menace. The dogs were taught to respect her; no man or boy about the place would have dreamed of throwing a stone at the famous pedigreed cat, and she had all the food she wanted, but still she was not happy. She was hankering for many things, she scarcely knew what. She had everything – yes, but she wanted something else. Plenty to eat and drink – yes, but milk does not taste the same when you can go and drink all you want from a saucer; it has to be stolen out of a tin pail when one is pinched with hunger, or it does not have the tang – it is not milk.

How pussy did hate it all! True, there was one sweet smelling shrub in the whole horrible place – one that she did enjoy nipping

and rubbing against it; it was the only bright spot in her country life.

One day, after a summer of discontent, a succession of things happened that stirred anew the slum instincts of the Royal prisoner. A great bundle of stuff from the docks had reached the country mansion. What it contained was of little moment, but it was rich with the most piquant of slum smells. The chords of memory surely dwell in the nose, and pussy's past was conjured up with dangerous force. Next day the cook left through some trouble. That evening the youngest boy of the house, a horrid little American with no proper appreciation of Royalty, was tying a tin to the blue-blooded one's tail, doubtless in furtherance of some altruistic project, when pussy resented it with a paw that wore five big fish-hooks for the occasion. The howl of down-trodden America roused America's mother; the deft and womanly blow she aimed with her book was miraculously avoided and pussy took flight, upstairs, of course. A hunted rat runs downstairs, a hunted dog goes on the level, a hunted cat runs up. She hid in the garret and waited till night came. Then, gliding downstairs, she tried the screen doors, found one unlatched and escaped into black August night. Pitch black to man's eyes, it was simply grey to her, and she glided through the disgusting shrubbery and flower-beds, had a final nip at that one little bush that had been an attractive spot in the garden, and boldly took her back track of the spring.

How could she take a back track that she never saw? There is in all animals some sense of direction. It is low in man and high in horses, but cats have a large gift, and this mysterious guide took her westward, not clearly and definitely, but with a general impulse that was made definite because the easiest travel was on the road. In an hour she had reached the Hudson River. Her nose had told her many times that the course was true. Smell after smell came back.

At the river was the railroad. She could not go on the water;; she must go north or south. This was a case where her sense of direction was clear: it said 'go south'; and Kitty trotted down the footpath between the iron rails and the fence.

LIFE III

Cats can go very fast up a tree or over a wall, but when it comes to the long, steady trot that reels off mile after mile, hour after hour, it is not the cat-hop but the dog-trot that counts. She became tired and a little footsore. She was thinking of a rest when a dog came running to the fence near by and broke out into such a horrible barking close to her ear that pussy leaped in terror. She ran as hard as she could down the path. The barking seemed to grow into a low rumble – a louder rumble and roaring – a terrifying thunder. A light shone; Kitty glanced back to see, not the dog, but a huge black thing with a blazing eye, coming on yowling and spitting like a yard full of tom cats. She put forth all her power to run, made such time as she never had made before, but dared not leap the fence. She was running like a dog – was flying, but all in vain: the monstrous pursuer overtook her, but missed her in the darkness, and hurried past to be lost in the night, while Kitty sat gasping for breath.

This was only the first encounter with the strange monsters – strange to her eyes – her nose seemed to know them, and told her that this was another landmark on the home trail. But pussy learned that they were very stupid and could not find her at all if she hid by slipping quietly under a fence and lying still. Before morning she had encountered many of them, but escaped unharmed from all.

About sunrise she reached a nice little slum on her home trail and was lucky enough to find several unsterilized eatables in an ash-heap. She spent the day around a stable. It was very like home, but she had no idea of staying there. She was driven by an inner craving that was neither hunger nor fear, and next evening set out as before. She had seen the 'One-eyed Thunder-rollers' all day going by, and was getting used to them. That night passed much like the first one. The days went by in skulking in barns, hiding from dogs and small boys, and the nights in limping along the track, for she was getting footsore; but on she went, mile after mile, southward, ever southward – dogs, boys, roarers, hunger – dogs, boys, roarers, hunger – but day after day with increasing weariness

on she went, and her nose from time to time cheered her by confidently reporting, 'This surely is a smell we passed last spring.'

So week after week went by, and pussy, dirty, ribbonless, footsore and weary, arrived at the Harlem Bridge. Though it was enveloped in delicious smells she did not like the look of that bridge. For half the night she wandered up and down the shore without discovering any other means of going south excepting some other bridges. Somehow she had to come back to it; not only its smells were familiar, but from time to time when a 'One-eye' ran over it there was the peculiar rumbling roar that was a sensation in the springtime trip. She leaped to the timber stringer and glided out over the water. She had got less than a third of the way over when a 'Thundering One-eye' came roaring at her from the opposite end. She was much frightened but, knowing their blindness, she dropped to a low side beam and there crouched in hiding. Of course, the stupid monster missed her and passed on, and all would have been well but it turned back, or another just like it, and came suddenly roaring behind her. Pussy leaped to the long track and made for the home shore. She might have got there, but a third of the red-eye terrors came roaring down at her from that side. She was running her hardest, but was caught between two foes. There was nothing for it but a desperate leap from the timbers into – she did not know what. Down – down – down – plop! splash! plunge – into the deep water, not cold, for it was August, but oh! so horrible. She spluttered and coughed and struck out for the shore. She had never learned to swim, and yet she swam, for the simple reason that a cat's position and attitude in swimming are the same as her position and attitude in walking. She had fallen into a place she did not like; naturally she tried to walk out, and the result was that she swam ashore. Which shore? It never fails – the south – the shore nearest home. She scrambled out all dripping wet, up the muddy bank and through coal-piles and dust-heaps, looking as black, dirty and unroyal as it was possible for a cat to look.

Once the shock was over the Royal pedigreed slummer began to feel better for the plunge. A genial glow without from the bath, a genial sense of triumph within, for had she not outwitted three of the big terrors?

Her nose, her memory and her instinct of direction inclined her to get on the track again, but the place was infested with the big thunder-rollers, and prudence led her to turn aside and follow the river bank with its musky home reminders.

She was more than two days learning the infinite dangers and complexities of the East River docks, and at length, on the third night, she reached familiar ground, the place she had passed the night of her first escape. From that her course was sure and rapid. She knew just where she was going and how to get there. She knew even the most prominent features in the dogscape now. She went faster, felt happier. In a little while she would be curled up in the old junk-yard. Another turn and the block was in sight –

But – what – it was gone. Kitty could not believe her eyes. There, where had stood, or leaned, or slouched, or straggled – the houses of the block – was a great broken wilderness of stone, lumber and holes in the ground.

Kitty walked all around it. She knew by the bearings and by the local colour of the pavement that she was in her home; that there had lived the bird-man, and there was the old junk-yard; but all were gone, completely gone, taking the familiar odours with them; and pussy turned sick at heart in the utter hopelessness of the case. Her home love was her master mood. She had given up all to come to a home that no longer existed, and for once her brave little spirit was cast down. She wandered over the silent heaps of rubbish and found neither consolation nor eatables. The ruin had covered several of the blocks and reached back from the water. It was not a fire. Kitty had seen one of these things once. Pussy knew nothing of the great bridge that was to rise from this very spot.

When the sun came up Kitty sought for cover. An adjoining block still stood with little change, and the Royal Analostan retired to that. She knew some of its trails, but once there was unpleasantly surprised to find the place swarming with cats that, like herself, were driven from their old grounds, and when the

garbage-cans came out there were several cats to each. It meant a famine in the land and pussy, after standing it a few days, set out to find her other home in Fifth Avenue. She got there to find it shut up and deserted, and the next night she returned to the crowded slum.

September and October wore away. Many of the cats died of starvation or were too weak to escape their natural enemies. But Kitty, young and strong, still lived.

Great changes had come over the ruined blocks. Though silent the night she saw them, they were crowded with noisy workmen all day. A tall building was completed by the end of October, and slum Kitty, driven by hunger, went sneaking up to a pail that a Negro had set outside. The pail, unfortunately, was not garbage, but a new thing in that region, a scrubbing-pail – a sad disappointment, but it had a sense of comfort: there was a trace of a familiar touch on the handle. While she was studying it the Negro elevator boy came out again. In spite of his blue clothes his odorous person confirmed the good impression of the handle. Kitty had retreated across the street. He gazed at her.

'Sho ef dat don't look like de Royal Ankalostan – Hya, pussy – pussy – pussy – pus-s-s-y, co-o-ome – pus-s-s-y, hya! I specs she's sho hungry.'

Hungry! She had not had a real meal for a month. The Negro went into the hall and reappeared with a portion of his own lunch.

'Hya, pussy, puss – puss – puss.' At length he laid the meat on the pavement and went back to the door. Slum Kitty came, found it savoury; sniffed at the meat, seized it, and fled like a little tigress to eat her prize in peace.

LIFE IV

This was the beginning of a new era. Pussy came to the door of the building now when pinched by hunger, and the good feeling for the Negro grew. She had never understood that man before. Now he was her friend, the only one she had.

One week pussy caught a rat. She was crossing the street in front of the new building when her friend opened the door for a well-dressed man to come out.

'Hell, look at that for a cat,' said the man.

'Yes, sah,' answered the Negro; 'cat's ma cat, sah; she's a terror on rats, sah. Hez 'em 'bout cleaned up, sah; dat's why she so thin.'

'Well, don't let her starve,' said the man, with the air of a landlord. 'Can't you feed her?'

'De liver-meat man comes reg'lar, sah, quatah dollar a week, sah,' said the Negro, realizing that he was entitled to the extra fifteen cents for 'the idea'.

'That's all right; I'll stand it.'

Since then the Negro has sold her a number of times with a perfectly clear conscience, because he knows quite well that it is only a question of a few days before the Royal Analostan comes back again. She has learned to tolerate the elevator and even to ride up and down on it. The Negro stoutly maintains that once she heard the meat man while she was on the top floor and managed to press the button that called the elevator to take her down.

She is sleek and beautiful again. She is not only one of 400 that form the inner circle about the liverman's barrow, but she is recognized as the star pensioner as well.

But in spite of her prosperity, her social position, her Royal name and fake pedigree, the greatest pleasure of her life is to slip out and go a-slumming in the gloaming, for now, as in her previous lives, she is at heart, and likely to be, nothing but a dirty little slum cat.

THE WHITE AND BLACK DYNASTIES

Théophile Gautier

A CAT BROUGHT FROM HAVANA by Mademoiselle Anïta de la Penuela, a young Spanish artist whose studies of white angoras may still be seen gracing the printsellers' windows, produced the daintiest little kitten imaginable. It was just like a swan's-down powder-puff, and on account of its immaculate whiteness it received the name of Pierrot. When it grew big this was lengthened to Don Pierrot de Navarre as being more grandiose and majestic.

Don Pierrot, like all animals which are spoilt and made much of, developed a charming amiability of character. He shared the life of the household with all the pleasure which cats find in the intimacy of the domestic hearth. Seated in his usual place near the fire, he really appeared to understand what was being said, and to take an interest in it.

His eyes followed the speakers, and from time to time he would utter little sounds, as though he too wanted to make remarks and give his opinion on literature, which was our usual topic of conversation. He was very fond of books, and when he found one open on a table he would lie on it, look at the page attentively, and turn over the leaves with his paw; then he would end by going to sleep, for all the world as if he were reading a fashionable novel.

Directly I took up a pen he would jump on my writing-desk and with deep attention watch the steel nib tracing black spider-legs on the expanse of white paper, and his head would turn each time I began a new line. Sometimes he tried to take part in the work, and would attempt to pull the pen out of my hand, no doubt in order to write himself, for he was an aesthetic cat, like Hoffman's Murr, and I strongly suspect him of having scribbled his memoirs at night on some house-top by the light of his phosphorescent eyes. Unfortunately these lucubrations have been lost.

Don Pierrot never went to bed until I came in. He waited for me inside the door, and as I entered the hall he would rub himself against my legs and arch his back, purring joyfully all the time. Then he proceeded to walk in front of me like a page, and if I had asked him, he would certainly have carried the candle for me. In this fashion he escorted me to my room and waited while I undressed; then he would jump on the bed, put his paws round my neck, rub noses with me, and lick me with his rasping little pink tongue, while giving vent to soft inarticulate cries, which clearly expressed how pleased he was to see me again. Then when his transports of affection had subsided, and the hour for repose had come, he would balance himself on the rail of the bedstead and sleep there like a bird perched on a bough. When I woke in the morning he would come and lie near me until it was time to get up. Twelve o'clock was the hour at which I was supposed to come in. On this subject Pierrot had all the notions of a concierge.

At that time we had instituted little evening gatherings among a few friends, and had formed a small society, which we called the Four Candles Club, the room in which we met being, as it happened, lit by four candles in silver candlesticks, which were placed at the corners of the table.

Sometimes the conversation became so lively that I forgot the time, at the risk of finding, like Cinderella, my carriage turned into a pumpkin and my coachman into a rat.

Pierrot waited for me several times until two o'clock in the morning, but in the end my conduct displeased him, and he went to bed without me. This mute protest against my innocent dissipation touched me so much that ever after I came home regularly at midnight. But it was a long time before Pierrot forgave me. He wanted to be sure that it was not a sham repentance; but when he

was convinced of the sincerity of my conversion, he deigned to take me into favour again, and he resumed his nightly post in the entrance-hall.

To gain the friendship of a cat is not an easy thing. It is a philosophic, well-regulated, tranquil animal, a creature of habit and a lover of order and cleanliness. It does not give its affections indiscriminately. It will consent to be your friend if you are worthy of the honour, but it will not be your slave. With all its affection, it preserves its freedom of judgement, and it will not do anything for you which it considers unreasonable; but once it has given its love, what absolute confidence, what fidelity of affection! It will make itself the companion of your hours of work, of loneliness, or of sadness. It will lie the whole evening on your knee, purring and happy in your society, and leaving the company of creatures of its own kind to be with you. In vain the sound of caterwauling reverberates from the house-tops, inviting it to one of those cats' evening parties where essence of red-herring takes the place of tea. It will not be tempted, but continues to keep its vigil with you. If you put it down it climbs up again quickly, with a sort of crooning noise, which is like a gentle reproach. Sometimes, when seated in front of you, it gazes at you with such soft, melting eyes, such a human and caressing look, that you are almost awed, for it seems impossible that reason can be absent from it.

Don Pierrot had a companion of the same race as himself, and no less white. All the imaginable snowy comparisons it were possible to pile up would not suffice to give an idea of that immaculate fur, which would have made ermine look yellow.

I called her Seraphita, in memory of Balzac's Swedenborgian romance. The heroine of that wonderful story, when she climbed the snow peaks of the Falberg with Minna, never shone with a more pure white radiance. Seraphita had a dreamy and pensive character. She would lie motionless on a cushion for hours, not asleep, but with eyes fixed in rapt attention on scenes invisible to ordinary mortals.

Caresses were agreeable to her, but she responded to them with great reserve, and only to those of people whom she favoured with her esteem, which it was not easy to gain. She liked luxury, and it was always in the newest armchair or on the piece of furniture best calculated to show off her swan-like beauty, that she was to be found. Her toilette took an immense time. She would carefully smooth her entire coat every morning, and wash her face with her paw, and every hair on her body shone like new silver when brushed by her pink tongue. If anyone touched her she would immediately efface all traces of the contact, for she could not endure being ruffled. Her elegance and distinction gave one an idea of aristocratic birth, and among her own kind she must have been at least a duchess. She had a passion for scents. She would plunge her nose into bouquets, and nibble a perfumed handkerchief with little paroxysms of delight. She would walk about on the dressing-table sniffling the stoppers of the scent-bottles, and she would have loved to use the violet powder if she had been allowed.

Such was Seraphita, and never was a cat more worthy of a poetic name.

Don Pierrot de Navarre, being a native of Havana, needed a hot-house temperature. This he found indoors, but the house was surrounded by large gardens, divided up by palings through which a cat could easily slip, and planted with big trees in which hosts of birds twittered and sang; and sometimes Pierrot, taking advantage of an open door, would go out hunting of an evening and run over the dewy grass and flowers. He would then have to wait till morning to be let in again, for although he might come mewing under the windows, his appeal did not always wake the sleepers inside.

He had a delicate chest, and one colder night than usual he took a chill which soon developed into consumption. Poor Pierrot, after a year of coughing, became wasted and thin, and his coat, which formerly boasted such a snowy gloss, now put one in mind of the lustreless white of a shroud. His great limpid eyes looked enormous in his attenuated face. His pink nose had grown pale, and he would walk sadly along the sunny wall with slow steps, and watch the yellow autumn leaves whirling up in spirals. He looked as though he were reciting Millevoye's elegy.

There is nothing more touching than a sick animal; it submits to suffering with such gentle, pathetic resignation.

Everything possible was done to try and save Pierrot. He had a very clever doctor who sounded him and felt his pulse. He ordered him asses' milk, which the poor creature drank willingly enough out of his little china saucer. He lay for hours on my knee like the ghost of a sphinx, and I could feel the bones of his spine like the beads of a rosary under my fingers. He tried to respond to my caresses with a feeble purr which was like a death rattle.

When he was dying he lay panting on his side, but with a supreme effort he raised himself and came to me with dilated eyes in which there was a look of intense supplication. This look seemed to say: 'Cannot you save me, you who are a man?' Then he staggered a short way with eyes already glazing, and fell down with such a lamentable cry, so full of despair and anguish, that I was pierced with silent horror.

He was buried at the bottom of the garden under a white rosebush which still marks his grave.

Seraphita died two or three years later of diphtheria, against which no science could prevail.

She rests not far from Pierrot. With her the white dynasty became extinct, but not the family. To this snow-white pair were born three kittens as black as ink.

Let him explain this mystery who can.

Just at that time Victor Hugo's *Misérables* was in great vogue, and the names of the characters in the novel were on everyone's lips. I called the two male kittens Enjolras and Gavroche, while the little female received the name of Eponine.

They were perfectly charming in their youth. I trained them like dogs to fetch and carry a bit of paper crumpled into a ball, which I threw for them. In time they learnt to fetch it from the tops of cupboards, from behind chests or from the bottom of tall vases, out of which they would pull it very cleverly with their paws. When they grew up they disdained such frivolous games, and acquired that calm philosophic temperament which is the true nature of cats.

To people landing in America in a slave colony all negroes are negroes, and indistinguishable from one another. In the same way, to careless eyes, three black cats are three black cats; but attentive observers make no such mistake. Animal physiognomy varies as much as that of men, and I could distinguish perfectly between those faces, all three as black as Harlequin's mask, and illuminated by emerald disks shot with gold.

Enjolras was by far the handsomest of the three. He was remarkable for his great leonine head and big ruff, his powerful shoulders, long back and splendid feathery tail. There was something theatrical about him, and he seemed to be always posing like a popular actor who knows he is being admired. His movements were slow, undulating and majestic. He put each foot down with as much circumspection as if he were walking on a table covered with Chinese bric-à-brac or Venetian glass. As to his character, he was by no

means a stoic, and he showed a love of eating which that virtuous and sober young man, his namesake, would certainly have disapproved. Enjolras would undoubtedly have said to him, like the angel to Swedenborg: 'You eat too much.'

I humoured this gluttony, which was as amusing as a gastronomic monkey's, and Enjolras attained a size and weight seldom reached by the domestic cat. It occurred to me to have him shaved poodle-fashion, so as to give the finishing touch to his resemblance to a lion.

We left him his mane and a big tuft at the end of his tail, and I would not swear that we did not give him mutton-chop whiskers on his haunches like those Munito wore. Thus tricked out, it must be confessed he was much more like a Japanese monster than an African lion. Never was a more fantastic whim carved out of a living animal. His shaven skin took odd blue tints, which contrasted strangely with his black mane.

Gavroche, as though desirous of calling to mind his namesake in the novel, was a cat with an arch and crafty expression of countenance. He was smaller than Enjolras, and his movements were comically quick and brusque. In him absurd capers and ludicrous postures took the place of the banter and slang of the Parisian gamin. It must be confessed that Gavroche had vulgar tastes. He seized every possible occasion to leave the drawing-room in order to go and make up parties in the backyard, or even in the street, with stray cats,

'De naissance quelconque et de sang peu prouvé,'

in which doubtful company he completely forgot his dignity as cat of Havana, son of Don Pierrot de Navarre, grandee of Spain of the first order, and of the aristocratic and haughty Doña Seraphita.

Sometimes in his truant wanderings he picked up emaciated comrades, lean with hunger, and brought them to his plate of food to give them a treat in his good-natured, lordly way. The poor creatures, with ears laid back and watchful side-glances, in fear of being interrupted in their free meal by the broom of the housemaid, swallowed double, triple, and quadruple mouthfuls, and, like the famous dog Siete-Aguas (seven waters) of Spanish posadas (inns), they licked the plate as clean as if it had been washed and polished by one of Gerard Dow's or Mieris's Dutch housewives.

Seeing Gavroche's friends reminded me of a phrase which illustrates one of Gavarni's drawings, 'Ils sont jolis les amis dont vous êtes susceptible d'aller avec!' ('Pretty kind of friends you like to associate with!')

But that only proved what a good heart Gavroche had, for he could easily have eaten all the food himself.

The cat named after the interesting Eponine was more delicate and slender than her brothers. Her nose was rather long, and her eyes slightly oblique, and green as those of Pallas Athene, to whom Homer always applied the epithet of *γλαυκωπις*. Her nose was of velvety black, with the grain of a fine Périgord truffle; her whiskers were in a perpetual state of agitation, all of which gave her a peculiarly expressive countenance. Her superb black coat was always in motion, and was watered and shot with shadowy markings. Never was there a more sensitive, nervous, electric animal. If one stroked her two or three times in the dark, blue sparks would fly crackling out of her fur.

Eponine attached herself particularly to me, like the Eponine of the novel to Marius, but I, being less taken up with Cosette than that handsome young man, could accept the affection of this gentle and devoted cat, who still shares the pleasures of my suburban retreat and is the inseparable companion of my hours of work.

She comes running up when she hears the front-door bell, receives the visitors, conducts them to the drawing-room, talks to them – yes, talks to them – with little chirruping sounds, that do not in the least resemble the language cats use in talking to their own kind, but which simulate the articulate speech of man. What does she say? She says in the clearest way, 'Will you be good enough to wait till monsieur comes down? Please look at the pictures, or chat with me in the meantime, if that will amuse you.' Then when I come in she discreetly retires to an armchair or a corner of the piano, like a well-bred animal who knows what is correct in good society. Pretty little Eponine gave so many proofs of intelligence,

good disposition and sociability, that by common consent she was raised to the dignity of a *person*, for it was quite evident that she was possessed of higher reasoning power than mere instinct. This dignity conferred on her the privilege of eating at table like a person instead of out of a saucer in a corner of the room like an animal.

So Eponine had a chair next to me at breakfast and dinner, but on account of her small size she was allowed to rest her two front paws on the edge of the table. Her place was laid, without spoon or fork, but she had her glass. She went right through dinner dish by dish, from soup to dessert, waiting for her turn to be helped, and behaving with such propriety and nice manners as one would like to see in many children. She made her appearance at the first sound of the bell, and on going into the dining-room one found her already in her place, sitting up in her chair with her paws resting on the edge of the tablecloth, and seeming to offer you her little face to kiss, like a well-brought-up little girl who is affectionately polite towards her parents and elders.

As one finds flaws in diamonds, spots on the sun, and shadows on perfection itself, so Eponine, it must be confessed, had a passion for fish. She shared this in common with all other cats. Contrary to the Latin proverb,

'Catus amat pieces, sed non vult tingere plantas,'

she would willingly have dipped her paw into the water if by so doing she could have pulled out a trout or a young carp. She became nearly frantic over fish, and, like a child who is filled with the expectation of dessert, she sometimes rebelled at her soup when she knew (from previous investigations in the kitchen) that fish was coming. When this happened she was not helped, and I would say to her coldly: 'Mademoiselle, a person who is not hungry for soup cannot be hungry for fish,' and the dish would be pitilessly carried away from under her nose. Convinced that matters were serious, greedy Eponine would swallow her soup in all haste, down to the last drop, polishing off the last crumb of bread or bit of macaroni, and would then turn round and look at me with pride, like someone who has conscientiously done his duty. She was then given her portion, which she consumed with great satisfaction, and after tasting of every dish in turn, she would finish up by drinking a third of a glass of water.

When I am expecting friends to dinner Eponine knows there is going to be a party before she sees the guests. She looks at her place, and if she sees a knife and fork by her plate she decamps at once and seats herself on a music-stool, which is her refuge on these occasions.

Let those who deny reasoning powers to animals explain if they can this little fact, apparently so simple, but which contains a whole series of inductions. From the presence near her plate of those implements which man alone can use, this observant and reflective cat concludes that she will have to give up her place for that day to a guest, and promptly proceeds to do so. She never makes a mistake; but when she knows the visitor well she climbs on his knee and tries to coax a tit-bit out of him by her pretty caressing ways.

THE CAT THAT WALKED BY HIMSELF

Rudyard Kipling

THIS BEFELL AND BEHAPPENED and became and was, O, my Best Beloved, when the tame animals were wild. The Dog was wild, and the Horse was wild, and the Cow was wild, and the Sheep was wild, and the Pig was wild – as wild as could be – and they walked in the wet wild woods by their wild ones, but the wildest of all the wild animals was the Cat. He walked by himself, and all places were alike to him.

Of course the Man was wild too. He was dreadfully wild. He didn't even begin to be tame till he met the Woman and she did not like living in his wild ways. She picked out a nice dry cave, instead of a heap of wet leaves, to lie down in, and she strewed clean sand on the floor, and she lit a nice fire of wood at the back of the cave, and she hung a dried Wild Horse skin, tail down, across the opening of the cave, and she said: 'Wipe your feet when you come in, and now we'll keep house.'

That night, Best Beloved, they ate Wild Sheep roasted on the hot stones and flavoured with wild garlic and wild pepper, and Wild Duck stuffed with wild rice, and wild fenugreek and wild coriander, and marrowbones of Wild Oxen, and wild cherries and wild granadillas. Then the Man went to sleep in front of the fire ever so happy, but the Woman sat up, combing. She took the bone of the shoulder of mutton, the big flat blade bone, and she looked at the wonderful marks on it, and she threw more wood on the fire and she made a magic. She made the first Singing Magic in the world.

Out in the wet wild woods all the wild animals gathered together where they could see the light of the fire a long way off, and they wondered what it meant.

Then Wild Horse stamped with his foot and said: 'O, my friends and my enemies, why have the Man and the Woman made that great light in that great cave, and what harm will it do us?'

Wild Dog lifted up his nose and smelled the smell of the roast mutton and said: 'I will go up and see and look and stay: for I think it is good. Cat, come with me.'

'Nenni,' said the Cat. 'I am the Cat who walks by himself, and all places are alike to me. I will not come.'

'Then we will never be friends again,' said Wild Dog, and he trotted off to the cave.

But when he had gone a little way, the Cat said to himself: 'All places are alike to me. Why should I not go too and see and look and come away?' So he slipped after Wild Dog softly, very softly, and hid himself where he could hear everything.

When Wild Dog reached the mouth of the cave he lifted up the dried Horse skin with his nose a little bit and sniffed the beautiful smell of the roast mutton, and the Woman heard him and laughed and said: 'Here comes the first wild thing out of the wild woods. What do you want?'

Wild Dog said: 'O, my enemy and wife of my enemy, what is this that smells so good in the wild woods?'

Then the Woman picked up a roasted mutton bone and threw it to Wild Dog and said: 'Wild thing out of the wild woods, taste and try.' Wild Dog gnawed the bone and it was more delicious than anything he had ever tasted, and he said: 'O, my enemy and wife of my enemy, give me another.'

The Woman said: 'Wild thing out of the wild woods, help my Man to hunt through the day and guard this cave at night and I will give you as many roast bones as you need.'

'Ah!' said the Cat listening, 'this is a very wise Woman, but she is not so wise as I am.'

Wild Dog crawled into the cave and laid his head on the Woman's lap and said: 'O, my friend and wife of my friend, I will help your Man to hunt through the day, and at night I will guard your cave.'

'Ah!' said the Cat listening, 'that is a very foolish Dog.' And he went back through the wet wild woods waving his tail and walking by his wild lone. But he never told anybody.

When the Man woke up he said: 'What is Wild Dog doing here?' And the Woman said: 'His name is not Wild Dog anymore, but the First Friend because he will be our friend for always and always and always. Take him with you when you go hunting.'

Next night the Woman cut great green armfuls of fresh grass from the water meadows and dried it before the fire so that it smelled like new-mown hay, and she sat at the mouth of the cave and plaited a halter out of horsehide, and she looked at the shoulder of mutton bone – at the big broad blade bone – and she made a magic. She made the second Singing Magic in the world.

Out in the wild woods all the wild animals wondered what had happened to Wild Dog, and at last Wild Horse stamped with his foot and said: 'I will go and see why Wild Dog has not returned. Cat, come with me.'

'Nenni,' said the Cat. 'I am the Cat who walks by himself, and all places are alike to me. I will not come.' But all the same he followed Wild Horse softly, very softly, and hid himself where he could hear everything.

When the Woman heard Wild Horse tripping and stumbling on his long mane she laughed and said: 'Here comes the second wild thing out of the wild woods. What do you want?'

Wild Horse said: 'O, my enemy and wife of my enemy, where is Wild Dog?'

The Woman laughed and picked up the blade bone and looked at it and said: 'Wild thing out of the wild woods, you did not come here for Wild Dog, but for the sake of this good grass.'

And Wild Horse, tripping and stumbling on his long mane, said: 'That is true, give it to me to eat.'

The Woman said: 'Wild thing out of the wild woods, bend your wild head and wear what I give you and you shall eat the wonderful grass three times a day.'

'Ah,' said the Cat listening, 'this is a clever Woman, but she is not so clever as I am.'

Wild Horse bent his wild head and the Woman slipped the plaited hide halter over it, and Wild Horse breathed on the woman's feet and said: 'O, my mistress and wife of my master, I will be your servant for the sake of the wonderful grass.'

'Ah,' said the Cat listening, 'that is a very foolish Horse.' And he went back through the wet wild woods, waving his wild tail and walking by his wild lone.

When the Man and the Dog came back from hunting, the Man said: 'What is Wild Horse doing here?' And the Woman said: 'His name is not Wild Horse anymore, but the First Servant because he will carry us from place to place for always and always and always. Take him with you when you go hunting.'

Next day, holding her wild head high that her wild horns should not catch in the wild trees, Wild Cow came up to the cave, and the Cat followed and hid himself just the same as before; and everything happened just the same as before; and the Cat said the same things as before, and when Wild Cow had promised to give her milk to the Woman every day in exchange for the wonderful grass, the Cat went back through the wet wild woods walking by his lone just the same as before.

And when the Man and the Hose and the Dog came home from hunting and asked the same questions, same as before, the Woman said: 'Her name is not Wild Cow anymore, but the Giver of Good Things. She will give us the warm white milk for always and always and always, and I will take care of her while you three go hunting.'

Next day the Cat waited to see if any other wild thing would go up to the cave, but no one moved, so the Cat walked there by himself, and he saw the Woman milking the Cow, and he saw the light

of the fire in the cave, and he smelled the smell of the warm white milk.

Cat said: 'O, my enemy and wife of my enemy, where did Wild Cow go?'

The Woman laughed and said: 'Wild thing out of the wild woods, go back to the woods again, for I have braided up my hair and I have put away the blade bone, and we have no more need of either friends or servants in our cave.'

Cat said: 'I am not a friend and I am not a servant. I am the Cat who walks by himself and I want to come into your cave.'

The Woman said: 'Then why did you not come with First Friend on the first night?'

Cat grew very angry and said: 'Has Wild Dog told tales of me?'

Then the Woman laughed and said: 'You are the Cat who walks by himself and all places are alike to you. You are neither a friend nor a servant. You have said it yourself. Go away and walk by yourself in all places alike.'

Then the Cat pretended to be sorry and said: 'Must I never come into the cave? Must I never sit by the warm fire? Must I never drink the warm white milk? You are very wise and very beautiful. You should not be cruel even to a Cat.'

Then the Woman said: 'I knew I was wise but I did not know I was beautiful. So I will make a bargain with you. If ever I say one word in your praise you may come into the cave.'

'And if you say two words in my praise?' said the Cat.

'I never shall,' said the Woman, 'but if I say two words you may sit by the fire in the cave.'

'And if you say three words?' said the Cat.

'I never shall,' said the Woman, 'but if I do you may drink the warm white milk three times a day for always and always and always.'

Then the Cat arched his back and said: 'Now let the curtain at the mouth of the cave, and the fire at the back of the cave, and the milk pots that stand beside the fire remember what my enemy and the wife of my enemy has said.' And he went away through the wet wild woods waving his wild tails and walking by his wild lone.

That night when the Man and the Horse and the Dog came home from hunting, the Woman did not tell them of the bargain that she had made because she was afraid that they might not like it.

Cat went far and far away and hid himself in the wet wild woods by his wild lone for a long time till the Woman forgot all about him. Only the Bat – the little upside-down Bat – that hung inside the cave knew where Cat hid, and every evening he would fly to Cat with the news.

One evening the Bat said: 'There is a Baby in the Cave. He is new and pink and fat and small, and the Woman is very fond of him.'

'Ah,' said the Cat listening, 'but what is the Baby fond of?'

'He is fond of things that are soft and tickle,' said the Bat. 'He is fond of warm things to hold in his arms when he goes to sleep. He is fond of being played with. He is fond of all those things.'

'Ah,' said the Cat, 'then my time has come.'

Next night Cat walked through the wet wild woods and hid very near the cave till morning time. The woman was very busy cooking, and the Baby cried and interrupted; so she carried him outside the cave and gave him a handful of pebbles to play with. But still the Baby cried.

Then the Cat put out his paddy-paw and patted the Baby on the cheek, and it cooed; and the Cat rubbed against its fat knees and tickled it under its fat chin with his tail. And the Baby laughed; and the Woman heard him and smiled.

Then the Bat – the little upside-down Bat – that hung in the mouth of the cave said: 'O, my hostess and wife of my host and mother of my host, a wild thing from the wild woods is most beautifully playing with your Baby.'

'A blessing on that wild thing whoever he may be,' said the Woman straightening her back, 'for I was a busy Woman this morning and he has done me a service.'

That very minute and second, Best Beloved, the dried horse-skin curtain that was stretched tail-down at the mouth of the cave fell

down – *So!* – because it remembered the bargain, and when the Woman went to pick it up – lo and behold! – the Cat was sitting quite comfy inside the cave.

'O, my enemy and wife of my enemy and mother of my enemy,' said the Cat, 'it is I, for you have spoken a word in my praise, and now I can sit within the cave for always and always and always. But still I am the Cat who walks by himself and all places are alike to me.'

The Woman was very angry and shut her lips tight and took up her spinning wheel and began to spin.

But the Baby cried because the Cat had gone away, and the Woman could not hush him for he struggled and kicked and grew black in the face.

'O, my enemy and wife of my enemy and mother of my enemy,' said the Cat, 'take a strand of the thread that you are spinning and tie it to your spindle wheel and drag it on the floor and I will show you a magic that shall make your Baby laugh as loudly as he is now crying.'

'I will do so,' said the Woman, 'because I am at my wits' end, but I will not thank you for it.'

She tied the thread to the little pot spindle wheel and drew it across the floor and the Cat ran after it and patted it with his paws, and rolled head over heels, and tossed it backward over his shoulder, and chased it between his hind legs, and pretended to lose it, and pounched down upon it again till the Baby laughed as loudly as he had been crying, and scrambled after the Cat and frolicked all over the cave till he grew tired and settled down to sleep with the Cat in his arms.

'Now,' said the Cat, 'I will sing the Baby a song that shall keep him asleep for an hour.' And he began to purr loud and low, low and loud, till the Baby fell fast asleep The Woman smiled as she looked down upon the two of them and said: 'That was wonderfully done. Surely you are very clever, O, Cat.'

That very minute and second, Best Beloved, the smoke of the fire at the back of the cave came down in clouds from the roof because it remembered the bargain, and when it had cleared away – lo and behold! – the Cat was sitting, quite comfy, close to the fire.

'O, my enemy and wife of my enemy and mother of my enemy,' said the Cat, 'it is I, for you have spoken a second word in my praise, and now I can sit by the warm fire at the back of the cave for always and always and always. But still I am the Cat who walks by himself and all places are alike to me.'

Then the Woman was very, very angry and let down her hair and

put more wood on the fire and brought out the broad blade bone of the shoulder of mutton and began to make a magic that should prevent her from saying a third word in praise of the Cat. It was not a Singing Magic, Best Beloved, it was Still Magic; and by and by the cave grew so still that a little we-wee Mouse crept out of a corner and ran across the floor.

'O, my enemy and wife of my enemy and mother of my enemy,' said the Cat, 'is that little Mouse part of your magic?'

'No,' said the Woman, and she dropped the blade bone and jumped upon a footstool in front of the fire and braided up her hair very quick for fear that the Mouse should run up it.

'Ah,' said the Cat listening, 'then the Mouse will do me no harm if I eat it?'

'No,' said the Woman, braiding up her hair; 'eat it quick and I will always be grateful to you.'

Cat made one jump and caught the little Mouse, and the Woman said: 'A hundred thanks to you, O, Cat. Even the First Friend is not quick enough to catch little Mice as you have done. You must be very wise.'

That very moment and second, O, Best Beloved, the milk pot that stood by the fire cracked in two pieces – *So!* – because it remembered the bargain, and when the Woman jumped down from the footstool – lo and behold! – the Cat was lapping up the warm white milk that lay in one of the broken pieces.

'O, my enemy and wife of my enemy and mother of my enemy,' said the Cat, 'it is I, for you have spoken three words in my praise, and now I can drink the warm white milk three times a day for always and always and always. But *still* I am the Cat who walks by himself and all places are alike to me.'

Then the Woman laughed and set him a bowl of the warm white milk and said: 'O, Cat, you are as clever as a Man, but remember that the bargain was not made with the Man or the Dog, and I do not know what they will do when they come home.'

'What is that to me?' said the Cat. 'If I have my place by the fire and my milk three times a day I do not care what the Man or the Dog can do.'

That evening when the Man and the Dog came into the cave the Woman told them all the story of the bargain, and the Man said: 'Yes, but he has not made a bargain with me or with all proper Men after me.' And he took off his two leather boots and he took up his little stone axe (that makes three) and he fetched a piece of wood and a hatchet (that is five altogether), and he set them out in a row and he said: 'Now we will make a bargain. If you do not catch Mice when you are in the cave, for always and always and always, I will throw these five things at you whenever I see you, and so shall all proper Men do after me.'

'Ah,' said the Woman listening. 'This is a very clever Cat, but he is not so clever as my Man.'

The Cat counted the five things (and they looked very knobby) and he said: 'I will catch Mice when I am in the cave for always and always and always: but still I am the Cat that walks by himself and all places are alike to me.'

'Not when I am near,' said the Man. 'If you had not said that I would have put all these things away (for always and always and always), but now I am going to throw my two boots and my little stone axe (that makes three) at you whenever I meet you and so shall all proper Men do after me.'

Then the Dog said: 'Wait a minute. He has not made a bargain with me.' And he sat down and growled dreadfully and showed all his teeth and said: 'If you are not kind to the Baby while I am in the cave for always and always and always I will chase you till I catch you, and when I catch you I will bite you, and so shall all proper Dogs do after me.'

'Ah,' said the Woman listening. 'This is a very clever Cat, but he is not so clever as the Dog.'

Cat counted the Dog's teeth (and they looked very pointed) and he said: 'I will be kind to the Baby while I am in the cave as long as he does not pull my tail too hard for always and always and always. But still I am the Cat that walks by himself and all places are alike to me.'

'Not when I am near,' said the Dog. 'If you had not said that I would have shut my mouth for always and always and always, but

now I am going to chase you up a tree whenever I meet you, and so shall all proper Dogs do after me.'

Then the Man threw his two boots and his little stone axe (that makes three) at the Cat, and the Cat ran out of the cave and the Dog chased him up a tree, and from that day to this, Best Beloved, three proper Men out of five will always throw things at a Cat whenever they meet him, and all proper Dogs will chase him up a tree. But the Cat keeps his side of the bargain too. He will kill Mice and he will be kind to Babies when he is in the house, as long as they do not pull his tail too hard. But when he has done that, and between times, he is the Cat that walks by himself and all places are alike to him, and if you look out at nights you can see him waving his wild tail and walking by his wild lone – just the same as before.

THE TOTEM OF AMARILLO

Emma-Lindsay Squier

PERHAPS YOU HAVE HEARD ME SPEAK of Amarillo before. He was a yellow cat who came to us from out of the woods when Brother and I still lived in the little log cabin on the shores of Puget Sound. And he was, in those days, our very special friend. His coming to our home was most spectacular, and his departure was equally dramatic. As for the grand finale of his story, as I learned it from those who cared for him in his last years, it is so curious and hints so much of melodrama that I am afraid that some will doubt it. I offer in explanation of my belief that it is true, only the fact that Amarillo was always a most unusual cat. And the proof of it is that he is perpetuated for ever in the village of Old Man House in a totem pole, carved and painted. Only the truly great are thus honoured by the tribe of Skokomish.

Amarillo, the yellow one, was born, I think, in the woods. And I further believe that complete savagery was only a short generation behind him. For his ears were tufted as are the ears of a bobcat, and his eyes were slanted and amber so that, in moments of complete repose, he resembled a Chinese mandarin pleasantly absorbed in thought.

He had grown up in a region where the law was that only the strongest survived. He had fought many battles and won them, and so had grown to a size unbelievable in an ordinary cat, another fact which hinted strongly at a parentage having nothing to do with domesticity and quiet firesides.

Still, he had within him the instinct of association with man. For when he first came to us, his lovely fur all draggled and covered with blood, he was sorely hurt and dragged a torn and wounded leg. He mewed pitifully and crawled to us, yet was afraid to let us touch him, and sprang back spitting venomously. But the instinct that had brought him down from the woods to the little cabin, where he knew he would find succour for his hurt, finally made him accept us. He let us examine the wounded leg, suffered us to bathe it and anoint it with salve. Then, being completely unable to hunt or care for himself, he allowed us to extend to him the hospitality of our home. He came to love us, and adopted us, and when he was well he stayed with us and became our friend.

Now Brother and I were so fond of Amarillo, the yellow cat, that we saw none of his faults; and when they were called to our attention by the grown-ups, we made excuses for them and pretended that they did not matter. For he was our constant companion during the day and, when I slept out of doors on the camp bed, I would, sometimes during the night, hear his soft 'Prr-t,' which signified that he was about to jump up beside me, and then feel the thud of his soft, heavy body, as he leaped. But the grown-ups did not share our unqualified approval of Amarillo and his ways. For he, never having had any knowledge of civilization, did not know, and could not be taught, that chickens were to be respected, and not stalked and devoured whenever he happened to be hungry. Neither was it permissible that he should molest the pigeons, climb up to the nests and kill their young. So, after all persuasion had failed and many attempts at discipline, it was decreed that Amarillo must go. And Brother and I were very sad because of it.

It was not hard to find a new home for him. He was admired by all who saw him and many places were open to our choosing. But it was deemed best that he be given into the kindly care of a fisherman friend of ours. A huge, dark man with kindly smiling eyes, a man whose descent was traced from Indian and Spanish blood, and whose wife and kinsfolk were of the tribe of Skokomish. They lived in the far-off village of Old Man House, called by the Indians, Suquamish.

They would, we knew, be kind to Amarillo. They had no chickens or pigeons for him to kill unlawfully, and there were rats and much small game in the woods to satisfy his hunting instincts.

So, on the day set for his departure, we took our friend, the Yellow One, down to the fishing launch which anchored at our float, and it was with heavy hearts that we set a dish of milk for him upon the deck. We hoped that eating would occupy his attention and that he would not realize until too late that he was going away from us. The Indian fisherman shoved off very gently from the wharf and did not start the engine until the launch had drifted for a hundred feet or more. But when the whirring of the fly wheel startled Amarillo, and the churning of the propeller whirled the water into eddies of white and green – then he knew that he was being taken away without his will or knowledge.

He sprang to the gunwale and stood, for an instant, gazing out at us, his slanted, amber eyes wide with alarm. The Indian fisherman spoke to him soothingly and moved towards him with friendly hand outstretched. But it was too late. For Amarillo, without an instant's hesitation, had leaped. We saw the flash of his yellow body as he sprang and the splash as he sank from sight. We cried out, because we thought he would drown. But he had no idea of coming to such an inglorious end. For the next instant he was swimming towards us, easily, powerfully, his tufted ears flattened back on his head, his body a lithe, yellow streak in the blueness of the water. When he reached the float, he climbed upon it, sat down with perfect composure, and commenced to wash himself with great earnestness and poise. He appeared to think nothing whatsoever of the swim he had taken. And that day, because of our entreaties, he was allowed to remain with us.

But it was, we knew, only a stay of sentence. On the next day we bade our friend goodbye once more. This time the Yellow One was fastened in a sack and, when the launch started its chugging way out into the blueness of the bay, we saw the frenzied contortions of the burlap bag and dimly heard protesting yowls above the throbbing of the engine. We watched sadly from the float until the fishing launch was but a speck of black athwart the jutting greenery of

the Point. Then it was lost to sight and we knew that Amarillo had gone from us for ever.

In the years that followed, we heard of our yellow friend from time to time. Once the Indian fisherman chugged around the Point and into our tiny cove specially to give us news of him. And once the old fisherman, who made his home with us, put into the village of Suquamish to learn at first hand of Amarillo's welfare. We were assured, each time, that the Yellow One was well and happy, and that he had established a kingship among the lesser cats of the village so that there was none to dispute his authority. But the details of his tempestuous life I did not fully learn until, grown out of childhood and many years away from the country of grey waters and singing pine trees, I came back to the woods and waters of Puget Sound; found at Suquamish our beloved old fisherman, with no trace of time upon the pinkness of his cheeks or within the clear twinkling of his eyes; found, too, the Indian fisherman and his wife who had given Amarillo shelter; and learned from him, and from the blind boy who was their son, the story of the Yellow One's tragic, triumphant career.

Now, the blind boy was a carver of totems. And in the great darkness, where there was no light, he found solace in bringing to remembrance the strange, almost forgotten tales of the Indians of the Sound. He made them live again, cunningly carved into symbols upon pine poles, and he painted them carefully, under the watchful eye of those who could see. There is today, in the open square of the village, a totem pole that the blind boy made. Upon it is depicted the story of how Teet' Motl, with his sweetheart, Hoo Han Hoo, rode upon a dolphin's back towards a far country where the Great Spirit promised them rest and prosperity. Their progress was barred by a school of blackfish, those tigers of the water called by the Indians 'killers'. But the brave dolphin, with a word of encouragement to those upon his back, dived into the depths of the sea, scraping up pebbles in his mouth. Then there came a great storm, and Teet' Motl and Hoo Han Hoo crept into the dolphin's mouth for safety. Inside they found the shining pebbles scraped up by the giant fish. And when at last the storm abated, the dolphin had indeed brought them safely to a pleasant country, green with trees and fruitful with berries. The Indians who inhabited the country used for currency shining pebbles. And Teet' Motl and Hoo Han Hoo, having many of them, were rich and for ever prosperous. Even to this day, said the blind boy, when the killers come from the south, then a storm will rise. So he portrayed upon the totem Teet' Motl and his sweetheart safe in the belly of the dolphin.

It was while the blind boy still carved the story upon the totem pole that Amarillo was brought into the household. And curiously enough, it was to the child who lived in darkness that the Yellow One gave his love and never-ending loyalty. He liked very well indeed the Indian fisherman and his wife, who was of the tribe of Skokomish. He obligingly caught the rats that had formerly made merry under the cabin, and once in the dead of night he gave alarm of fire that had started from a chance spark, by mewing and rubbing his cold nose against the Indian fisherman's face. He repaid the hospitality they offered him with a friendship that was staunch and true. But it was only the blind boy that he loved – and I believe, and would have you believe, that it was because he knew of the darkness in which the blind boy lived, and because he knew that in some ways his friend was helpless.

But because he loved the little blind boy so well, Amarillo was jealous of everything to which he gave his attention. During the long evenings, when the blind boy carved the totem pole, the Yellow One would sit on the table beside him, watching with slanted amber eyes, while the childish, sensitive fingers crept over the long pine pole, feeling out with a sharp knife the contours of the dolphin, the killer blackfish, and the rude figures of Teet' Motl and his sweetheart. When Amarillo thought his friend given too much attention to the work of carving, he would reach out a padded, yellow paw and pat the blind boy's hand. If there was no response, he would yawn prodigiously, get up and stretch, and rub his broad back against the blind boy's face, deliberately walking on the pole, so that he could not carve. Then, if his friend persisted in his work, Amarillo would mew sharply, a little angry sound that ended in a

snarl. He would switch his tail violently, jump down from the table with a loud thump, and sulk under the stove, refusing to come out for commands or cajoling words.

Now, Amarillo was not the only four-footed guest in the household of the Indian fisherman and his wife. The hospitality of their little cabin was offered freely to any living thing that needed shelter or aid, and there was rarely a time when they were not caring for some boarder from the wood who had come to grief. Once they found a pheasant's nest with the mother's dead body beside it, bullet-riddled, and the tiny, brown chicks scarcely out of their shells. They took the tiny things to their cabin and fed them so carefully that all of them lived, and would have grown eventually to adult pheasanthood – had it not been for Amarillo.

At first, it was not difficult to keep the wee brown pheasant chicks secluded. They learned very soon to run briskly to the door of their wire coop when they heard a footstep approaching, and they were as friendly as if their parents had never lived in the wilds. Amarillo watched them with sullen, amber eyes, his tail twitching ever so little, his shoulder muscles moving slightly whenever he saw the baby pheasants running about in the safety of the wire enclosure. But he never attempted to molest them. And even when they grew so large that the coop was deemed too small to hold them comfortably, and so were permitted to roam at liberty, he did not try to pounce upon them – having perhaps in mind the punishment meted out to him at our cabin the day when he tried to kill the chickens.

But upon the day when the little blind boy made his way out to the wire enclosure and called to the pheasants, who came running to peck at the crumbs he held in his hand – upon that day did Amarillo declare war upon the brown invaders. Never did the Indian fisherman or his wife actually catch him doing violence to the pheasant boarders, but one by one they disappeared with only a bunch of feathers left to tell of their passing. And once the Yellow One came into the cabin with one tiny feather still hanging from his whiskers – he had forgotten to remove the evidence. It was the last feather of the last pheasant. So they spanked him soundly, and he snarled and spat, and ran away into the woods, and did not come back for two days, during which time the blind boy missed him sorely. When he returned, it was with sullen, padding steps, and his amber eyes were rather furtive as if he doubted whether he would be welcomed. But the family forgave him the pheasants, and made much of him, and the blind boy cried, holding the yellow cat close against his cheek. So Amarillo purred deeply, like an organ, and dug his toes comfortably into his friend's shoulders, and that night slept upon the blind boy's bed, unrebuked. For a week he would not let the child go out of his sight, but followed him like a dog, and every evening sat near him when he carved upon the totem pole.

It was soon after the incident of the pheasants that another woods friend was brought into the kindly care of the Indian fisherman and his wife. One day the Indian fisherman saw in the woods, near the village of Suquamish, a little lady racoon who had been caught in a trap such as they set for racoons in the Puget Sound country. A hole had been bored in a small log, and honeycomb had been put deep inside it. Then nails had been set in such a way that a racoon hand, reaching inside for the honeycomb, could not pull itself out without tearing the skin completely away. So the Indian fisherman found the racoon lady with one arm inside the hole, her bright eyes blinking worriedly through the black marking that ran completely across her face like a highwayman's mask. She was really very foolish to have kept her clutch on the honeycomb, for by releasing it and squeezing her little black hand together, she could have brought it through the nail barricade without mishap. But she wanted the honeycomb and so she kept her hold of it, thus keeping herself prisoner – as, indeed, those who set the trap knew she would do.

But the Indian fisherman could not bear to see the little lady racoon thus a captive. For she was soon to have babies. He drew out the nails, very carefully, while she stood rigidly alert to all he was doing, but stubbornly refusing to let go her hold on the sweetness that was in the hole. He slipped his hat over her; then, in her sudden alarm, she withdrew her hand, all sticky with honeycomb, and the Indian fisherman brought her to the cabin, wriggling and squeaking in protest.

He saw to it that she had a comfortable pen to live in, and all the family made much of her. By the time her tiny children were born, she was quite at home in her new environment, and accepted philosophically all the kindly attentions bestowed upon her.

They named her Betty, and her children were born in a box behind the kitchen stove. Soon afterwards she was put into a comfortable cage in the woodshed. But one day she escaped from the pen and came into the house, with her three babies following her in single file, their tails curled up high over their backs as if they had been taught just the correct way of holding them thus, and on every tiny face was a black mask through which bright eyes blinked in friendly curiosity at the new world in which they found themselves.

Now, Amarillo saw this strange procession with astonishment not unmixed with alarm. He had been away hunting in the woods when Betty was brought to the cabin and the Indian fisherman had taken care that he had had no access to her cage or to her box behind the kitchen stove. Certainly he had never seen a racoon baby, with a black mask on its face and its tail curling up neatly over its head. He leaped upon a chair and spat vigorously as the little procession trundled across the kitchen floor to a saucer of milk behind the stove. Betty took no notice of him and pursued her even course, her three babies following in a line, one directly behind the other.

Amarillo leaned over the edge of the chair and growled terrifically. Betty looked up at him from behind her highwayman's mask, and her eyes glittered at him. She showed a line of white, menacing teeth. The Yellow One continued to snarl deep in his throat, but made no move, except to settle down on his haunches and watch and speculate. If Betty and her babies had been out in the open, he would have set upon them without delay. But their presence in the kitchen disturbed him, made him vaguely uncertain as to their standing. For he had been punished many times for interfering with domestic friends. He licked his chops and continued to growl.

Then, suddenly, his temper getting the better of him – he sprang. The Indian Fisherman moved to protect the racoon lady, whose life he thought in peril. But Betty was quite capable of defending herself and her family. Although she had apparently given no heed to the yellow cat, yet she was ready for his pounce. She gave a shrill squeal and darted to one side so quickly that even Amarillo's swiftness was not equalled by it. Before the yellow cat could realize what had happened, she was upon him, her black little hands clutching at his neck, her sharp teeth digging through his thick fur and into the flesh beneath. Amarillo snarled and yowled with pain. He rolled over and over, seeking vainly to fasten his claws on the alert, darting body of the lady racoon. The racoon babies scuttled under the

stove where they sat and peeped with bright, inquisitive eyes at the rolling, scrambling whirlwind of fur – yellow fur and brown. It was Amarillo who finally cried 'enough' in the unequal battle. His authority had been undisputed for such a long time that it made his surrender the more complete. He bolted for the open door, yowling in wholehearted terror, with Betty astride him like a jockey, her hands deep in his fur, her eyes viciously sardonic through the black highwayman's mask.

Amarillo finally rid himself of his unwelcome rider by rolling with despairing energy. Having freed himself, he climbed a tree, spitting at every step, and found shelter on a limb, very high above the ground, where he snarled and spat, and licked his wounds, and had many harsh and bitter thoughts towards racoons and the world in general.

Betty, on the other hand, took her victory with modest simplicity. She curled her tail high over her head and marched sedately back to the kitchen and her babies. And after taking a refreshing drink of milk from the saucer, she proceeded to give her children their lunch, while she tidied her disordered coat, pulling from it the bits of twigs and tufts of yellow fur that had clung to it in the battle.

Amarillo went away into the woods, as was his custom when insulted, and he stayed so long that the family feared that his nose had been put permanently out of joint. But he came back at last, very sulky and bad-tempered until he found that he was really welcomed, especially by the blind boy who had missed him greatly. So he purred and rolled on the floor like a kitten, and slept at night on the little boy's bed. The racoon family – who now lived under the house – he did not molest. Betty and her children came at will into the kitchen and the room adjoining, they even received food from the hand of the blind boy – and Amarillo did not seek to prevent them. Sometimes he would growl and spit softly, but when Betty glanced at him sharply from behind her menacing mask, he would blink and look away, and pretend that he had not said a word.

The racoons were very cleanly folk. There was a big pan of water for them always upon the black porch, and into it they would dip every morsel of food before they ate it. They would bathe regularly, too, sitting up around the pan like little, furry toys, dipping their black hands in the water and washing their faces and necks very daintily and properly. They knew where the Indian fisherman beached the flat-bottomed boat in which he carried fish to sell. It was his custom to leave a few small fish in it after the day's work, just for the pleasure of seeing Betty lead her children down through the woods to the gravelled shore, the four of them in single file with their tails curled over their heads, and all of them humming a curious little monotone of a song, such as racoons sing when they are journeying and are contented with life.

When the fall came the racoon babies, quite well grown by that time, went away, into the woods, and later Betty, too, slipped away, to be gone for the whole winter. They expected that she would return in the spring. But she did not, and they never knew what became of the intrepid little lady.

Her absence, as you can readily imagine, was no grief at all to Amarillo. His kingship was once more undisputed, and he was happy in the friendship of the Indian fisherman and his wife, and in the affection that the blind boy gave him. The two were more inseparable than ever. It was rarely now that the Yellow One went away to hunt in the woods. He preferred, instead, to remain with the little boy he loved, to follow when the child walked about in the yard with the halting, uncertain steps of those who cannot see, and to sleep on his bed at night.

In due course of time he found a lady cat to his liking, and he brought her to live at the cabin of the Indian fisherman. Only one kitten did the lady cat give birth to, a kitten who was almost as golden in colour as Amarillo himself. And Amarillo as a father, I am glad to say, emulated his savage ancestors rather than his immediate domestic forebears. He cared for the kitten much more tenderly than the mother cat did, for she proved after all to be a careless jade, totally unworthy of Amarillo's affections. Soon after her daughter was weaned she went away into the woods and the kitten, to whom the Indian fisherman gave the outrageous name of 'Whiskey Susan', grew up entirely under her father's supervision.

Whiskey Susan was the only one beside himself whom Amarillo would suffer the family to pet. He was not jealous of the affection they gave her, and even the blind boy could hold the snuggling, yellow kitten in his lap while he carved upon the totem pole, and Amarillo would sit on the table beside him, purring deep in his throat, his eyes closed to mere slits of contentment.

But one day, many months later, there came another, and this time a final, disturbing factor in the life of the Yellow One. The Indian fisherman had found a small mallard duck caught in the meshes of his nets, and one leg had been broken so that he floundered there, helpless, beating the water with his wings. The Indian fisherman released him gently and brought him to the cabin where his wife took kindly charge of the invalid, set the hurt leg in splints, and tended to his wants. It was upon the first evening of his stay that Amarillo, coming in from out-of-doors, spied the newcomer. The blind boy, who could not see the Yellow One's approach, was bending over the wounded duck, stroking him gently. And at the sight Amarillo hissed sharply – and sprang. His leap did no more than knock the astonished duck over on the floor, but the Fisherman's wife was impatient that her invalid should be so treated. She cuffed Amarillo sharply and he stared at her with furious, amber eyes, then laid his ears back on his head and trotted out of the house, his fur in thick, outraged ruffles, and headed straight for the woods.

He did not come back for one week, nor for the two weeks. And the blind boy grew daily more worried and more lonely. He took to wandering about the yard, calling for Amarillo, and when his mother was busy, so that he could not prevent him, he would feel his way through the gate and set off up the trail that led into the deep woods, walking very slowly with his hands outstretched before him, calling Amarillo's name, hoping that the yellow cat would hear and come to him.

Now, it was not safe to go alone or unarmed into the thickness of those forests, for many dangers lurked in the shadowed depths of them and many were the tales told of bold attacks made by cougars and bobcats driven down from the high mountains by hunger or forest fires. Yet always the blind boy came back safely, for he ventured only a little way and returned before his absence could be noticed.

But one day he slipped away, having acquired some confidence in his knowledge of the trail. He went farther and farther, calling to Amarillo with louder tones as he felt himself out of hearing distance from the cabin. The trail became rougher and was unfamiliar to his feet. But still he went on and, at last, he realized that there was a chill in the air that spoke of coming night. The woods were very still, with only the light dropping of pine needles to dot the silence, or the distant call of a heron flying to a tall pine-tree nest. A little frightened, the blind boy turned towards home. But his feet had lost their confidence. He turned into a ragged, wandering trail that led away from the true path. And as the night grew colder, and his feet stumbled over sprawling roots, and low-hanging branches struck his face, he knew that he was lost, lost and helpless.

Then he ceased to call for Amarillo, but sent up his voice in a thin, wavering cry such as the Indians use. It is a sound which carries clearly across great spaces, and the Indians know it for a signal of distress.

Down in the cabin it was nearly sunset before the absence of the blind boy had been discovered, for both the Indian fisherman and his wife were at work mending nets upon the beach. When evening came, and they returned home, they looked at each other with startled eyes, and a great fear was in their hearts. For they knew the menace of the dark woods behind them.

The Indian fisherman called the others of the tribe of Skokomish and, with that cunning that Indians possess, they found the child's light, halting footprints in the softness of the earth, and followed them into the forest, until it was too dark for them to see further.

They listened, and presently, from far away, a thin, wavering cry came to their ears. They responded mightily and plunged along the trail, the glimmering of their lanterns throwing dark, grotesque shadows on the path before them.

But suddenly they heard another cry, and they stood breathless for a moment, tingling cold with horror. For it was the savage,

hunting cry of the bobcat – the cry he gives as he springs upon his prey.

Firing their guns and shouting fiercely, they set off at a run towards the direction from which the two cries – the call for help and the call of death – had come. It was easy to guide themselves so, for the woods were alive with the savage sounds of fighting – eerie screams that set the birds to twittering nervously and made the men grit their teeth with fear at what they should find.

When they turned down the ragged, wandering trail, they heard above the snarls and shrieks a child's voice sobbing in fear. And the gleam of the lanterns caught a wild tangle of blazing eyes, white, snapping teeth, and rolling, twisting, furry bodies upon the ground. The blind boy crouched in the ferns at the side of the trail and crawled towards them, his arms lifted to his unseen rescuers. His father caught him up with a fierce sobbing of breath. And there came a fusillade of shots barking viciously into the whirl of writhing bodies. There was a sharp, sudden silence. The bodies dropped down loosely, twitched for a moment, then lay still.

Then the child screamed sharply. 'Don't shoot,' he cried, 'don't shoot – you'll hurt Amarillo!'

The men stared. And for once the Indian fisherman was glad that his child could not see. For there before them, in the trail, lay the tawny, dead body of a bobcat its cruel claws clenched about the yellow body of a cat – the gallant body of Amarillo. The body of the Yellow One was torn almost to shreds, and he lay in a pool of blood. But the wildcat had suffered too, for Amarillo's teeth were buried in his throat and even death had not sufficed to loosen the hold.

They carried the poor, torn body very tenderly back to the cabin, and the blind boy sobbed on his father's shoulder. He told them later how, in that cold darkness, he had heard a light swishing of leaves, and then a well-known 'Prr-t,' which told him that Amarillo had heard him at last and was coming to him. But even as he had knelt, his arms outstretched to welcome the Yellow One to his heart, there had come a stirring in the branches over his head – and the wild, savage shriek of a bobcat. Then had come the leap that had knocked him upon his face. But before the bloodthirsty creature could spring again, Amarillo was upon him, fighting savagely, and the bobcat, surprised at the sudden attack, had fought back, for the moment forgetting the human prey whom he had stalked.

So it was that many years later, when I came to the village of Old Man House, known by the Indians as Suquamish, I found the old fisherman, and the Indian fisherman, and his wife who was of the tribe of Skokomish. I met the blind boy, grown now almost to manhood, and I saw in the open square of the village the totem telling the story of how Teet' Motl and Hoo Han Hoo found the promised land.

There, in the cabin yard, is a little grave. It bears no headstone, such as a white man would erect to a well-remembered friend. It has a nobler, more fitting monument of gratitude and love – a carved and painted totem pole. At the bottom of the totem is the fierce, snarling face of a wildcat with white, cruel fangs displayed. Over the snarling face sits the stolid figure of a mallard duck, with one leg stiffly wrapped in splints. Above this are two closed eyes – eyes that cannot see the light. And at the very top, in the place of honour, is the carved portrait of Amarillo himself – his yellow face benign and almost smiling – his tufted ears erect and alert . . .

If he could know this, I am sure he would be proud. For only the truly great are thus honoured by the tribe of Skokomish.

MRS BOND'S CATS

James Herriot

'I WORK for cats.' That was how Mrs Bond introduced herself on my first visit, gripping my hand firmly and thrusting out her jaw defiantly as though challenging me to make something of it. She was a big woman with a strong, high-cheekboned face and a commanding presence and I wouldn't have argued with her anyway, so I nodded gravely as though I fully understood and agreed, and allowed her to lead me into the house.

I saw at once what she meant. The big kitchen-living room had been completely given over to cats. There were cats on the sofas and chairs and spilling in cascades on to the floor, cats sitting in rows along the window sills and, right in the middle of it all, little Mr Bond, pallid, wispy-moustached, in his shirt sleeves reading a newspaper.

It was a scene which was going to become very familiar. A lot of the cats were obviously uncastrated Toms because the atmosphere was vibrant with their distinctive smell – a fierce pungency which overwhelmed even the sickly wisps from the big saucepans of nameless cat food bubbling on the stove. And Mr Bond was always there, always in his shirt sleeves and reading his paper, a lonely little island in a sea of cats.

I had heard of the Bonds, of course. They were Londoners who for some obscure reason had picked on North Yorkshire for their retirement. People said they had a 'bit o' brass' and they had bought an old house on the outskirts of Darrowby where they kept themselves to themselves – and the cats. I had heard that Mrs Bond was in the habit of taking in strays and feeding them and giving them a home if they wanted it and this had predisposed me in her favour, because in my experience the unfortunate feline species seemed to be fair game for every kind of cruelty and neglect. They shot cats, threw things at them, starved them and set their dogs on them for fun. It was good to see somebody taking their side.

My patient on this first visit was no more than a big kitten, terrified little blob of black and white crouching in a corner.

'He's one of the outside cats,' Mrs Bond boomed.

'Outside cats?'

'Yes. All these you see here are the inside cats. The others are the really wild ones who simply refuse to enter the house. I feed them of course but the only time they come indoors is when they are ill.'

'I see.'

'I've had frightful trouble catching this one. I'm worried about his eyes – there seemed to be a skin growing over them, and I do hope you can do something for him. His name, by the way, is Alfred.'

'Alfred? Ah yes, quite.' I advanced cautiously on the little half-grown animal and was greeted by a waving set of claws and a series of open-mouthed spittings. He was trapped in his corner or he would have been off with the speed of light.

Examining him was going to be a problem. I turned to Mrs Bond. 'Could you let me have a sheet of some kind? An old ironing sheet would do. I'm going to have to wrap him up.'

'Wrap him up?' Mrs Bond looked very doubtful but she disappeared into another room and returned with a tattered sheet of cotton which looked just right.

I cleared the table of an amazing variety of cat feeding dishes, cat books, cat medicines and spread out the sheet, then I approached my patient again. You can't be in a hurry in a situation like this and it took me perhaps five minutes of wheedling and 'Puss-pussing' while I brought my hand nearer and nearer. When I got as far as being able to stroke his cheek I made a quick grab at the scruff of his neck and finally bore Alfred, protesting bitterly and lashing out in all directions, over to the table. There, still

holding tightly to his scruff, I laid him on the sheet and started the wrapping operation.

This is something which has to be done quite often with obstreperous felines and, although I say it, I am rather good at it. The idea is to make a neat, tight roll, leaving the relevant piece of cat exposed; it may be an injured paw, perhaps the tail, and in this case of course the head. I think it was the beginning of Mrs Bond's unquestioning faith in me when she saw me quickly enveloping that cat till all you could see of him was a small black and white head protruding from an immovable cocoon of cloth. He and I were now facing each other, more or less eyeball to eyeball, and Alfred couldn't do a thing about it.

As I say, I rather pride myself on this little expertise and even today my veterinary colleagues have been known to remark: 'Old Herriot may be limited in many respects but by God he can wrap a cat.'

As it turned out, there wasn't a skin growing over Alfred's eyes. There never is.

'He's got a paralysis of the third eyelid, Mrs Bond. Animals have this membrane which flicks across the eye to protect it. In this case it hasn't gone back, probably because the cat is in low condition – maybe had a touch of cat flu or something else which has weakened him. I'll give him an injection of vitamins and leave you some powder to put in his food if you could keep him in for a few days. I think he'll be all right in a week or two.'

The injection presented no problems with Alfred furious but helpless inside his sheet and I had come to the end of my first visit to Mrs Bond's.

It was the first of many. The lady and I established an immediate rapport which was strengthened by the fact that I was always prepared to spend time over her assorted charges; crawling on my stomach under piles of logs in the outhouses to reach the outside cats, coaxing them down from trees, stalking them endlessly through the shrubbery. But from my point of view it was rewarding in many ways.

For instance there was the diversity of names she had for her cats. True to her London upbringing she had named many of the

Toms after the great Arsenal team of those days. There was Eddie Hapgood, Cliff Bastin, Ted Drake, Wilf Copping, but she did slip up in one case because Alex James had kittens three times a year with unfailing regularity.

Then there was her way of calling them home. The first time I saw her at this was on a still summer evening. The two cats she wanted me to see were out in the garden somewhere and I walked with her to the back door where she halted, clasped her hands across her bosom, closed her eyes and gave tongue in a mellifluous contralto.

'Bates, Bates, Bates, Ba-hates.' She actually sang out the words in a reverent monotone except for a delightful little lilt on the 'Be-hates'. Then once more she inflated her ample rib cage like an operatic prima donna and out it came again, delivered with the utmost feeling.

'Bates, Bates, Bates, Ba-hates.'

Anyway it worked, because Bates the cat came trotting from behind a clump of laurel. There remained the other patient and I watched Mrs Bond with interest.

She took up the same stance, breathed in, closed her eyes, composed her features into a sweet half-smile and started again.

'Seven-times-three, Seven-times-three, Seven-times-threehee.' It was set to the same melody as Bates with the same dulcet rise and fall at the end. She didn't get the quick response this time, though, and had to go through the performance again and again, and as the notes lingered on the still evening air the effect was startlingly like a muezzin calling the faithful to prayer.

At length she was successful and a fat tortoiseshell slunk apologetically along the wall-side into the house.

'By the way, Mrs Bond,' I asked, making my voice casual. 'I didn't quite catch the name of that last cat.'

'Oh, Seven-times-three?' She smiled reminiscently. 'Yes, she is a dear. She's had three kittens seven times running, you see, so I thought it rather a good name for her, don't you?'

'Yes, yes, I do indeed. Splendid name, splendid.'

Another thing which warmed me towards Mrs Bond was her concern for my safety. I appreciated this because it is a rare trait among animal owners. I can think of the trainer after one of his

Mrs Bond's Cats

racehorses had kicked me clean out of a loose box examining the animal anxiously to see if it had damaged its foot; the little old lady dwarfed by the bristling, teeth-bared Alsatian saying: 'You'll be gentle with him won't you and I hope you won't hurt him – he's very nervous'; the farmer, after an exhausting calving which I feel certain has knocked about two years off my life expectancy, grunting morosely: 'I doubt you've tired that cow out, young man.'

Mrs Bond was different. She used to meet me at the door with an enormous pair of gauntlets to protect my hands against scratches and it was an inexpressible relief to find that somebody cared. It became part of the pattern of my life; walking up the garden path among the innumerable slinking, wild-eyed little creatures which were the outside cats, the ceremonial acceptance of the gloves at the door, then the entry into the charged atmosphere of the kitchen with little Mr Bond and his newspaper just visible among the milling furry bodies of the inside cats. I was never able to ascertain Mr Bond's attitude to cats – come to think of it he hardly ever said anything – but I had the impression he could take them or leave them.

The gauntlets were a big help and at times they were a veritable godsend. As in the case of Boris. Boris was an enormous blue-black member of the outside cats and my bête noire in more senses than one. I always cherished a private conviction that he had escaped from a zoo; I had never seen a domestic cat with such sleek, writhing muscles, such dedicated ferocity. I'm sure there was a bit of puma in Boris somewhere.

It had been a sad day for the cat colony when he turned up. I have always found it difficult to dislike any animal; most of the ones which try to do us a mischief are activated by fear, but Boris was different; he was a malevolent bully and after his arrival the frequency of my visits increased because of his habit of regularly beating up his colleagues. I was forever stitching up tattered ears, dressing gnawed limbs.

We had one trial of strength fairly early. Mrs Bond wanted me to give him a worm dose and I had the little tablet all ready held in forceps. How I ever got hold of him I don't quite know, but I hustled him on to the table and did my wrapping act at lightning speed, swathing him in roll upon roll of stout material. Just for a few

seconds I thought I had him as he stared up at me, his great brilliant eyes full of hate. But as I pushed my loaded forceps into his mouth he clamped his teeth viciously down on them and I could feel claws of amazing power tearing inside the sheet. It was all over in moments. A long leg shot out and ripped its way down my wrist, I let go my tight hold of the neck and in a flash Boris sank his teeth through the gauntlet into the ball of my thumb and was away. I was left standing there stupidly, holding the fragmented worm tablet in a bleeding hand and looking at the bunch of ribbons which had once been my wrapping sheet. From then on Boris loathed the very sight of me and the feeling was mutual.

But this was one of the few clouds in a serene sky. I continued to enjoy my visits there and life proceeded on a tranquil course except, perhaps, for some legpulling from my colleagues. They could never understand my willingness to spend so much time over a lot of cats. And of course this fitted in with the general attitude because Siegfried didn't believe in people keeping pets of any kind. He just couldn't understand their mentality and propounded his views to anybody who cared to listen. He himself, of course, kept five dogs and two cats. The dogs, all of them, travelled everywhere with him in the car and he fed dogs and cats every day with his own hands – wouldn't allow anybody else to do the job. In the evening all seven animals would pile themselves round his feet as he sat in his chair by the fire. To this day he is still as vehemently anti-pet as ever, though another generation of waving dogs' tails almost obscures him as he drives around and he also has several cats, a few tanks of tropical fish and a couple of snakes.

Tristan saw me in action at Mrs Bond's on only one occasion. I was collecting some long forceps from the instrument cupboard when he came into the room.

'Anything interesting, Jim?' he asked.

'No, not really. I'm just off to see one of the Bond cats. It's got a bone stuck between its teeth.'

The young man eyed me ruminatively for a moment. 'Think I'll come with you. I haven't seen much small animal stuff lately.'

As we went down the garden at the cat establishment I felt a twinge of embarrassment. One of the things which had built up my happy relationship with Mrs Bond was my tender concern for her charges. Even with the wildest and the fiercest I exhibited only gentleness, patience and solicitude; it wasn't really an act, it came quite naturally to me. However, I couldn't help wondering what Tristan would think of my cat bedside manner.

Mrs Bond in the doorway had summed up the situation in a flash and had two pairs of gauntlets waiting. Tristan looked a little surprised as he received his pair but thanked the lady with typical charm. He looked still more surprised when he entered the kitchen, sniffed the rich atmosphere and surveyed the masses of furry creatures occupying almost every available inch of space.

'Mr Herriot, I'm afraid it's Boris who has the bone in his teeth,' Mrs Bond said.

'Boris!' My stomach lurched. 'How on earth are we going to catch him?'

'Oh I've been rather clever,' she replied. 'I've managed to entice him with some of his favourite food into a cat basket.'

Tristan put his hand on a big wicker cage on the table. 'In here, is he?' he asked casually. He slipped back the catch and opened the lid. For something like a third of a second the coiled creature within and Tristan regarded each other tensely, then a sleek black body exploded silently from the basket past the young man's left ear on to the top of a tall cupboard.

'Christ!' said Tristan. 'What the hell was that?'

'That,' I said, 'was Boris, and now we've got to get hold of him again.' I climbed on to a chair, reached slowly on to the cupboard top and started 'Puss-puss-puss'ing in my most beguiling tone.

After about a minute Tristan appeared to think he had a better idea; he made a sudden leap and grabbed Boris's tail. But only briefly, because the big cat freed himself in an instant and set off on a whirlwind circuit of the room; along the tops of cupboards and dressers, across the curtains, careering round and round like a wall-of-death rider.

Tristan stationed himself at a strategic point and as Boris shot past he swiped at him with one of the gauntlets.

'Missed the bloody thing!' he shouted in chagrin. 'But here he comes again . . . take that, you black sod! Damn it, I can't nail him!'

The docile little inside cats, startled by the scattering of plates and tins and pans and by Tristan's cries and arm wavings, began to run around in their turn, knocking over whatever Boris had missed. The noise and confusion even got through to Mr Bond because just for a moment he raised his head and looked around him in mild surprise at the hurtling bodies before returning to his newspaper.

Tristan, flushed with the excitement of the chase, had really begun to enjoy himself. I cringed inwardly as he shouted over to me happily.

'Send him on, Jim, I'll get the bugger next time round!'

We never did catch Boris. We just had to leave the piece of bone to work its own way out, so it wasn't a successful veterinary visit. But Tristan as we got back into the car smiled contentedly.

'That was great, Jim. I didn't realize you had such fun with your pussies.'

Mrs Bond on the other hand, when I next saw her, was rather tight-lipped over the whole thing.

'Mr Herriot,' she said, 'I hope you aren't going to bring that young man with you again.'

THE CAT IN THE FIG TREE

Charles McPhee

THE GREAT LEADER was weary. He ceased to listen. It was so seldom anyone said anything to him any more that he wished to hear. He yawned widely, revealing strong yellow teeth. It was going to be a long day. There was the parade and then the presentation of medals, and then, of course, the speech from the balcony, without which no Nation Day was complete. The Great Leader pushed aside his chair and walked over to the French windows. He had seen a flash of orange in the green of the fig tree and wanted to know what it was. The chief of police was always telling him to keep away from the windows but what was the point of being all-powerful if you could not look through your own windows?

The minister of the interior, who had been addressing him on the water shortage as though he were a public meeting, faltered, lost the thread of what he was saying and came to a halt. He stared vacantly at The Great Leader's back, seeing how the sweat had soaked through his shirt and had stained it. The minister was nervous. It was so unlike the chief to be inattentive and he wondered if he had heard a rumour. He had known him so well and for so long but still he could not always guess what he was thinking. Only a few minutes before, he had been expressing his undying loyalty to The Great Leader whom he had helped to power all those years before, but now he wondered if he had been too fervent, too sincere. He regretted the need to betray him.

The Great Leader did know his old friend was conspiring to kill him. It did not worry him unduly, though it saddened him that

even those closest to him were disloyal. There was always someone conspiring against him. The last attempt to assassinate him had been less than a year before and, without knowing he did so, The Great Leader stroked the scar on his hand where he had warded off the knife. It was a fact of life and, in the end, of death that they would try again to kill him.

The chief of police was waiting for the right moment to arrest the conspirators but, in the meantime, The Great Leader thought he would probably be bored to death. There were so many speeches, so many words and really, there was nothing to be done. The water was not his to command, though no doubt he should not have given his mistress a house with a swimming-pool on the hill above the shanty town. They would murder her, the people for whom he had ceased to struggle, and he would be sorry.

The figs on the tree looked purple-ripe and succulent, like so much bruised flesh. He stepped through the windows on to the gravel pathway. He almost stumbled over the slight step and this annoyed him. He was getting old and his bones ached. He walked over to the tree, his feet crunching loudly on the loose stone. He picked one of the figs and bit into it. The red juice refreshed him. He let it dribble down his mouth and chin.

On closer inspection, the orange in the fig tree proved to be a cat. It was a one-eyed brute, probably of great age and scarred by innumerable fights. As he stretched out his hand to it, the cat scrambled down the trunk fluttering the leaves and knocking unripe figs on to the ground. The Great Leader liked cats. They were mostly silent and demanded so little of the humans with whom they chose to lodge. He had an immediate sympathy for this predatory old rogue. He too was predatory but he wondered for just how long he could be bothered to fight off the young cats who seemed to want so badly to have him dead. In his haste, the cat had dropped a pathetic little bundle of feathers. It had been munching on a fledgling. The Great Leader was not censorious. Was there any difference between the violence of the animal kingdom and the savagery of his own kind? He did not think so. Or rather, at least the cat's mauling of the small bird was dictated by a natural desire to assuage his hunger. His own savagery, he recalled, had been premeditated and in the pursuit of power for its own sake.

Across the city a man, naked to the waist, was oiling a rifle with loving care. As he moved his hand over the black metal, so pure and so cool against his palm, he smelt his own sweat, sour and stale. There had been no water in the apartment for three days and the bottled water, warm and brackish, he reserved for drinking. He could not leave his room during the hours of daylight and, at night, he only dared creep out for a quick breath of fresh air, all the time listening for the armoured police-cars which leaped out of the night without warning, sirens screaming. If it was so hot now in the early morning, surely the heat at midday would be intolerable. He thought he might risk letting in a little air. He cautiously unbolted the heavy wooden shutters. As he did so, a breeze touched his face and cooled his brow. He stepped out on to the balcony, forgetting for a moment the need for secrecy. His room overlooked Freedom Square and was exactly opposite the mausoleum, upon the roof of which The Great Leader would make his speech.

A sudden pain brought his hand to his cheek. Blood trickled warmly between his fingers. For a second he believed he had been shot. Then he saw the cat looking at him with one malevolent eye from across the balcony. Where the other eye had been, there was only an ugly, empty socket. He swore and aimed a kick at it but, tail waving angrily, it evaded his boot and jumped on to the narrow ledge between the man's balcony and that of the apartment next door. He had no idea where the animal had sprung from or why it had attacked him. The city was crawling with wild cats and he knew he should have the scratch dressed in case it became infected. It must wait, of course, until the job was done and he could get out of the city.

The Great Leader dismissed the minister and went back to his apartment to dress. Magnificent though the palace was, the Great Leader's bedroom was cell-like. Apart from the narrow iron bedstead, the only furniture was a wooden rocking chair and a bedside table bearing a ewer of water and a cracked mirror. There was, however, a dressing-room next door where his servant slept. It con-

tained a huge wardrobe with all his uniforms, rank after rank of them. He was not given to introspection but he sometimes wondered why he had collected all these meaningless uniforms, each of which was hung with equally meaningless decorations.

As a child, he had read how the English admiral, Nelson, had insisted on wearing his uniform on the quarterdeck of his ship *Victory* at the battle of Trafalgar. He wore it out of vanity but also to make his presence known to as many of his sailors as possible in the heat of battle. He had read how a French sharpshooter, perched on the mizzen top of the *Redoutable*, had picked him out of the smoke of battle by reason of this peacock display and shot him down. The Great Leader, even when he had first read the story, had been puzzled as to what moral to draw but, from that time, he had eagerly sought out occasions on which he too could wear gleaming medals, gold epaulettes and shiny, black-leather boots. Despite what had happened to Nelson, wearing one of his uniforms made him feel invulnerable.

His servant brought him a dish of eggs and ham, and soft cheese wrapped in vine leaves. He drank moderately of a light dry wine his country exported to many other countries, one of its few economic achievements. The servant asked him if he wanted a girl but he said he didn't. He would rest for an hour before the duties of the afternoon. The servant was to wake him when it was time to prepare himself. Without taking off his boots, he lay on his bed and, as it creaked under him, the orange cat he had seen in the fig tree dived out from underneath it and came to a shuddering halt by the door. The Great Leader, at first startled and then amused, tried to tempt it with what remained of his meal but the cat arched its back and spat contemptuously. The Great Leader, in his mind, named it Nelson.

After another minute had passed, the cat jumped on to the table, knocking over the wineglass with his tail. Turning round, the cat seemed to understand what he had done and began to lick the wine as it seeped into the linen cloth. The Great Leader filled an ashtray with wine from the bottle and the cat, with evident enjoyment, began to lap at it as though it were milk. 'At least you are not bothered by the water shortage, Nelson,' thought The Great Leader, wryly.

When the wine was finished, the cat stretched and yawned and curled himself up on the little bed and was soon fast asleep. The Great Leader sat in the rocking chair watching the cat and smoking a cigar. Eventually, trying not to disturb the cat, he took off his boots and got under the bed cover. The warmth of the cat on his feet was curiously comforting and The Great Leader, who had the gift shared by many military men of falling asleep whenever he chose, was soon breathing deeply and evenly.

Across the city, the man with the damaged face could not sleep. His face throbbed and he thought he might have a temperature. He peered in the mirror on the wall. The razor-sharp claws had only just missed his eye and had striated his cheek as a butcher might

slash porkskin. In the square below, the tarmac boiled and only the noise of the occasional motor car broke the midday silence.

At two, The Great Leader was woken. He noticed with regret that the one-eyed cat had not waited to see him in full fig. He washed and dressed. He wore one of his favourite uniforms, that of Admiral of the Fleet. It particularly appealed to him in this landlocked country to wear the uniform of a non-existent navy. A small group of ministers was waiting for him and he noticed that the minister of defence was sweating heavily and the minister of the interior was rubbing at a pimple on his face with nervous irritation. He smiled and this seemed to make the two men even more uneasy. The Great Leader supposed the chief of police knew what he was doing but, in any case, he was not sure he really cared. There was at least some little excitement in being so much at the mercy of fate.

He got into his black bulletproof limousine and was driven to the stand in the square where he was to take the salute. The crowds seemed thinner and more sullen than usual. Freedom Square was still a furnace. Some soldiers fainted. Nevertheless, other soldiers marched and the tanks, imported from a more developed dictatorship, did not break down. Three obsolete fighter-jets raced above his head. There was only enough fuel for one such demonstration and it was quickly over. The Youth Guard marched past singing. Their optimism struck him as misplaced.

He pinned medals on the breasts of those who had shot dead striking miners in the north of the country, and an 'eagle', the country's highest honour, on the soldier who had helped disarm the knife-wielding lunatic. Each time he attached the shiny medallion which bore a representation of his face in profile to the coarse cloth, he kissed the soldier, first the right cheek, then the left. The smell of garlic and cheap cigarettes which emanated from these loyal veterans choked him.

Then, with his minsters, he walked into the mausoleum which housed the body of the Hero of the Revolution. He climbed slowly up the grand staircase and on to the flat roof. There, behind a balustrade, he stood to attention, his ministers in a line on either side of him. The Great Leader had had to shoot the Hero in the back the day after the Revolution. Though many suspected what he had done, only the chief of police knew for certain. Together, they had dragged the Hero's body into the palace and concocted the story which the children read in the country's history books.

The man in the room across the square sweated. He put the rifle to his cheek and winced from the pain. The scratch made by the cat's claws was beginning to suppurate. He adjusted the telescopic sights. First he saw several men in suits then the all too familiar face: the noble Roman nose, the grey eyes beneath bushy eyebrows, and the small toothbrush moustache. He lowered the rifle half an inch. The medals on The Great Leader's breast filled his vision. There was a noise in the apartment below his and then shouts. He could hear feet on the stone stairs and hoarse voices as he squeezed the trigger.

The Great Leader, standing erect and motionless, wondered if he was going to die. The hairs on the back of his neck stood up and tickled him, always a sign his life was in danger. He glanced sideways at the minister of the interior who was standing beside him. A flash of orange at his feet made him look down. It was the cat. On impulse he leant down to pick it up. He felt the wind as the bullet all but scraped his scalp. He did not see it strike the minister of the interior who had moved to one side, also surprised by the cat's unexpected appearance. He did, however, see him collapse and the phrase that came unbidden into his mind was 'as though all the stuffing had been knocked out of him.'

Letting go of the cat, he knelt beside the dying man and lifted his head off the cold stone. He saw that he was trying to say something and he wondered what words were worth this supreme effort. He lowered his face to his old friend's and saw that he was smiling.

'Curse the cat . . .' whispered the minister. 'Cheek of it . . . mine once . . . followed me everywhere . . . betrayed me . . .'

Then, blood frothed on his lips and trickled down his chin and The Great Leader was reminded of the fig he had eaten in the morning.

CATS OF MY CHILDHOOD

May Eustace

THE NOSTALGIC LONGING for childhood days superimposes itself on everything I write.

> Why do I write,
> What sin to me unknown,
> Dipt me in ink,
> My parents' or my own?
>
> *Alexander Pope*

Looking back on my yesterdays is to me an exercise in solace and inspiration. No other human experience fills me with such delight. When I reminisce I forget all the cares of the world. I forget that I am getting old. I forget that I am now nearly altogether alone. I forget that I have tax forms to fill in and pension books to sign. I forget all the irritations of the present and enjoy again the old familiar haunts, with the old folks and the animals who first taught me how to live.

> I remember, I remember,
> The house where I was born,
> The little windows where the sun,
> Came peeping in at dawn.

Yes, those were the days. Clearly, as through a looking-glass, I see the old home, the gardens, the paddocks and rivulets. And I see the pathway, too, which leads to the river and the woods carpeted with bluebells, primroses and cowslips. And then – as if I ever could forget – I see my mother and father again.

Mother's long black skirt is trailing in the dust and my father's moustache seems longer and bushier than before. They are speaking in whispers, as if they still have some unfinished business in hand. It was the business of love and sex. Our family was not yet complete.

And, fortunately for us children, our parents were so taken up with each other that they left us very much to our own devices. Within reason we could do what we liked. The same good fortune followed the cats. They were everywhere, males and females together, just living their own lives in their own sweet ways. I know that mother never had a kitten destroyed and there were many of them coming and going in all directions. If I had today's official standards of points I am sure I would have found, amongst them, Rexes and Havanas, Silver Tabbies and British Blues and Bicoloureds galore.

I was only a small child when the seeds of cat enchantment were sown within me. Not in a namby-pamby way but in a studious and interested fashion, more becoming to an older child. And I repeat again that cats were everywhere. On a sunny day they came out in number, each selecting its very own sheltered and sunny spot. Ostensibly, none of these outdoor cats could claim from us a roof for their heads. We had our own recognized cat dynasty, which included the cat belonging to Rosey, our old housekeeper, and one or two others who scrounged their own kind of living. But we had plenty of surplus rations which we handed out freely to the strays.

But how many of these multi-coloured or self-coloured cats were really strays? There was one little tabby who always had her afternoon nap on my window sill. She basked in the sunshine like an oriental goddess. She felt and smelled good. Her ears stood up sharply and she had wisdom written all over her little striped face. She had a cute black nose which seemed to direct her always to the sun. I would not say that she was an over-friendly cat. She did not permit too many familiarities – one or two little rubs, a tickle under her chin, a gentle touch to her little thick tail. No more. She let me know she did not like my overtures and stood up and went away. I thought that an apt name for her would be Winny Silly.

Our next sunbather was the doorstep cat. He was pure black and every inch a male. I was sure of this because I often heard Rosey using bad language towards him; nevertheless, he sat it out though his noxious presence angered the humans. He was quite an agreeable old fellow and permitted me to rub him down and tickle his chin. We called him Steptoe, not after the TV character we know today, but because of his location preference and also after our uncle. He was a very rich farmer and came to Kilkenny once a year. He did not trust anyone to do his buying and selling and when he came down the road on a fair day he had the biggest herd of cattle of all the farmers. He specialized in the Herefordshires and congratulated himself on being a quality breeder. He had only one weakness: he always celebrated a good sale with a good drink. He liked his whiskey neat and always ordered it in doubles. Mother did not seem to mind for she said it was his own money he spent and he could do what he liked with it – his pockets always bulged with £5 and £10 notes. When my father helped him into his cart he just dropped down in the straw like an asphyxiated pig and the pony went along home without any direction, keeping to his own side of the road and negotiating his entrance to the drive carefully.

But Steptoe held onto the step no matter who was coming and going, so long as it was sunny and warm. You were at liberty to step over him but not to displace him.

The barn cat was a black and white one and the most determined sunbather of the lot. He was not so distinguished-looking as Steptoe. His coat was rather coarse, there were odd smudges of white on his tummy and the tip of his tail was white for a good half-inch. He was domesticated, too, and never objected to having his whiskers pulled. Like the others, whose names were associated with their own selected habitat, we found that Barny was a heaven-ordained name for him. He always hung round the barn and it would appear that he had a special friendship for the little black Kerry cow who was housebound until her calf was born. She was known to wander and had her calves in the most unlikely places. Once she actually gave birth while standing in a stream. Only by the merest fluke was she found in time. In the meantime, if the sun shone, Barny came out to enjoy it and, if the weather was bad, he went into the straw with the cow. Sometimes we did not see him around for a couple of weeks. He did not smell so much of cat as of cow dung.

With regard to smells and scents country folk are more discriminating than those born in towns. The scents of lilacs and roses could never obliterate the smells associated with animals. But Rosey had a town nose, really, and particularly disliked tom cat odour. If she got the slightest whiff she was away for the dog or for her switch.

Then there was the most beautiful of all the cats – the white Persian. I say 'beautiful', but I ought to have said 'could have been beautiful', for her coat was always very dirty. Her lovely fan-like tail was trailed in the dirt too. I am absolutely certain that she had blue eyes which she used to advantage – if ever a cat winked an acknowledgment it was Persi. Her favourite haunt was the stable where we kept the big brown stallion. He was an enormous fellow and generated a special kind of heat which appealed to cats. Persi did not have to cuddle up to him; you could always see the perspiration coming

from his body. Though he was a noble beast, full of puissance and fertility, the occasion for him to prove himself never arose.

Besides those named there were also more cats hiding in the hay lofts and it only needed the sun to bring them out. It was interesting to see how the various cats reacted to weather changes. I do not know what Kilkenny weather is like now but I remember that, half a century ago, it was always raining. My mother pointed out that the ever-green grass and the lush vegetation everywhere was the result of the pleasant moist climate. She loved the rain. Once she went on a holiday to her brother in Wembley and she said the weather was too clammy and dry; she longed for the drip, drip, drip, that seemed to be going on forever round our old home. I can remember standing so often in the porch waiting for the sun to shine and my pal and I chanted the popular dirge, 'Rain, rain, go to Spain, and never come back again'. During these wet periods the cats disappeared altogether. All, of course, except our own cats who had managed to sequester themselves in some quiet corners. But no stray cats were allowed the comfort of Rosey's kitchen. She did not keep her hearth so beautifully polished and the surrounding brasses so exquisitely radiant and shining to dazzle the eyes of the strays. This inviting spot was hers and for her little cat alone. Even the house dogs on the payroll were not encouraged to loiter in the comforting glow from the turf fire and the logs.

It was really Nan that set our project in action. Nan was one of the songsters who was with me singing in the rain. She was also one of my best school friends and had a big heart for all cats.

'Where is Winny Silly today?' she asked, seeing the vacant corner.

'Funny you should ask as I was just wondering the same myself. Every time it rains she goes away. Suppose we try to find out where her second home is?' I replied.

'Yes,' said Nan, 'we will run after her next time she comes and decides to leave.'

'And there are others, too, who sit around in the sun for days at a time and as soon as the weather breaks – away they go. It would be fun to find out where they all live.' And there and then we embarked on a project which would establish for all time the true homes of all our visiting felines.

It was quite a few days before we could get our plan started. The weather had been most inviting and we saw all the cats in their sunbathing haunts. I told Nan that mother had prophesied that the low clouds now in the sky meant that rain was on the way. And she was right. Nan had barely arrived when the first drops fell. The first to really get the message was Winny Silly. She was away in a flash with the two of us after her. She jumped over the garden gate like a born athlete, wound her way along the hedge, through the woodside, in and out amongst the trees. We were both out of breath trying to keep up with her. To make matters worse Nan fell down a marshy slope and commenced to cry, 'I think I will go home. We'll never catch her, and I am so tired.'

But I dismissed her complaints and she soon stopped them and came running on with the same zest as she had at the start. We had Winny in sight when she took a sharp turn into the lane leading to the priest's house. We watched her let herself in through the window with such aplomb that we knew she was home. We waited round for a bit and she did not come out. So that was that. Our first query was solved: Winny Silly was the priest's cat. Sunbathing on my windowsill meant nothing to her. She was there because she liked the shelter it afforded her. She had no love for stray humans. When life suddenly became hard, and the cruel winds of winter buffeted her about, she knew where she could find comfort – on the welcoming knees of the priest's housekeeper. Here food was plentiful and warmth abundant.

Finding Steptoe's domicile took a more exhaustive search. In the first place a few drops of rain were not enough to displace him. We watched him while he crouched miserably against the wall, while the rain lashed all about him.

'Come on Nan,' I whispered, 'I think he has had enough.' Yes. That was so. He was moving. First, he looked appealingly into Rosey's kitchen. The fire was sending out rays of warmth and light which made Steptoe's skin tickle in anticipation. But before he had as much as put a foot forward Rosey was after him like a ton of bricks.

'No stray cats here, please!' said Rosey in a language that Steptoe understood. He walked sulkily away. We wore heavy rain wear and Wellington boots and continued in Steptoe's wake. Once again he took the same route as Winny, but this time he passed the priest's house and went in the direction of the river. It was like a funeral march for, rain or no rain, Steptoe was in no hurry. He stopped several times for a smell of this and that. Then, quite unexpectedly, he stood in front of his own halldoor but this time it was not the usual kind of door – it was a door that one had to jump over and this abode was a houseboat of sorts. There didn't seem to be any welcoming hands coming out to fondle him; nevertheless, he climbed into the cabin, displaying a proprietorial air, and sat himself down. It was evident that this was his real home. No matter how desolate and dreary everything looked in the rain, we were satisfied that this was where Steptoe lived. Later, mother told us that an old fellow known as Joxer had laid claim to the boat after the death of the real owner. He was known to be respectable and did odd jobs for the farmers. He did quite a good bit of fishing, too, and if anyone wanted a nice fresh trout Joxer was their man.

We were very pleased to have found Steptoe's home. Now we had traced back two of our sunbathers. After that I often purloined some of Rosey's cat food for poor Steptoe because I felt he had a lean time on the boat. Miss Winny Silly needed no extra rations for she lived the life of a lady when she was not on our windowsill. She was well fed and well nourished from the generous table of the fat parish priest.

Now for Barny. His conduct was not always predictable. Sometimes for days he disappeared and then we saw him surreptitiously climb through the window of the cow shed. It was certain there was some sort of affinity between the little Kerry cow and him. When we did approach him he was always amiable and we were sure that he was not an abandoned stray. He was never ravenously hungry like Steptoe, so Nan and I agreed that he came from a good home. Yet we had not a single clue. Finding his home would be a hit-or-miss matter. Unlike Winny and Steptoe he was not driven away by the rain. When his sunbathing was disturbed he just went inside and played the waiting game with the little cow. He lay comfortably in the straw as if time did not matter. Nan and I decided that all we could do was wait. Surely this was wise, for by waiting we found out all we wanted to know about Barny. We were coming home from school one day when a little fellow called Tommy Docherty asked us if we would play a game of marbles with him. As we had never before been asked favours from boys, we agreed to do this.

'Hold on a minute,' said Tommy, 'I see Jimmy, our cat, coming home for his dinner.' And at that very moment we looked into the eyes of Cowshed Barny. So that was that, Barny – alias Jimmy – had a good home.

As we walked back Nan and I congratulated ourselves on establishing the real identity of Cat Number Three – Barny of the old barn – a cat who had fallen in love with our little cow.

The fourth cat, the dirty white Persian, was the most difficult of all to trace, for she never left the stable. When she was not sunbathing on the roof she was inside with the big horse. She really was a homeless stray as she never left our yard and she was the one cat that was never missing. She was always hungry and ate ravenously in a manner more becoming to a waif and stray than to her Persian forebears. I could never catch her. Nan and I saw her several times a day and we decided that, if we could catch her and clean her up, she would gain entry in to any society – and most certainly into Rosey's kitchen. The word 'Persian' was magic.

We told mother of the lovely white cat we saw in the stable and we were sure she was a Persian.

'Persian, indeed,' said mother, 'and how could a Persian cat be turned into a waif or stray?'

So 'Persian, indeed' was our most difficult quarry. To trace her was not going to be easy.

About this time Nan and I started our education proper at the convent school. No more frolics with Tommy Docherty and his kind. Every morning we walked nearly two miles, along footpaths, leafy lanes, through the woods and fields, passing the old church and graveyard, and up the hill to the convent. A little later mother

got us our own pony and trap and we took him to school every day. It was very difficult getting permission to tie him up at the back gate and there was one thing we had to promise and that was that we must clean up every evening. The little nun who was in charge of the roses welcomed the good manure we placed so liberally on her rose trees. Driving backwards and forwards to school, with a car full of scholars, was amongst the proudest and happiest experiences of my early school life.

And soon, very soon indeed, there occurred the last and final key to our cat project. Reverend Mother's first address to the assembly included a request pupils to keep an eye out for her own very special white Persian cat, which had been missing for about a month.

'Did you hear that, Nan?' I whispered. 'Could it possibly be Persi?'

Trembling all over I put my hand up to speak. 'Please, Mother, I think I know where there is a white Persian.'

'Speak up, child,' was her reply but I was not able to speak any louder and I was summoned to the table.

Then everything changed. Suddenly her voice sounded more kindly and the next thing I knew was that I was being sent home with big Alice, the convent cook. Yes, she immediately identified Fluffie, the convent cat. While the chase was on she told mother that she was a very special cat, having been imported (or rather smuggled in) from the home of a viscount in Le Mans – a special gift to Reverend Mother for services rendered to his daughter while boarding in the convent. Then Alice took mother aside and said that, being a female, she was becoming a real annoyance, especially when the male cat population of the town serenaded her all night. It took quite a little while to catch Fluffie as her month's freedom and life as a waif and stray had whetted her appetite for adventure. With the whole of our working staff guarding every exit from the stable, Alice dived headlong under the horse's belly and emerged with a much-bedraggled Fluffie.

Instead of settling down to be the angelic, white-robed creature she used to be, her stay in the outside world had unsettled her. She was no longer content to listen quietly to the angelus bells and the clanking of the rosary beads as the nuns came and went from their devotions. Celibate and happy though her owners might be, Fluffie was now rebellious. The quiet of the convent was shaken. After a serious conference in the community it was decided that Fluffie would have to move on – not as a horse's mate in a dull and depressing stable but as a companion for someone of importance in the town.

When Reverend Mother's wishes were made public the convent bell rang loud and often as hopeful hearts sought ownership of the most important cat in town. From several applicants Fluffie was presented to the mayor, for who better than the first citizen to win such a prize?

But now the real fun started. On the night of arrival Fluffie escaped up the chimney and it looked as if she would be impossible to catch, so the First Lady sent out a series of SOS. The mayor himself was quickly on the scene and, when he looked up the chimney, he was soon blinded by soot that had been displaced by the cat. More and more SOS to civic dignitaries and others. The district nurse outran the doctor and arrived in time to shout: 'Oh, your Lordship! Your poor, dear Lordship! Water, soap, castor oil and brandy! Quick!'

It did not take Ellen, the district nurse, many minutes to get things under control. She cleaned up the mayor, cheered up the mayoress, nipped the wee brandy and went after the cat. By this time Fluffie was in a more agreeable mood and was not so difficult to catch.

'You may take her if you want,' stammered the mayor, 'she is too much for me with my civic duties.'

And so Fluffie became the nurse's cat.

It is so many years ago that I cannot remember all the details but I know that, after her weekly bath, her coat was as white as snow. She was as sweet as she was handsome – and nurse watched carefully over her morals. The occasional tom who picked up her trail ran for his life if ever he saw nurse appear, so there were never any little Fluffies to carry on the name.

And that was how it was in my youth. Cats and everything to do with them were so much fun.

CHILDHOOD OF MISS CHURT

F. R. Buckley

MISS CHURT – British, like everyone else aboard the *Malvern* – sat on the storm sill of the galley and with glazed eyes surveyed the North Atlantic.

Miss Churt was meditating sombrely on the rump steak the cook had given her. 'Eat it up, Kitty; good!' the cook had said, and Miss Churt had followed the suggestion.

Now – although the steak had been delicious – Miss Churt was experiencing certain qualms; a sensation, as of cannon balls in the midriff, had assailed her....

Miss Churt decided that she would get a little fresh air and drop in on her friend Mr Wharton.

She dropped from her perch and, with tail at its meridian height, walked unsteadily toward the cuddy stairway.

The *Malvern* was moving unsteadily also, and likewise because of a heavy feeling in the midriff; caused not by cannon balls but by much more modern munitions of war. Never on very cordial terms with her rudder, she had now been be-shelled and be-packing-cased and be-airplane-parted until she would just as soon go anywhere as anywhere else, and was constantly trying to do so.

In a room on the boat deck, the first officer and the chief engineer were discussing this phenomenon and others related to the comfort and well-being of the ship's company. Mr McIvor, who was naturally the engineer, had joined in New York and was absorbing pessimism from Mr Wharton.

'He's a kind of mixed product of the flu and the board room,' said the first mate, alluding to his captain. 'He's – well, you saw him.'

'I saw *something*,' said Mr McIvor, cautiously.

'That'd be him. Chairman's nephew; on the beach for years; war come along – old Stokes gets flu – harnd o' Providence – an' here I am sayin' "Aye, aye, sir!" to *that*. If he'd got eyelashes I wouldn't mind it so much, but –'

Mr McIvor nodded, and his unclean pipe said, 'Cluck, cluck.'

'Have any trouble comin' over?'

'Subs, you mean? Naw. Hello, sweetheart! Hello! Come to see Poppa?'

Mr McIvor, thunderstruck, made an instinctive motion to smooth his hair, but it was only Miss Churt. Mr Wharton went over, picked her up out of the aperture of the hooked door and before sitting down again on his berth spread a month-old newspaper carefully on the carpet. The page uppermost bore a picture of Lady Somebody's wedding to Captain Gossakes-Whosis of the guards; Mr Wharton, bending with Miss Churt sprawled over his palm, surveyed orange blossoms, smiles, teeth, tonsils and the arch of swords with a nitric eye.

'There, sweetheart,' he said, putting Miss Churt down on them.

'You a morried mon?' asked Mr McIvor.

'Nah. But I *will* be. That's her.'

The engineer rolled an eye at the picture on the bureau.

'Nice gurrul.'

'You said it. Canon Hobson an' all. Speakin' of cannon, have you seen our 4.7 on the poop deck?'

'To my grief. But what's this,' said Mr McIvor, whose intake of personal news was disproportionate to his output, 'aboot a canon? The young leddy's no got a smash on um?'

'On old Hobson? Not *that* kind,' said Mr Wharton; and his look made Mr McIvor wonder whether he should have asked. 'Fact is – that's a good little sweetheart! Come to Poppa! 'At's a girlie!'

'Ye seem fond o' yon kitten.'

'I'm mad about her. And she's just wild about Harry, aren't you, pet?'

Miss Churt licked a gnarled and knotted hand. It tasted something like the rump steak, flavoured with tar, salt, tobacco and Mallinson's Wonder Ointment for superficial cuts and bruises. . . .

'Then whaur *does* this canon come in?'

'All the girls round our way in Liverpool are mad about him. See – he had us all in Sunday school; children's choral guild, he called it; us boys got away after we'd been confirmed, of course, but you can believe it or not, I've never been the swearer I ought to have.'

'I noticed that when we was warpin' into the stream,' said Mr McIvor. 'I thocht maybe ye was a nance.'

A sudden squeezing of Miss Churt's ribs evoked a mew.

'Did I hurt ums bellah?' asked Mr Wharton. 'Dere Snuzzle down, a good girlie; such a full ickle tummy . . . Ho, you did, hah?'

'Until we met,' said Mr McIvor in haste. 'But – he canna be a young mon, this parson?'

'Canon,' said Mr Wharton. 'New, an' he's no beauty neither. But he's the bee's knees so far's Annie's concerned, an' she's goin' to be married by him or nobody, so so far it's been nobody – an' now they go an' put this pink-whiskered nincompoop in over my head –'

'What's it matter who morries ye? It takes no longer than havin' a tooth out.'

'Ho, doesn't it? That's where *you* drop your tow. Old Hobson's strong for the ritual and all that; and that means veils an' orange flowers for Annie an' a top hat an' tails for me.'

'But not in wartime!'

'How do you know?'

'I'd go,' said Mr McIvor after reflection, 'an' see the old mon an' say "Fush!" to um.'

'You would *not*,' said Mr Wharton darkly, 'not if you saw him. He's only five foot six, but I've seen him sober, an' askin' for coffee. He's got one o' those kissers you carve out o' granite with a road drill. Looks something like you.'

The chief engineer considered this judicially, and put his glass down.

'Awheel,' he said, rising. 'It's the wull o' Allah, I suppawse, that some of us should be morried an' hae bairns, while ithers lovish their possions on tobby cots. Guid nicht, Mr Wharton.'

In the doorway he turned to see the burst of this Glaswegian bomb. Miss Churt, who had been awakened by something that felt like an earth tremor, blinked at him and went to sleep again.

'We've naval ratings aboard to work yon gun?' McIvor asked, to cover his more morbid curiosity.

'We have,' said Mr Wharton, 'an' if anybody asks you who's in command o' that gun crew, it's me. Naval reserve.'

'You bein' in turn commanded by Captain Timbs. Weel – guid nicht.'

'You heard about that timber ship gettin' torpedoed?' Wharton asked.

'No. What was that?'

'Oh, just that they thought she mightn't have sunk properly, an' be derelict hereabouts. Timbs has been radioin' everybody bar Churchill an' President Roosevelt, but nobody's seen her. Dark night, too. Well – pleasant dreams.'

A certain pensiveness marked Mr McIvor's departure but the first mate seemed to feel better.

He extracted Miss Churt gently from the land of nod, held her up with forelegs dangling, treated her to a gigantic smile and kissed her unhygienically on the nose.

'Azza booful girlie!' said Mr Wharton. 'You like Poppa go home to his other girl an' get married, please, an' zen you have lovely house an' garden to scratch in?'

Miss Churt was exceedingly drowsy; moreover that rump steak seemed still to be clogging her articulation. She opened her pink mouth, but no sound issued.

'I'll bet you,' said Mr Wharton. 'And that reminds me –'

He had just risen to pick up the newspaper with the wedding on it when from for'ard, out in the starry dark, there came a thunderous crash.

The *Malvern* stopped in her tracks like a dowager smitten in the breadbasket.

Simultaneously, the lights went out.

It was, of course, that derelict, floating bottom up at what the French so prettily call the flower of the water, or, in Anglo-Saxon sea talk, awash.

Having accomplished the destiny given her by those heavenly lights overhead – Neptune afflicted by Mars, perhaps; who knows? – and buckled the *Malvern*'s blunt bows backward like the bellows of a concertina, the timber ship rolled, spewed a few hundred thousand board feet from a new gash and sank; while down behind the fore-peak of the Malvern, Mr Wharton and a number of nearly naked shipmates strove to save their tub from doing likewise.

It was a question of strengthening a bulkhead, and strengthening bulkheads is uneasy work in the pitch dark.

It was an hour before Mr McIvor and his horde got the uprooted dynamo going again; and then what was revealed by hand lights led into the hold was the reverse of encouraging.

Not only was the bulkhead spouting water through the holes of deracinated rivets; it was bulging bodily and visibly inward, so that it was obvious that no time remained for carpenter work and fancy shoring.

Mr Wharton's eyes, under a mop of embattled hair, shuttled desperately about the hold. The port and starboard sides were solid-packed with minor munitions, forming admirable buttresses for the wings of the forward wall. But in the midst stood two cases that had taxed the stevedores; they were large and heavy enough to have contained whippet tanks, and the *Malvern*'s notorious instability had caused them to be stowed well aft of the bulkhead.

The space between was filled with this and that, in packets weighing mere hundreds of pounds.

'Get that junk out o' the way!' roared Mr Wharton. 'C'mon, boys!'

He himself was about to seize a crate when the third mate grabbed his shoulder.

'I say – Wharton –'

'The hell you do. Muck in an' shift something. I'm going' to shove these locomotives up, or whatever they are'.

'Listen! The Old Man's in a sweat of funk – sendin' out SOS till the ether's got clots in it –'

'To hell with him!'

'An' now he's getting ready to abandon ship.'

Mr Wharton disposed of his current crate and dashed forward to cut the key case out of a jam. Somehow or other his shirt had disintegrated, and his trousers consisted of but a breechclout and one leg, but still he was not swearing.

Canon Hobson, at that moment asleep in far-off Liverpool, his craglike nose in a soft pillow made for him by a parishioner, would have been gratified could he have known.

'What are you going' to do?' demanded the third officer. 'He's got all the ship's papers ready, an' he says his duty's to his men, an' unless we get help by dawn he's gonna take to the boats.'

'If you don't get outa my dog-rammed way we won't be afloat till dawn,' said Mr Wharton. 'Hey –'

'But you got to stop him!'

'An' risk my ticket – mutiny? No, sir; I obey – get that stuff movin', you bunch o' lobsters! Come along aft here, you knobeyed slackers – want me to shove this myself? You Fawdry – you Wilson –'

A cleared space now lay between the bulkhead and the first tank, which, of course, was not really a tank, it just felt like one. Anyway, the problem was to get it up to that bulkhead – and the other one up behind it, if possible. And the bulkhead was remarking, in the language of tortured steel, that it would be damned if it was going to wait for such support much longer.

'You can't shift 'em,' said the third mate weakly, 'an' if you do, you'll shove her bow down an' we'll slide.'

'Like the *Tornado* at Coney Island,' gasped Mr Wharton, grinning. ' "Down went McGinty" – ready, boys? Line up, get your shoulders against it. It's shove or grow gills! Now – one – two –'

The case didn't move.

'The Old Man says –' gasped the third mate.

'Give us a shanty,' grunted one of the men; and Mr Wharton obliged. It might almost be said that out of the fullness of the heart the mouth spoke. It could hardly be called singing, and the verbiage was bald and incomplete; yet in topicality, direction and – yes – the passion of love denied, Mr Wharton's shanty might have claimed kinship with the romances of the troubadours.

'Ca-a-a-ptain Ti-i-i-mbs,' he emitted in a wavering roar, 'is a son of a – *heave!*'

The men had had their leave stopped in Staten Island.

'Ca-a-a-ptain Ti-i-i-mbs,' they agreed fulsomely, 'is a son of a – *heave!*'

The case budged.

'Ca-a-a-ptain Timbs – *heave!*'

It moved six inches.

' – son of a – *heave!*'

Six inches more.

Up on the bridge, the subject of the shanty was talking to three naval ratings who seemed not to like him. They were the men responsible for the 4.7 aft, and they seemed to be suffering from the spirit of Nelson, or Collingwood or somebody.

All they did about it, though, was to say they didn't think – 'You don't have to think!' said Captain Timbs.

'You're not our officer, sir,' said the senior rating.

'You're under my orders! If I say to abandon ship, we'll abandon ship!'

This made it the turn of the junior rating.

'Aye, aye, sir,' said he. 'If you say so.'

Captain Timbs swallowed a large and visible lump in the throat. 'That's the order,' he said. 'Soon's it's dawn. We're ripped wide open.'

'Roughish sea, sir,' said the senior rating impassively.

'I've got a Swedish freighter on the radio – she'll be here by then, standing by. Who the hell are you, questioning my orders?'

'Nobody, sir,' said the second rating.

'Get to hell out!'

'Aye, aye, sir,' said the third; and out they went.

What they said as they went below is nobody's business; such low speculations about the sums payable by government to bereaved ship owners; so much plain, vulgar swearing. One may, however, make extracts to the extent that the senior remarked that dawn was breaking already; the second said that the old gal felt like taking the high dive, at that; while the junior, peering aft, remarked sentimentally that anyhow she'd go down with her flag up and her gun shotted.

'Might go an' fire her off for once,' said he.

'Might go down an' give Wharton a hand,' said his senior severely; and so they did.

Some time later, Miss Churt, whose rump steak had filled slumber with dreams of gigantic rats chasing her down unending alleyways, awoke with a start and a bad taste in her mouth.

She yawned and decided that a little fresh air, again, would do her good. Jumping down from the settee, she found that the floor

was not exactly where she had left it – it sloped downward now, and before she could correct her stance her for'ard legs had given way and she had rolled into a corner.

Picking herself thence, and reaching the door-sill, she rolled forth in search of company. It was light, so she gave the yawn and stretch by which cats thank God for each night spent in shelter – but something appeared to be wrong.

Where was everybody, to start with?

And why wasn't the deck vibrating as it always had, except just before and after mother left? And then the cargo winches had been working, with a roar that set one's ears back; now there was stillness – and behold! as one crossed behind the charthouse the bulwark of boats was gone and the wind smote one unimpeded.

Just some ropes trailing . . .

Miss Churt walked forward a few more paces and sat down, like the treble clef in a musical stave. Far in the misty distance she could see a ship standing still; and as for the *Malvern*'s boats, they were on the water – swimming, actually, and swimming away from her.

And in one of them, along with the three naval ratings and some other able-bodied gentlemen who disapproved of Captain Timbs and were saying so, Mr Wharton was at this identical moment remembering that he had left Miss Churt aboard.

'Noah's nails!' he ejaculated; and Canon Hobson, still sleeping, smiled in his distant dreams. 'Why –'

The oars lifted.

'Forgot something, sir?' asked the senior rating.

'Forgotten something?' said Mr Wharton. 'I've left my cat behind!'

From the bow of the boat came an imperfectly stifled chuckle.

'You laugh at me and I'll put a head on you,' said the first officer; and silence redescended on the ocean.

'Want to go back, sir?'

'I – think I will,' said Mr Wharton. 'If we're to save our dirty hides when there's no need to, I don't see why a poor dumb animal should suffer. Unless these gentlemen object? Pull stabbud, back port! Come on, you bunch of tailors!'

'Captain's boat's stopped rowin', sir,' said the bow oar.

'Ne'er mind,' said Mr Wharton, 'we can rat just as well in ten minutes' time. An' that Swede can wait. Some expensive nephew for – c'mon, put some beef into it!'

A distant hail came over the water – which, by the way, was now astonishingly calm.

'I'll just swarm up the falls an' be back in a jiffy,' said Mr Wharton – not knowing that a mile the other side of the *Malvern* the sea, hidden from him by the wallowing bulk of that ship, was just being broken by the conning tower of a submarine.

Her commander, a pleasant enough fellow named Koenig, usually resident in Munich, Glocknergasse No. 8, had heard the frantic distress signals wirelessed by Captain Timbs and had wondered if perchance they might portend something in his line of business. There was, he knew, a temporary scarcity of destroyers in this area, but the event was turning out better than his hopes. Through the periscope he had watched the crew abandoning ship, and, when the *Malvern* failed to slide precipitately out of sight, had commented soul-ticklingly to his men on the unsea-to-dare-worthiness of British sailors.

That this was no Q-ship he was well assured, both by the presence of the Swedish ship and the perilous trim of the *Malvern* herself. So it was his intent to combine business with pleasure by letting the fleeing crew watch him use their vessel for target practice. He thought he would use percussion fuse and blow the funnel out of her first.

As the submarine came awash her gun crew tumbled up, ran for'ard and proceeded to clear their gun.

And simultaneously, the longing gaze of Miss Churt was gratified by the spectacle of Mr Wharton, shaggier than ever. Miss Churt liked shagginess, it gave one more corners to nestle in.

Her master, landing on the boat deck from the falls, didn't seem as cheery as usual; something seemed to be bothering him; he didn't smile.

But Miss Churt knew how to remedy that. When anybody looked sad, she ran away, and Mr Wharton ran after her and

picked her up and called her a little devil and corrected himself and said 'weevil' and kissed her on the end of the nose.

Miss Churt therefore ran away now, skidding slightly because of the slant of the deck; her ears cocked for the sound of beloved footsteps pursuing.

And here they came.

But here came something else.

Something terrible. A long, increasing noise, coming out of the middle of a distant thump, boring into her ears – so terrifying – and then – a vast flash of light, taking up the whole world and tearing it to pieces, shaking her stomach so that the steak didn't matter any more. . . .

Mr Wharton, rushing from behind the wireless house, paused a moment.

He saw a very large scorched hole in the boat deck planking, around which he had to pick his way.

While thus engaged, he saw Captain Koenig's submarine, lying perhaps three quarters of a mile off.

But what he was looking for was a small ball of soiled fur; and this he found, very limp, just for'ard of the bridge deck ladder. The curious thing is that Captain Koenig also adored cats, and had three at home in the Glocknergasse.

But that's war.

Mr Wharton took up in his very large hand what war had left of Miss Churt, and he laid the other hand over her like the lid of a little coffin and cursed Captain Koenig and his superiors and inferiors; and then he lifted both his arms and, still holding the limp form in his right hand, raised in a voice that almost carried the distance.

Indeed – in St Mary's Rectory, Canon Hobson awoke with a start; looked at his bedside clock and found it was 5.25; rolled over – but somehow was disinclined to go to sleep again.

'You bloody, sneaking *bloody* butcher!' Mr Wharton was now shouting; and there came a sudden crack in his voice. 'My little –'

A voice spoke from just behind him. It had not seemed quite proper to the naval ratings that their officer should go aboard without escort, so they had swarmed up the falls also and here they were. The voice was the voice of the senior rating, as was proper.

'How about giving 'em a packet, sir?' he inquired.

Mr Wharton had forgotten the 4.7 gun aft. Now he remembered and gave a perfect snarl of assent.

The body of Miss Churt he crammed into the side pocket of his coat; and then down the ladder he went, and after him came the ratings.

They had to descend another ladder and cross the aft welldeck and then climb the poop; and it was now that Captain Koenig saw them.

With a welter of ow sounds and a swamp of terminations in ch, he directed his men to shift target and give Wharton *et al.* a packet; so that the question resolved itself roughly into one of who should give whom a packet first.

The U-boat, being in the groove, got her shot off the earlier; but the hastily altered aim was high and the shell went to miss the Swedish ship by no more than half a mile. (Memorandum of 27 March 1940, paragraph 2.)

Meantime, the senior rating had done various manipulations of various things; and now, with a nod of the head, he expressed himself satisfied. Quite unnecessarily, he looked at Mr Wharton, opened his mouth and was just about to ask if he should open fire when the officer (not a regular navy man, of course) shoved him aside, seized the firing lever and got the shot off himself.

It was just luck, blind luck, for all concerned; but the fact remains that the unconventional, almost illegitimate, shell flew as through a tube to the barrel of the U-boat's gun, bent it, zoomed thereoff without touching Captain Koenig or his men, and smote the lip of the conning tower, where it exploded with the abandon peculiar to high explosive.

Nobody was hurt, save Seaman Albrecht Otto of Bremen (deafness and scratches) – but the conning tower was impossible to close. That meant no submersion –

And on the southern sky line there had appeared, and was approaching, a smudge of smoke, which betokened destroyers. The ratings pointed this out to one another.

Meanwhile Mr Wharton, at the other rail, was expressing his completely berserk opinion of Captain Timbs and all men who would take to boats leaving cats on perfectly sound ships full of badly needed munitions.

This expression, in addition to blistering (if the third officer may be believed) the paint on the thwarts of Lifeboat No. 1, left Mr Wharton rather exhausted. And softened in mood.

He put his hand into his pocket and pulled out the mortal envelope of Miss Churt. The bluish eyes were closed, the furry head rolled on the neck, and all her whiskers had been singed away.

'You want us to come back, sir?' came a hail from the boats.

'You can go to hell!' roared Mr Wharton; so they started toward him.

But a voice pitched to carry a quarter of a mile is tremendous at close range.

Miss Churt vibrated in every cell.

Her stomach began to trouble her again. There was a familiar smell in her nostrils, seeping past the stench of burned whiskers – tobacco, tar and Mallinson's –

She opened her eyes and said: 'Mew!'

For all it was wartime, the parish church of St Mary's was properly decorated for this wedding; though in view of the circumstances, Canon Hobson had consented to relax the clothing rules so far as the bridegroom was concerned.

Miss Woollard, however, was in the prescribed raiment even down to the seventy-ninth orange blossom; albeit inclined, apparently, to take nervous bites out of her veil. She was more nervous than brides usually are; more nervous even than seemed warranted by the fact that her bridegroom had three best men – the senior, junior and middle naval ratings, all with medals but one degree inferior to that which had been bestowed on Mr Wharton.

The cause for this uneasiness came to light when Canon Hobson, opening his prayer book, first glanced, then looked, then stared at the bridegroom's right-hand coat pocket.

It should perhaps be mentioned here that in addition to a granite face and an extraordinarily soft heart, the reverend gentleman was equipped with eyes that seemed to have been chipped out of adamant and ground to fine points.

He furled the prayer book and spoke in a low, dazed voice.

'Henry,' said he, while the congregation craned, 'that cannot be a cat you have in your coat pocket? Not a *cat?*'

This was rather an exaggeration of the status of Miss Churt, who was six weeks old that day and had just put her shellshaven face out for a little air. But the general proposition was undeniable.

'Yes,' said Mr Wharton. 'It is.'

'He *would* bring it – he *would* – I said –' quavered the bride; but Canon Hobson paid no attention to her, though she began to sob.

Meeting the bluish eyes of Miss Churt, however, his adamantine orbs underwent a peculiar process. First they flickered from their condemning stare; then, as it were, they liquefied, so that their penetrative qualities became nil.

He spoke:

'Am I to presume that – this – is some kind of mascot? Connected perhaps with the recent – ? What has happened to her whiskers?'

'I'll tell you about it in the vestry,' said Mr Wharton; and, meeting the canon's gaze, mourned for the misjudgments of his youth.

Canon Hobson nodded; opened the book which he had closed on a probationary thumb, and cleared his throat.

'Dearly beloved,' he proclaimed, 'we are gathered together –'

Miss Churt could not quite identify all the smells (largely lilies) or sounds (mostly Canon Hobson) that were going on.

They were interesting, and she had a vague idea that something of the same general purport might be her personal concern one day.

But not now.

Not for a long time yet.

And meantime she had had enough air.

She withdrew her head from the atmosphere of St Mary's into the warm tweediness of Mr Wharton's pocket and composed herself to sleep.

THE ACHIEVEMENT OF THE CAT

Saki
(Hector Hugo Munro)

THE ANIMAL which the Egyptians worshipped as divine, which the Romans venerated as a symbol of liberty, which Europeans in the ignorant Middle Ages anathematized as an agent of demonology, has displayed to all ages two closely blended characteristics – courage and self-respect. No matter how unfavourable the circumstances, both qualities are always to the fore.

Confront a child, a puppy, and a kitten with a sudden danger; the child will turn instinctively for assistance, the puppy will grovel in abject submission to the impending visitation, the kitten will brace its tiny body for a frantic resistance. And disassociate the luxury-loving cat from the atmosphere of social comfort in which it usually contrives to move, and observe it critically under the adverse conditions of civilization – that civilization which can impel a man to the degradation of clothing himself in tawdry ribald garments and capering mountebank dances in the streets for the earning of the few coins that keep him on the respectable, or non-criminal, side of society. The cat of the slums and alleys, starved, outcast, harried, still keeps amid the prowlings of its adversity the bold, free, panther-tread with which it paced of yore the temple courts of Thebes, still displays the self-reliant watchfulness which man has never taught it to lay aside.

And when its shifts and clever managings have not sufficed to stave off inexorable fate, when its enemies have proved too strong or too many for its defensive powers, it dies fighting to the last, quivering with the choking rage of mastered resistance, and voicing in its death-yell that agony of bitter remonstrance which human animals, too, have flung at the powers that may be; the last protest against a destiny that might have made them happy – and has not.

THE UNDOING OF MORNING GLORY ADOLPHUS

N. Margaret Campbell

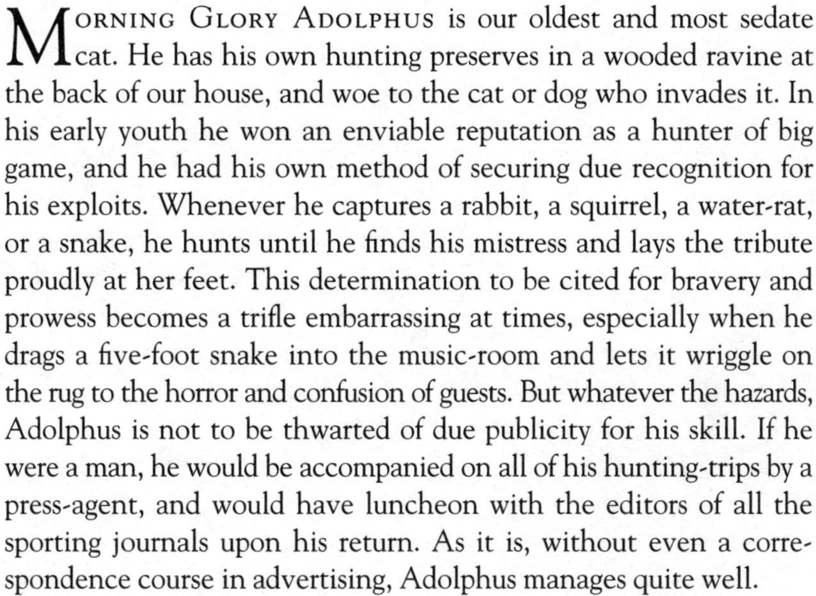

MORNING GLORY ADOLPHUS is our oldest and most sedate cat. He has his own hunting preserves in a wooded ravine at the back of our house, and woe to the cat or dog who invades it. In his early youth he won an enviable reputation as a hunter of big game, and he had his own method of securing due recognition for his exploits. Whenever he captures a rabbit, a squirrel, a water-rat, or a snake, he hunts until he finds his mistress and lays the tribute proudly at her feet. This determination to be cited for bravery and prowess becomes a trifle embarrassing at times, especially when he drags a five-foot snake into the music-room and lets it wriggle on the rug to the horror and confusion of guests. But whatever the hazards, Adolphus is not to be thwarted of due publicity for his skill. If he were a man, he would be accompanied on all of his hunting-trips by a press-agent, and would have luncheon with the editors of all the sporting journals upon his return. As it is, without even a correspondence course in advertising, Adolphus manages quite well.

For the study of majestic dignity, tinged on occasions with lofty disdain, interpreters of muscular expression would do well to seek out Adolphus. He walks the highway without haste or concern for his personal survival in the midst of tooting automobiles and charging dogs. When a strange dog appears and mistakes Adolphus for an ordinary cat who may be chased for the sport of the thing, it is the custom of Adolphus to slow his pace somewhat and stretch out in the path of the oncoming enemy, assuming the pose and the expression of the sphinx. He is the graven image of repose and perfect muscular control. Only his slumbrous amber eyes burn unblinkingly, never leaving the enraged countenance of his enemy, who bears down upon him with exposed fangs and hackles erect. When the assault is too ferocious to be in good taste even among dogs, accompanied by hysterical yapping and snapping, Adolphus has been known to yawn in the face of his assailant, quite deliberately and very politely, as a gentleman of good breeding might when bored by an excessive display of emotion. Usually the dog mysteriously halts within a foot or so of those calm yellow eyes and describes a semi-circle within the range of those twin fires, filling the air with defiant taunts that gradually die away to foolish whimpering as he begins an undignified withdrawal, while Adolphus winks solemnly and stares past his cowering foe into a mysterious space undesecrated by blustering dogs.

A few dogs there have been who have failed to halt at the hypnotic command of those yellow eyes. Then there came a lightning-like flash of fur through the air, and Adolphus landed neatly on his victim's neck, his great claws beginning to rip with businesslike precision through the soft ears and forehead of the terrified dog. Perhaps the rumour of these encounters spread among the canine population of our neighbourhood, for it is never counted against the reputation of any dog as a fighter if he makes a wide detour of the regions frequented by Adolphus.

For years the rule of Adolphus among the cats of his own household had been undisputed. Then came Silver Paws, a handsome young rogue whose satiny coat was beautiful with broken silver and blue lights. There was no question about it, Silver Paws had a way with the ladies. While Adolphus still looked upon him as a frolicsome kitten whose sense of humour was unbalanced by a proper sense of dignity, he artfully won all hearts and easily became the centre of attraction wherever he appeared. It was plainly disgusting to Adolphus to see the way the conceited young thing arched his

Ivy

'Come, lovely cat, and rest upon my heart,
And let my gaze dive in the cold
Live pools of thine enchanted eyes that dart
Metallic rays of green and gold.'
BAUDELAIRE

The Flower-Pot Cat

'Let me warn you not to put too much stock in the theory that animals do not think and that they act only by instinct.'
My Boss the Cat

My Bathroom Cat

'Cats, incidentally, are a great warm-up for a successful marriage – they teach you your place in the household.'
My Boss the Cat

Susie's Window

'I had only one desire, one dream, and that was to slip out of the upper window and escape on to the roofs.'
THE CAT'S PARADISE

back expectantly whenever a human hand came near enough to caress him.

If Adolphus had had the small mind of a punster, he might have observed, after the cynical manner of others who have lost their place in the public affections to an unworthy rival, that the glory was passing out of his name. But he was never one to surrender without a struggle. He went to his nightly hunt with cold murder in his heart and a high resolve to force the spotlight back upon himself. Daily he laid at the feet of his mistress older and wilder rabbits, fiercer-eyed rats, and longer snakes. All to no purpose. He even played the heroic role of the deliverer when his hated rival was treed by the grocer's dog. He simply walked calmly up to the tree where the dog was dancing wildly under the limb where the trembling Silver Paws clung, and the dog suddenly remembered that he really ought to catch up to the grocer's wagon and it wasn't much fun to bark at a silly kitten, anyway! When the frightened Silver Paws slid down the tree, Adolphus walked up to him with the self-righteous air of a benevolent gentleman who has rescued a lost soul not because the soul deserved it, but because he himself was made that way. This magnanimous act gave Adolphus a momentary advantage over his rival, but the fickle attentions of the household were soon centred upon the handsome young charmer again. Then Adolphus took to sitting about the house, gazing solemnly past the spot where Silver Paws was receiving the choicest bits of meat with many endearing words, and smoothing his whiskers with a reflective paw.

It was about this time that Silver Paws, to the consternation of the household, disappeared. A search was instituted in the neighbourhood, but he was gone without a trace, just as though he had been whisked away on a magic broom. Mournfully we gathered up the playthings he had left scattered over the house – a bit of fur on a string, a bright-coloured ball, some dried beans that rattled in the pod when batted about by a velvet paw – and of these remembrances we made a heap in his favourite rocking-chair. 'He'll want them if he ever comes back,' we said.

A remarkable change had come over Morning Glory Adolphus. We had long honoured him as a crafty hunter and first-rate fighting-man, but we had judged him to be somewhat lacking in sentiment, a trifle indifferent and unresponsive, as was natural enough in one who had achieved no small amount of fame. What was our astonishment to find that he had become, overnight, warmly demonstrative in his affections and sympathetically desirous of turning our thoughts from useless brooding over the lost one. It was really touching to see the way he followed us about the house, sitting at our feet to sing with rapturous abandon wherever we happened to pause. Forgotten were the joys of the chase, the pleasant pastime of disciplining unmannerly dogs. For three whole days he gave himself up wholly to the business of love-making. If we attempted to ignore him, he threw himself at our feet and lay on his back at our mercy, as one who would say that he bared his faithful heart that we might kill him if we could not love him. He walked about the house with the proudly possessive air of a haughty ruler who has returned to his domains after an enforced absence, and he curled up blissfully on the cushions where his late rival had been accustomed to take his ease. Once we found him stretched contemptuously over the playthings that lay in a little heap in the rocking-chair. It must have been a bumpy sort of bed, but Adolphus looked happy and comfortable.

Suspicion instantly seized upon his mistress. 'Adolphus,' she said sternly, 'I believe you know what has become of our beautiful Silver Paws!' The accused rose stiffly to his full height, regarded her with the gravely innocent expression of an outraged deacon, and then, turning his back deliberately upon her, gave himself up again to the slumbers of the just.

But the suspicions of the household were not laid. 'Adolphus is trying too hard to be good,' they argued. 'It is not natural. There must be something on his conscience!' For this was Adolphus's way of raising a smoke-screen, as it were, to hide his evil deeds. They had observed this in the past. It was all very humiliating to a proud soul like Adolphus, and he showed his resentment by stalking out of the house and letting the screen-door slam behind him after the manner of any offended male.

The household followed him from afar. He walked straight to the

ravine, where he was accustomed to hunt, and stood peering intently down into it over the edge of a cliff, his ears pricked forward, every line of him expressing gloating satisfaction, from his agitated whiskers to the tip of his quivering tail. It was hard to believe that he was the same kindly creature who had been making affectionate advances to us a few hours before. As we drew near we could hear a faint crying, pleading and pitiful, and down among the bushes we discovered our lost Silver Paws, too weak from loss of food to stand, and rather battered from the rough treatment he had received from his jailor.

The moment that Adolphus saw us looking into the ravine he withdrew in disgust, for he knew that his game was up. With lofty scorn he watched us gather up his banished rival, revive him with warm milk, caress and comfort him. With what dire threats had Adolphus kept his captive down in the ravine, within sound of our voices, all the long hours while he wooed us at his leisure, and what spell had he cast over him that the hungry kitten had not dared to come at our call?

While we rejoiced and scolded, the grocer's dog was observed coming around the corner of the house. He had grown bold during those days of weakness when Adolphus had been courting the ladies. But one look into the amber eyes of Adolphus, and he was off with a shriek, for he could see that the fighter was once more the master of his emotions.

THE HOME LIFE OF A HOLY CAT

Arthur Wiegall

ONE SUMMER during a heat wave, when the temperature in the shade of my veranda in Luxor was 125° Fahrenheit, I went down to cooler Lower Egypt to pay a visit to an English friend of mine stationed at Zagazig, the native city which stands beside the ruins of ancient Bubastis.

He was about to leave Egypt and asked me whether I would like to have his cat, a dignified, mystical-minded, long-legged, small-headed, green-eyed female, whose orange-yellow hair, marked with greyish-black stripes in tabby pattern, was so short that she gave the impression of being naked – an impression, however, which did not in any way detract from her air of virginal chastity.

Her name was Basta, and though her more recent ancestors had lived wild amongst the ruins, she was so obviously a descendant of the holy cats of ancient times, who were incarnations, of the goddess Basta, that I thought it only right to accept the offer and take her up to Luxor to live with me. To be the expert in charge of Egyptian antiquities and not have an ancient Egyptian cat to give an air of mystery to my headquarters had, indeed, always seemed to me to be somewhat wanting in showmanship on my part.

Thus it came about that, on my departure, I drove off to the railroad station with the usually dignified Basta bumping around and uttering unearthly howls inside a cardboard hat box, in the side of which I had cut a small round hole for ventilation. The people in the streets and on the station platform seemed to be under the impression that the noises were digestive and that I was in dire need of a doctor; and it was a great relief to my embarrassment when the hot and panting train steamed into Zagazig.

Fortunately, I found myself alone in the compartment, and the hatbox at my side had begun to cause me less anxiety, when suddenly Basta was seized with a sort of religious frenzy. The box rocked about, and presently out through the airhole came a long, snake-like paw which waved weirdly to and fro in space for a moment and then was withdrawn, its place being taken by a pink nose which pushed itself outward with such frantic force that the sides of the hole gave way, and out burst the entire sandy, sacred head.

She then began to choke, for the cardboard was pressing tightly around her neck; and to save her from strangulation I was obliged to tear the aperture open, whereupon she wriggled out, leaped in divine frenzy up the side of the carriage and prostrated herself on the network of the baggage-rack, where her hysteria caused her to lose all control of her internal arrangements if and I say modestly that she was overcome with nausea, I shall be telling but a part of the dreadful tale.

The rest of the journey was like a bad dream; but at the Cairo terminus, where I had to change into the night express for Luxor, I got the help of a native policeman who secured a large laundry basket from the sleeping-car department, and after a prolonged struggle, during which the train was shunted into a distant siding, we imprisoned the struggling Basta again.

The perspiring policeman and I then carried the basket at a run along the tracks back to the station in the sweltering heat of the late afternoon, and I just managed to catch my train; but during this second part of my journey Basta travelled in the baggage-van whence, in the hot and silent night, whenever we were at a standstill, her appalling incantations came drifting to my ears.

I opened the basket in an unfurnished spare room in my house, and like a flash Basta was up the bare wall and on to the curtain pole above the window. There she remained all day, in a sort of hypnotic trance; but at sunset the saucer of milk and plate of fish

which I had provided for her at last enticed her down, and in the end she reconciled herself to her new surroundings and indicated by her behaviour that she was willing to accept my house as her earthly temple.

With Pedro, my pariah dog, there was not the slightest trouble; he had no strong feelings about cats, and she on her part graciously deigned to acknowledge his status – as, I believe, is generally the case in native households. She sometimes condescended to visit my horse and donkey in their stalls; and for Laura, my camel, she quickly developed a real regard, often sleeping for hours in her stable.

I was not worried as to how she would treat the chickens and pigeons, because her former owner at Zagazig had insisted upon her respecting his hen coop and pigeon cote; but I was a little anxious about the ducks, for she had not previously known any, and in ancient times her ancestors used to be trained to hunt wild geese and ducks and were fed with *pâté de foie gras*, or whatever it was called then, on holy days and anniversaries.

In a corner of the garden I had made a miniature duck pond which was sunk rather deeply in the ground and down to which I had cut a narrow, steeply sloping passage, or gangway. During the day, after the ducks had been up and down this slope several times, the surface used to become wet and slippery, and the ducks, having waddled down the first few inches, were forced to toboggan down the rest of it on their tails, with their two feet sticking out in front of them and their heads well up.

Basta was always fascinated by this slide and by the splash at the bottom, and used to sit and watch it all for hours, which made me think at first that she would one day spring at one of them; but she never did. Field mice, and water rats down by the Nile, were her only prey; and in connection with the former I may mention a curious occurrence.

One hot night I was sitting smoking my pipe on the veranda when my attention was attracted by two mice which had crept into the patch of brilliant moonlight before my feet and were boldly nibbling some crumbs left over from a cracker thrown to Pedro earlier in the evening. I watched them silently for a while and did not notice that Basta had seen them and was preparing to spring, nor did I observe a large white owl sitting aloft amongst the overhanging roses and also preparing to pounce.

Suddenly, and precisely at the same moment, the owl shot down on the mice from above and Basta leaped at them from beside me. There was a collision and a wild scuffle; fur and feathers flew; I fell out of my chair; and then the owl made off screeching in one direction and the cat dashed away in the other; while the mice, practically clinging to each other, remained for a moment or so too terrified to move.

During the early days of her residence in Luxor, Basta often used to go down to the edge of the Nile to fish with her paw; but she never caught anything, and in the end she got a fright and gave it up. I was sitting by the river watching her trying to catch one of a little shoal of small fish which were sunning themselves in the shallow water when there came swimming into view a twelve or fourteen-inch fish which I recognized (by its whiskers and the absence of a dorsal fin) as the electric cat fish, pretty common in the Nile – a strange creature able to give you an electric shock like hitting your funny bone.

These fish obtain their food in a curious way: they hang round any shoal of small fry engaged in feeding, and then glide quietly into their midst and throw out this electric shock, whereupon the little fellows are all sick to the stomach, and the big fellow gets their disgorged dinners.

I was just waiting to see this happen with my own eyes – for it had always seemed a bit far-fetched – when Basta made a dart at the intruder with her paw and got a shock. She uttered a yowl as though somebody had trodden on her and leaped high in the air; and never again did she put her foot near the water. She was content after that with our daily offering of a fish brought from the market and fried for her like a burnt sacrifice.

Basta had a most unearthly voice, and when she was feeling emotional would let out a wail which at first was like the crying of a phantom baby and then became the tuneless song of a lunatic, and finally developed into the blood-curdling howl of a soul in torment.

And when she spat, the percussion was like that of a spring-gun.

There were some wild cats or, rather, domestic cats who, like Basta's own forebears, had taken to a wild life, living in a grove of trees beside the river just beyond my garden wall; and it was generally the proximity of one of these which started her off; but sometimes the outburst was caused by her own unfathomable thoughts as she went her mysterious ways in the darkness of the night.

I think she must have been clairvoyant, for she often seemed to be seeing things not visible to me. Sometimes, perhaps when she was cleaning fish or mouse from her face, she would pause with one foot off the ground and stare in front of her, and then back away with bristling hair or go forward with friendly little mewing noises; and sometimes she would leap off a chair or sofa, her tail lashing and her green eyes dilated. But it may have been worms.

Once I saw her standing absolutely rigid and tense on the lawn, staring at the rising moon; and then all of a sudden she did a sort of dance such as cats sometimes do when they are playing with other cats. But there was no other cat and, any way, Basta never played; she never forgot that she was a holy cat.

Her chaste hauteur was so great that she would not move out of the way when people were walking about, and many a time her demoniacal shriek and perhaps a crash of breaking glass informed the household that somebody had tripped over her. It was astonishing, however, how quickly she recovered her dignity and how well she maintained the pretence that whatever happened to her was at her own celestial wish and was not our doing.

If I called her she would pretend not to hear, but would come a few moments later when it could appear that she had thought of doing so first; and if I lifted her off a chair she would jump back on to it and then descend with dignity as though of her own free will. But in this, of course, she was more like a woman than like a divinity.

The Egyptian cat is a domesticated species of the African wild-cat, and no doubt its strange behaviour and its weird voice were the cause of it being regarded as sacred in ancient times; but, although the old gods and their worship have been forgotten these many centuries, the traditional sanctity of the race has survived.

Modern Egyptians think it unlucky to hurt a cat and, in the native quarters of Cairo and other cities, hundreds of cats are daily fed at the expense of benevolent citizens. They say that they do this because cats are so useful to mankind in killing off mice and other pests; but actually it is an unrecognized survival of the old beliefs.

In the days of the Pharaohs, when a cat died the men of the household shaved off their eyebrows and sat around wailing and rocking themselves to and fro in simulated anguish. The body was embalmed and buried with solemn rites in the local cats' cemetery, or was sent down to Bubastis to rest in the shadow of the temple of their patron goddess. I myself have dug up hundreds of mummified cats; and once, when I had a couple of dozen of the best specimens standing on my veranda waiting to be dispatched to the Cairo Museum, Basta was most excited about it, and walked around sniffing at them all day. They certainly smelled awful.

On my lawn there was a square slab of stone which had once been the top of an altar dedicated to the sun god, but was now used as a sort of low garden table; and sometimes when she had caught a mouse she used to deposit the chewed corpse upon this slab – nobody could think why, unless, as I always told people, she was really making an offering to the sun. It was most mysterious of her; but it led once to a very unfortunate episode.

A famous French antiquarian, who was paying a polite call, was sitting with me beside this sacred stone, drinking afternoon tea and eating fresh dates, when Basta appeared on the scene with a small dead mouse in her mouth, which in her usual way she deposited upon the slab – only on this occasion she laid it on my guest's plate, which was standing on the slab.

We were talking at the moment and did not see her do this and, anyhow, the Frenchman was as blind as a bat; and, of course, as luck would have it, he immediately picked up the wet, mole-coloured mouse instead of a ripe brown date, and the thing had almost gone into his mouth before he saw what it was and, with a yell, flung it into the air.

It fell into his upturned sun helmet which was lying on the grass beside him; but he did not see where it had gone and, jumping

angrily to his feet in the momentary belief that I had played a schoolboy joke on him, he snatched up his helmet and was in the act of putting it on his head when the mouse tumbled out on to the front of his shirt and slipped down inside his buttoned jacket.

At this he went more or less mad, danced about, shook himself, and finally trod on Basta, who completed his frenzy by uttering a fiendish howl and digging her claws into his leg. The dead mouse, I am glad to say, fell on to the grass during the dance without passing through his roomy trousers, as I had feared it might; and Basta, recovering her dignity, picked it up and walked off with it.

It is a remarkable fact that, during the five or six years she spent with me, she showed no desire to be anything but a spinster all her life, and when I arranged a marriage for her she displayed such dignified but violent antipathy towards the bridegroom that the match was a failure. In the end, however, she fell in love with one of the wild cats who lived among the trees beyond my wall, and nothing could prevent her going off to visit him from time to time, generally at dead of night.

He did not care a hoot about her sanctity, and she was feminine enough to enjoy the novelty of being roughly treated. I never actually saw him, for he did not venture into the garden, but I used to hear him knocking her about outside my gates; and when she came home, scratched and bitten and muttering something about holy cats, it was plain that she was desperately happy. She licked her wounds, indeed, with deep and voluptuous satisfaction.

A dreadful change came over her. She lost her precious dignity and was restless and inclined to be savage; her digestion played embarrassing tricks on her; and once she mortally offended Laura by clawing her nose. There was a new glint in her green eyes as she watched the ducks sliding into the pond; the pigeons interested her for the first time; and for the first time, too, she *ate* the mice she had caught.

Then she began to disappear for a whole day or night at a time, and once when I went in search of her amongst the trees outside and found her sharpening her claws on a branch above my head, she put her ears back and hissed at me until I could see every one of her teeth and halfway down her pink throat. I tried by every method to keep her at home when she came back, but it was all in vain, and at last she left me forever.

Weeks afterwards I caught sight of her once again amongst the trees, and it was evident that she was soon to become a mother. She gave me a friendly little mew this time, but she would not let me touch her; and presently she slipped away into the undergrowth. I never knew what became of her.

MIDSHIPMAN, THE CAT

John Coleman Adams

THIS IS A TRUE STORY about a real cat who, for aught I know, is still alive and following the sea for a living. I hope to be excused if I use the pronouns 'who' and 'he' instead of 'which' and 'it,' in speaking of this particular cat; because although I know very well that the grammars all tell us that 'he' and 'who' apply to persons, while 'it' and 'which' apply to things, yet this cat of mine always seemed to us who knew him to be so much like a human being that I find it unsatisfactory to speak of him in any other way. There are some animals of whom you prefer to say 'he,' just as there are persons whom you sometimes feel like calling 'it.'

The way we met this cat was after this fashion: It was back somewhere in the seventies, and a party of us were cruising east from Boston in the little schooner-yacht *Eyvor.* We had dropped into Marblehead for a day and a night, and some of the boys had gone ashore in the tender. As they landed on the wharf, they found a group of small boys running sticks into a woodpile, evidently on a hunt for something inside.

'What have you in there?' asked one of the yachtsmen.

'Nothin' but a cat,' said the boys.

'Well, what are you doing to him?'

'Oh, pokin' him up! When he comes out we'll rock him,' was the answer, in good Marblehead dialect.

'Well, don't do it anymore. What's the use of tormenting a poor cat? Why don't you take somebody of your size?'

The boys slowly moved off, a little ashamed and a little afraid of the big yachtsman who spoke; and when they were well out of sight the yachtsmen went on, too, and thought no more about the cat they had befriended. But when they had wandered about the tangled streets of the town for a little while, and paid the visits which all good yachtsmen pay, to the grocery and the post office and the apothecary's soda fountain, they returned to the wharf and found their boat. And behold, there in the stern sheets sat the little gray-and-white cat of the woodpile! He had crawled out of his retreat and made straight for the boat of his champions. He seemed in no wise disturbed or disposed to move when they jumped on board, nor did he show anything but pleasure when they stroked and patted him. But when one of the boys started to put him ashore, the plucky little fellow showed his claws; and no sooner was he set on his feet at the edge of the wharf than he turned about and jumped straight back into the boat.

'He wants to go yachting,' said one of the party, whom we called 'the Bos'n.'

'Ye might as wal take the cat,' said a grizzly old fisherman standing on the wharf. 'He doesn't belong to anybody, and ef he stays here the boys'll worry him t'death.'

'Let's take him aboard,' said the yachtsmen. 'It's good luck to have a cat on board ship.'

Whether it was good luck to the ship or not, it was very clear that pussy saw it meant good luck to him, and curled himself down in the bottom of the boat, with a look that meant business. Evidently he had thought the matter all over and made up his mind that this was the sort of people he wanted to live with; and, being a Marblehead cat, it made no difference to him whether they lived afloat or ashore; he was going where they went, whether they wanted him or not. He had heard the conversation from his place in the woodpile, and had decided to show his gratitude by going to sea with these protectors of his. By casting in his lot with theirs he was paying them the highest compliment of which a cat is capable. It would have been the height of impoliteness not to recognize his distinguished appreciation. So he was allowed to remain in the boat, and was taken off to the yacht.

Upon his arrival there, a council was held, and it was unanimously decided that the cat should be received as a member of the crew; and as we were a company of amateur sailors, sailing our own boat, each man having his particular duties, it was decided that the cat should be appointed midshipman, and should be named after his position. So he was at once and ever after known as 'Middy.' Everybody took a great interest in him, and he took an impartial interest in everybody – though there were two people on board to whom he made himself particularly agreeable. One was the quiet, kindly professor, the captain of the *Eyvor*; the other was Charlie, our cook and only hired hand. Middy, you see, had a seaman's true instinct as to the official persons with whom it was his interest to stand well.

It was surprising to see how quickly Middy made himself at home. He acted as if he had always been at sea. He was never seasick, no matter how rough it was or how uncomfortable any of the rest of us were. He roamed wherever he wanted to, all over the boat. At mealtimes he came to the table with the rest, sat up on a valise, and lapped his milk and took what bits of food were given him, as if he had eaten that way all his life. When the sails were hoisted it was his especial joke to jump upon the main gaff and be hoisted with it; and once he stayed on his perch till the sail was at the masthead. One of us had to go aloft and bring him down. When we had come to anchor and everything was snug for the night, he would come on deck and scamper out on the main boom, and race from there to the bowsprit end as fast as he could gallop, then climb, monkey-fashion, halfway up the masts, and drop back to the deck or dive down into the cabin and run riot among the berths.

One day, as we were jogging along, under a pleasant southwest wind, and everybody was lounging and dozing after dinner, we heard the Bos'n call out, 'Stop that, you fellows!' and a moment after, 'I tell you, quit! Or I'll come up and make you!'

We opened our lazy eyes to see what was the matter, and there sat the Bos'n, down in the cabin, close to the companionway, the tassel of his knitted cap coming nearly up to the combings of the hatch; and on the deck outside sat Middy, digging his claws into the tempting yarn, and occasionally going deep enough to scratch the Bos'n's scalp.

When night came and we were all settled down in bed, it was Middy's almost invariable custom to go the rounds of all the berths, to see if we were properly tucked in, and to end his inspection by jumping into the captain's bed, treading himself a comfortable nest there among the blankets, and curling himself down to sleep. It was his own idea to select the captain's berth as the only proper place in which to turn in.

But the most interesting trait in Middy's character did not appear until he had been a week or so on board. Then he gave us a surprise. It was when we were lying in Camden Harbor. Everybody was going ashore to take a tramp among the hills, and Charlie, the cook, was coming too, to row the boat back to the yacht.

Middy discovered that he was somehow 'getting left.' Being a prompt and very decided cat, it did not take him long to make up his mind what to do. He ran to the low rail of the yacht, put his forepaws on it, and gave us a long, anxious look. Then as the boat was shoved off he raised his voice in a plaintive mew. We waved him a good-bye, chaffed him pleasantly, and told him to mind the anchor, and have dinner ready when we got back.

That was too much for his temper. As quick as a flash he had dived overboard, and was swimming like a water spaniel, after the dinghy!

That was the strangest thing we had ever seen in all our lives! We were quite used to elephants that could play at seesaw, and horses that could fire cannon, to learned pigs and to educated dogs; but a cat that of his own accord would take to the water like a full-blooded Newfoundland was a little beyond anything we had ever heard of. Of course the boat was stopped, and Middy was taken aboard drenched and shivering, but perfectly happy to be once more with the crew. He had been ignored and slighted; but he had insisted on his rights, and as soon as they were recognized he was quite contented.

Of course, after that we were quite prepared for anything that Middy might do. And yet he always managed to surprise us by his

bold and independent behavior. Perhaps his most brilliant performance was a visit he paid a few days after his swim in Camden Harbor.

We were lying becalmed in a lull of the wind off the entrance to Southwest Harbor. Near us, perhaps a cable's-length away, lay another small yacht, a schooner hailing from Lynn. As we drifted along on the tide, we noticed that Middy was growing very restless; and presently we found him running along the rail and looking eagerly toward the other yacht. What did he see – or smell – over there which interested him? It could not be the dinner, for they were not then cooking. Did he recognize any of his old chums from Marblehead? Perhaps there wee some cat friends of his on the other craft. Ah, that was it! There they were on the deck, playing and frisking together – two kittens! Middy had spied them, and was longing to take a nearer look. He ran up and down the deck, mewing and snuffing the air. He stood up in his favorite position when on lookout, with his forepaws on the rail. Then, before we realized what he was doing, he had plunged overboard again, and was making for the other boat as fast as he could swim! He had attracted the attention of her company, and no sooner did he come up alongside than they prepared to welcome him. A fender was lowered, and when Middy saw it he swam toward it, caught it with his forepaws, clambered along it to the gunwale, and in a twinkling was over the side and on the deck scraping acquaintance with the strange kittens.

How they received him I hardly know, for by that time our boat was alongside to claim the runaway. And we were quite of the mind of the skipper of the *Winnie L.*, who said, as he handed our bold midshipman over the side, 'Well, that beats all *my* going a-fishing!'

Only a day or two later Middy was very disobedient when we were washing decks one morning. He trotted about in the wet till his feet were drenched, and then retired to dry them on the white spreads of the berths below. That was quite too much for the captain's patience. Middy was summoned aft, and, after a sound rating, was hustled into the dinghy which was moored astern, and shoved off to the full length of her painter. The punishment was a severe one for Middy, who could bear anything better than exile from his beloved shipmates. So of course he began to exercise his ingenious little brain to see how he could escape. Well under the overhang of the yacht he spied, just about four inches out of water, a little shoulder of the rudder. That was enough for him. He did not stop to think whether he would be any better off there. It was a part of the yacht, and that was home. So overboard he went, swam for the rudder, scrambled on to it, and began howling piteously to be taken on deck again; and, being a spoiled and much-indulged cat, he was soon rescued from his uncomfortable roosting place and restored to favor.

I suppose I shall tax your powers of belief if I tell you many more of Middy's doings. But truly he was a strange cat, and you may as well be patient, for you will not soon hear of his equal. The captain was much given to rifle practice, and used to love to go ashore and shoot at a mark. On one of his trips he allowed Middy to accompany him, for the simple reason, I suppose, that Middy decided to go, and got on board the dinghy when the captain did. Once ashore, the marksman selected a fine large rock as a rest for his rifle, and opened fire upon his target. At the first shot or two Middy seemed a little surprised, but showed no disposition to run away. After the first few rounds, however, he seemed to have made up his mind that since the captain was making all the racket it must be entirely right and proper, and nothing about which a cat need bother his head in the least. So, as if to show how entirely he confided in the captain's judgment and good intentions, that imperturbable cat calmly lay down, curled up, and went to sleep in the shade of the rock over which the captain's rifle was blazing and cracking about once in two minutes. If anybody was ever acquainted with a cooler or more self-possessed cat I should be pleased to hear the particulars.

I wish that this chronicle could be confined to nothing but our shipmate's feats of daring and nerve. But, unfortunately, he was not always blameless in his conduct. When he got hungry he was apt to forget his position as midshipman, and to behave just like any cat with an empty stomach. Or perhaps he may have done just what any hungry midshipman does under the circumstances; I do not quite know what a midshipman does under all circumstances and so I cannot say. But here is one of this cat midshipman's exploits. One

afternoon, on our way home, we were working along with a head wind and sea toward Wood Island, a haven for many of the small yachts between Portland and the Shoals. The wind was light and we were a little late in making port. But as we were all agreed that it would be pleasanter to postpone our dinner till we were at anchor, the cook was told to keep things warm and wait till we were inside the port before he set the table. Now, his main dish that day was to be a fine piece of baked fish; and, unfortunately, it was nearly done when we gave orders to hold back the dinner. So he had closed the drafts of his little stove, left the door of the oven open, and turned into his bunk for a quiet doze – a thing which every good sailor does on all possible occasions; for a seafaring life is very uncertain in the matter of sleep, and one never quite knows when he will lose some, nor how much he will lose. So it is well to lay in a good stock of it whenever you can.

It seems that Middy was on watch, and when he saw Charlie fast asleep he undertook to secure a little early dinner for himself. He evidently reasoned with himself that it was very uncertain when we should have dinner and he'd better get his while he could. He quietly slipped down to the stove, walked coolly up to the oven, and began to help himself to baked haddock.

He must have missed his aim or made some mistake in his management of the business, and, by some lucky chance for the rest of us, waked the cook. For, the first we knew, Middy came flying up the cabin companionway, followed by a volley of shoes and spoons and pieces of coal, while we could hear Charlie, who was rather given to unseemly language when he was excited, using the strongest words in his dictionary about 'that thief of a cat!'

'What's the matter?' we all shouted at once.

'Matter enough, sir!' growled Charlie. 'That little cat's eaten up half the fish! It's a chance if you get any dinner tonight, sir.'

You may be very sure that Middy got a sound wigging for that trick, but I am afraid the captain forgot to deprive him of his rations as he threatened. He was much too kindhearted.

The very next evening Middy startled us again by a most remarkable display of coolness and courage. After a weary thrash to windward all day, under a provokingly light breeze, we found ourselves under the lee of the little promontory at Cape Neddick, where we cast anchor for the night. Our supply of water had run very low, and so, just after sunset, two of the party rowed ashore in the tender to replenish our water keg, and by special permission Middy went with them.

It took some time to find a well, and by the time the jugs were filled it had grown quite dark. In launching the boat for the return to the yacht, by some ill luck a breaker caught her and threw her back upon the beach. There she capsized and spilled out the boys, together with their precious cargo. In the confusion of the moment, and the hurry of setting matters to rights, Middy was entirely forgotten, and when the boat again was launched, nobody thought to look for the cat. This time everything went well, and in a few minutes the yacht was sighted through the dusk. Then somebody happened to think of Middy! He was nowhere to be seen. Neither man remembered anything about him after the capsize. There was consternations in the hearts of those unlucky wights. To lose Middy was almost like losing one of the crew.

But it was too late and too dark to go back and risk another landing on the beach. There was nothing to be done but to leave poor Middy to his fate, or at least to wait until morning before searching for him.

But just as the prow of the boat bumped against the fender on the yacht's quarter, out from under the stern sheets came a wet, bedraggled, shivering cat, who leaped on board the yacht and hurried below into the warm cabin. In that moist adventure in the surf, Middy had taken care of himself, rescued himself from a watery grave, got on board the boat as soon as she was ready, and sheltered himself in the warmest corner. All this he had done without the least outcry, and without asking any help whatever. His self-reliance and courage were extraordinary.

Well, the pleasant month of cruising drew to a close, and it became a question what should be done with Middy. We could not think of turning him adrift in the cold world, although we had no fears but that so bright and plucky a cat would make a living any-

where. But we wanted to watch over his fortunes, and perhaps take him on the next cruise with us when he should have become a more settled and dignified Thomas. Finally, it was decided that he should be boarded for the winter with an artist, Miss Susan H——, a friend of one of our party. She wanted a studio cat, and would be particularly pleased to receive so accomplished and traveled a character as Middy. So when the yacht was moored to the little wharf at Annisquam, where she always ended her cruises, and we were packed and ready for our journey to Boston, Middy was tucked into a basket and taken to the train. He bore the confinement with the same good sense which had marked all his life with us, though I think his feelings were hurt at the lack of confidence we showed in him. And, in truth, we were a little ashamed of it ourselves, and when once we were on the cars somebody suggested that he be released from his prison just to see how he would behave. We might have known he would do himself credit. For when he had looked over his surroundings, peeped above the back of the seat at the passengers, taken a good look at the conductor, and counted the rest of the party to see that none of us was missing, Middy snuggled down upon the seat, laid his head upon the captain's knee, and slept all the way to Boston.

That was the last time I ever saw Middy. He was taken to his new boarding place in Boylston Street, where he lived very pleasantly for a few months, and made many friends by his pleasing manners and unruffled temper. But I suppose he found it a little dull in Boston. He was not quite at home in his aesthetic surroundings. I have always believed he sighed for the freedom of a sailor's life. He loved to sit by the open window when the wind was east, and seemed to be dreaming of faraway scenes. One day he disappeared. No trace of him was ever found. A great many things may have happened to him. But I never could get rid of the feeling that he went down to the wharves and the ships and the sailors, trying to find his old friends, looking everywhere for the stanch little *Eyvor*; and, not finding her, I am convinced that he shipped on some East Indianman and is now a sailor cat on the high seas.

THE STORY OF WEBSTER

P. G. Wodehouse

'CATS are not dogs!'

There is only one place where you can hear good things like that thrown off quite casually in the general run of conversation, and that is the bar parlour of the 'Angler's Rest'. It was there, as we sat grouped about the fire, that a thoughtful Pint of Bitter had made the statement just recorded.

Although the talk up to this point had been dealing with Einstein's Theory of Relativity, we readily adjusted our minds to cope with the new topic. Regular attendance at the nightly sessions over which Mr Mulliner presides with such unfailing dignity and geniality tends to produce mental nimbleness. In our little circle I have known an argument on the Final Destination of the Soul to change inside forty seconds into one concerning the best method of preserving the juiciness of bacon fat.

'Cats', proceeded the Pint of Bitter, 'are selfish. A man waits on a cat hand and foot for weeks, humouring its lightest whim, and then it goes and leaves him flat because it has found a place down the road where the fish is more frequent.'

'What I've got against cats', said a Lemon Sour, speaking feelingly, as one brooding on a private grievance, 'is their unreliability. They lack candour and are not square shooters. You get your cat and you call him Thomas or George, as the case may be. So far, so good. Then one morning you wake up and find six kittens in the hat-box and you have to reopen the whole matter, approaching it from an entirely different angle.'

'If you want to know what's the trouble with cats,' said a red-faced man with glassy eyes, who had been rapping on the table for his fourth whisky, 'they've got no tact. That's what's the trouble with them. I remember a friend of mine had a cat. Made quite a pet of that cat, he did. And what occurred? What was the outcome? One night he came home rather late and was feeling for the keyhole with his corkscrew; and, believe me or not, his cat selected that precise moment to jump on the back of his neck out of a tree. No tact.'

Mr Mulliner shook his head.

'I grant you all this,' he said, 'but still, in my opinion, you have not got to the root of the matter. The real objection to the great majority of cats is their insufferable air of superiority. Cats, as a class, have never completely got over the snootiness caused by the fact that in Ancient Egypt they were worshipped as gods. This makes them too prone to set themselves up as critics and censors of the frail and erring human beings whose lot they share. They stare rebukingly. They view with concern. And on a sensitive man this often has the worst effects, inducing an inferiority complex of the gravest kind. It is odd that the conversation should have taken this turn,' said Mr Mulliner, sipping his hot Scotch and lemon, 'for I was thinking only this afternoon of the rather strange case of my cousin Edward's son, Lancelot.'

'I knew a cat –' began a Small Bass.

My cousin Edward's son, Lancelot (said Mr Mulliner) was, at the time of which I speak, a comely youth of some twenty-five summers. Orphaned at an early age, he had been brought up in the home of his Uncle Theodore, the saintly Dean of Bolsover; and it was a great shock to that good man when Lancelot, on attaining his majority, wrote from London to inform him that he had taken a studio in Bott Street, Chelsea, and proposed to remain in the metropolis and become an artist.

The Dean's opinion of artists was low. As a prominent member of the Bolsover Watch Committee, it had recently been his distasteful duty to be present at a private showing of the super-super-film, *Palettes of Passion*; and he replied to his nephew's communication with a vibrant letter in which he emphasized the grievous pain it gave him to think that one of his flesh and blood should deliberately be embarking on a career which must inevitably lead sooner or later to the painting of Russian princesses lying on divans in the semi-nude with their arms round tame jaguars. He urged Lancelot to return and become a curate while there was yet time.

But Lancelot was firm. He deplored the rift between himself and a relative whom he had always respected; but he was dashed if he meant to go back to an environment where his individuality had been stifled and his soul confined in chains. And for four years there was silence between uncle and nephew.

During these years Lancelot had made progress in his chosen profession. At the time at which this story opens, his prospects seemed bright. He was painting the portrait of Brenda, only daughter of Mr and Mrs B. B. Carberry-Pirbright, of 11 Maxton Square, South Kensington, which meant thirty pounds in his sock on delivery. He had learned to cook eggs and bacon. He had practically mastered the ukulele. And, in addition, he was engaged to be married to a fearless young *vers libre* poetess of the name of Gladys Bingley, better known as The Sweet Singer of Garbidge Mews, Fulham – a charming girl who looked like a pen-wiper.

It seemed to Lancelot that life was very full and beautiful. He lived joyously in the present, giving no thought to the past.

But how true it is that the past is inextricably mixed up with the present and that we can never tell when it may spring some delayed bomb beneath our feet. One afternoon, as he sat making a few small alterations to the portrait of Brenda Carberry-Pirbright, his fiancée entered.

He had been expecting her to call, for today she was going off for a three weeks' holiday to the South of France, and she had promised to look in on her way to the station. He laid down his brush and gazed at her with a yearning affection, thinking for the thousandth time time how he worshipped every spot of ink on her nose. Standing there in the doorway with her bobbed hair sticking out in every direction like a golliwog's, she made a picture that seemed to speak to his very depths.

'Hullo, Reptile!' he said lovingly.

'What ho, Worm!' said Gladys, maidenly devotion shining through the monocle which she wore in her left eye. 'I can stay just half an hour.'

'Oh, well, half an hour soon passes,' said Lancelot. 'What's that you've got there?' 'A letter, ass. What did you think it was?' 'Where did you get it?' 'I found the postman outside.' Lancelot took the envelope from her and examined it. 'Gosh!' he said. 'What's the matter?' 'It's from my Uncle Theodore.' 'I didn't know you had an Uncle Theodore.' 'Of course I have. I've had him for years.' 'What's he writing to you about?' 'If you'll kindly keep quiet for two seconds, if you know how,' said Lancelot, 'I'll tell you.' And in a clear voice which, like that of all the Mulliners, however distant from the main branch, was beautifully modulated, he read as follows:

The Deanery,
Bolsover, Wilts.

My dear Lancelot,

As you have, no doubt, already learned from your *Church Times*, I have been offered and have accepted the vacant Bishopric of Bongo-Bongo, in West Africa. I sail immediately to take up my new duties, which I trust will be blessed.

In these circumstances it becomes necessary for me to find a good home for my cat Webster. It is, alas, out of the question that he should accompany me, as the rigours of the climate and the lack of essential comforts might well sap a constitution which has never been robust.

I am dispatching him, therefore, to your address, my dear boy, in a straw-lined hamper, in the full confidence that you will prove a kindly and conscientious host.

With cordial good wishes,

Your affectionate uncle,

Theodore Bongo-Bongo

For some moments after he had finished reading this communication, a thoughtful silence prevailed in the studio. Finally Gladys spoke.

'Of all the nerve!' she said. 'I wouldn't do it.'

'Why not?'

'What do you want with a cat?'

Lancelot reflected.

'It is true,' he said, 'that, given a free hand, I would prefer not to have my studio turned into a cattery or cat-bin. But consider the special circumstances. Relations between Uncle Theodore and self have for the last few years been a bit strained. In fact, you might say we had definitely parted brass-rags. It looks to me as if he were coming round. I should describe this letter as more or less what you might call an olive-branch. If I lush this cat up satisfactorily, shall I not be in a position later on to make a swift touch?'

'He is rich, this bean?' said Gladys, interested.

'Extremely.'

'Then', said Gladys, 'consider my objections withdrawn. A good stout cheque from a grateful cat-fancier would undoubtedly come in very handy. We might be able to get married this year.'

'Exactly,' said Lancelot. 'A pretty loathsome prospect, of course; but still, as we've arranged to do it, the sooner we get it over, the better, what?'

'Absolutely.'

'Then that's settled. I accept custody of cat.'

'It's the only thing to do,' said Gladys. 'Meanwhile, can you lend me a comb? Have you such a thing in your bedroom?'

'What do you want with a comb?'

'I got some soup in my hair at lunch. I won't be a minute.'

She hurried out, and Lancelot, taking up the letter again, found that he had omitted to read a continuation of it on the back page.

It was to the following effect:

> PS. In establishing Webster in your home, I am actuated by another motive than the simple desire to see to it that my faithful friend and companion is adequately provided for.
>
> From both a moral and an educative standpoint, I am convinced that Webster's society will prove of inestimable value to you. His advent, indeed, I venture to hope, will be a

turning-point in your life. Thrown, as you must be, incessantly among loose and immoral Bohemians, you will find in this cat an example of upright conduct which cannot but act as an antidote to the poison cup of temptation which is, no doubt, hourly pressed to your lips.

PPS. Cream only at midday, and fish not more than three times a week.

He was reading these words for the second time, when the front doorbell rang and he found a man on the steps with a hamper. A discreet mew from within revealed its contents, and Lancelot, carrying it into the studio, cut the strings.

'Hi!' he bellowed, going to the door.

'What's up?' shrieked his betrothed from above.

'The cat's come.'

'All right. I'll be down in a jiffy.'

Lancelot returned to the studio.

'What ho, Webster!' he said cheerily. 'How's the boy?'

The cat did not reply. It was sitting with bent head, performing that wash and brush up which a journey by rail renders so necessary.

In order to facilitate these toilet operations, it had raised its left leg and was holding it rigidly in the air. And there flashed into Lancelot's mind an old superstition handed on to him, for what it was worth, by one of the nurses of his infancy. If, this woman had said, you creep up to a cat when its leg is in the air and give it a pull, then you make a wish and your wish comes true in thirty days.

It was a pretty fancy, and it seemed to Lancelot that the theory might as well be put to the test. He advanced warily, therefore, and was in the act of extending his fingers for the pull, when Webster, lowering the leg, turned and raised his eyes.

He looked at Lancelot. And suddenly with sickening force there came to Lancelot the realization of the unpardonable liberty he had been about to take.

Until this moment, though the postscript to his uncle's letter should have warned him, Lancelot Mulliner had had no suspicion of what manner of cat this was that he had taken into his home.

Now, for the first time, he saw him steadily and saw him whole.

Webster was very large and very black and very composed. He conveyed the impression of being a cat of deep reserves. Descendant of a long line of ecclesiastical ancestors who had conducted their decorous courtships beneath the shadow of cathedrals and on the back walls of bishops' palaces, he had that exquisite poise which one sees in high dignitaries of the Church. His eyes were clear and steady, and seemed to pierce to the very roots of the young man's soul, filling him with a sense of guilt.

Once, long ago, in his hot childhood, Lancelot, spending his summer holidays at the deanery, had been so far carried away by ginger-beer and original sin as to plug a senior canon in the leg with his air-gun – only to discover, on turning, that a visiting archdeacon had been a spectator of the entire incident from his immediate rear. As he had felt then, when meeting the archdeacon's eye, so did he feel now as Webster's gaze played silently upon him.

Webster, it is true, had not actually raised his eyebrows. But this, Lancelot felt, was simply because he hadn't any.

He backed, blushing.

'Sorry!' he muttered.

There was a pause. Webster continued his steady scrutiny. Lancelot edged towards the door.

'Er – excuse me – just a moment . . .' he mumbled. And, sidling from the room, he ran distractedly upstairs.

'I say,' said Lancelot.

'Now what?' asked Gladys.

'Have you finished with the mirror?'

'Why?'

'Well, I – er – I thought', said Lancelot, 'that I might as well have a shave.'

The girl looked at him, astonished.

'Shave? Why, you shaved only the day before yesterday.'

'I know. But, all the same . . . I mean to say, it seems only respectful. That cat, I mean.'

'What about him?'

'Well, he seems to expect it, somehow. Nothing actually said,

don't you know, but you could tell by his manner. I thought a quick shave and perhaps a change into my blue serge suit –'

'He's probably thirsty. Why don't you give him some milk?'

'Could one, do you think?' said Lancelot doubtful. 'I mean, I hardly seem to know him well enough.' He paused. 'I say, old girl,' he went on, with a touch of hesitation.

'Hullo?'

'I know you won't mind my mentioning it, but you've got a few spots of ink on your nose.'

'Of course I have. I always have spots of ink on my nose.'

'Well . . . you don't think . . . a quick scrub with a bit of pumice-stone . . . I mean to say, you know how important first impressions are. . . .'

The girl stared.

'Lancelot Mulliner,' she said, 'if you think I'm going to skin my nose to the bone just to please a mangy cat –'

'Sh!' cried Lancelot, in agony.

'Here, let me go down and look at him,' said Gladys petulantly.

As they re-entered the studio, Webster was gazing with an air of quiet distaste at an illustration from *La Vie Parisienne* which adorned one of the walls. Lancelot tore it down hastily.

Gladys looked at Webster in an unfriendly way.

'So that's the blighter!'

'Sh!'

'If you want to know what I think,' said Gladys, 'that cat's been living too high. Doing himself a dashed sight too well. You'd better cut his rations down a bit.'

In substance, her criticism was not unjustified. Certainly, there was about Webster more than a suspicion of *embonpoint*. He had that air of portly well-being which we associate with those who dwell in cathedral closes. But Lancelot winced uncomfortably. He had so hoped that Gladys would make a good impression, and here she was, starting right off by saying the tactless thing.

He longed to explain to Webster that it was only her way; that in the Bohemian circles of which she was such an ornament genial chaff of a personal order was accepted and, indeed, relished. But it was too late. The mischief had been done. Webster turned in a pointed manner and withdrew silently behind the chesterfield.

Gladys, all unconscious, was making preparations for departure.

'Well, bung-oh,' she said lightly. 'See you in three weeks. I suppose you and that cat'll both be out on the tiles the moment my back's turned.'

'Please! Please!' moaned Lancelot. 'Please!'

He had caught sight of the tip of a black tail protruding from behind the chesterfield. It was twitching slightly, and Lancelot could read it like a book. With a sickening sense of dismay, he knew that Webster had formed a snap judgement of his fiancée and condemned her as frivolous and unworthy.

It was some ten days later that Bernard Worple, the neo-Vorticist sculptor, lunching at the Puce Ptarmigan, ran into Rodney Scollop, the powerful young surrealist. And after talking for a while of their art:

'What's all this I hear about Lancelot Mulliner?' asked Worple. 'There's a wild story going about that he was seen shaved in the middle of the week. Nothing in it, I suppose?'

Scollop looked grave. He had been on the point of mentioning Lancelot himself, for he loved the lad and was deeply exercised about him.

'It is perfectly true,' he said.

'It sounds incredible.'

Scollop leaned forward. His fine face was troubled.

'Shall I tell you something, Worple?'

'What?'

'I know for an absolute fact', said Scollop, 'that Lancelot Mulliner now shaves every morning.'

Worple pushed aside the spaghetti which he was wreathing about him and through the gap stared at this companion.

'Every morning?'

'Every single morning. I looked in on him myself the other day, and there he was, neatly dressed in blue serge and shaved to the core. And, what is more, I got the distinct impression that he had used talcum powder afterwards.'

'You don't mean that!'

'I do. And shall I tell you something else? There was a book lying open on the table. He tried to hide it, but he wasn't quick enough. It was one of those etiquette books!'

'An etiquette book!'

'*Polite Behaviour*, by Constance, Lady Bodbank.'

Worple unwound a stray tendril of spaghetti from about his left ear. He was deeply agitated. Like Scollop, he loved Lancelot.

'He'll be dressing for dinner next!' he exclaimed.

'I have every reason to believe', said Scollop gravely, 'that he does dress for dinner. At any rate, a man closely resembling him was seen furtively buying three stiff collars and a black tie at Hope Brothers in the King's Road last Tuesday.'

Worple pushed his chair back, and rose. His manner was determined.

'Scollop,' he said, 'we are friends of Mulliner's, you and I. It is evident from what you tell me that subversive influences are at work and that never has he needed our friendship more. Shall we not go round and see him immediately?'

'It was what I was about to suggest myself,' said Rodney Scollop.

Twenty minutes later they were in Lancelot's studio, and with a significant glance Scollop drew his companion's notice to their host's appearance. Lancelot Mulliner was neatly, even foppishly, dressed in blue serge with creases down the trouser-legs, and his chin, Worple saw with a pang, gleamed smoothly in the afternoon light.

At the sight of his friends' cigars, Lancelot exhibited unmistakable concern.

'You don't mind throwing those away, I'm sure,' he said pleadingly.

Rodney Scollop drew himself up a little haughtily.

'And since when', he asked, 'have the best fourpenny cigars in Chelsea not been good enough for you?'

Lancelot hastened to soothe him.

'It isn't me,' he exclaimed. 'It's Webster. My cat. I happen to know he objects to tobacco smoke. I had to give up my pipe in deference to his views.'

Bernard Worple snorted.

'Are you trying to tell us', he sneered, 'that Lancelot Mulliner allows himself to be dictated to by a blasted cat?'

'Hush!' cried Lancelot, trembling. 'If you knew how he disapproves of strong language!'

'Where is this cat?' asked Rodney Scollop. 'Is that the animal?' he said, pointing out of the window to where, in the yard, a tough-looking Tom with tattered ears stood mewing in a hard-boiled way out of the corner of its mouth.

'Good heavens, no!' said Lancelot. 'That is an alley cat which comes round here from time to time to lunch at the dustbin. Webster is quite different. Webster has a natural dignity and repose of manner. Webster is a cat who prides himself on always being well turned out and whose high principles and lofty ideals shine from his eyes like beacon fires....' And then suddenly, with an abrupt change of manner, Lancelot broke down and in a low voice added: 'Curse him! Curse him! Curse him! Curse him!'

Worple looked at Scollop. Scollop looked at Worple.

'Come, old man,' said Scollop, laying a gentle hand on Lancelot's bowed shoulder. 'We are your friends. Confide in us.'

'Tell us all,' said Worple. 'What's the matter?'

Lancelot uttered a bitter, mirthless laugh.

'You want to know what's the matter? Listen, then. I'm cat-pecked!'

'Cat-pecked?'

'You've heard of men being hen-pecked, haven't you?' said Lancelot with a touch of irritation. 'Well, I'm cat-pecked.'

And in broken accents he told his story. He sketched the history of his association with Webster from the latter's first entry into the studio. Confident now that the animal was not within earshot, he unbosomed himself without reserve.

'It's something in the beast's eye,' he said in a shaking voice. 'Something hypnotic. He casts a spell upon me. He gazes at me and disapproves. Little by little, bit by bit, I am degenerating under his influence from a wholesome, self-respecting artist into . . . well, I don't know what you call it. Suffice it to say that I have given up smoking, that I have ceased to wear carpet slippers and go about

without a collar, that I never dream of sitting down to my frugal evening meal without dressing, and' – he choked – 'I have sold my ukulele.'

'Not that!' said Worple, paling.

'Yes,' said Lancelot. 'I felt he considered it frivolous.'

There was a long silence.

'Mulliner,' said Scollop, 'this is more serious than I had supposed. We must brood upon your case.'

'It may be possible', said Worple, 'to find a way out.'

Lancelot shook his head hopelessly..

'There is no way out. I have explored every avenue. The only thing that could possibly free me from this intolerable bondage would be if once – just once – I could catch that cat unbending. If once – merely once – it would lapse in my presence from its austere dignity for but a single instant, I feel that the spell would be broken. But what hope is there of that?' cried Lancelot passionately. 'You were pointing just now to that alley cat in the yard. There stands one who has strained every nerve and spared no effort to break down Webster's inhuman self-control. I have heard that animal say things to him which you would think no cat with red blood in its veins would suffer for an instant. And Webster merely looks at him like a Suffragan Bishop eyeing an erring choirboy and turns his head and falls into a refreshing sleep.'

He broke off with a dry sob. Worple, always an optimist, attempted in his kindly way to minimize the tragedy.

'Ah, well,' he said. 'It's bad, of course, but still, I suppose there is no actual harm in shaving and dressing for dinner and so on. Many great artists . . . Whistler, for example –'

'Wait!' cried Lancelot. 'You have not heard the worst.'

He rose feverishly, and, going to the easel, disclosed the portrait of Brenda Carberry-Pirbright.

'Take a look at that,' he said, 'and tell me what you think of her.'

His two friends surveyed the face before them in silence. Miss Carberry-Pirbright was a young woman of prim and glacial aspect. One sought in vain for her reasons for wanting to have her portrait painted. It would be a most unpleasant thing to have about any house.

Scollop broke the silence.

'Friend of yours?'

'I can't stand the sight of her,' said Lancelot vehemently.

'Then', said Scollop, 'I may speak frankly. I think she's a pill.'

'A blister,' said Worple.

'A boil and a disease,' said Scollop, summing up.

Lancelot laughed hackingly.

'You have described her to a nicety. She stands for everything most alien to my artist soul. She gives me a pain in the neck. I'm going to marry her.'

'What!' cried Scollop.

'But you're going to marry Gladys Bingley,' said Worple.

'Webster thinks not,' said Lancelot bitterly. 'At their first meeting he weighed Gladys in the balance and found her wanting. And the moment he saw Brenda Carberry-Pirbright he stuck his tail up at right angles, uttered a cordial gargle, and rubbed his head against her leg. Then turning, he looked at me. I could read that glance. I knew what was in his mind. From that moment he has been doing everything in his power to arrange the match.'

'But, Mulliner,' said Worple, always eager to point out the bright side, 'why should this girl want to marry a wretched, scrubby, hard-up footler like you? Have courage, Mulliner. It is simply a question of time before you repel and sicken her.'

Lancelot shook his head.

'No,' he said. 'You speak like a true friend, Worple, but you do not understand. Old Ma Carberry-Pirbright, this exhibit's mother, who chaperones her at the sittings, discovered at an early date my relationship to my Uncle Theodore, who, as you know, has got it in gobs. She knows well enough that some day I shall be a rich man. She used to know my Uncle Theodore when he was Vicar of St Botolph's in Knightsbridge, and from the very first she assumed towards me the repellent chumminess of an old family friend. She was always trying to lure me to her At Homes, her Sunday luncheons, her little dinners. Once she actually suggested that I should escort her and her beastly daughter to the Royal Academy.'

He laughed bitterly. The mordant witticisms of Lancelot Mulliner at

the expense of the Royal Academy were quoted from Tite Street in the south to Holland Park in the north and eastward as far as Bloomsbury.

'To all these overtures', resumed Lancelot, 'I remained firmly unresponsive. My attitude was from the start one of frigid aloofness. I did not actually say in so many words that I would rather be dead in a ditch than at one of her At Homes, but my manner indicated it. And I was just beginning to think I had choked her off when in crashed Webster and upset everything. Do you know how many times I have been to that infernal house in the last week? Five. Webster seemed to wish it. I tell you, I am a lost man.'

He buried his face in his hands. Scollop touched Worple on the arm, and together the two men stole silently out.

'Bad!' said Worple.

'Very bad,' said Scollop.

'It seems incredible.'

'Oh, no. Cases of this kind are, alas, by no means uncommon among those who, like Mulliner, possess to a marked degree the highly-strung, ultra-sensitive artistic temperament. A friend of mine, a rhythmical interior decorator, once rashly consented to put his aunt's parrot up at his studio while she was away visiting friends in the north of England. She was a woman of strong evangelical views, which the bird had imbibed from her. It had a way of putting its head on one side, making a noise like someone drawing a cork from a bottle, and asking my friend if he was saved. To cut a long story short, I happened to call on him a month later and he had installed a harmonium in his studio and was singing hymns, ancient and modern, in a rich tenor, while the parrot, standing on one leg on its perch, took the bass. A very sad affair. We were all much upset about it.'

Worple shuddered.

'You appal me, Scollop! Is there nothing we can do?'

Rodney Scollop considered for a moment.

'We might wire Gladys Bingley to come home at once. She might possibly reason with the unhappy man. A woman's gentle influence. . . . Yes, we could do that. Look in at the post office on your way home and send Gladys a telegram. I'll owe you for my half of it.'

In the studio they had left, Lancelot Mulliner was staring dumbly at a black shape which had just entered the room. He had the appearance of a man with his back to the wall.

'No!' he was crying. 'No! I'm dashed if I do!'

Webster continued to look at him.

'Why should I?' demanded Lancelot weakly.

Webster's gaze did not flicker.

'Oh, all right,' said Lancelot sullenly.

He passed from the room with leaden feet, and, proceeding upstairs, changed into morning clothes and a top hat. Then, with a gardenia in his buttonhole, he made his way to 11 Maxton Square, where Mrs. Carberry-Pirbright was giving one of her intimate little teas ('just a few friends') to meet Clara Throckmorton Stooge, authoress of *A Strong Man's Kiss*.

Gladys Bingley was lunching at her hotel in Antibes when Worple's telegram arrived. It occasioned her the gravest concern.

Exactly what it was all about she was unable to gather, for emotion had made Bernard Worple rather incoherent. There were moments, reading it, when she fancied that Lancelot had met with a serious accident; others when the solution seemed to be that he had sprained his brain to such an extent that rival lunatic asylums were competing eagerly for his custom; others, again, when Worple appeared to be suggesting that he had gone into partnership with his cat to start a harem. But one fact emerged clearly. Her loved one was in serious trouble of some kind, and his best friends were agreed that only her immediate return could save him.

Gladys did not hesitate. Within half an hour of the receipt of the telegram she had packed her trunk, removed a piece of asparagus from her right eyebrow, and was negotiating for accommodation on the first train going north.

Arriving in London, her first impulse was to go straight to Lancelot. But a natural feminine curiosity urged her, before doing so, to call upon Bernard Worple and have light thrown on some of the more abstruse passages in the telegram.

Worple, in his capacity of author, may have tended towards

obscurity, but, when confining himself to the spoken word, he told a plain story well and clearly. Five minutes of his society enabled Gladys to obtain a firm grasp on the salient facts, and there appeared on her face that grim, tight-lipped expression which is seen only on the faces of fiancées who have come back from a short holiday to discover that their dear one has been straying in their absence from the straight and narrow path.

'Brenda Carberry-Pirbright, eh?' said Gladys, with ominous calm. 'I'll give him Brenda Carberry-Pirbright! My gosh, if one can't go off to Antibes for the merest breather without having one's betrothed getting it up his nose and starting to act like a Mormon Elder, it begins to look a pretty tough world for a girl.'

Kind-hearted Bernard Worple did his best.

'I blame the cat,' he said. 'Lancelot, to my mind, is more sinned against than sinning. I consider him to be acting under undue influence or duress.'

'How like a man!' said Gladys. 'Shoving it all off on to an innocent cat!'

'Lancelot says it has a sort of something in its eye.'

'Well, when I meet Lancelot,' said Gladys, 'he'll find that I have a sort of something in my eye.'

She went out, breathing flame quietly through her nostrils. Worple, saddened, heaved a sigh and resumed his neo-Vorticist sculpting.

It was some five minutes later that Gladys, passing through Maxton Square on her way to Bott Street, stopped suddenly in her tracks. The sight she had seen was enough to make any fiancée do so.

Along the pavement leading to No. 11 two figures were advancing. Or three, if you counted a morose-looking dog of a semi-dachshund nature which preceded them, attached to a leash. One of the figures was that of Lancelot Mulliner, natty in grey herringbone tweed and a new Homburg hat. It was he who held the leash. The other Gladys recognized from the portrait which she had seen on Lancelot's easel as that modern Du Barry, that notorious wrecker of homes and breaker-up of love-nests, Brenda Carberry-Pirbright.

The next moment they had mounted the steps of No. 11, and had gone in to tea, possibly with a little music.

It was perhaps an hour and a half later that Lancelot, having wrenched himself with difficulty from the lair of the Philistines, sped homeward in a swift taxi. As always after an extended *tête-à-tête* with Miss Carberry-Pirbright, he felt dazed and bewildered, as if he had been swimming in a sea of glue and had swallowed a great deal of it. All he could think of clearly was that he wanted a drink and that the materials for the drink were in the cupboard behind the chesterfield of his studio.

He paid the cab and charged in with his tongue rattling dryly against his front teeth. And there before him was Gladys Bingley, whom he had supposed far, far away.

'You!' exclaimed Lancelot.

'Yes, me!' said Gladys.

Her long vigil had not helped to restore the girl's equanimity. Since arriving at the studio she had had leisure to tap her foot three thousand, one hundred and forty-two times on the carpet, and the number of bitter smiles which had flitted across her face was nine hundred and eleven. She was about ready for the battle of the century.

She rose and faced him, all the woman in her flashing from her eyes.

'Well, you Casanova!' she said.

'You who?' said Lancelot.

'Don't you say "Yoo-hoo!" to me!' cried Gladys. 'Keep that for your Brenda Carberry-Pirbright. Yes, I know all about it, Lancelot Don Juan Henry the Eighth Mulliner! I saw you with her just now. I hear that you and she are inseparable. Bernard Worple says you said you were going to marry her.'

'You mustn't believe everything a neo-Vorticist sculptor tells you,' quavered Lancelot.

'I'll bet you're going back to dinner there tonight,' said Gladys.

She had spoken at a venture, basing the charge purely on a possessive cock of the head which she had noticed in Brenda Carberry-Pirbright at their recent encounter. There, she had said to herself at the time, had gone a girl who was about to invite – or had just invited – Lancelot Mulliner to dine quietly and take her to the pictures afterwards. But the shot went home. Lancelot hung his head.

'There was some talk of it,' he admitted.

'Ah!' exclaimed Gladys.

Lancelot's eyes were haggard.

'I don't want to go,' he pleaded. 'Honestly, I don't. But Webster insists.'

'Webster!'

'Yes, Webster. If I attempt to evade the appointment, he will sit in front of me and look at me.'

'Tchah!'

'Well, he will. Ask him for yourself.'

Gladys tapped her foot six times in rapid succession on the carpet, bringing the total to three thousand, one hundred and forty-eight. Her manner had changed and was now dangerously calm.

'Lancelot Mulliner,' she said, 'you have your choice. Me, on the one hand, Brenda Carberry-Pirbright on the other. I offer you a home where you will be able to smoke in bed, spill the ashes on the floor, wear pyjamas and carpet slippers all day and shave only on Sunday mornings. From her, what have you to hope? A house in South Kensington – possibly the Brompton Road – probably with her mother living with you. A life that will be one long round of stiff collars and tight shoes, of morning coats and top hats.'

Lancelot quivered, but she went on remorselessly.

'You will be at home on alternate Thursdays, and will be expected to hand the cucumber sandwiches. Every day you will air the dog, till you become a confirmed dog-airer. You will dine out in Bayswater and go for the summer to Bournemouth or Dinard. Choose well, Lancelot Mulliner! I will leave you to think it over. But one last word. If by seven-thirty on the dot you have not presented yourself at 6a Garbidge Mews ready to take me out to dinner at the Ham and Beef, I shall know what to think and shall act accordingly.'

And brushing the cigarette ashes from her chin, the girl strode haughtily from the room.

'Gladys!' cried Lancelot.

But she had gone.

For some minutes Lancelot Mulliner remained where he was, stunned. Then, insistently, there came to him the recollection that he had not had that drink. He rushed to the cupboard and produced the bottle. He uncorked it, and was pouring out a lavish stream, when a movement on the floor below him attracted his attention.

Webster was standing there, looking up at him. And in his eyes was that familiar expression of quiet rebuke.

'Scarcely what I have been accustomed to at the Deanery,' he seemed to be saying.

Lancelot stood paralysed. The feeling of being bound hand and foot, of being caught in a snare from which there was no escape, had become more poignant than ever. The bottle fell from his nerveless fingers and rolled across the floor, spilling its contents in an amber river, but he was too heavy in spirit to notice it. With a gesture such as Job might have made on discovering a new boil, he crossed to the window and stood looking moodily out.

Then, turning with a sigh, he looked at Webster again – and, looking, stood spellbound.

The spectacle which he beheld was of a kind to stun a stronger man than Lancelot Mulliner. At first, he shrank from believing his eyes. Then, slowly, came the realization that what he saw was no mere figment of a disordered imagination. This unbelievable thing was actually happening.

Webster sat crouched upon the floor beside the widening pool of whisky. But it was not horror and disgust that had caused him to crouch. He was crouched because, crouching, he could get nearer to the stuff and obtain crisper action. His tongue was moving in and out like a piston.

And then abruptly, for one fleeting instant, he stopped lapping and glanced up at Lancelot, and across his face there flitted a quick smile – so genial, so intimate, so full of jovial camaraderie, that the young man found himself automatically smiling back, and not only smiling but winking. And in answer to that wink Webster winked too – a whole-hearted, roguish wink that said as plainly as if he had spoken the words:

'How long has this been going on?'

Then with a slight hiccough he turned back to the task of getting his drink before it soaked into the floor.

Into the murky soul of Lancelot Mulliner there poured a sudden flood of sunshine. It was as if a great burden had been lifted from his shoulders. The intolerable obsession of the last two weeks had ceased to oppress him, and he felt a free man. At the eleventh hour the reprieve had come. Webster, that seeming pillar of austere virtue, was one of the boys, after all. Never again would Lancelot quail beneath his eye. He had the goods on him.

Webster, like the stag at eve, had now drunk his fill. He had left the pool of alcohol and. was walking round in slow, meditative circles. From time to time he mewed tentatively, as if he were trying to say 'British Constitution'. His failure to articulate the syllables appeared to tickle him, for at the end of each attempt he would utter a slow, amused chuckle. It was about this moment that he suddenly broke into a rhythmic dance, not unlike the old Saraband.

It was an interesting spectacle, and at any other time Lancelot would have watched it raptly. But now he was busy at his desk, writing a brief note to Mrs Carberry-Pirbright, the burden of which was that if she thought he was coming within a mile of her foul house that night or any other night she had vastly underrated the dodging powers of Lancelot Mulliner.

And what of Webster? The Demon Rum now had him in an iron grip. A lifetime of abstinence had rendered him a ready victim to the fatal fluid. He had now reached the stage when geniality gives way to belligerence. The rather foolish smile had gone from his face, and in its stead there lowered a fighting frown. For a few moments he stood on his hind legs, looking about him for a suitable adversary: then, losing all vestiges of self-control, he ran five times round the room at a high rate of speed and, falling foul of a small footstool, attacked it with the utmost ferocity, sparing neither tooth nor claw.

But Lancelot did not see him. Lancelot was not there. Lancelot was out in Bott Street, hailing a cab.

'6A Garbidge Mews, Fulham,' said Lancelot to the driver.

THE YELLOW TERROR

W. L. Alden

'SPEAKING OF CATS,' said Captain Foster, 'I'm free to say that I don't like 'em. I don't care to be looked down on by any person, whether he be man or cat. I know I ain't the President of the United States, nor yet a millionaire, nor yet the Boss of New York, but all the same I calculate that I'm a man, and entitled to be treated as such. Now, I never knew a cat yet that didn't look down on me, same as cats do on everybody. A cat considers that men are just dirt under his or her paws, as the case may be. I can't see what it is that makes a cat believe that he is so everlastingly superior to all the men that have ever lived, but there's no denying the fact that such is his belief, and he acts accordingly. There was a Professor here one day, lecturing on all sorts of animals, and I asked him if he could explain this aggravating conduct of cats. He said that it was because cats used to be gods, thousands of years ago in the land of Egypt; but I didn't believe him. Egypt is a Scripture country, and consequently we ought not to believe anything about it that we don't read in the Bible. Show me anywhere in the Bible that Egyptian cats are mentioned as having practised as gods, and I'll believe it. Till you show it to me, I'll take the liberty of disbelieving any worldly statements that Professors or anybody else may make about Egypt.

'The most notorious cat I ever met was old Captain Smedley's Yellow Terror. His real legal name was just plain Tom: but being yellow, and being a holy terror in many respects, it got to be the fashion among his acquaintances to call him "The Yellow Terror".

He was a tremendous big cat, and he had been with Captain Smedley for five years before I saw him.

'Smedley was one of the best men I ever knew. I'll admit that he was a middling hard man on his sailors, so that his ship got the reputation of being a slaughter-house, which it didn't really deserve. And there is no denying that he was a very religious man, which was another thing which made him unpopular with the men. I'm a religious man myself, even when I'm at sea, but I never held with serving out religion to a crew, and making them swallow it with belaying pins. That's what old Smedley used to do. He was in command of the barque *Medford*, out of Boston, when I knew him. I mean the city of Boston in Massachusetts, and not the little town that folks over in England call Boston: and I must say that I can't see why they should copy the names of our cities, no matter how celebrated they may be. Well! The *Medford* used to sail from Boston to London with grain, where she discharged her cargo and loaded again for China. On the outward passage we used to stop at Madeira, and the Cape, and generally Bangkok, and so on to Canton, where we filled up with tea, and then sailed for home direct.

'Now thishyer Yellow Terror had been on the ship's books for upwards of five years when I first met him. Smedley had him regularly shipped, and signed his name to the ship articles, and held a pen in his paw while he made a cross, same as if he had been a Dago. You see, in those days the underwriters wouldn't let a ship go to sea without a cat, so as to keep the rats from getting at the cargo. I don't know what a land cat may do, but there ain't a seafaring cat that would look at a rat. What with the steward, and the cook and the men forrard, being always ready to give the ship's cat a bite, the cat is generally full from kelson to deck, and wouldn't take the trouble to speak to a rat, unless one was to bite her tail. But, then, underwriters never know anything about what goes on at sea, and it's a shame that a sailorman should be compelled to give in to their ideas. The Yellow Terror had the general idea that the *Medford* was his private yacht, and that all hands were there to wait on him. And Smedley sort of confirmed him in that idea, by treating him with more respect than he treated his owners, when he was ashore. I don't blame the cat,

and after I got to know what sort of a person the cat really was, I can't say as I blamed Smedley to any great extent.

'Tom, which I think I told you was the cat's real name, was far and away the best fighter of all cats in Europe, Asia, Africa, and America. Whenever we sighted land he would get himself up in his best fur, spending hours brushing and polishing it, and biting his claws so as to make sure that they were as sharp as they could be made. As soon as the ship was made fast to the quay, or anchored in the harbour, the Yellow Terror went ashore to look for trouble. He always got it too, though he had such a reputation as a fighter, that whenever he showed himself, every cat that recognised him broke for cover. Why, the gatekeeper at the London Docks – I mean the one at the Shadwell entrance – told me that he always knew when the *Medford* was warping into dock, by the stream of cats that went out of the gate, as if a pack of hounds were after them. You see that as soon as the *Medford* was reported, and word passed among the cats belonging to the ships in dock that the Yellow Terror had arrived, they judged that it was time for them to go ashore, and stop till the *Medford* should sail. Whitechapel used to be regularly overflowed with cats, and the newspapers used to have letters from scientific chaps trying to account for what they called the wave of cats that had spread over East London.

'I remember that once we laid alongside of a Russian brig, down in the basin by Old Gravel Lane. There was a tremendous big black cat sitting on the poop, and as soon as he caught sight of our Tom, he sung out to him, remarking that he was able and ready to wipe the deck up with him at any time. We all understood that the Russian was a new arrival who hadn't ever heard of the Yellow Terror, and we knew that he was, as the good book says, rushing on his fate. Tom was sitting on the rail near the mizzen rigging when the Russian made his remarks, and he didn't seem to hear them. But presently we saw him going slowly aloft till he reached our cross-jack yard. He laid out on the yard arm till he was near enough to jump on to the mainyard of the Russian, and the first thing that the Russian cat knew Tom landed square on his back. The fight didn't last more than one round, and at the end of that, the remains of the

Russian cat sneaked behind a water cask, and the Yellow Terror came back by the way of the crossjack yard and went on fur brushing, as if nothing had happened.

'When Tom went ashore in a foreign port he generally stopped ashore till we sailed. A few hours before we cast off hawsers, Tom would come aboard. He always knew when we were going to sail, and he never once got left. I remember one time when we were just getting up anchor in Cape Town harbour, and we all reckoned that this time we should have to sail without Tom, he having evidently stopped ashore just a little too long. But presently alongside comes a boat, with Tom lying back at full length in the sternsheets, for all the world like a drunken sailor who has been delaying the ship, and is proud of it. The boatman said that Tom had come down to the pier and jumped into his boat, knowing that the man would row him off to the ship, and calculating that Smedley would be glad to pay the damage. It's my belief that if Tom hadn't found a boatman, he would have chartered the government launch. He had the cheek to do that or anything else.

'Fighting was really Tom's only vice; and it could hardly be called a vice, seeing as he always licked the other cat, and hardly ever came out of a fight with a torn ear or a black eye. Smedley always said that Tom was religious. I used to think that was rubbish; but after I had been with Tom for a couple of voyages I began to believe what Smedley said about him. Every Sunday when the weather permitted, Smedley used to hold service on the quarter-deck. He was a Methodist, and when it came to ladling out Scripture, or singing a hymn, he could give odds to almost any preacher. All hands, except the man at the wheel, and the lookout, were required to attend service on Sunday morning, which naturally caused considerable grumbling, as the watch below considered they had a right to sleep in peace, instead of being dragged aft for service. But they had to knock under, and what they considered even worse, they had to sing, for the old man kept a bright lookout while the singing was going on, and if he caught any man malingering and not doing his full part of the singing he would have a few words to say to that man with a belaying pin, or a rope's end, after the service was over.

'Now Tom never failed to attend service, and to do his level best to help. He would sit somewhere near the old man and pay attention to what was going on better than I've seen some folks do in first-class churches ashore. When the men sang, Tom would start in and let out a yell here and there, which showed that he meant well even if he had never been to a singing-school, and didn't exactly understand singing according to Gunter. First along, I thought that it was all an accident that the cat came to service, and I calculated that his yelling during the singing meant that he didn't like it. But after a while I had to admit that Tom enjoyed the Sunday service as much as the Captain himself, and I agreed with Smedley that the cat was a thoroughgoing Methodist.

'Now after I'd been with Smedley for about six years, he got married all of a sudden. I didn't blame him, for in the first place it wasn't any of my business; and, in the next place, I hold that a ship's captain ought to have a wife, and the underwriters would be a sight wiser if they insisted that all captains should be married, instead of insisting that all ships should carry cats. You see that if a ship's captain has a wife, he is naturally anxious to get back to her, and have his best clothes mended, and his food cooked to suit him. Consequently he wants to make good passages and he don't want to run the risk of drowning himself, or of getting into trouble with his owners, and losing his berth. You'll find, if you look into it, that

married captains live longer, and get on better than unmarried men, as it stands to reason that they ought to do.

'But it happened that the woman Smedley married was an Agonyostic, which is a sort of person that doesn't believe in anything, except the multiplication table, and such-like human vanities. She didn't lose any time in getting Smedley round to her way of thinking, and instead of being the religious man he used to be, he chucked the whole thing, and used to argue with me by the hour at a time, to prove that religion was a waste of time, and that he hadn't any soul, and had never been created, but had just descended from a family of seafaring monkeys. It made me sick to hear a respectable sailorman talking such rubbish, but of course, seeing as he was my commanding officer, I had to be careful about contradicting him. I wouldn't ever yield an inch to his arguments, and I told him as respectfully as I could, that he was making the biggest mistake of his life. "Why, look at the cat," I used to say, "he's got sense enough to be religious, and if you was to tell him that he was descended from a monkey, he'd consider himself insulted." But it wasn't any use. Smedley was full of his new agonyostical theories, and the more I disagreed with him, the more set he was in his way.

'Of course he knocked off holding Sunday morning services; and the men ought to have been delighted, considering how they used to grumble at having to come aft and sing hymns, when they wanted to be below. But there is no accounting for sailors. They were actually disappointed when Sunday came and there wasn't any service. They said that we should have an unlucky voyage, and that the old man, now that he had got a rich wife, didn't consider sailors good enough to come aft on the quarter-deck, and take a hand in singing. Smedley didn't care for their opinion, but he was some considerable worried about the Yellow Terror. Tom missed the Sunday morning service, and he said so as plain as he could. Every Sunday, for three or four weeks, he came on deck, and took his usual seat near the captain, and waited for the service to begin. When he found out that there was no use in waiting for it, he showed that he disapproved of Smedley's conduct in the strongest way. He gave up being intimate with the old man, and once when Smedley tried to

pat him, and be friendly, he swore at him, and bit him on the leg – not in an angry way, you understand, but just to show his disapproval of Smedley's irreligious conduct.

'When we got to London, Tom never once went ashore, and he hadn't a single fight. He seemed to have lost all interest in worldly things. He'd sit on the poop in a melancholy sort of way, never minding how his fur looked, and never so much as answering if a strange cat sang out to him. After we left London he kept below most of the time, and finally, about the time that we were crossing the line, he took to his bed, as you might say, and got to be as thin and weak as if he had been living in the forecastle of a lime-juicer. And he was that melancholy that you couldn't get him to take an interest in anything. Smedley got to be so anxious about him that he read up in his medical book to try and find out what was the matter with him; and finally made up his mind that the cat had a first-class disease with a big name something like spinal menagerie. That was some little satisfaction to Smedley, but it didn't benefit the cat any; for nothing that Smedley could do would induce Tom to take medicine. He wouldn't so much as sniff at salts, and when Smedley tried to poultice his neck, he considered himself insulted, and roused up enough to take a piece out of the old man's ear.

'About that time we touched at Funchal, and Smedley sent ashore to lay in another tom-cat, thinking that perhaps a fight would brace Tom up a little. But when the new cat was put down alongside of Tom, and swore at him in the most impudent sort of way, Tom just turned over on his other side, and pretended to go asleep. After that we all felt that the Yellow Terror was done for. Smedley sent the new cat ashore again, and told me that Tom was booked for the other world, and that there wouldn't be any more luck for us on that voyage.

'I went down to see the cat, and though he was thin and weak, I couldn't see any signs of serious disease about him. So I says to Smedley that I didn't believe the cat was sick at all.

' "Then what's the matter with him?" says the old man. "You saw yourself that he wouldn't fight, and when he's got to that point I consider that he is about done with this world and its joys and sorrows."

' "His nose is all right," said I. "When I felt it just now it was as cool as a teetotaller's."

' "That does look as if he hadn't any fever to speak of," says Smedley, "and the book says that if you've got spinal menagerie you're bound to have a fever."

' "The trouble with Tom," says I, "is mental: that's what it is. He's got something on his mind that is wearing him out."

' "What can he have on his mind?" says the captain. "He's got everything to suit him aboard this ship. If he was a millionaire he couldn't be better fixed. He won all his fights while we were in Boston, and hasn't had a fight since, which shows that he can't be low-spirited on account of a licking. No, sir! You'll find that Tom's mind is all right."

' "Then what gives him such a mournful look out of his eyes?" says I. "When you spoke to him this morning he looked at you as if he was on the point of crying over your misfortunes – that is to say, if you've got any. Come to think of it, Tom begun to go into thishyer decline just after you were married. Perhaps that's what's the matter with him."

'But there was no convincing Smedley that Tom's trouble was mental, and he was so sure that the cat was going to die, that he got to be about as low-spirited as Tom himself. "I begin to wish," says Smedley to me one morning, "that I was a Methodist again, and believed in a hereafter. It does seem kind of hard that a first-class cat-fighter like Tom shouldn't have a chance when he dies. He was a good religious cat if ever there was one, and I'd like to think that he was going to a better world."

'Just then an idea struck me. "Captain Smedley," says I, "you remember how Tom enjoyed the meetings that we used to have aboard here on Sunday mornings!"

' "He did so," said Smedley. "I never saw a person who took more pleasure in his Sunday privileges than Tom did."

' "Captain Smedley," says I, putting my hand on the old man's sleeve. "All that's the matter with Tom is seeing you deserting the religion that you was brought up in, and turning agonyostical, or whatever you call it. I call it turning plain infidel. Tom's mourning

about your soul, and he's miserable because you don't have any more Sunday morning meetings. I told you the trouble was mental, and now you know it is."

' "Mebbe you're right," says Smedley, taking what I'd said in a peaceable way, instead of flying into a rage, as I expected he would. "To tell you the truth, I ain't so well satisfied in my own mind as I used to be, and I was thinking last night, when I started in to say 'Now I lay me' – just from habit you know – that if I'd stuck to the Methodist persuasion I should be a blamed sight happier than I am now."

' "To-morrow's Sunday," says I, "and if I was you, Captain, I should have the bell rung for service, same as you used to do, and bring Tom up on deck, and let him have the comfort of hearing the rippingest hymns you can lay your hand to. It can't hurt you, and it may do him a heap of good. Anyway, it's worth trying, if you really want the Yellow Terror to get well."

' "I don't mind saying," says Smedley, "that I'd do almost anything to save his life. He's been with me now going on for seven years, and we've never had a hard word. If a Sunday morning meeting will be any comfort to him, he shall have it. Mebbe if it doesn't cure him, it may sort of smooth his hatchway to the tomb."

'Now the very next day was Sunday, and at six the Captain had the bell rung for service, and the men were told to lay aft. The bell hadn't fairly stopped ringing, when Tom comes up the companion way, one step at a time, looking as if he was on his way to his own funeral. He came up to his usual place alongside of the capstan, and lay down on his side at the old man's feet, and sort of looked up at him with what anybody would have said was a grateful look. I could see that Smedley was feeling pretty serious. He understood what the cat wanted to say, and when he started in to give out a hymn, his voice sort of choked. It was a ripping good hymn, with a regular hurricane chorus, and the men sung it for all they were worth, hoping that it would meet Tom's views. He was too weak to join in with any of his old-time yells, but he sort of flopped the deck with his tail, and you could see he was enjoying it down to the ground.

'Well, the service went on just as it used to do in old times, and

Smedley sort of warmed up as it went along, and by and by he'd got the regular old Methodist glow on his face. When it was all through, and the men had gone forrard again, Smedley stooped down, and picked up Tom, and kissed him, and the cat nestled up in the old man's neck and licked his chin. Smedley carried Tom down into the saloon, and sung out to the steward to bring some fresh meat. The cat turned to and ate as good a dinner as he'd ever eaten in his best days, and after he was through, he went into Smedley's own cabin, and curled up in the old man's bunk, and went to sleep purring fit to take the deck off. From that day Tom improved steadily, and by the time we got to Cape Town he was well enough to go ashore, though he was still considerable weak. I went ashore at the same time, and kept an eye on Tom, to see what he would do. I saw him pick out a small measly-looking cat, that couldn't have stood up to a full-grown mouse, and lick him in less than a minute. Then I knew that Tom was all right again, and I admired his judgment in picking out a small cat that was suited to his weak condition. By the time that we got to Canton, Tom was as well in body and mind as he had ever been; and when we sailed, he came aboard with two inches of his tail missing, and his starboard ear carried away, but he had the air of having licked all creation, which I don't doubt he had done, that is to say, so far as all creation could be found in Canton.

'I never heard any more of Smedley's agonyostical nonsense. He went back to the Methodists again, and he always said that Tom had been the blessed means of showing him the error of his ways. I heard that when he got back to Boston, he gave Mrs Smedley notice that he expected her to go to the Methodist meeting with him every Sunday, and that if she didn't, he should consider that it was a breach of wedding articles, and equivalent to mutiny. I don't know how she took it, or what the consequences were, for I left the *Medford* just then, and took command of a barque that traded between Boston and the West Indies. And I never heard of the Yellow Terror after that voyage, though I often thought of him, and always held that for a cat he was the ablest cat, afloat or ashore, that any man ever met.'

PARTICULARLY CATS

Doris Lessing

I CAME TO LIVE in a house in cat country. The houses are old and they have narrow gardens with walls. Through our back windows show a dozen walls one way, a dozen walls the other, of all sizes and levels. Trees, grass, bushes. There is a little theatre that has roofs at various heights. Cats thrive here. There are always cats on the walls, roofs, and in the gardens, living a complicated secret life, like the neighbourhood lives of children that go on according to unimagined private rules the grown-ups never guess at.

I knew there would be a cat in the house. Just as one knows, if a house is too large people will come and live in it, so certain houses must have cats. But for a while I repelled the various cats that came sniffing around to see what sort of a place it was.

During the whole of that dreadful winter of 1962, the garden and the roof over the back verandah were visited by an old black-and-white tom. He sat in the slushy snow on the roof; he prowled over the frozen ground; when the back door was briefly opened, he sat just outside, looking into the warmth. He was most unbeautiful, with a white patch over one eye, a torn ear, and a jaw always a little open and drooling. But he was not a stray. He had a good home in the street, and why he didn't stay there, no one seemed able to say.

That winter was further education into the extraordinary voluntary endurances of the English.

These houses are mostly L.C.C. owned, and by the first week of the cold, the pipes had burst and frozen, and people were waterless.

The system stayed frozen. The authorities opened a main on the street corner, and for weeks the women of the street made journeys to fetch water in jugs and cans along pavements heaped with feet of icy slush, in their house slippers. The slippers were for warmth. The slush and ice were not cleared off the pavement. They drew water from the tap, which broke down several times, and said there had been no hot water but what they boiled on the stove for one week, two weeks – then three, four and five weeks. There was, of course, no hot water for baths. When asked why they didn't complain, since after all they paid rent, they paid for water hot and cold, they replied the L.C.C. knew about their pipes, but did not do anything. The L.C.C. had pointed out there was a cold spell; they agreed with this diagnosis. Their voices were lugubrious, but they were deeply fulfilled, as this nation is when suffering entirely avoidable acts of God.

In the shop at the corner an old man, a middle-aged woman and a small child spent the days of that winter. The shop was chilled colder even than the below-zero weather nature was ordaining, by the refrigeration units; the door was always open into the iced snowdrifts outside the shop. There was no heating at all. The old man got pleurisy and went to hospital for two months. Permanently weakened, he had to sell the shop that spring. The child sat on the cement floor and cried steadily from the cold, and was slapped by its mother who stood behind the counter in a light wool dress, man's socks and a thin cardigan, saying how awful it all was, while her eyes and nose ran and her fingers swelled into chilblains. The old man next door who works as a market porter slipped on the ice outside his front door, hurt his back, and was for weeks on unemployment pay. In that house, which held nine or ten people, including two children, there was one bar of electric fire to fight the cold. Three people went to hospital, one with pneumonia.

And the pipes stayed burst, sealed in jagged stalactites of ice; the pavements remained ice slides; and the authorities did nothing. In middle-class streets, of course, snow was cleared as it fell, and the authorities responded to angry citizens demanding their rights and threatening lawsuits. In our area, people suffered it out until the spring.

Surrounded by human beings as winterbound as if they were cave dwellers of ten thousand years ago, the peculiarities of an old tomcat who chose an icy roof to spend its nights on lost their force.

In the middle of that winter, friends were offered a kitten. Friends of theirs had a Siamese cat, and she had a litter by a street cat. The hybrid kittens were being given away. Their flat is minute, and they both worked all day; but when they saw the kitten, they could not resist. During its first weekend it was fed on tinned lobster soup and chicken mousse, and it disrupted their much-married nights because it had to sleep under the chin, or at least, somewhere against the flesh, of H., the man. S., his wife, announced on the telephone that she was losing the affections of her husband to a cat, just like the wife in Colette's tale. On Monday they went off to work leaving the kitten by itself, and when they came home it was crying and sad, having been alone all day. They said they were bringing it to us. They did.

The kitten was six weeks old. It was enchanting, a delicate fairy-tale cat, whose Siamese genes showed in the shape of the face, ears, tail, and the subtle lines of its body. Her back was tabby: from above or the back, she was a pretty tabby kitten, in grey and cream. But her front and stomach were a smoky-gold, Siamese cream, with half-bars of black at the neck. Her face was pencilled with black – fine dark rings around the eyes, fine dark streaks on her cheeks, a tiny cream-coloured nose with a pink tip, outlined in black. From the

front, sitting with her slender paws straight, she was an exotically beautiful beast. She sat, a tiny thing, in the middle of a yellow carpet, surrounded by five worshippers, not at all afraid of us. Then she stalked around that floor of the house, inspecting every inch of it, climbed up on to my bed, crept under the fold of a sheet, and was at home.

S. went off with H. saying: Not a moment too soon, otherwise I wouldn't have a husband at all.

And he went off groaning, saying that nothing could be as exquisite as being woken by the delicate touch of a pink tongue on his face.

The kitten went, or rather hopped, down the stairs, each of which was twice her height: first front paws, then flop, with the back; front paws, then flop with the back. She inspected the ground floor, refused the tinned food offered to her, and demanded a dirt box by mewing for it. She rejected wood shavings, but torn newspaper was acceptable, so her fastidious pose said, if there was nothing else. There wasn't: the earth outside was frozen solid.

She would not eat tinned cat food. She would not. And I was not going to feed her lobster soup and chicken. We compromised on some minced beef.

She has always been as fussy over her food as a bachelor gourmet. She gets worse as she gets older. Even as a kitten she could express annoyance, or pleasure, or a determination to sulk, by what she ate, half-ate, or chose to refuse. Her food habits are an eloquent language.

But I think it is just possible she was taken away from her mother too young. If I might respectfully suggest it to the cat experts, it is possible they are wrong when they say a kitten may leave its mother the day it turns six weeks old. This cat was six weeks, not a day more, when it was taken from its mother. The basis of her dandyism over food is the neurotic hostility and suspicion towards it of a child with food problems. She had to eat, she supposed; she did eat; but she has never eaten with enjoyment, for the sake of eating. And she shares another characteristic with people who have not had enough mother-warmth. Even now she will instinctively creep under the fold of a newspaper, or into a box or a basket – anything

that shelters, anything that covers. More; she is overready to see insult; overready to sulk. And she is a frightful coward.

Kittens who are left with their mother seven or eight weeks eat easily, and they have confidence. But of course, they are not as interesting.

As a kitten, this cat never slept on the outside of the bed. She waited until I was in it, then she walked all over me, considering possibilities. She would get right down into the bed, by my feet, or on to my shoulder, or crept under the pillow. If I moved too much, she huffily changed quarters, making her annoyance felt.

When I was making the bed, she was happy to be made into it; and stayed, visible as a tiny lump, quite happily, sometimes for hours, between the blankets. If you stroked the lump, it purred and mewed. But she would not come out until she had to.

The lump would move across the bed, hesitate at the edge. There might be a frantic mew as she slid to the floor. Dignity disturbed, she licked herself hastily, glaring yellow eyes at the viewers, who made a mistake if they laughed. Then, every hair conscious of itself, she walked to some centre stage.

Time for the fastidious pernickety eating. Time for the earth box, as exquisite a performance. Time for setting the creamy fur in order. And time for play, which never took place for its own sake, but only when she was being observed.

She was as arrogantly aware of herself as a pretty girl who has no attributes but her prettiness: body and face always posed according to some inner monitor – a pose which is as good as a mask: no, no, this is what I am, the aggressive breasts, the sullen hostile eyes always on the watch for admiration.

Cat, at the age when, if she were human, she would be wearing clothes and hair like weapons, but confident that any time she chose she might relapse into indulged childhood again, because the role had become too much of a burden – cat posed and princessed and preened about the house and then, tired, a little peevish, tucked herself into the fold of a newspaper or behind a cushion, and watched the world safely from there.

Her prettiest trick, used mostly for company, was to lie on her back under a sofa and pull herself along by her paws, in fast sharp rushes, stopping to turn her elegant little head sideways, yellow eyes narrowed, waiting for applause. 'Oh beautiful kitten! Delicious beast! Pretty cat!' Then on she went for another display.

Or, on the right surface, the yellow carpet, a blue cushion, she lay on her back and slowly rolled, paws tucked up, head back, so that her creamy chest and stomach were exposed, marked faintly, as if she were a delicate subspecies of leopard, with black blotches, like the roses of leopards. 'Oh beautiful kitten, oh you are so beautiful.' And she was prepared to go on until the compliments stopped.

Or she sat on the back verandah, not on the table, which was unadorned, but on a little stand that had narcissus and hyacinth in earthenware pots. She sat posed between spikes of blue and white flowers, until she was noticed and admired. Not only by us, of course; also by the old rheumatic tom who prowled, grim reminder of a much harder life, around the garden where the earth was still frostbound. He saw a pretty half-grown cat, behind glass. She saw him. She lifted her head, this way, that way; bit off a fragment of hyacinth, dropped it; licked her fur, negligently; then with an insolent backwards glance, leaped down and came indoors and out of his sight. Or, on the way upstairs, on an arm or a shoulder, she would glance out of the window and see the poor old beast, so still that sometimes we thought he must have died and been frozen there. When the sun warmed a little at midday and he sat licking himself, we were relieved. Sometimes she sat watching him from the window, but her life was still to be tucked into the arms, beds, cushions, and corners of human beings.

Then the spring came, the back door was opened, the dirt box, thank goodness, made unnecessary, and the back garden became her territory. She was six months old, fully grown, from the point of view of nature.

She was so pretty then, so perfect; more beautiful even than that cat who, all those years ago, I swore could never have an equal. Well of course there hasn't been; for that cat's nature was all tact, delicacy, warmth and grace – so, as the fairy tales and the old wives say, she had to die young.

Our cat, the princess, was, still is, beautiful, but, there is no glossing it, she's a selfish beast.

The cats lined up on the garden walls. First, the sombre old winter cat, king of the back gardens. Then, a handsome black-and-white from next door, his son, from the look of it. A battle-scarred tabby. A grey-and-white cat who was so certain of defeat that he never came down from the wall. And a dashing tigerish young tom that she clearly admired. No use, the old king had not been defeated. When she strolled out, tail erect, apparently ignoring them all, but watching the handsome young tiger, he leaped down towards her, but the winter cat had only to stir where he lay on the wall, and the young cat jumped back to safety. This went on for weeks.

Meanwhile, H. and S. came to visit their lost pet. S. said how frightful and unfair it was that the princess could not have her choice; and H. said that was entirely as it should be: a princess must have a king, even if he was old and ugly. He has such dignity, said H.; he has such presence; and he had earned the pretty young cat because of his noble endurance of the long winter.

By then the ugly cat was called Mephistopheles. In his own home, we heard, he was called Billy. Our cat had been called various names, but none of them stuck. Melissa and Franny; Marilyn and Sappho; Circe and Ayesha and Suzette. But in conversation, in love-talk, she miaowed and purred and throated in response to the long-drawn-out syllables of adjectives – beeecooti-ful, delicious puss.

On a very hot weekend, the only one, I seem to remember, in a nasty summer, she came in heat.

H. and S. came to lunch on the Sunday, and we sat on the back verandah and watched the choices of nature. Not ours. And not our cat's, either.

For two nights the fighting had gone on, awful fights, cats wailing and howling and screaming in the garden. Meanwhile grey puss had sat on the bottom of my bed, watching into the dark, ears lifting and moving, tail commenting, just slightly at the tip.

On that Sunday, there was only Mephistopheles in sight. Grey cat was rolling in ecstasy all over the garden. She came to us and rolled around our feet and bit them. She rushed up and down the tree at the bottom of the garden. She rolled and cried, and called, and invited.

'The most disgraceful exhibition of lust I've ever seen,' said S. watching H., who was in love with our cat.

'Oh poor cat,' said H. 'If I were Mephistopheles I'd never treat you so badly.'

'Oh, H.,' said S., 'you are disgusting, if I told people they'd never believe it. But I've always said, you're disgusting.'

'So that's what you've always said,' said H., caressing the ecstatic cat.

It was a very hot day, we had a lot of wine for lunch, and the love play went on all afternoon.

Finally, Mephistopheles leaped down off the wall to where grey cat was wriggling and rolling – but alas, he bungled it.

'Oh my God,' said H., genuinely suffering. 'It is really not forgivable, that sort of thing.'

S., anguished, watched the torments of our cat, and doubted, frequently, dramatically and loudly, whether sex was worth it. 'Look at it,' said she, 'that's us. That's what we're like.'

'That's not at all what we're like,' said H. 'It's Mephistopheles. He should be shot.'

Shoot him at once, we all said; or at least lock him up so that the young tiger from next door could have his chance.

But the handsome young cat was not visible.

We went on drinking wine; the sun went on shining; our princess danced, rolled, rushed up and down the tree, and, when at last things went well, was clipped again and again by the old king.

'All that's wrong,' said H., 'is that he's too old for her.'

'Oh my God,' said S., 'I'm going to take you home. Because if I don't, I swear you'll make love to that cat yourself.'

'Oh I wish I could,' said H. 'What an exquisite beast, what a lovely creature, what a princess, she's wasted on a cat, I can't stand it.'

Next day winter returned; the garden was cold and wet; and grey cat had returned to her fastidious disdainful ways. And the old king lay on the garden wall in the slow English rain, still victor of them all, waiting.

COME, LOVELY CAT

Charles Baudelaire

Come, lovely cat, and rest upon my heart,
   And let my gaze dive in the cold
Live pools of thine enchanted eyes that dart
   Metallic rays of green and gold.

My fascinated hands caress at leisure
   Thy head and supple back, and when
Thy soft electric body fills with pleasure
   My thrilled and drunken fingers, then

Thou changest to my woman; for her glance,
   Like thine, most lovable of creatures,
Is icy, deep, and cleaving as a lance.

   And round her hair and sphinx-like features
And round her dusky form float, vaguely blent,
   A subtle air and dangerous scent.

THE FAT OF THE CAT

Gottfried Keller

I

In Seldwyla, when someone has made a bad bargain, people say, 'He has tried to buy the fat off the cat!' It is a queer saying and a puzzling one. But there is an old, half-forgotten story which tells how it first came to be used and what it really means.

Several hundred years ago, so runs the tale, there lived in Seldwyla an old, old lady whose only companion was a handsome grey cat. This fine creature was always to be seen with his mistress; he was quiet and clever, and never harmed anyone who let him alone. 'Everything in moderation' was his motto – everything, that is, except hunting, which was his one great enjoyment. But even in this sport he was never savage or cruel. He caught and killed only the most impudent and troublesome mice; the others he merely chased away. He left the small circle in which he hunted only once in a while, when some particularly bold mouse roused his anger. Then there was no stopping him! He would follow the foolhardy nibbler everywhere. And if the mouse tried to hide at some neighbour's place, the cat would walk up to the owner, make a deep bow and politely ask permission to hunt there. And you may be sure he was always allowed to do so, for he never disturbed anything in the house. He did not knock over the butter-crocks, never stole milk from pails, never sprang up on the sides of ham which hung against the wall. He went about his business very quietly, very carefully; and, after he had captured his mouse, disappeared

just as quietly as he came. He was neither naughty nor wild, but friendly to everyone. He never ran away from well-behaved children and allowed them to pinch his ears a little without scratching them. Even when stupid people annoyed him, he would simply get out of their way or thump them over the hand if they tried to take liberties with him.

Glassy – for this was the name that was given him on account of his smooth and shiny fur – lived his days happily in comfort and modesty. He did not sit on his mistress's shoulder just to snatch a piece of food from her fork, but only when he saw that it pleased her to have him there. He was neither selfish nor lazy, but only too happy to go walking with his mistress along the little river that flowed into the lake near by. He did not sleep the whole day long on his warm pillow behind the stove. Instead, he loved to lie wide-awake, thinking out his plans, at the foot of the stairs, or prowling along the edge of the roof, considering the ways of the world like the grey-haired philosopher that he was. His calm life was interrupted only in spring, when the violets blossomed, and in autumn, when the warm days of Indian summer imitated Maytime. At such times Glassy would stroll over the roofs like an inspired poet and sing the strangest and most beautiful songs. He had the wildest adventures during these nights, and when he would come home after his reckless wanderings, he looked so rough and towsled that his mistress used to say, 'Glassy, how *can* you behave that way! Aren't you ashamed of yourself?' But Glassy felt no shame; he thought he was now a regular man-of-the-world. Never answering a word, he would sit quietly in his corner, smoothing his fur and washing himself behind the ears, as innocently as if he had never stirred from the fireside.

One day this pleasant manner of life came to an unhappy end. Just as Glassy became a full-grown cat, his mistress died of old age, leaving him an unprotected orphan. It was Glassy's first misfortune, and his piercing cries and long wailing showed how deep was his grief. He followed the funeral part of the way down the street and then returned to the house, wandering helplessly from room to room. But his good sense told him he must serve the heirs of his mistress as faithfully as he did her – he must continue to keep the mice in their place, be ever watchful and ready, and (whenever necessary) give the new owners good advice. But these foolish people would not let Glassy get near them. On the contrary, whenever they saw him, they threw the slippers and the foot-stool of his departed mistress at his bewildered head. After eight days of quarrelling among themselves, they boarded up the windows, closed the house, and – while they went to court to see who really owned it – no one was allowed to set foot inside the doors.

Poor Glassy, thrown into the street, sat on the doorstep of his old home and no one took the slightest notice of him. All day long he sat and he sat and he sat. At night he roamed about the roofs and, at first, he spent a great part of the time hidden and asleep, trying to forget his cares. But hunger drove him to people again, to be at hand whenever there might be a chance of getting a scrap of something to eat. As food grew scarcer, his eyes grew sharper; and, as his whole attention was given to this one thing, he ceased to look like his old self. He ran from door to door and stole about the streets, sometimes pouncing gladly upon a greasy morsel that, in the old days, he would never even have sniffed at. Often, indeed, he found nothing at all. He grew hungrier and thinner from day to day; he who was once so plump and proud became scraggy and timid. All his courage, his dignity, his wisdom and his philosophy vanished. When the boys came from school, he crawled behind a barrel or into an old can, daring to stick his head out only to see whether one of them would throw away a crust of bread. In the old days he could look the fiercest dog straight in the eye, and many was the time he punished them severely. Now he ran away from the commonest cur. And while, in the times gone by, he used to run away from rough and unpleasant people, now he would let them come quite near, not because he liked them any better, but because – who knows? – they might toss him something to chew on. Even when, instead of feeding him, coarse men would strike him or twist his tail, still he would not cry. He would just sit there and look longingly at the hand which had hurt him, but which had such a heavenly smell of sausage or herring.

Wisteria Cat

'He is the graven image of repose and perfect muscular control.'
MORNING GLORY ADOLPHUS

Konstantinopel Market-Cats

'As we called up a tender greeting to them, we saw an expression of horror come over their faces. "Great heavens! Run!"'

MY BOSS THE CAT

Toby's Cat

'To gain the friendship of a cat is not an easy thing . . .
It does not give its affections indiscriminately.'
THE WHITE AND BLACK DYNASTIES

Brush Creek Cat, 1995

'He could content himself for hours at a low window, looking into the ravine and at the great trees, noting the smallest stir there.'

CALVIN, THE CAT

The wise and gentle Glassy had, indeed, come down in the world. He was starving as he sat one day, on his stone, dreaming and blinking in the sunlight. As he lay there, the town-wizard, a sly magician by the name of Pineiss, came that way, noticed the cat and stopped in front of him. Hoping for something good, Glassy sat meekly on his stone, waiting to see what Pineiss would do or say. At the first words, Glassy lost hope, for Pineiss said, 'Well, cat, would you like to sell your fat?' He thought that the magician was only making fun of his skinny appearance. But still he answered demurely, 'Ah, Master Pineiss likes to joke!'

'But I am serious!' the wizard replied, 'I need cat's fat in my witchery; I work wonders with it. But it must be taken only if the cat is willing to give it – otherwise the magic will not work. I am thinking if ever a cat was in a position to make a good bargain, you're the very one! Come into my service; I'll feed you as you never have been fed. I'll give you the richest of warm milk and the sweetest of cakes. You will grow fat as a dumpling on juicy sausages, chicken livers and roast quail. On my enormous roof – which is well known as the greatest hunting-ground in the world for cats – there are hundreds of interesting corners and inviting dark holes. And there, on the top of that old roof, there grows a wonderful grass, green as an emerald. When you play in it, you will think you are a tiger in the jungle, and – if you have eaten too many rich things – a few nibbles of it will cure the worst stomach-ache. My mice are the tenderest – and the slowest – in the country, and catnip grows in the back of my garden. Thus, you see, *you* will be happy and healthy, and *I* will have a good supply of useful fat. What do you say?'

Glassy had listened to this speech with ears pricked up and his mouth watering. But he was so weak that he did not quite understand the bargain, and he said, 'That isn't half bad, Master Pineiss. If I only understood how I could hold on to my reward! If I have to lose my life to give you my fat, how am I to enjoy all these fine things when I am dead?'

'Hold on to your reward?' answered the magician, impatiently. 'Your reward is in the enjoyment of all you can eat and drink *while* you are alive. That ought to be clear enough. But I don't want to force you!' And he shrugged his shoulders and made as if he were going to walk off.

But Glassy cried, quickly and eagerly, 'Wait! Wait! I will say yes on one condition. You must wait a few days *after* I have reached my roundest and fattest fullness before you take my life: I must have a little time so that I am not torn away too suddenly when I am so happy, so full of food and contentment.'

'So be it!' said Pineiss with seeming generosity. 'Until the next full-moon you shall enjoy yourself as much as you like. But it cannot last a minute longer than that. For, when the moon begins to wane, the fat will grow less powerful and my well-earned property will shrink.'

So they came to an agreement. Pineiss disappeared for a moment. Then he came running back with a great quill-pen and an enormous roll of paper. This was the contract, and it was so large because it was full of queer words that lawyers are fond of – words like 'whereas' and 'notwithstanding' and 'herinbefore' and '"hereunto' and 'party-of-the-second-part' and others too long and expensive to print here. Without stopping to read it through, Glassy signed his name neatly on the dotted line, which proved how well he had been brought up.

'Now you can come and have lunch with me,' said the magician. 'We dine at twelve, sharp.'

'Thanks,' replied the famished cat, 'I will be pleased to accept your invitation,' and a few minutes before noon he was waiting at the table of Master Pineiss.

From that moment Glassy began to enjoy a wonderful month. He had nothing else to do but to eat all the delicate dishes that were put before him, to watch the magician at work and go climbing about the roof. It was really a most heavenly sort of roof – dark, high and pointed like a steeple – just the sort of a top for a house of magic and mystery.

II

But you should know something about the town-magician. Master Pineiss was a jack-of-all-trades. He did a thousand different things. He cured sick people, removed warts, cleared houses of rats, drove out roaches, pulled teeth, loaned money, and collected bills. He took charge of all the orphans and widows, made black ink out of charcoal and, in his spare time, cut quill-pens, which he sold twelve for a penny. He sold ginger and pepper, candy and axle-grease, shoe-nails and perfume, books and button-hooks, sausages and string. He repaired clocks, extracted corns, painted signs, delivered papers, forecasted the weather, and prepared the farmer's almanac. He did a great many good things in the daytime very cheaply; and, for much higher prices, he did other things (which are not spoken about) after it grew dark. Although he was a magician, his principal business was not witchcraft; he made magic and worked spells only for household use. The people of Seldwyla needed *someone* who would do all sorts of unpleasant jobs and mysterious things for them, so they had elected him town-wizard. And, for many years, Pineiss had worked hard, early and late, to do whatever they wished – and a few things to please himself.

In this house, full of all sorts of curious objects, Glassy had plenty of time to see, smell, and taste everything. Tired out with doing nothing, he lay on large, soft cushions all day long. At first he paid attention to nothing else but eating. He devoured greedily whatever Pineiss offered him and could scarcely wait from one meal to the next. Often, indeed, he ate too much, and then he would have to go and chew the green grass on the roof to be well enough – so he could eat still more. His master was well pleased with this hunger, and thought to himself, 'That cat will soon be round and fat – and the more I give him now the less he will be able to eat later.'

So Pineiss built a little countryside for Glassy. He planted a tiny forest of a dozen baby pine-trees, made a few hills of stones and moss, and scooped out a hole with water so there would be a lake. In the trees he stuck sweet roast finches, stuffed larks, baked sparrows, and small potted pigeons. The hills were full of the most exciting mouse-holes; and inside them Pineiss had hidden more than a hundred juicy mice, which had been fattened on wheat-flour and broiled in bacon. Some of these delicious mice were easily within reach of Glassy's paw; others (to give him more of an appetite) had to be dug for, but all were on strings so that Glassy could play he was chasing without losing them. The little lake was filled with fresh milk every morning and, as Glassy was fond of fishing, young sardines and tender goldfish floated in that delightful pool.

It was Glassy's idea of Paradise, a cat's heaven on earth. He ate and ate and ate. And in between his meals, he nibbled. When he did not eat, he rested. And *how* he slept! It got so that the mice began to gather about his pillow where he lay and mock at him. And Glassy never stirred – not even when their tails whisked across his whiskers! Now that Glassy could eat all he wanted and whenever he wished to, his whole appearance changed. He looked like his old self: his fur became glossy and smooth again, his eyes grew large and fiery, and his mind acted more cleverly than before. He stopped being greedy; he no longer stuffed himself just for the pleasure of eating. He began to think seriously about life in general – and about his own in particular. One day, as he was thoughtfully tearing apart a cooked quail, he saw that the little insides of the bird were packed with unspoilt food. Some green herbs, black and white seeds, a few crumbs, grains of corn and one bright red berry were crowded together – just as tight as a mother packs her boy's lunch-basket when he goes off for the day. As Glassy saw this, he grew still more thoughtful. And the more thoughtful he grew, the sadder he became. At last he began to think out aloud. 'Poor bird,' he said, scratching his head, 'what good did all this fine food do you? You had to search so hard for these crumbs, fly who knows how many miles to find those grains of corn. That red berry was snatched at great risk from the bird-catcher's trap. And all for what? You thought you ate to keep yourself alive, but the fatter you grew, the nearer you came to your end.... Ah, me,' he sighed deeply, 'why did I ever make such a wretched bargain! I did not think – I was too foolish with hunger. And now that I can think again, all I can see is

that I will end like this poor quail. When I am fat enough, I will have to die – for no other reason except that I will be fat enough! A fine end for a lively and intelligent cat-of-the-world! Oh, if I could only get out of this fix!'

He kept on brooding and worrying, yet he could think of no way to escape his fate. But, like a wise man, he controlled himself and his appetite and tried to put off the final day as long as possible. He refused to lie on the great cushions, which Pineiss had placed all over so that he could sleep a great deal and get fat quicker. Instead of soft places, he rested himself on the cold sill or lay down on the hard stones whenever he was tired. Rather than munch the roasted birds and stuffed mice, he began to hunt in earnest on the tall roof-top. And the living mice he caught with his own efforts tasted far better to him than all the rich goodies from Pineiss's kitchen – especially since they did not make him so fat. The constant exercise made him strong and slender – much to Pineiss's astonishment. The magician could not understand how Glassy remained so active and healthy; he expected to see a great clumsy animal that never moved from its pillows and was just one enormous roll of fat.

After some time had passed and Glassy, instead of wallowing in fat, grew still stronger and handsomer without losing his slender figure, Pineiss determined to do something. 'What is the matter, Glassy?' he harshly inquired one day. 'What is wrong with you? Why don't you eat the good things that I prepare for you with such care? Why don't you fetch the roast birds down from the trees? Why don't you dig the dainty broiled mice out of their holes? Why have you stopped fishing in the milky sea? Why don't you take better care of yourself? Why do you refuse to lie on the nice, soft cushions? Why do you wear yourself out instead of resting comfortably and growing good and round?'

'Because, Master Pineiss,' answered Glassy, 'I feel much better this way! I have only a little while to live – and shouldn't I enjoy that short time in the way it suits me?'

'Not at all!' exclaimed Pineiss. 'You should live the sort of life that will make you thick and soft! But I know what you are driving at! You think you'll make a monkey of me and prevent me from doing what we have agreed upon. You think I'll let you go on like this for ever? Don't you believe it! I tell you it is your duty to eat and drink and take care of yourself so that you'll grow layer upon layer of fat! I tell you to stop behaving the way you have been doing! And if you don't act according to the contract, I'll have something still more serious to say!'

Glassy stopped purring (which he had begun only to show how calm he was) and said quietly, 'I don't remember a single word in the contract against my being healthy or living the kind of life I liked. There was nothing in the agreement that did not allow me to eat whatever food I wished, and even chase after it if I cared to! If the town-magician took it for granted that I was a lazy, greedy, good-for-nothing, that is not my fault! You do a thousand good things every day, so do this one also – let us remain good friends as we are. And don't forget that you can only use my fat if you get it by fair means!'

'Stop your chattering!' cried Pineiss angrily. 'Don't you dare to lecture me! Perhaps I had better put an end to you at once!' He seized Glassy sharply, whereupon the surprised cat struck out and scratched him sharply on the hand. Pineiss looked thoughtful for a moment. Then he said, 'Is that the way things are, you beast? Very well. Then I declare that, according to our agreement, I consider you fat enough. I am satisfied with the way you are, and I will act according to the contract. In five days the moon will be full, and until then you can live the way you wish, just as it is written down. You can do exactly as you please until then – and not one minute longer!'

With this, he turned his back and left the cat to his own thoughts.

These thoughts, as you can believe, were painful and gloomy. Was the time really so near when Glassy would have to lose his skin? And, with all his cleverness, was there nothing he could do? What miracle could save him now? Sighing, he climbed up to the roof, whose pointed ridge rose like a threatening sign against the happy autumn sky. It was early evening and the moon began to climb up the other side of the roof. Soon the whole town was

flooded with blue light and a sweet song sounded in Glassy's ears. It was the voice of a snow-white puss whose body was shining like silver on a neighbouring roof. Immediately Glassy forgot the thought of death and answered with his loudest and loveliest notes. Still singing, he hurried to her side and soon was engaged in the most terrific battle with three other gallant cats. After he had defeated his rivals, he turned to his lady, who met his ardent glance with a modest but encouraging miaow.

Glassy was charmed. He remained with the white stranger day and night, and was her devoted slave. Without giving a single thought to Pineiss, he never came home, but remained close to his lady-love. He sang like a nightingale every moonlight night, went on wild hunts with his fair companion, and was in continual fights with other tom-cats who wanted to come too close. Many times he was almost clawed to pieces, many times he was tumbled from the roof; but he only shook his towsled fur and came back to the struggle as hardy as ever. All these adventures – moments of peaceful talk and hours of angry quarrels, love and jealousy, friendship and fights – all of these exciting days made a great change in Glassy. The wild life showed its effects. And finally, when the moon was full, the poor animal looked wilder, tougher and thinner than ever.

At this moment, Pineiss (who had not seen his cat for almost a week) leaned out of the window and cried, 'Glassy, Glassy! Where are you? Don't you know it's time to come home!' And Glassy, leaving his partner, who trotted off contentedly, came back to the magician's house. It was dark as he entered the kitchen and Pineiss came towards him, rustling the paper contract, and saying, 'Come, Glassy, good Glassy.' But as soon as the magician had struck a light and saw the cat sitting there defiantly, nothing but a bundle of bones and ragged hair, he flew into a terrible rage. Jumping up and down with anger, he screamed, 'So that's the way you tried to cheat me! You villain, you ragamuffin! You evil parcel of bones! Wait! I'll show you!' Beside himself with fury, he seized a broom and sprang at Glassy. But the desperate cat was no longer frightened. With his back high in the air, he faced his maddened owner. His hair stood up straight, sparks flew from his green eyes, and his appearance was so terrifying that Pineiss retreated two or three steps. The town-wizard began to be afraid; for it suddenly struck him that this might also be a magician, and a more powerful one than himself. Uncertain and anxious, he asked in a low voice, 'Is the honourable gentleman perhaps in the same profession as myself? Ah, it must be a very learned enchanter who can not only put on the appearance of a cat, but change his size whenever he wishes – large and strong one minute, then suddenly as skinny as a skeleton!'

Glassy calmed himself and spoke honestly. 'No, Master Pineiss, I am no magician. It is nothing but my wildness, my love of life, which has taken away my, I mean your, fat. Let us start over again, and this time I promise you I will eat anything and everything you bring me. Fetch out your longest sausage – and you will see!'

Still angry, Pineiss picked Glassy up by his collar and threw him into the goose-pen, which was empty, and cried, 'Now see if your love of life will help you. Let's see if your wildness is greater than my witchcraft! Now, my plucked bird, you'll remain in your cage – and there you will eat or die!'

Pineiss began at once to broil a huge sausage that had such a heavenly flavour that he himself had to taste it before he stuck it between the bars. Glassy finished it, skin and all, without stopping for breath. And, as he sat comfortably cleaning his whiskers and smoothing his fur, he said to himself, 'Ah, this love of life is a fine thing, after all! Once again it has saved me from a cruel fate. Now I will rest awhile and keep my wits about me. This prison is not so bad, and something good may come of having nothing to do but to think and eat for a change. Everything has its time. Yesterday a little trouble; today a little quiet; tomorrow something different. Yes, life is a very interesting affair.'

Now Pineiss saw to it that no time was wasted. All day long he chopped and seasoned and mixed and boiled and basted and stewed and baked and broiled and roasted and fried. In short, he cooked such delicious meals that Glassy simply could not resist. The delighted cat ate and ate until Pineiss was afraid that there would not be enough left in the house for the smallest mouse to nibble at.

When, finally, Glassy seemed fat enough, Pineiss did not delay a moment. Right in front of his victim's eyes, he set out pots and pans and made a great fire in the stove. Then he sharpened a large knife, lifted the latch of Glassy's cell, pulled the poor cat out (first taking care to lock the kitchen door) and said cheerfully, 'Come, my young friend. Now to business! First, we shall cut your head off; then, when that's done, we shall skin you. Your fur will make a nice warm cap for me and maybe even a pair of gloves. Or shall I skin you first and then cut off your head?'

'No,' answered Glassy meekly, 'if it's the same to you, I 'd rather have my head off first.'

'Right you are, poor fellow,' said Pineiss, putting some more wood on the big fire, 'I don't want to hurt you more than necessary. Let us do only what is right.'

'That is a true saying,' said Glassy' with a deep sigh, and hung his head. 'Oh, if I had only remembered that – if I only had done what was right, I could die with a clear conscience, for I die willingly. But a wrong which I have done makes it hard for me.'

'What sort of a wrong?' asked Pineiss inquisitively.

'Ah, what's the use of talking about it now,' sighed Glassy. 'What's done is done, and it's too late to cry over it.'

'You rascal!' Pineiss went on. 'You must indeed be a wicked scoundrel who richly deserves to die. But what did you really do? Tell me at once! Have you hid anything of mine? Or stolen something? Have you done me a great injury which I know nothing about? Confess your crimes immediately or I'll skin and boil you alive! Will you talk – or die a horrible death?'

'But you don't understand,' said Glassy. 'It isn't anything about you that troubles my conscience. It concerns the ten thousand gold guldens of my poor dear mistress. . . . But what's the sense of talking! Only – when I look at you, I think perhaps it is not too late, after all. When I look at you, I see a handsome man still in the prime of life, wise and active and . . . Tell me, Master Pineiss, have you never cared to marry – to come into a good family and a fortune? But what am I talking about! Such a smart and busy man as you has no time for such idle thoughts. Why should such a learned magician think about silly women! Of course, it's no good denying the fact that a woman is very comforting to have around the house. To be sure, a wife can be a great help to a busy man – obliging in her manner, careful about his tastes, sparing with his money and extravagant only in his praise. A good wife will do a thousand things to please to her husband. When he is downcast, she will make him happy; when he is happy, she will make him happier. She will fetch his slippers when he wants to be comfortable, stroke his beard and kiss him when he wants to be petted. When he is working, she will let nobody disturb him, but go quietly about her household duties or tell the neighbours what a wonderful man she has.... But here I am talking like a fool at the very door of death! How could such a wise man care for such vanities! . . . Excuse me, Master Pineiss, and cut my head off.'

But Pineiss spoke up quickly, 'Wait a moment, can't you! Tell me, where is such a woman? And are you sure she has ten thousand gold guldens?'

'Ten thousand gold guldens?' asked Glassy.

'Yes,' answered Pineiss, impatiently. 'Isn't that what you were just talking about?'

'Oh, those are two separate things. The money lies buried in a certain place.'

'And what is it doing there? Who does it belong to?' Pineiss asked eagerly.

'To nobody – that's just what is on my conscience! I should have seen to it that the money was put in good hands. Really, the guldens belong to the man who marries the woman I have described. But how is a person to bring those three things together in this stupid town: a fair white lady, ten thousand guldens, and a wise and upright man? That is too hard a task for one poor cat!'

'Now listen,' advised Pineiss. 'If you don't tell me the whole story in the proper order, I'll cut off your tail and both your ears to start with! So begin!'

'Well, if you wish it, I will go ahead,' said Glassy, and sat down on his haunches, 'although this delay only makes my troubles worse. But still, I am willing to live a little longer – for your sake, Master Pineiss.'

The magician stuck his sharp knife in the bare boards between Glassy and himself, sat down on a barrel, and the cat told the following story.

III

'You may know, Master Pineiss,' he began, 'that the good lady who used to be my mistress died unmarried. She was a quiet person – people knew her only as an old maid who did good to a great many and harm to none. But she was not always so plain and quiet. As a young girl, she was the most beautiful creature for miles around and young men came flocking from far and wide. Everyone who saw her dancing eyes and laughing mouth fell in love with her at once. She had hundreds of offers of marriage and many a duel was fought on her account. She, too, had decided to marry – and she had enough candidates to choose from. There came bold suitors and shy ones,

honest lovers and sly ones, merchants, cavaliers, landowners, loud wooers and silent adorers, suitors who were boastful, suitors who were bashful – in short, the lady had as great a choice as any girl could wish. But she had one great fault: she was suspicious of everybody. Besides her beauty, she had a fortune of many thousand gold guldens – and it was just because of this that she never could decide which man to marry. She had managed her affairs so shrewdly that her property had grown still larger, and (as people always judge others by themselves) she thought that the suitors only wanted her because of her fortune. If a man happened to be rich, she thought, "Oh, he only wants to increase his wealth. He wouldn't look at me if I were poor." If a poor man proposed to her, she would think, "Ah, he's only after my gold guldens." The foolish lady did not realize that she was thinking about her money much more than the suitors did, and what she believed to be their greed for gold was really something in her own nature. Several times she was as good as engaged, but at the last minute something in her lover's face would convince her that he, too, was only after her wealth. And so, with a heavy heart, but a stubborn will, she would have no more to do with him.

'When they brought her presents or gave feasts in her honour, she would say, "I am not so foolish a fish to be caught with such bait!" And she would give their gifts to the poor and send the givers off. In fact, she put them to so many tests and treated them so badly that, after a time, all of the right sort of men stayed away. The only men that came to win her were sharp and cunning fellows, and this made her more suspicious than ever. So, in the end, she who was only looking for an honest heart, found herself surrounded by mean and dishonest persons. She could not bear it any longer. One day she sent all the grasping suitors from her doors, locked up the house and set out for Italy, for the city of Milan, where she had a cousin. Her thoughts were heavy and sorrowful as she travelled across the Alps, and her eyes were blind to those great mountains, standing like proud kings with sunset crowning their happy heads. Even in Italy, beneath the bluest skies, she remained pale; no matter how light the heavens were, her thoughts were dark.

'But one day the clouds began to lift from her heart, and the winds (which had never spoken to her before) whispered little songs in her ear. For a young man had come to visit at her cousin's house, a young man who looked so fair and talked so pleasantly that she fell in love with him at once. He was a handsome youngster, well educated and of fine family, not too rich and not too poor. He had just ten thousand guldens (which had been left to him by his parents) and with this sum he was going to start a silk business in Milan. Highly educated though he was, he seemed as innocent as a child, and, though only a merchant, he carried his sword with a knightly air. All of this so pleased the fair lady that she could scarcely contain herself. She was happy again – and if she had little moments of sadness, it was only when she feared that the young man might not return her affection. The lovelier she grew, the more she worried whether or not she made a good impression on him.

'As for the young merchant, he had never seen anyone so charming and (to tell the truth) he was even more in love with her than she was with him. But he was very shy and most modest. "How can any man," he said to his anxious heart, "hope to win such beauty for himself? How can I expect one so far beyond me even to consider me? No, no, I must not think of it; it is impossible." For several weeks he tried to conquer his love or, at least, to hide it from the world. But his nature was so warm and sincere he could not disguise it. Whenever he was near his adored one, or even when her name was mentioned, he trembled, grew confused; and it was easy to see where his thoughts were. His very timid manner made my mistress still fonder of him – especially since he was so different from all her other suitors of the past – and her love grew greater with every day.

'Here was a peculiar situation. Two hearts were on fire; cupids were fanning the blaze – and yet nothing happened. Here were two people head-over-heels in love with each other – and remaining as distant as strangers. He, for his part, was too bashful to declare his desire; she, naturally, was too modest to speak of hers. It was a curious comedy, and the people of Milan watched it being played with keen enjoyment. It must be confessed that she helped him a bit – not, of course, with words, but with smiles and little expressions of pleasure whenever he gave her some trifle, and with a hundred unspoken hints that women understand so well. Things could not go on like this much longer. Finally the day came. People were beginning to gossip, and he felt it was not fair to her to let matters stand as they were. "Better put an end to it," he thought, "even though it will kill my last hope!" So he came to her and, frightened but desperate, blurted out his love in a few words. He gave her little time to consider, his sentences came so fast. It never occurred to him that a young lady might like to delay the happy moment before answering; he did not know that women, even when they are most in love, say "no" at first when they expect to say "yes" afterwards. He just poured out his heart in one burst, ending with, "Do not keep me in agony! If I have spoken rashly, let the blow fall at once! With me it is one thing or the other: life or death, yes or no! Speak – which is it to be?"

'Just as she was about to open her arms to him as an answer, her old distrust overcame her. The old suspicion flashed on her that, maybe, like all the others, he only cared for her fortune. "Possibly," an evil thought nudged her, "he is only saying this to get your money into his business. Don't yield to your impulse too quickly. Think it over. Test him first!" Therefore, instead of telling him the truth and completing her happiness, she listened to the voice of doubt and decided to put her lover to a severe test. As he stood waiting for her answer, she put a sad expression on her face and made up the following story.

'She was sorry, she said, that she could not say "yes" to him because (here she blushed at her falsehood) because she was already engaged to marry a man in her own country. "I am very fond of you, as you can tell," she continued, "and you see I confide in you. I regard you as a brother – but my heart belongs to the man who is waiting for me in my own land. It is a secret that nobody knows – how deeply I love this man and how impossible it would be for me to marry anyone else. We would have been married long ago, but my lover is a poor merchant and he expected to start in business with the money I was to bring him as a bridal gift. Everything was ready; he had started a shop; our wedding was to be celebrated in a

few days – when hard times came and, overnight, most of my fortune was lost. My poor lover was beside himself; he did not know where to turn. As I said, he had already made preparations for a large business, and ordered supplies, had bought goods, and he owed for all of it, mostly to merchants in Italy. The day of payment is dose at hand, and that is the reason I came here – in the hope of getting help from my relatives. But I see I have come at a bad time; nobody here can do anything for me – even my uncle will not risk his money. And if I return without assistance, I think I will die."

'She finished and buried her face in her hands, but watched between her fingers to see what effect this tale would have on the young man. During her story, he had grown pale and, as she ended, he was as white as a new napkin. But he did not utter a sound of complaint or speak another word about himself or his love. He only asked, with a sadness he tried to hide, what was the amount of money owed by her fiancé? "Ten thousand gold guldens," she answered, in a still sadder voice. The young merchant stood up, advised her to be of good cheer, and left the room without telling her how deeply her story had moved him.

The poor fellow, of course, believed every word of it and his affection for her was so great that he made up his mind to help her, even though she was (as he thought) going to marry another. Her happiness – not his – was the only thing he now considered. So he gathered together everything he possessed – all the money with which he was going to start in business – and in a few hours' time he was back again. He offered the money and asked her, as a great favour to him, to accept it until things improved after her marriage and her husband could afford to pay it back.

'Her eyes danced and her heart beat faster with a joy such as she had never felt before. She did not doubt any longer. "But where," she inquired, as if she could not imagine, "where did you get all this money?"

'"Oh," he replied, "I have had a lot of luck lately. Business has been very good with me, and I can spare this amount without any trouble."

'She looked closely at him and knew at once that he was lying:

she realized it was his entire fortune he was sacrificing for her sake. Still, she pretended to believe him and thanked him heartily for his kindness. But, she said, she would accept his generous offer only on one condition: that, on a certain day, he would come to her wedding, as he was her best friend and, also, because he had made her marriage possible.

"No, no; do not ask me that," he pleaded, "ask me anything else!"

"'And why not?" she inquired, looking offended.

'He grew red and could scarcely speak for a moment. Finally, he said, "There are many reasons why I cannot come to your wedding. In the first place, my business demands me here. In the second place, I haven't the time to go to Switzerland. And," he added honestly, "there are other reasons."

'But she would not listen to him. "Unless you do as I ask, I will not accept a single one of these gold-pieces," she said firmly, and pushed the money towards him.

'So finally he consented, and she made him give her his hand in promise. As soon as he left her, she locked the treasure in her trunk and placed the key in the bosom of her dress. She did not stay in Milan more than a few days more, but travelled quickly back to Switzerland. Crossing the Alps was a far different experience than the first time; instead of shedding tears or carrying a dark expression, she laughed and sunshine leaped out of her eyes. It was a happy voyage and a happier home-coming. She aired the house from top to bottom, threw the doors wide open, had the floors polished and decorated the rooms as if she were expecting a royal prince. But at the head of her bed she placed the precious bag with the ten thousand gold gulden, and every night her happy head rested on it as comfortably as though the hard bundle were stuffed with the softest feathers. She could scarcely wait until the day came when he was expected, the day of beautiful surprises, when she would give him not only his own ten thousand gold guldens, but many times that amount, as well as her whole household and (here she must have blushed sweetly) herself. He would surely come; for she knew, no matter what happened, he would never break his word.

'But the day came and her beloved did not appear. And many days passed and many weeks, and still he did not come. She began to tremble, and all her hours were filled with fear. Her messengers searched for him on every highway. She stood at the window of her topmost balcony from daybreak till night blotted out the whitest roads. She sent despatches to Milan, letter after letter – to him, to relatives, to strangers – all without result. No answer came; no one could tell where he was to be found.

'At last, quite by accident,' continued Glassy, taking a breath in the midst of his long story, 'she learned that her beloved had gone to the wars and that his body had been found, full of wounds, on the field of battle. Just before he died, he had turned to the man lying next to him – a Swiss soldier who happened to come from Seldwyla and who had not been so badly hurt – and had given him this message. "If you ever return to Seldwyla," he said, "seek out my love and ask her to forgive me for breaking my word. Tell her I loved her so much that I could not bear to go to her wedding and see her married to another. She will forgive me, I know – if she still remembers me – for she has also suffered because of love. Tell her I wish her a long lifetime of happiness."

'As soon as the soldier from Seldwyla reached home, he repeated these words (which, like a true Swiss, he had carefully put down in his note-book) to my mistress. The poor girl scarcely listened till he had finished the sad message. She beat her breast, tore her clothes and began to cry in such a loud voice that people far down the street thought that someone was being murdered. Her reason almost left her. She carried his bag of gold guldens about with her as tenderly as if it were a baby. At other times she would scatter the coins on the ground and throw herself, weeping, upon them. She lay there, day and night, without eating or drinking, kissing the cold metal, which was all she had left of him. Suddenly, one dark midnight, she gathered the treasure together, tied up the bag, and, carrying it into her garden, threw it down a deep well so that it should never belong to anyone else.'

As soon as Glassy had finished this sorrowful tale, Pineiss broke in eagerly, 'And is the money still there?'

'Yes,' replied Glassy, 'it is lying just where she dropped it. But don't forget that I am the person who was supposed to see that it was given to the right man – and my conscience is troubled because I have failed to do this.'

'Quite right,' Pineiss added hastily, 'your interesting story made me forget all about you. What you say makes me feel that, after all, it might not be a bad thing to have a wife with ten thousand guldens around the house. But she would have to be very pretty! . . . But there must be more to your story. Go on with the rest of it so I can see how it hangs together.'

Glassy continued, 'It was many years later that I first came to know the unfortunate lady I have been telling you about. She was a lonely old maid when she took me into her household, and I allow myself to believe that I was her best friend and her only comfort to the end of her days. As she saw this end drawing near, she related the whole story of her youth to me and told me, with many tears, how she had lost her whole life's happiness because of suspicion and distrust. "Let it be a warning to others," she said to me. "Ah, if I could only save some other girl from my fate!" It was then that she thought of a way to use the gold guldens lying in the well. "Promise me, Glassy, you will do just what I tell you?" she said to me one day, as I sat perched on her work-basket. And when I had promised, she spoke as follows: "Look around, keep your eyes open, until you find a beautiful girl who has no suitors because she is too poor. Then, if she should meet an honest, hardworking, handsome man – and the man loves her for herself alone – then you must help her. If the man will take an oath always to cherish and protect the girl, you are to give her the ten thousand gold guldens which are in the well; so that, on her wedding-day, the bride can surprise her husband by giving him this wedding-present." Those were almost the last words of my dear mistress. She died soon after speaking them. And, because of my bad luck, I have never been able to carry out her wishes.'

IV

There was a moment's silence as Glassy finished. Then Pineiss, with a greedy look and a distrustful voice, said, 'I'd like to believe you were telling me the truth. And maybe I would believe it – if you could let me have a peep at the place.'

'Why not?' answered Glassy. 'Only I warn you not to try to take the treasure out of its hiding-place. In the first place, the gold can only be removed at the right time; in the second place, it lies in a very dangerous part and you would be sure to break your neck if you tried to go after it.'

'Who said anything about taking it out?' protested Pineiss, somewhat frightened. 'Just lead me there so I can see whether you are telling the truth. Or, better still, I will lead you on a stout string so that you won't try to run away.'

'As you like!' replied Glassy. 'But take a long rope and a lantern with you, for it's a very deep and dark well.'

Pineiss followed this advice and led the cat to the garden of his dead mistress. They climbed over a crumbling wall and through an overgrown path which was almost blotted out by bushes and weeds. Finally they reached the spot. Pineiss tied the lantern to the rope and dropped it part of the way down the well, still holding Glassy with the other hand. Pineiss leaned over and trembled as he caught the glint of something shining in the depths.

'Sure enough!' he cried, excitedly. 'I see it! It's there, all right! Glassy, you are a wonder!' Then, looking eagerly down again, 'Are you sure there are ten thousand?'

'I can't swear to that,' replied Glassy, 'I have not been down there and I have never counted them! Also, the poor lady may have dropped a few when she carried them here, as she was so worried and nervous at the time.'

'Well, if there are two or three less,' said Pineiss, rubbing his chin, 'I will have to be satisfied.' He sat down on the rim of the well; Glassy also seated himself there and began to lick his paws. Pineiss scratched his head and began again. 'There is the treasure, and here is the man. But where is the girl?'

'What do you mean?' inquired Glassy.

'I mean there is only one thing missing to fulfil the old lady's wishes – the girl who is to give her husband the ten thousand guldens as a wedding-present and who has also all the other good qualities you spoke about.'

'Hum!' replied Glassy, with a wide yawn. 'The facts are not exactly the way you state them. The treasure is there, as you have seen, and the girl is ready, for I have already found her. But where can I find the right man who will marry under such conditions? For he will come into a great deal of money, and money brings with it a lot of cares and troubles. The man who has such a fortune has so much to keep him busy. He will have fine horses and many servants. He will have velvet suits and fresh linen sheets, cattle and hunting-dogs, oak furniture and a kitchen full of copper pots. He will have to remember what to tell his gardener to plant, will have to think of his property, his flowers, his wife, his crops, his armour, his old wines, his carriages, his rare books, his games – always his and his and his, from dawn till dark. Yes, owning things is a lot of trouble for a wealthy man. Then there are his rich clothes, his fat cows, his –'

But Pineiss interrupted him. 'Enough, you chatterbox! Will you ever stop babbling?' he cried, tugging at the string until Glassy miaowed with pain. For, you can imagine, Pineiss would gladly have had all these 'troubles' – and the more he heard about what such a fortune would bring, the more his mouth watered. 'Where is the young woman you have found?' he asked, suddenly.

Glassy acted as if he were astonished. 'Would you really care to try it? Are you sure?'

'Of course I am sure! Who else but I should have the fortune? Tell me, where is she?' demanded Pineiss.

'So that you can go there and be her suitor?' inquired Glassy.

'Absolutely.

'Understand, then,' Glassy declared, 'the business can only be conducted through me. You must deal with me, if you want the gold and the girl!'

'I see,' said Pineiss slowly. 'You are trying to get me to give up our contract so you can save your head?'

'Is that so unnatural?' inquired Glassy, and began to wash his ears with wet paws.

'You think, you sly scoundrel, you'll cheat me in the end!' cried Pineiss.

'Is that possible?' mocked Glassy.

'I tell you, don't you dare betray me!'

'All right, then I won't,' said Glassy.

'If you do!' threatened Pineiss.

'Then I will.'

'Don't torture me like this!' said the excited Pineiss, almost crying.

And Glassy answered seriously. 'You are a remarkable man, Master Pineiss! You have me on a string and you pull on it until I can scarcely breathe. You have kept the sword of death hanging over me for two hours – what am I saying! – for two years, for two eternities! And now you say, "Don't torture me like this!" You ask that of me! . . . With your permission, let me tell you something,' Glassy continued in a calmer key. 'I would be only too happy to carry out the wishes of my late mistress and find the man fit for the lovely girl I spoke of – and you seem to be the right sort in every way. But it will not be easy for me to persuade the young lady. It is a difficult task. And if I must die . . . ! No, I tell you frankly, Mr Pineiss, I must have my freedom before I speak another word. Therefore, take the cord from my neck and lay the contract here on the well-curb, or cut my head off – one or the other!'

'Why so excited and hot-headed?' asked Pineiss. 'Let us talk this thing over.'

But Glassy sat there, motionless, and for three or four minutes neither uttered a word. Then Pineiss, afraid that he might lose the fortune, reached into his pocket, took out the precious piece of paper, unfolded it, read it through once more and put it slowly down in front of the cat. The paper had scarcely reached the stone-curb before Glassy pounced upon it, chewing up every morsel. And, although he almost choked on some of the large words, he still considered it the best, the most wholesome meal he had ever enjoyed – and hoped it would make him healthy and fat!

As he finished this very satisfying dish, he turned to the magician ceremoniously and said, 'You will hear from me without fail, Master Pineiss. I promise to deliver the treasure as well as the lovely lady. Therefore, make yourself ready: prepare to receive your future wife, who is as good as yours already, and be happy. Finally, allow me to thank you for your care and hospitality, and kindly excuse me while I take leave of you for a little while.'

So saying, Glassy went his way and rejoiced at the stupidity of the town-wizard who thought he could fool everyone. This man even tried to fool himself, thought Glassy, by declaring he was going to marry the girl for herself alone, whereas all he cared about was the sack of money. Glassy was already thinking of who the bride would be as he passed the street where the magician lived.

V

Across the way from the worker-in-magic, stood a house whose plaster front was whiter than milk and whose windows were always washed till they shone. The curtains were equally white and prim, and everything that one could see was as clean and stiffly ironed as the linen head-dress and collar worn by the woman who lived in this house. She was an old woman, very pious and very ugly. The starched edges and corners of her clothes were sharp; but they were no sharper than her long nose, her pointed chin, her spiteful tongue or her cutting glance. Yet she scarcely ever spoke to people, for she was so stingy she would not even spend her breath on them. Her neighbours disliked her intensely, but they had to admit she was religious – at least she seemed to be. Three times a day they watched her go to church; and every time the children saw her long nose coming down the street, they ran to get out of her way. Even the grown people ducked behind their doors if they had time. But still, even if nobody cared to go near her, she had a good reputation because of her continual prayers and church-going. So the strict old woman lived – never smiling, never mingling with other people – from one day to the other, at peace and utterly alone. And if the neighbours

had nothing to do with her, she, for her part, never concerned herself about them. The only person she ever paid any attention to was Pineiss – and him she hated. Whenever he appeared, she would throw a terrible look and pull her curtains together quickly; while he, who feared her like fire, hid himself away from her.

As I have said, the part of her house that faced the street was neat and clean. But as white as was the front, so dark, so gloomy, so queer and so evil-smelling was the back. Built in the corner of an old wall, it was so black and lost in shadows that it could only be seen by the birds in the air and the cats on the roof. Under the eaves, in a place that no man had ever seen, hung filthy bundles, torn scraps of clothing, ragged underwear, broken baskets, bags of strange herbs. On top of the roof was a little forest of thorn-bushes and mosses., from the centre of which a thin chimney stretched its length like a lean and wicked finger. And out of this chimney, when the nights were darkest, a witch would often rise – young and fair and without a stitch of clothing – and go riding about on a broomstick. Thus, by the power of her secret magic, the old woman would disguise herself as a young girl. She would laugh lightly as she galloped through the air on her one-footed steed; her lips would shine like polished cherries and her long, black hair would flutter in the night-wind like a flag.

In a hole in the chimney sat an old owl. And it was to this wise bird that Glassy came as soon as he was freed, carrying a fat mouse in his jaws.

'Good evening, dear Madam Owl,' said Glassy. 'Still busy keeping watch?'

'I have to,' replied the owl. 'And good evening to you. You have not given your friends the pleasure of your company for a long time.'

'There were reasons, as I will tell you. Have you had your supper yet? No? Here is a mouse; nothing much, but it is all I could find on the way. I hope you won't refuse it. And has your mistress gone out riding?'

'Not yet,' answered the owl. 'She will wait another hour until it is almost morning. Thanks for the fine mouse. And here I have a small sparrow laid aside; it happened to fly too close to me. Try it, just to please me. And how have things gone with you?'

'Wonderfully. You would hardly believe it. If you care to listen, I'll tell you.' And so, while the two good friends enjoyed their little meal, Glassy told the whole tale how he came to make the fearful contract, how Pineiss had almost killed him, and how, in the end, he had saved himself.

After Glassy had finished, the owl said, 'Well, I congratulate you! And I wish you the best of luck. Now you are a free man again; you can go where you please and do whatever you wish!'

'But not right away,' objected Glassy. 'First, Pineiss must have his lady and the ten thousand gold guldens.'

'Are you crazy?' screamed the owl. 'Surely, you are only joking! You certainly are not going to reward the man who wanted to take the very skin off your back?'

'Yes, he was about to do that. But if I can pay him back in the same coin, why shouldn't I? The story I told him was a pure fairy tale; I made the whole thing up myself from beginning to end. My mistress was a simple body; she was quite plain, had never been in love, and no suitors ever came near her all her life. As to the treasure, there really are some guldens at the bottom of the well. But it is stolen money, and my mistress would never touch it. "Let it lie there," she used to say to me, "for there is a curse on it. Whoever takes it out and uses it will be unlucky!" That shall be Master Pineiss's "reward"!'

'Ah,' the owl chuckled, 'that's different! You're a deep one! But where is the promised lady going to come from?'

'From this chimney!' answered Glassy. 'That is the reason I came here. Let us talk it over like two sensible people.

Wouldn't you like to be free of this witch who is always making you work for her? And wouldn't it be a lovely thing to get these two old villains married to each other? But first, we must catch our witch. And that's no easy matter. Stir your brains; think how we can manage it!'

For a while there was nothing but silence in the night. Then the owl whispered, 'I think I have it! As soon as you are here with me, my brain begins to work!'

'Good,' said Glassy. 'Soon we will have a plan.'

'I have a plan already,' continued the owl. 'Everything joins together nicely.'

'When do we begin?' asked Glassy, eagerly.

'At once!' said the owl.

'And how are we going to catch her?' inquired Glassy, with eyes that burned like green fire.

'With a net for catching snipe, a fine new net made of the toughest hemp. It must have been woven by a twenty-year-old hunter's son who has never once looked at a woman. The night-dew must have fallen three times upon it where it lay without having caught a single snipe. And it must have lain there because of three good deeds. Only such a net is strong enough to catch witches!'

'But I am curious to know where such a net can be found,' said Glassy. 'There must be one somewhere in the world, I suppose, because I have never known you to say a foolish thing. But where,' repeated the puzzled animal, 'are we ever to find such a remarkable affair?'

'It has been found already, just as if it were made for us,' replied the owl. 'Listen. In a wood, not far from here, there sits the twenty-year-old son of a hunter who has never looked at a woman as much as once. He was born blind. There's your first requirement. Being blind, he cannot do much except weave yarn and, a few days ago, he finished a fine net for catching snipe. As the old hunter was about to spread it out to trap the birds, a woman came along who wanted him to go with her and join a band of wealthy robbers. But she was so hideous that he dropped everything in fright and ran away. So the hempen net lay in the dew without catching a snipe, and a good motive was the cause of it. The next day, as the old bunter returned to stretch the net, a horseman rode past carrying a heavy bundle behind him. In this bundle was a small hole, and, from time to time, a gold-piece fell out of it. The hunter dropped the net again and ran hotly after the horseman, picking up the gold pieces and putting them in his own hat – until suddenly the horseman turned around, saw what the hunter had been doing, and charged angrily down upon him. Fearing for his life, the hunter bowed suddenly, snatched his cap from his head and said, "Allow me – you have been losing your money, and I have run all the way after so I could give it back to you." This was the second "good" act, and, as the hunter was by this time far away from the net, it lay a second night without being used as a trap. Finally on the third day, which was yesterday, as he came to the place, he met a young woman who carried a basketful of delicious home-cooked sausages and cakes. She was a pleasant girl, and when she invited the hunter to come to her sister's wedding, where there was to be a great feast that evening, he accepted gladly and said, "Oh, let the snipes go! One ought to take pity on the animals! Besides, who cares for snipes when there's a goose?" And because of these three good acts, the net has lain for three nights in the dew without being used – quite ready for us. All I have to do is fetch it.'

'Fetch it quickly, then,' cried Glassy. 'It is the very thing we need!'

'I will get it at once,' said the owl. 'You keep watch for me here, and if my mistress should call up the chimney asking if the coast is clear, answer her in my voice and say, "No, it is not foul enough!"'

Glassy thereupon took his friend's place, and the owl flew over the town towards the wood. In fifteen minutes she was back, carrying the snipe-net in her beak. 'Has she called out?' asked the owl. 'Not yet,' said Glassy.

Then they stretched the closely woven trap over the chimney and sat down to wait for whatever might happen. The night was pitch dark and an early morning wind blew out two or three pale stars. Suddenly they heard the witch's voice: 'Is the coast clear?' And the owl answered, 'Quite clear. The air is fine and foul!'

As soon as the words were said, a white form rose from the chimney – and the next moment the witch was squirming in the snare, while the two animals pulled and tied it together. The witch raged and kicked and flopped and floundered like a gleaming fish in a net, but 'Hold fast!' cried the owl, and 'Tie it tight!' called Glassy. And the net held. Finally, seeing she was helpless, the witch grew quiet and asked, 'What do you want of me, you strange creatures?'

'Let me leave your service and give me my freedom,' said the owl.

'Such a great boast for such a little roast!' said the witch, using an old Swiss proverb. 'Why all this trouble? You are free. Now open the net.'

'Wait a moment,' cried Glassy, 'before we let you out you must promise to marry the town-wizard, Pineiss, in the way we shall explain to you.'

'Marry that man? Never!' replied the witch, and began to fume again.

But Glassy continued quietly. 'Would you like the whole town to know who you are? If you don't do exactly as we say, we will hang the net – and all that is inside of it – right under the part of your roof which faces the street. Tomorrow morning the villagers will

pass this house on their way to work. When they look up, they'll see you caught here and everybody will know who the witch is! Besides,' Glassy went on in a more persuading tone of voice, 'just think how easily you will be able to rule Master Pineiss after you are his wife!'

It is hard to say which of these two arguments convinced the witch. At any rate, after a long pause, she said with a sigh, 'Tell me, then, what you want me to do.' And Glassy told her the plan he had in mind and explained to her exactly how it was to be carried out. 'Very well, then, as I cannot help myself, I agree,' said the sorceress, and pledged her word with the strongest magic known to witchcraft. Then she mounted her broom, the owl settled herself on the handle, Glassy perched securely behind on the straw bottom, and so they flew through the air to the old well. The witch descended it, took out the treasure, and the three parted company for the time being.

Early next morning Glassy appeared before Pineiss and informed him that he could see the promised lady. She was so poor and lonely that she had no suitors and was sitting underneath a willow in front of the town-gate, crying bitterly. As soon as Pineiss heard this, he was overjoyed and his dark room seemed lighter. He ran to his mirror, took off his shabby working clothes, put on his yellow velvet doublet (which he only wore on holidays), his silk hose (which he always thought too good to wear), his best fur-cap, and stuck a

coloured handkerchief in his pocket. As if this were not enough, he sprinkled perfume on himself, sent a boy out for a big bouquet of flowers, carried a pair of green gloves, and, thus magnificently attired, went with Glassy to the town-gate. There he saw a girl seated under a willow-tree weeping as if her heart would break. She was the loveliest person he had ever seen, even though her dress was so torn that it barely covered her. Pineiss could scarcely take his eyes off her, and it was some time before he could speak. The girl was really too beautiful. But she dried her eyes as he comforted her, and when he asked her to marry him, she even laughed in musical tones and said yes. Quickly Pineiss provided her with a wedding-dress and a bridal veil as long as a waterfall. She looked lovelier than ever, so radiant that when they passed the town the men sitting outside raised their glasses and cheered. Afraid that she might change her mind, Pineiss hurried to an old hermit and, within an hour, the town-magician and the fair unknown were made man and wife. Candles were lit, merry cupids seemed to be singing in the air, and, with downcast eyes, the lovely bride entered her new home. The wedding-feast was celebrated in the wizard's house without any other guests except the owl and the cat, who had asked permission to come. The ten thousand gold guldens were in a bowl upon the table and Pineiss's greedy eyes kept looking from his beloved gold to the lovely girl and back again from the girl to the gold. She sat, in sea-blue velvet, with pearls around her slender neck and her eyes brighter than diamonds. But Pineiss cared most for her piled-up yellow hair, for it looked to him like a great mass of glittering gold-pieces.

It was a merry dinner, spiced with Glassy's witty remarks, flavoured with the owl's wise sayings and sweetened with the smiles of the beautiful bride. When the meal was over, the two animals sang a few duets and, as it was beginning to grow dark, prepared to leave their host. Pineiss took them, with a light, to the door, thanked Glassy again and wished them both goodnight. Then, gleefully rubbing his hands together, he went back to the room, congratulating himself on his clever bargain. He closed the door, letting his greedy eyes drink in the happy sight.

There, in the bowl, sparkled the yellow money. But, as his eyes went further, his heart almost stopped beating. Something had gone wrong! There, at the head of the table, instead of the young bride, sat his neighbour, the horrible old woman, frowning at him with a look of hate! She rose from her chair, picked up a broomstick and rode on it in all her hideousness. Imps and demons appeared in every corner, goblins ran about, kobolds sprang on top of the stove. The room was full of strange sounds and queer lights. The very air flickered. Dazzled and scarcely able to see, Pineiss let the candle fall and leaned, trembling, against the wall. His jaw dropped and his whole face grew as white and sharp as the old witch's. They were two of a kind – and the town-wizard richly deserved his 'reward'.

When the marriage became known, the townspeople said, 'Still waters run deep! Who would have thought that the pious old lady would have married the master-magician! Well, they are a well-matched pair – if not very handsome!'

From that time on, Pineiss lived a hard life. His wife learned all his secrets and kept him busy from morning to night. She ruled him with an iron hand; there was not an idle minute he could call his own. And whenever Glassy happened to pass by, the cat would smile cheerfully and say, 'Always busy – eh, Master Pineiss? That's the way – always keep busy!'

And so in Seldwyla, even today, whenever a person has made a bad bargain, they say, 'Too bad! But he should never have tried to buy the fat off the cat!'

ACKNOWLEDGMENTS

The Publisher has made every effort to contact the Copyright holders, but wishes to apologise to those he has been unable to trace. Grateful acknowledgment is made for permission to reprint the following:

'Amours' from *Les Vrilles de la Vigne* by Colette. Reproduced by permission of John Johnson Ltd. Translation copyright © 1992 by Michael O'Mara Books Ltd.

'Incident on East Ninth' by Jill Drower. Reproduced by permission of the author.

'Olly and Ginny' by James Herriot from *James Herriot's Cat Stories* (Michael Joseph Ltd). Reproduced by permission of David Higham Associates/St Martin's Press, Inc., New York and McClelland & Stewart, Inc., Canada. Copyright © by James Herriot 1994.

'My Boss the Cat' by Paul Gallico. Reproduced by permission of Aitken and Stone and Harold Ober Associates, Inc.

'Ming's Biggest Prey' from *The Animal Lover's Book of Beastly Murder* by Patricia Highsmith. Copyright © 1975 by Diogenes Verlag AG, Zürich.

'Mrs Bond's Cats' from *All Things Bright and Beautiful* by James Herriot. Reproduced by permission of David Higham Associates Ltd and St Martin's Press, Inc., New York. Copyright © 1973, 1974 by James Herriot.

'The Cat that Walked by Himself' by Rudyard Kipling. Reproduced by permission of A. P. Watt Ltd on behalf of The National Trust.

Acknowledgments

'The Story of Webster' from *Mulliner Nights* by P. G. Wodehouse. Reproduced by permission of A. P. Watt Ltd on behalf of the Trustees of the Wodehouse Trust and Hutchinson Ltd.

'Particularly Cats' by Doris Lessing. Copyright © 1967 by Doris Lessing Productions Ltd. Reproduced by kind permission of Jonathan Clowes Ltd, London and Michael Joseph Ltd.

040–866–1